TRIPLE CROSS

TRIPLE CROSS

The First Three Kate Fansler Mysteries

AMANDA CROSS

GARDEN CITY, NEW YORK

This book club edition was compiled from:
In the Last Analysis © 1964 by Carolyn Heilbrun
The James Joyce Murder © 1967 by The MacMillan Company
Poetic Justice © 1970 by Carolyn Heilbrun

ISBN: 1-56865-744-7

PRINTED IN THE UNITED STATES OF AMERICA

CONTENTS

Introduction

It was 35 years ago that I wrote the first of these three novels, and as it seems to me now, that was in a different lifetime, and I was a different person. It is only with difficulty that I resurrect that time and that Amanda Cross.

It was 1963. I was in my late 30s, the mother of three children under eight, assistant professor of English literature at Columbia University, the owner of a large dog and, not least, the wife of a man who had gone back to school for his Ph.D., having earlier been employed at a satisfactorily remunerative position at the Chase Bank (as it then was). Why did I begin writing mysteries then? A neighbor had sardonically remarked when we acquired the large dog: "Time was hanging heavy on your hands, Mrs. Heilbrun?"

There were a lot of reasons for my foray into mystery fiction, some of which I have already mentioned in *Writing a Woman's Life*: I needed something very private to do, something secretive, something that was, in a busy life full of the demands and needs of others, just mine. And there were other reasons: if I wanted to move up the academic scale beyond assistant professor, I had to publish detective novels secretly; such frivolity was not academically admired, especially in the young.

I had long read with passion the detective stories of English writers, delighting in the wit, the conversation, above all, in the lack of mayhem and misogyny that so sharply characterized the American detective story. It is, indeed, questionable whether I should ever have made it through to graduation from Wellesley College if I had not had British detective novels, and particularly the works of Dorothy L. Sayers, to read. I would hide out in the Wellesley library, the campus and the dormitories forgotten, enjoying my "real" life in England. And so I lived for hours each day with Lord Peter Wimsey and Harriet Vane in London and Cambridge, and with the many other English, appealingly unmacho detectives created by Ngaio Marsh, Nicholas Blake (C. Day-Lewis), Cyril Hare, Michael Gilbert, Michael Innes, Christina Brand, Margery Allingham, and others.

And then suddenly, by 1963, it seemed they were no longer writing mysteries, or no longer writing in sufficient numbers to satisfy my longing. P. D. James, in fact, published her first novels more or less simultaneously with mine. Had I previously read her elegant works I would probably have been discouraged from attempting my own versions of the mystery novels. (The dazzling Sarah Caudwell was to come along decades later when I had, so to speak, gotten into my stride.) As it was, I forged ahead unaware of such daunting competition.

Also, I wanted to create a female detective and there were so few of those around as to suggest a positive dearth. The fact was that when *In the Last Analysis* was published in 1964, Carol Brener, the owner of New York City's first mystery book shop, Murder Ink, told me that there was no other American woman detective in print, and few enough in English, Agatha Christie's Miss Marple being the only one to come to mind.

People have often asked why I picked the name Amanda Cross, and I have more times than I care to remember told the story of how my husband and I were marooned in our car in Nova Scotia facing a sign reading "MacCharles Cross." My husband suggested that we use that as a pseudonym, should either of us ever require one; I was, however, told by the publisher that my novel required an author with a female name, hence Amanda. There is, however, a later bit to this story that I have not yet revealed in print. One day, I was visiting a mystery bookstore in Tucson, Arizona, with a wonderful name: "They Were the Footprints of an Enormous Hound." (The bookstore, no doubt inspired by its name, was home to a huge Irish wolfhound, but that has nothing to do with this story except perhaps that I am enamored of Irish wolfhounds and may have gone to the bookstore in the first place to meet him.)

There came into the bookstore a lady who told me, graciously but with great firmness, that she came from Nova Scotia, and that there was no such place as MacCharles Cross. "It wasn't exactly a place," I told her, "it was a crossroads." She repeated that she had never heard of it, but would look into the matter. I received the distinct impression that her research would prove me a purveyor of untruth; she was too ladylike to use the word "liar." She took my address, promising to report her findings to me.

Months passed. Then one day came a letter from this lady, apologizing for having doubted me, and enclosing a letter she had written to the President (or was he the Prime Minister?) of Nova Scotia inquiring about MacCharles Cross. He had replied to her, assuring her that there was such a place, and enclosing a map with "my" crossroads carefully circled in red. I thought the lady most honorable to have sent me these materials.

My first novel showed the influence of Dorothy L. Sayers on every page. People raised their hands to summon brandy from waiters and performed other upper-class English gestures. I don't think my novel suffered from this nor, apparently, did others think so. Dorothy Salisbury Davis, later to receive a Grand Master Award from the Mystery Writers of America (hereafter referred to as the MWA), gave me a blurb that certainly helped my book along. And the following spring, my book was short-listed for the Best First Novel Edgar. What should have been delight was terror; I could hardly cling to my anonymity as the winner of an Edgar. Happily for me and him, the award went to the first of the Rabbi mysteries, and my real name was left undisclosed. The MWA has never nominated me for an award since, so clearly I have come down in the world. The truth is that my rather quiet mysteries, devoid of painstakingly depicted violence and suffering from a dearth of blood and bodies, have won no prizes from any mystery organization, except for one from the Nero Wolfe Pack, which in 1981 awarded me a Rex Stout gold-colored metal bookmark for *Death in a Tenured Position*; I'm exceedingly grateful to them still.

By my second novel I had traded Sayers for James Joyce, though this was not to remain with me as a permanent literary swap. James Joyce had been forced upon me—forced, as in forced feeding—so continuously in graduate school that I developed a kind of allergic reaction to him. Not, I hasten to say, to Leopold Bloom in the first three chapters of *Ulysses* and the next to last, "Ithaca," or to that magnificent story, "The Dead." It had become clear to me, however, that Joyce had, I believed intentionally and knowingly, designed himself as the perfect subject for close analysis by English graduate students and that he had succeeded magnificently in his aim. I developed, and have never lost, an affection for writers who are read just for pleasure or because they enhance the reader's sense of life's possibilities. Virginia Woolf, except perhaps for *The Waves* (which I happen to cherish), is such a writer; Joyce is not. Deconstructing Joyce, like writing a bad review, is mainly a chance to show off.

Back in the '60s, however, I still pretended to enjoy Joyce—I pretended a lot of things in the '60s: that I liked to cook, that feminists were too "shrill," that my husband would become mysteriously demasculinized if he did anything approximating an equal share of parenting and housework. Still, the '60s were fast becoming a hell of a lot better than the '50s, and I got even with Joyce without even suspecting that I disliked him by using his *Dubliners* for my second mystery. I didn't actually admire most of the stories in *Dubliners*, but I was still fond of Leopold Bloom, which was why Kate's nephew was named Leo. The fact is I used *Dubliners* as scaffolding as T. S. Eliot had taught me Joyce had used the *Odyssey* in *Ulysses*. *The James Joyce Murder*, incidentally, was the only one of my novels that did not immediately get published in paperback; the title was too erudite. My husband suggested I retitle it *Love in the Haystack*, which would have been appropriate enough, but cowardly. Eventually my novel was reissued in hardcover and then in paperback. They also publish who only stand and wait.

One personage I did by the '60s stop pretending wholeheartedly to admire was Freud. In my first novel, I was still acting as though not believing everything Freud claimed was tantamount to not believing in God, and I even accepted Freud's belated declaration that children who claimed to have been sexually abused were having wishful fantasies. Almost every male my husband and I knew in those days was a psychoanalyst of the New York Psychoanalytic Institute ilk—that was the group that had thrown Karen Horney out on her ear for questioning the holy writ about penis envy—and I guess I had to pretend to admire them before I began to appreciate the damage they could do and had done to people I knew. So I had a lot of lovely things to say about Freud and psychoanalysts in that first novel, and they're still there; I refuse to revise the Amanda Cross of those days, however gullible I find her now. I'm a total disbeliever in the revision of their early works by aging authors, who are different people and should mind their own business.

In any case, since my first books the wonderful emergence of therapists and psychologists who can really help people without forcing them to relive every minute of their childhoods (Freud believed people over 50 couldn't be analyzed because they wouldn't be able to remember their childhoods in detail) has fulfilled one long-held dream of mine. My other fervent long-held wish was that there would be more successful fictional women detectives. Life doesn't answer most of our wishes, but it certainly answered these, to my infinite satisfaction.

One humorous response I remember to *The James Joyce Murder* came from my mother. There is a scene where Kate and Reed go off for a walk, which is more than likely to end in their making love, but that is never demonstrated. "Well," my mother commented, "I see you have to put sex in your books to make them sell." My mother was very down-to-earth about sex and most other things, but her literary taste had been formed by 19th-century novelists, subsequently extended to include those writing before World War II. I once, at her request, borrowed *Portnoy's Complaint* for her, and some hours after I had delivered it to her, she telephoned me to insist upon my getting it out of her house within the hour; it was polluting the atmosphere. Well, as I said, I began writing mystery novels 35 years ago, and the world has changed since then, largely for the better, in my opinion.

I am aware that anyone reading these three novels will notice that there are no other professional women or friends in *In the Last Analysis*, but there are three such women in *The James Joyce Murder*. My feminism, like my awareness of politics, was beginning to ripen. By my third novel, *Poetic Justice*, I had become a political person. I was at Columbia during the two student demonstrations, the first against the Vietnam War and the unresponsive Columbia administration, the second against the bombing in Cambodia. Students kept telling me that the Government lied, that the CIA and FBI were involved in illegal actions, stuff like that, and I didn't believe them at first, but time proved the students right. I became a political person overnight, and a little of this creeps into my third novel.

Perhaps more significantly in my third novel, I allowed myself to praise a poet I had always genuinely admired: W. H. Auden. I heard that he was embarrassed by my adoring use of his poems, but my esteem was sincere. There was an amusing outcome of my Auden use 20 years after the novel's publication. *Poetic Justice* was being translated into German, and the publisher or translator suggested that since such excellent German versions had been made of Auden's poems, perhaps I could tell them the titles of the poems from which the quoted lines had been plucked. Twenty years later, I could hardly remember; what to do? And then I bethought me of my colleague in the Columbia English Department, Edward Mendelson, who was Auden's literary executor, chosen, gossip had it, because he knew Auden's poetry better than Auden did. Indeed, Ed Mendelson has demonstrated that Auden made an excellent choice for his literary executor, and it was also a choice that served me. I called up Ed, threw myself on his mercy, and asked for the poems from which I had, so long ago, extracted the lines. He identified them all, and the Germans and I were much relieved.

As I have said, these three early novels might be called prefeminist; they were, in fact, prefeminist. That is why some readers prefer them, and others like to see how far I've come in three decades. Feminism in ways both obvious and subtle, transformed the mystery novel more thoroughly than any other event, except possibly, in America, Dashiell Hammett's much earlier employment by the Pinkerton agency. Even the male novelists changed their female characters from hangers-on, rejected bitches and tiresome hags to professionals with their own lives. Dare I suggest that the immense popularity of the detective novel is not unconnected with this transformation?

Not that awards for mystery writers have gone to feminists; they haven't. One Edgar went to a feminist novel—by which I mean one in which a professional, independent, saucy woman is the protagonist—and that was Margaret Maron's splendid *Bootlegger's Daughter* in 1992. A recent Edgar went to a novel by a woman in which a grossly fat woman did or did not murder her mother and sister and then carve them into pieces like fried chicken. I hated that novel for its violence and indecisiveness about guilt, but was alone in that opinion; a television version was made in England and shown on PBS in a series that had previously featured Morse, Dalgleish, Poirot, Rumpole, Miss Marple and the wonderful Helen Mirren in *Prime Suspect*. Ruth Rendell, one of the most highly praised of mystery writers, also upset me by publishing an antifeminist novel that was worthy of Rush Limbaugh. P. D. James, on the other hand, who is a Baroness and would probably not like to be labeled as a feminist, has created at least three perfectly marvelous important female characters and brought them back for repeat performances. Currently, Elizabeth George and Anne Perry are also honorable in their views on gender, without arousing any suspicion of having an "agenda."

Amanda Cross has changed greatly since that first novel, and so has Kate Fansler. We have continued to be lucky in our publishers and in our readers. There are, of course, those who cannot abide either of us, which does not bother me a bit. No one can write for everyone, but only for those, as they said in my youth, on the same wavelength. I hope to be successful enough to encourage someone to publish my next novel; in fact, I have always been suspicious of, and have never desired, fame, one of those ''gifts'' that, like Faust's, turn out to be a lousy bargain, for which the devil asks too high a price.

I do not read reviews, which most people disbelieve, but it is the truth. I think that Robert Parker doesn't read his either. More writers are made miserable by reviews than are kicked by donkeys each year, and that, I understand, is an impressive number. Bad reviews cause everything from dismay to death and good reviews inspire a much less extensive response. Evil is, everywhere, more powerful than good, and why encourage it? Also, as a professor of literature, I have read several volumes of a series called *The Critical Heritage*, which lists the reviews of books now considered classics. The idiocy of the reviewers is monumental, and the sadness of the authors deep. Reviewers too often—and far more frequently these days—have an ax to grind, and the author who lets them grind it against his or her personal happiness is not wise. Bad reviews cause us to hate the reviewer, and to persist in that hatred. To offer something of the self and have it stomped to bits is hard to bear, let alone with equanimity.

What I do appreciate are letters from readers who liked my books, and I always answer them, which I understand is not a usual practice. Perhaps you will conclude, with reason, that I am old-fashioned, and in certain ways I am. But Kate Fansler and I, who share a taste for courtesy and kindness if little else, are old-fashioned only in that. She and I grow older—she less rapidly than I—and together we become sad at times and with a sense of a certain futility and hopelessness. But it doesn't last long, in either of us, because there is, in this naughty world, so much needing to be seen to. We both meddle in villainous situations that are brought sharply to our attention; we leave the world changed, only slightly perhaps, but, we hope, for the better. And we learn a lot and talk a lot along the way.

Amanda Cross

In the Last Analysis

Prologue

"I didn't say I objected to Freud," Kate said. "I said I objected to what Joyce called freudful errors—all those nonsensical conclusions leaped to by people with no reticence and less mind."

"If you are going to hold psychiatry responsible for sadistic parlor games, I see no point in continuing the discussion," Emanuel answered. But they would continue the discussion nonetheless; it had gone on for years, and showed no signs of exhausting itself.

"By the way," Kate said, "I've sent you a patient. At any rate, a student asked me to recommend a psychoanalyst, and I gave her your name and address. I have no idea if she'll call, but I rather expect she will. Her name is Janet Harrison." Kate walked to the window and looked out on the raw and blustery weather. It was the sort of January day when even she, who loathed spring, longed for it.

"Considering your opinion of psychiatry," Nicola said, "Emanuel should feel duly honored. Look honored, Emanuel!" Nicola, Emanuel's wife, followed these discussions rather as the spectator at a tennis match follows the ball, her head turning from one to the other. Having managed to place her faith in psychiatry without withdrawing her right to criticize, she applauded the good shots and groaned at the misses. Kate and Emanuel, charmed with Nicola as audience, enjoyed the matches not only for the occasional insights which emerged from them, but also because they shared the knack of irritating without ever offending each other. Nicola smiled on them both.

"It isn't Freud himself one quarrels with," Kate said, "nor even the great body of theory he evolved. It's the dissemination of his ideas in the modern world. I'm always reminded of the story of the

Japanese gentleman and the Trinity: 'Honorable Father, very good; Honorable Son, very good; but Honorable Bird I do not understand at all' ''

''Your quotations,'' Emanuel said, ''always enliven the conversation without in any way advancing the discussion.''

''The only quotation I can think of,'' said Nicola, in her turn walking to the window, ''is 'If Winter comes, can Spring be far behind?' ''

Which, as it turned out, was the most significant remark anybody made that afternoon.

1

SOMEONE had chalked "April is the cruelest month" on the steps of Baldwin Hall. Kate, unimpressed by the erudition, agreed with the sentiment. Spring on an American campus, even as urban a campus as this one, inevitably drove the faculty into a mood compounded of lassitude, irritation and fastidiousness. Perhaps, Kate thought, it is because we are getting old, while the students, like Caesar's crowds on the Appian Way, are always the same age. Gazing at the students who sprawled, or made love, on every available patch of grass, Kate longed, as she did each spring, for a statelier, less untidy era. "The young in one another's arms," Yeats had complained.

She mentioned this to Professor Anderson, who had stopped too, pondering the chalk inscription. "This time of year," he said, "I always want to shut myself up in a dark room, with the curtains drawn, and play Bach. Really, you know," he said, still regarding Eliot's line, "Millay put it better: 'To what purpose, April, do you return again?'" Kate was startled by Professor Anderson, who was an eighteenth century man with a strong distaste for all female writers since Jane Austen. Together they entered the building and mounted the stairs to the English department on the next floor. That was it, really. However expected, April was always startling.

On the bench outside Kate's office, waiting for her office hours, sat a line of students. This too was a spring symptom. The good students either vanished from the campus altogether, or appeared at odd moments to argue some abstruse point of interpretation. The mediocre, particularly the poor ones, began to worry about marks. April, stirring their dull senses, reminded them that the time of marks was near and the B they had faithfully promised themselves dismally remote. They had come to talk it out. Kate sighed as she unlocked the door to her office, and then stopped, in surprise and annoyance. A man standing at the window turned as she entered.

"Please come in, Miss Fansler. Perhaps I should say Doctor, or Professor; I am Acting Captain Stern, Detective from the Police Department. I've shown my credentials to the secretary in the office, who suggested that I had perhaps better wait in here. She was kind enough to let me in. I haven't disturbed anything. Won't you sit down?"

"I assure you, Captain," Kate said, sitting down at her desk, "I know very little about the personal lives of my students. Has one of them got into trouble?" She regarded the detective with interest. An avid reader of detective stories, she had always suspected that in real life detectives were desperately ordinary men, the sort who coped well with short-answer exams (corrected by machine) but were annoyed by complex ideas, literary or otherwise; the sort who liked the hardness of facts and found the need for ambivalence distasteful.

"Would you be good enough to tell me, Miss Fansler, what you were doing yesterday morning until noon?"

"What I was *doing?* Really, Captain Stern, I do assure you that . . ."

"If you will just be good enough to answer my questions, Miss Fansler, I will explain the reasons for them very shortly. Yesterday morning?"

Kate stared at him, and then shrugged. As is the unfortunate habit of the literary person, she already imagined herself retelling this extraordinary event. She caught the detective's eye, and reached for a cigarette. He lit it for her, waiting patiently. "I don't teach on Tuesdays," she said. "I am writing a book, and I spent all yesterday morning in the stacks of the library, looking up articles in nineteenth century periodicals. I was there until a little before one, when I went to wash, and then to meet Professor Popper for lunch. We ate in the faculty club."

"Do you live alone, Miss Fansler?"

"Yes."

"What time did you arrive in the 'stacks'?"

"The stacks, Captain Stern, are the inner floors of the library, on which the books are kept." Why is it, she wondered, that women are always annoyed at being asked if they live alone? "I got to the library at about nine-thirty."

"Did anyone see you in the stacks?"

"Anyone who could give me an 'alibi'? No. I found the volumes I wanted, and worked with them at the small tables along the wall provided for that purpose. Several people must have seen me there, but whether they recognized me, or remembered me, I couldn't say."

"Do you have a student named Janet Harrison?"

In books, Kate thought, detectives were always enthusiastically interested in their work, rather like knights on a quest. It had never really occurred to her before with what fervor they attacked their work. Some of the time, of course, they were related to, or in love with, the accused or murdered, but whether being a detective was their job or avocation, they seemed vehemently to care. She wondered what, if anything, Acting Captain Stern cared about. Could she ask him if he lived alone? Certainly not. "Janet Harrison? She used to be a student of mine; that is, she took one of my classes, on the nineteenth century novel. That was last semester; I haven't seen her since." Kate thought longingly of Lord Peter Wimsey; at this point, surely, he would have paused to discuss the nineteenth century novel. Captain Stern seemed never to have heard of it.

"Did you recommend that she attend a psychoanalyst?"

"Good God," Kate said, "is that what this has to do with? Surely the police are not checking up on all people who attend analysts. I didn't 'recommend' that she attend an analyst; I would consider it improper to do any such thing. She came to me having already decided, or been advised, to go to an analyst. She asked me if I could recommend a good one, since she had heard of the importance of finding a properly qualified man. Now that you mention it, I don't quite know why she came to me; I suppose we are all too willing to assume that others recognize us as monuments of good sense and natural authorities on most things."

There was no answering smile from Captain Stern. "Did you in fact recommend a psychoanalyst?"

"Yes, in fact, I did!"

"What was the name of the analyst you recommended?"

Kate was suddenly angry. Glancing out of the window, where April was breeding desire all over the place, did nothing to improve her mood. She averted her eyes from the campus and looked at the detective, who appeared unmoved by April. Undoubtedly he found all months equally cruel. Whatever this was about—and her curiosity had been greatly diluted by annoyance—was there any purpose in dragging Emanuel into it? "Captain Stern," she asked, "am I required to answer that question? I'm not at all certain of the legal rights in this matter, but wouldn't I be 'booked,' or told what this is all about, if I'm to answer questions? Would it suffice for now if I were to assure you (though I cannot prove it) that yesterday morning until one o'clock I was involved in no way whatever with any human being other than Thomas Carlyle, whose death well over half a century ago precludes the possibility of my having been in any way involved in it?''

Captain Stern ignored this. "You say you did recommend a psychoanalyst to Janet Harrison. Did she find him satisfactory; did she plan to continue with him for very long?''

"I don't know," Kate said, feeling somewhat ashamed of her outburst into sarcasm, "I don't even know if she went to him. I gave her his name, address and telephone number. I mentioned the matter to him. From that moment to this I haven't seen the girl, nor given her a moment's thought.''

"Surely the analyst would have mentioned the matter to you, if he had taken her as a patient. Particularly,'' Captain Stern added, revealing for the first time a certain store of knowledge, "if he were a good friend.''

Kate stared at him. At least, she thought, we are not playing twenty questions. "I can't make you believe it, of course, but he did not mention it, nor would a first-rate analyst do so, particularly if I had not asked him. The man in question is a member of the New York Psychoanalytic Institute, and it is against their principles ever to discuss a patient. This may seem strange; nonetheless, it is the simple truth.''

"What sort of girl was Janet Harrison?''

Kate leaned back in the chair, trying to gauge the man's intelligence. She had learned as a college teacher that if one simplified what one wished to say, one falsified it. It was possible only to say what one meant, as clearly as possible. What could this Janet Harrison have done? Were they trying to establish her instability? Really, this laconic policeman was most trying.

"Captain Stern, while the students are attending classes here, their lives are going on; most of these students are not isolated in dormitories, they are not away from family pressure, financial pressures, emotional pressures of all sorts. They are at an age when, if they are not married—and that is a state which brings its own problems—they are suffering from love or the lack of it. They are going to bed with someone they love, which is to be in one emotional state, or they are going to bed with someone they do not love, which is to be in another, or they are going to bed with no one at all, which is to be in still another. Sometimes they are colored, or the unreligious children of religious parents, or the religious children of unreligious parents. Sometimes they are women torn between mind and family. Often they are in trouble, of one sort or another. As teachers, we know little of this, and if we catch a hint of some of it we are—how shall I put it—not the priest, but the church: we are there; we continue. We speak for something that goes on—art, or science, or history. Of course, we get the occasional student who tells you about himself even as he breathes; for the most part, we get only the most general impression, apart, of course, from the student's actual work.

"You ask what sort of girl was Janet Harrison? I tell you all this so that you will understand my answer. I have only an impression. If you ask, Was she the sort to hold up a bank? I would say No, she didn't seem to me the sort, but I'm not sure I could tell you why. She was an intelligent student, well above the average; she gave me the impression of being able to do excellent work, should she put her mind to it, but her whole mind was never put to it. It was as though a part of her was off somewhere, waiting to see what would happen. Yet you know," Kate added, "till you asked me, I had not thought of it quite that way."

"Didn't you have any idea why she would want to go to a psychoanalyst?"

"No, I did not. People today turn to analysis as they used to turn to—what? God, their minister, their families; I don't pretend to know. I have heard people say, and only half in fun, that parents had better save now for their child's analysis as they used to save for his college education. A youngster today, moving in intellectual circles, will, in trouble, turn to psychiatry, and his parents will often help him if they can."

"And a psychiatrist, a psychoanalyst, will accept any patient who comes to him?"

"Of course not," Kate said. "But surely you haven't come here to learn about these matters from me. There are many people competent to discuss . . ."

"You sent this girl to a psychoanalyst, and he took her as a patient. I would like to know why you thought she should go to an analyst, and why you thought this analyst would take her."

"This is my office hour," Kate said. Not that she minded, on this particular April day, missing the students ("I'm a provisional student, Professor Fansler, and if I don't get a B− in this course . . .''), but the thought of the students patiently waiting on the bench, perhaps now overflowing it . . . but Captain Stern had no objection, obviously, to displacing the students. Perhaps she should send Captain Stern to Emanuel. All at once, the thought of sitting in her office on a spring day, discussing psychiatry with a police detective, struck her as ludicrous. "Look here, Captain Stern," she said, "what is it you want to know? Before a good analyst will take on a patient, he must be certain that the patient is qualified for analysis. The patient must be of sufficient intelligence, with certain kinds of problems, with a certain possibility for free development. A psychotic, even certain neurotics, are not proper subjects. Most of all, a patient must *want* to go into analysis, must *want* to be helped. On the other hand, most analysts that I have met believe that any intelligent person can be helped, can be given a greater freedom of activity by a good analysis. If I am asked to recommend a good analyst, I recommend a good one, knowing that a good analyst will only take a patient suitable to analysis, and suitable to analysis by this particular analyst. I can't be any clearer than that on a subject about which I know remarkably little, and any psychiatrist hearing me now would probably scream in horror and say I'd got it all wrong, which I probably have. Now what in the world has Janet Harrison done?''

"She has been murdered.''

Captain Stern left the words hanging in the air. From outside came the campus noises of spring. Some fraternity boys were selling raffle tickets on a car. The shadow of someone, probably a student, passed back and forth behind the glass door to Kate's office.

"Murdered?'' Kate said. "But I knew nothing about her. Was she attacked in the street?'' Suddenly the girl seemed born again in Kate's memory, sitting where Captain Stern now sat. *Thou art a scholar; speak to it, Horatio.*

"You said, Miss Fansler, she seemed to be waiting to see what would happen. What did you mean by that?''

"Did I say that? I don't know what I meant. A way of speaking.''

"Was there *anything* of a personal nature between you and Janet Harrison?''

"No. She was a student.'' Suddenly, Kate remembered his first question: *What were you doing yesterday morning?* "Captain Stern, what has this to do with me? Because I gave her the name of an analyst, because she was my student, am I supposed to know who murdered her?''

Captain Stern rose to his feet. "Forgive me for taking the time from your students, Miss Fansler. If I have to see you again, I will try to make it at a more convenient hour. Thank you for answering my questions.'' He paused a moment, as though arranging his sentences.

"Janet Harrison was murdered in the office of the psychoanalyst to whom you sent her. Emanuel Bauer is his name. She had been his patient for seven weeks. She was murdered on the couch in his office, the couch on which, as I understand it, patients lie during their analytic hour. She was stabbed with a knife from the Bauer kitchen. We are anxious, of course, to find out all we can about her. There seems to be remarkably little information available. Goodbye for now, Miss Fansler.''

Kate stared after him as he left, closing the door behind him. She had underestimated his flair for the dramatic; that much was clear. *I've sent you a patient, Emanuel.* What had she sent him? Where was he now? Surely the police could not imagine that Emanuel had stabbed a patient on his own couch? But how then had the murderer got in? Had Emanuel been there? She picked up the receiver and dialed 9 for an outside line. What was his number? She would not thumb through a phone book. It surprised her to notice, as she dialed 411 for information, that her hand was shaking. "Can you give me the number, please, of Mrs. Nicola Bauer, 879 Fifth Avenue?'' Emanuel's office number was under his name, his home phone under Nicola's, she remembered that: to prevent patients calling him at home. "Thank you, operator.'' She did not write it down, but repeated it over and over to herself. Trafalgar 9. But she had forgotten to dial 9 again for an outside line. Begin again and take it slowly. *Emanuel, what have I done to you?* "Hello.'' It was Pandora, the Bauers' maid. What an amusing name it had once seemed! "Pandora, this is Miss Fansler, Kate Fansler. Please tell Mrs. Bauer that I must speak to her.''

"Just a minute, Miss Fansler, I'll see.'' The phone was laid down. Kate could hear one of the Bauer boys. Then there was Nicola.

"Kate. I suppose you've heard.''

"A detective's been here; I'm in my office. Efficient, laconic, and, I suspect, superficial. Nicki, are they letting you stay there?''

"Oh, yes. Thousands of men have been through the whole place, but they say we can stay. Mother said we should go home with her, but once the policemen cleared out, it seemed better somehow to stay. As though if we left, we might never come back, Emanuel might never come back. We've even kept the boys here. It does seem crazy, I suppose.''

"No, Nicki. I understand. You stay. Can I come and see you? Will you tell me what's happened? Will they let me come?''

"They've only left a policeman outside, to cope with the mobs. There've been reporters. We'd like to see you, Kate.''

"You sound exhausted, but I'm coming anyway.''

"I'd like to see you. I don't know about Emanuel. Kate, I think they think we did it, in Emanuel's office. Kate, don't you know an Assistant District Attorney? Maybe you could . . .''

"Nicki, I'll be right over. I'll do anything I can. I'm leaving now.''

Outside the office a few students still waited. Kate rushed past them down the stairs. On that bench, how many months ago, Janet Harrison had waited. *Professor Fansler, could you recommend a good psychiatrist?*

2

THERE is no real reason why psychiatrists should confine themselves to the most elegant residential section of the city. Broadway, for example, is accessible by subway, while Fifth, Madison, Park Avenue, and the side streets which connect them can be reached only by taxi, bus or on foot. But no psychiatrist would dream of moving west, with the exception of a few brave souls on Central Park West, who apparently find sufficient elegance in the sight of Fifth Avenue across the park. Whether this has formed itself as an equation: East Side = style, psychiatry = style, therefore psychiatry = East Side; whether it is that the West Side and success are unthinkable together, whatever the reason, psychiatrists find themselves, and their patients find them, in the sixties, seventies, perhaps the low eighties, between the avenues. The area is known, in certain circles, as psychiatrists' row.

The Bauers lived in a ground-floor apartment in the sixties, just off Fifth Avenue. The building itself was on Fifth Avenue, but Dr. Emanuel Bauer's office address was 3 East. This added, for some mysterious reason, a note of elegance, as though, living on Fifth Avenue, it was more couth if one did not say so in so many words. What the Bauers' rent was, Kate had never dared to imagine. Nicola, of course, had money, and since Emanuel's office was in the apartment, a percentage of the rent was tax deductible. Kate herself lived in a large four-room apartment overlooking the Hudson River, not, as some of her friends said, because she was a reverse snob, but because the old apartments on the East Side were unavailable, and as for the new ones—Kate would rather have pitched a tent than live with a windowless kitchen, with walls so thin one listened, perforce, to the neighbors' television, with Muzak in the elevators, and goldfish in the lobby. Her ceilings were high, her walls thick, and her elegance faded.

As Kate's taxi wove in and out of traffic, carrying her to the Bauers', she thought, not of their rent, but of the apartment's layout, its convenience for a murderer. In fact, the apartment, when one came to think of it, was designed for intrusion of any sort. The entrance from the street led one into a short hall, with the Bauer apartment on one side, another doctor's office (he was not in psychiatry, Kate seemed to remember) on the other. Beyond these two entrances, the hall widened into a small lobby, with a bench, an elevator and a door beyond it to the garage. Although the main lobby of the building was stiff with attendants, this small one boasted only the elevator man who, in keeping with his kind, spent a good part of his time going up to, or down from, the upper floors. When he was in his elevator, the lobby was empty. Neither the Bauers' apartment nor the office across the hall was locked during the day. Emanuel's patients simply walked in and waited in a small waiting room until summoned by Emanuel into his office. Theoretically, if the elevator were up, one could walk in unobserved at any time.

But, of course, there would be other people about. Not to mention the other doctor and his patients and nurse, who seemed to do rather a lot of going and coming, there were Emanuel himself, his patients, possibly one in the office and one waiting, Nicola, the maid, the Bauer boys, Simon and Joshua, friends of Nicola's, friends of the boys, and of course, Kate realized, anyone living on the upper floors who had entered the building by the side entrance and waited in the small lobby for the elevator. It was becoming increasingly clear to Kate, and probably already clear to the police, that whoever had done this knew the place and the habits of the Bauers. It was a disquieting thought, but Kate refused at this point to give way to its depressing implications. Perhaps, Kate thought, the murderer had been seen. Yet in fact she doubted it. And if he or she had been seen, he or she had probably looked like a quite ordinary tenant, or visitor, or patient, and was therefore quite unmemorable, in fact invisible.

Kate found Nicola stretched out on her bed in the back of the apartment. Kate had walked in unnoticed by anyone except the policeman in the hall, a fact which depressed her still further, though whether she was upset by the ease of her intrusion or the presence of the policeman she could not have said. Nicola was usually to be found in the back. The Bauer living room, visible from the foyer through which the patients passed, was not used during the day or

the early hours of the evening when Emanuel had patients. Great
care, in fact, as all Nicola's friends knew, was taken to make sure
that the patients saw no one in Emanuel's household. And even the
boys had become expert at dodging back and forth between the bedroom part of the apartment and the kitchen without meeting a patient.

"Is Emanuel working?" Kate asked.

"Yes. They've let him have the office again, though of course it
will be in the papers, and whether the patients will come back, or
what they will think if they do, I can't imagine. I suppose actually it
will bring up all sorts of fascinating material, if they care to talk
about it; but it is *not* the best thing for transference during an analysis,
at least not for *positive* transference, to have one's analyst's office
the scene of a murder, with the analyst himself as the chief suspect.
I mean, patients may have fantasies about being attacked on an analyst's couch—I'm sure most of them do—but it is best *not* to have
someone actually stabbed there."

Nothing, Kate noticed thankfully, nothing could stop the flow of
Nicola's talk. Except when she talked about her children (and the
only way to keep from being boring on that subject, Kate believed,
was to avoid it), Nicola was never dull, partly because her talk came
from a joy in life that was more than egocentricity, and partly because
she not only talked, she listened, listened and cared. Kate often
thought that Emanuel had married Nicki largely because her language, flowing over him in waves, catching up every imaginable,
every unprofound subject, buoyed him up despite the heaviness of
his own mind. For the only thing which drove Emanuel eagerly to
talk was an abstract idea, and, oddly, this anomaly suited them. Like
most male followers of Freud, like Freud himself, if it came to that,
Emanuel needed and sought the company of intellectual women but
avoided any contractual alliance with them.

"And, of course," Nicki went on, "patients shouldn't know *anything* about their analyst, personally, and even if the police do their
best—as they have promised—the papers are bound to print that he
has a wife and two children, let alone is suspected of stabbing a
patient on the couch, and I can't imagine how we shall ever recover
from this, even if Emanuel isn't sent to jail, though they could doubtless use a brilliant psychoanalyst in jail, but if Emanuel had wanted
to study the criminal mind he would have gone in for that in the first
place. Perhaps if he *had,* he could figure out who did it. I keep telling
him it *must* have been one of his patients, and he keeps saying, 'Let's
not discuss it, Nicola,' and I'm not supposed to talk to anyone really,

except perhaps Mother, who wants to rally round, but insists on looking so *brave,* but Emanuel has said I can talk to you because you
know how to keep your mouth shut, and you'll be a good outlet. For
me, I mean.''

"Let me get you some sherry," Kate said.

"Now, don't start being sensible, or I shall scream. Pandora is
being sensible with the boys; of course I am too, but I just want
someone who will sit down with me and *wail.*''

"I am not being sensible, merely selfish. I could use a drink
myself. In the kitchen? All right, stay there, I'll get it; you plan how
you can tell me all this starting right at the beginning . . .''

"I know, go on till I get to the end, and then stop. We do need
the Red King, don't we? It is rather like that."

As Kate walked to the kitchen and back with the drinks, peeking
first through the doors to make sure the path was clear (it would not
do to meet a patient with a glass of liquor firmly grasped in each
hand), Kate clarified in her own mind the sort of fact she would have
to elicit from Nicki if she were to make any sense of the entire affair.
She had already determined to call Reed at the D.A.'s office and
blackmail him (if it should come to that) into telling her what the
police knew, but meanwhile the sensible thing was to get the facts.
With that odd ability to see herself from the outside, Kate noticed
with interest that she had already accepted the murder as fact, that
the shock had passed, that she had now reached the state where co-
herent action was possible.

"Well," Nicki said, sipping her sherry automatically, "it began
like any other day." (Days always do, Kate thought, but we notice
it only when they don't end like any other day.) "Emanuel got up
with the boys. It's the only time he really gets to see them, except
for odd moments during the day, and they all had breakfast together
in the kitchen. Because he had an eight o'clock patient, at ten minutes
of he shoved the boys into their room, where they played, though
quiet play is clearly beyond them, and I continued to sleep my fitful
sleep until nine . . .''

"Do you mean Emanuel has a patient at eight o'clock in the
morning?''

"Of course, it's the most popular hour of all. People who work
have to come either before they go to work, or in their lunch hour,
or just after work at night, which is why Emanuel's day, and I suppose every psychiatrist's, stretches out so at both ends. Of course, at
the moment Emanuel's got five patients in the morning, but that's a

very bad arrangement, and he's planning—well, he *was* planning—to move the ten o'clock patient over to the afternoon as soon as he, the patient, could arrange his schedule to come in the afternoon. Now the eleven o'clock patient is gone, possibly to be followed by all the others.''

"The eleven o'clock patient was Janet Harrison?''

"Kate, do you think she had a past? She *must* have had a past, mustn't she, if someone tracked her down and killed her in Emanuel's office? I keep pointing out that someone in analysis is very likely to mention her past, and why in hell doesn't Emanuel tell the police about her, but of course it's like the secrets of the confessional; still, the girl is dead, and Emanuel in danger . . .''

"Nicki, dear, she doesn't have to have had a past; a present will do, even a future someone wanted to avoid. I only hope whoever did it wanted to murder *her*. I mean, if the police have to find a homicidal maniac who was overcome at the sight of a girl on a couch, and who just happened to wander in, who never knew who she was—well, of course, that idea is preposterous. Let's get back to yesterday. Emanuel had patients at eight, nine, ten, eleven and twelve?''

"He *expected* to have; as it turned out the eleven and twelve o'clock patients canceled, or Emanuel *thought* they canceled, though of course they came, that was how I happened to find the body, because the twelve o'clock patient . . .''

"Nicki, please, let's stick to the proper order. The point is, don't leave out anything, however ordinary, however insignificant. How many patients does Emanuel have altogether, by the way; I mean, how many *did* he have, as of yesterday morning?''

"I don't know, exactly. Emanuel never talks about his work. I know he never has more than eight a day, but of course they can't all afford to come every day, so the total probably comes to ten or twelve; I don't know, you'll have to ask Emanuel.''

"All right, we're up to nine o'clock yesterday morning, when you arose from your fitful sleep.''

"Nine-fifteenish, really. Then the children and I make a dash for the kitchen, where I have a first breakfast, and they have a second. We tend to dawdle, actually, and usually I make lists, either of marketing I have to do, or errands of some other sort, and I telephone the butcher, and sometimes Mother, and so on. *You* know what mornings are like.''

"When does Pandora come?''

"Oh, Pandora's come already. Sorry, I keep forgetting things.

Pandora comes at nine; she's usually in the kitchen when I get there
with the boys. After they've sampled most of my breakfast, she's
stacked the dishes, and so on, she dresses the boys and they go out,
unless of course it's raining. Pandora has a kind of colony she meets
in the Park; I've no idea what age, or sex, or nationality the other
children are, but the boys seem to like it, and Pandora, of course, is
a positive monument of good sense, particularly now she's been . . .''

"It is about ten o'clock in the morning, and the children have
just gone out with Pandora."

"A little after ten, actually, as a general rule. Then I begin throwing on my clothes, and so on, since I have to leave at least by twenty
of eleven to get to my analytic hour, though usually I leave a bit
earlier to do an errand or two on the way." Nicki, too, was in analysis, though exactly why Kate had never been able to determine. It
had something to do with understanding and sympathizing with her
husband, but apparently Nicki had felt also a great need to work out
certain problems, the chief of which seemed to be what Nicki referred
to as "anxiety attacks." Kate could never discover precisely *what* an
anxiety attack was, though she gathered that it was terrifying, and
that its chief characteristic seemed to be the fact that there was nothing, at the time, to be anxious about. Nothing rational, that is. For
example, Nicki had explained, a person might get an anxiety attack
in an elevator; he would become violently anxious about the elevator's falling, but if you could *prove* to him absolutely that the elevator
couldn't fall, and he might know perfectly well that it *can't,* none of
that would prevent the anxiety attack. Nor, Kate had further gathered,
did it mean that he (the victim of the anxiety attack) had ever been
in a falling elevator, had ever known anyone who had been in a
falling elevator, had ever, in fact, had anything superficially to do
with elevators at all. Nicki's anxiety attacks were not associated with
elevators—a pity, really, since she lived on the ground floor—but
were connected, apparently, with public transportation. Not for the
first time, Kate reflected that while she was impressed profoundly
with the genius of Freud, the ineffectual groping, the combination of
muddle and doctrine which marked clinical analysis today left her
unimpressed in the extreme. The trouble was, among other things,
that if Freud were to return to earth today, he would still be a better
psychiatrist than anybody else; Einstein, before he died, could not
understand the work then being done in physics, and this, Kate
thought, was proper, and as it should be. Psychiatry, which had begun

with Freud, seemed largely to have ended there; but perhaps it was too early to tell.

"Actually, I left at ten-thirty yesterday," Nicki said.

"Meanwhile, Emanuel was having patients in his office."

"Yes. In between the nine and ten o'clock patients, he came into the back of the apartment to say hello and to go to the bathroom. Everything was still all right then. I didn't see him again till . . ."

"Wait a minute, Nicki. Let's get this straight now. By ten-thirty, Emanuel was in his office with a patient (the patient, incidentally, whom he wanted to switch to the afternoon—does that possibly matter? I wonder if he knew the girl), Pandora had gone out with the children, and you were leaving for your eleven o'clock appointment and an errand. When you left, there would be no one in the apartment but Emanuel and his patient, who would be shut up in the office?"

"Yes. It sounds a bit dramatic, of course, but that's perfectly true. The police seemed very interested in all this too."

"Anyone who had observed the household would know that this is what actually happened, or what inevitably happened, unless someone was sick, or it rained?"

"Yes. But who would observe the apartment? Kate, don't you see, the whole point is precisely that."

"Nicki, please. Let's stick to the chronological report for a minute. At eleven, then, the girl Janet Harrison, would have come; the previous patient would have left. You would be at your analyst's, the children and Pandora would be in the park, and for an hour this situation would continue?"

"For fifty minutes, anyway. The fifty-minute hour, you know. The patients leave at ten of, and the hour begins on the hour. But you see the problem the police have. I mean, one can see their point of view, even if one knows oneself that Emanuel could never have stabbed a patient in his own office, on his own couch; the whole idea is insane. There he was, or at least, they think he was, though of course he wasn't, but I mean, there they *think* he was, in a soundproof office with a girl, no one else about, and he claims that someone else came in and stabbed her on the couch and that he wasn't there at all. From their point of view, I suppose it does sound fishy, to say the least. Of course, Emanuel has told them perfectly clearly that . . ."

"Why is the room soundproofed, by the way?"

"For the patient's peace of mind, really. If a patient sitting in the waiting room should hear a sound, any sound at all, from the office, he would leap to the conclusion that *he* could be heard, and this might have dreadful inhibiting effects. So Emanuel decided to have it sound-proofed—I think most psychiatrists do—and he sat in every possible place in the waiting room, while I lay on the couch in the office and screamed I LOVE MY MOTHER AND HATE MY FATHER over and over, though of course the patients don't scream, and they would never say that, but we did have to be sure, and Emanuel didn't hear a thing."

"Let's skip a minute, Nicki. Let's go on to twelve o'clock, when you found the body. Why you? Do you usually go into Emanuel's office?"

"Never during the day, really. At night I go in to dust and empty the ashtrays, since Pandora doesn't really have a chance, and in the summer sometimes, in the evenings before we go away, we sit in there because it's the only air-conditioned room in the house. But during the day none of us ever goes near it. We try even not to go back and forth too much when there's a patient in the waiting room, though Emanuel has them trained to shut the hall door behind them, so technically they couldn't see us anyway, unless they were going in or out. I know a lot of psychiatrists disapprove of an analyst having his office in his house, but they don't realize how little the patients do see of what goes on. Although Emanuel's patients probably assume he's married, only one of them has ever seen me in all these years, and he may have thought I was another patient. None of them has ever seen, I think, even an indication of the children. The office is definitely out of bounds, and I would no more go into it than I would go into Emanuel's office if it were somewhere else; probably less so."

"Suppose for some reason you have to talk to him during the day."

"If it's important, I wait till he comes back, which he often does between patients. If there is a rush, I telephone him. He has his own office phone, of course."

"But you went into the office yesterday at twelve o'clock."

"Not at twelve, no; I'm usually not home before twelve-thirty, though yesterday I was a little early. Some days I meet someone for lunch, or go downtown, and don't come home in the early afternoon at all. But yesterday, thank God—I suppose, thank God—I came home early. As I walked into the house, the twelve o'clock patient . . . ."

"Did you recognize him?"

"No, of course not; I'd never seen him before. I mean, the man

I later learned was the twelve o'clock patient stuck his head out the
hall door and asked if the doctor was meeting his patients. It was
twenty-five of one, and the doctor hadn't come to call him in. Well,
you know, Kate, that was extremely odd. Emanuel has never in his
life stood up a patient. I knew he had had an eleven o'clock patient
(Janet Harrison), and he never tries to dash out in the ten minutes
between patients. I wondered what could have happened to him.
Could he be in his office, feeling, for some reason, unable to meet a
patient? I dialed his office phone from the telephone in the kitchen,
and after three rings, the service answered, so I knew he wasn't there,
or wasn't answering, and then I became worried. Meanwhile, I'd
coaxed the patient back into the waiting room. Of course, I was
having all sorts of fantasies about his having had a heart attack in
the office, or having been unable to get rid of the eleven o'clock
patient—one does have the oddest fantasies at these times—Pandora
was in the kitchen with the boys getting lunch, and I went and
knocked on the office door. I knew the patient in the waiting room
was aware of what I was doing, though he couldn't see me, but I had
to do something, and naturally, no one answered the knock, so I
opened the door a bit and stuck my head in. She was right there on
the couch, which is near the door; I couldn't possibly miss seeing
her. At first I thought, She's fallen asleep, but then I saw the knife
sticking out of her chest. And Emanuel nowhere to be found. I did
have the presence of mind to close the office door and tell the patient
he'd better go. He was curious, and clearly reluctant to leave a scene
which he sensed was fraught with drama, but I ushered him out. I
was extremely calm, as one often is right after a shock.''

"And then you sent for the police?"

"No. Actually I never thought of the police, not then."

"What *did* you do?"

"I rushed into the office across the hall and got the doctor. He
was very nice and came right away, even though he had an office
full of patients. His name is Barrister, Michael Barrister. He told me
she was dead.''

3

"DINNER seems to be served," said Emanuel, coming into the bedroom. "Hello, Kate. Pandora has set a place for you. How that woman carries on like this, I don't know, but she has never had any use for the police."

"You carry on fairly well yourself," Kate said.

"Today, after all, was still a bit of the old life for me. The patients didn't know yet, at least not till the last one at six o'clock. He had an evening paper."

"Do the papers mention it?" Nicola asked.

"Mention it! I'm afraid at the moment we *are* the news. Pyschiatry, couches, female patients, male doctors, knives—one can scarcely blame them. Let's say good night to the boys and have some dinner."

But it was not until dinner was over, and they were in the living room, that they talked again of the murder. Kate had half expected Emanuel to disappear, but he seemed to want to talk. Usually some inner need to "get something done," to "make use of time," either drove him from social occasions, or subjected him, if he remained, to the pressure of a mounting inner tension. Yet tonight, with a real problem looming, as it were, in the external world, Emanuel seemed, almost with thankfulness, to have relaxed in the contemplation of something beyond his control. The very externality of the murder gave him a kind of relief. Kate, recognizing this, knew the police would mistake his calm for some symptom, some indication of guilt, when in fact, if they only knew, it was the assurance of his innocence. Had he murdered the girl, the problem would not, of course, have been outside. Yet what policeman in the world could one convince of all this? Stern? Kate forced her thoughts back to the facts.

"Emanuel," she asked, "where were you between ten of eleven and twelve-thirty? Don't tell me you suffered a blow on the head and simply wandered about, uncertain of who you were."

Emanuel looked at her, and then at Nicola, and said to Kate, "How much has she told you?"

"Only the normal routine of the day, really, plus a word or two on the finding of the body. We had, for the moment, skipped over the magic hour."

"Magic is the word," Emanuel said. "It was all done with such cleverness that really, you know, I don't blame the police for suspecting me; I almost suspect myself. When you add to the quite justified suspicions of police, the mysterious and still, I fear, not quite fully American profession of psychiatry, it's no wonder they assume that I went mad and stabbed the girl on my couch. I don't think they have any doubts."

"Why haven't they arrested you?"

"I wondered that myself, and decided finally that there really isn't, yet, quite enough evidence. I don't know much about the ins and outs of this, but I gather the D.A.'s office has to be convinced they've got enough evidence to have a good chance for conviction before they'll allow an arrest and trial. A really clever lawyer (which it is assumed I could afford with ease) would make mincemeat of what they've got so far. As I see it, there are two problems: what this will do to me professionally, which I prefer for the moment to ignore, and the fact that as long as they believe I did it they will not really work to find who did. In that case I am doomed, either way."

Kate felt a great surge of admiration and affection for this deeply intelligent and honest man. No one knew better than she (or, perhaps, did Nicola?) his failure to meet the day-to-day demands of a personal relationship, but at that still center of himself she recognized, as in every crisis she always would, an honor, an identity, that nothing would shatter. She had lived long enough to know that when you find intelligence and integrity in the same individual, you have found a prize.

"I'm surprised they let you go on seeing your patients, even today," said Nicola, in tones of sarcasm. "Perhaps you might go mad, since we are apparently to consider it a symptom of your profession, and stab another victim. Wouldn't they look foolish then?"

"On the contrary," Kate said lightly. "They'd have their case wrapped up. I imagine that partly they are hoping he will do it again, and cast away all doubt, and partly even they, in their dim, methodical way, suspect somewhere in the depths of their beings that Emanuel didn't do it.'' Her eyes met Emanuel's and then dropped, but he had seen the faith, and it had strengthened him.

"The irony great enough to make Shakespeare howl,'' Emanuel said, "is that the girl had recently become very angry, which means transference. When she canceled today, I assumed it was because of that, and didn't feel surprised. How clever we like to think we are!''

"Did she call you to cancel the appointment?''

"I didn't speak to her, but in the normal course of events that is hardly surprising. She and the twelve o'clock patient—who later showed up and catapulted Nicki into finding the body—both of them, I learned at about five of eleven, had canceled their appointments.''

"Isn't that a bit unusual?''

"Not really. As a rule, of course, two patients don't cancel in a row, but it's by no means extraordinary. Sometimes patients hit a patch of difficult material, and just can't face it for a while. It happens in the course of every analysis. Or they tell themselves they're too tired, or too busy, or too upset. Freud came to understand this very early. It's one of the reasons we insist on charging patients for canceled appointments, even where they appear to have, do have, a perfectly legitimate excuse. People who don't understand psychiatry are always shocked and think we are moneygrubbers, but the whole mechanism of paying, and even sacrificing to pay for an analysis, is an important part of the therapy.''

"How did you learn at five of eleven that they had both canceled?''

"I called the exchange and they told me.''

"The exchange is the answering service? Do you call them every hour?''

"Not unless I know there's been a call.''

"You mean while you were in there with a patient, the phone rang, and you didn't answer it?''

"The phone doesn't ring; it has a yellow light which flashes on and off instead of a ring. The patient can't see it from the couch. If I don't answer after three rings, or three flashes, the exchange answers. Of course, I don't interrupt patients by answering the phone.''

"Did you find out who spoke to the exchange to cancel the appointments? Was it a man and a woman, or a man for both, or what?''

"I thought of that, of course, first thing, but when I got to the exchange someone else was on duty, and they don't keep any record of the voice they spoke to, merely the message and the time. Doubtless the police will look into it more carefully."

Nicola, who had been sitting quietly during this exchange, whirled around to face Kate. "Before you ask another question, let me ask you something. This is the part that sticks in the throats of the police; I know it is, but maybe Emanuel has talked to enough people about it so that they'll find out it's probably true, and anyway we've met other psychiatrists who do the same things because they feel so shut up."

"Nicki, dear," Kate said, "not to mention your pronouns, I haven't an idea in the world what you're talking about."

"Of course not; I haven't asked you the question yet. Here it is: If a patient of Emanuel's canceled, what would Emanuel do?"

"Go somewhere. No matter where, just go."

"You see," Nicola said. "Everyone knows that. I'd guess you'd go down to Brentano's to browse among the paper books, and my mother, when I asked her that question, decided he'd think of an errand, somewhere, he simply had to do, but the important point is that the police cannot understand that a psychiatrist, who must sit quietly all day listening, relaxes by moving. They think if he wasn't harboring nefarious plans, he would have stayed nicely in his office like any other sane person, catching up on his correspondence. At his *most* abandoned, they are convinced he would have called up a friend and had lunch downtown with two vodka cocktails first. It's no good telling them that Emanuel never eats lunch, *certainly* never eats it with anyone else, and in any case is not geared to calling people up for lunch because he's never, except for a fluke like this— and now that I think of it, it isn't a fluke, it was planned—free for lunch."

"What did you do, Emanuel?" Kate asked.

"I walked around the reservoir; round and round and round, at a kind of trot."

"I know; I've seen you; I've trotted too." It had been long ago, before Nicola, when she was still young enough to run just for the hell of it.

"It was spring; the spring was in my blood." Kate thought of the chalk inscription. She seemed to have viewed it in another lifetime. She was suddenly dog tired, and felt herself collapse, like one of those cartoon figures she remembered from her childhood who discovered they were sitting on nothing, and then fell to the floor.

From the first emotional shock of Detective Stern's announcement—
She has been murdered—until this moment, she had allowed no feeling to cluster about the idea of Emanuel's situation. Particularly, she
had excluded from her attention the question of responsibility for this
situation. She was sufficiently logical, even in this state of emotional
and physical exhaustion, not to hold herself wholly to blame. She
could not have known the girl would be murdered, could not have
guessed—indeed, could not have imagined—that she would be murdered in Emanuel's office. Had such an idea crossed her mind, Kate
would have decided that, in Nicola's language, she was "hallucinating."

Yet if Kate was no more than a single link in the chain of events
which had led to this disaster, she had, nonetheless, a responsibility,
not only to Emanuel and Nicola, but to herself, perhaps also to Janet
Harrison.

"Do you remember that joke of a few years ago?" she said to
them, "the one about the two psychiatrists on the stairs, and one of
them gooses the other. The goosed one is at first rather angry, and
then, shrugging his shoulders, dismisses the incident. 'After all,' he
is supposed to have said, 'it's *his* problem.' Well, I can't do the same;
it's my problem too, even if you were not my friends."

From the way in which Emanuel and Nicola avoided looking at
each other, or at her, she knew this point had been at least mentioned
between them. "In fact," she continued, "regarded in a certain light,
shall we say the light of the police, I'm a rather nice suspect myself.
The detective who came to see me asked what I was doing yesterday
morning. It may have been what they call 'routine'; it may not."

Emanuel and Nicola stared at her. "That's absolute nonsense,"
Emanuel said.

"No more nonsense, really, than that you should have murdered
her in your own office, or that Nicola might have. Look at it from
Detective Stern's point of view: I know the routine, more or less, of
your household and office. As it happens, I didn't know about your
telephone, about its lighting up instead of ringing, or about your not
answering when a patient is there, but there's only my word for that.
I sent the girl to Emanuel. Perhaps I was madly jealous of her, or
had stolen her money, or one of her literary ideas, and seized the
chance to kill her."

"But you didn't have any personal connection with her, did
you?" Nicola asked.

"Of course I didn't. But neither, I assume, did Emanuel. Yet the police must suppose there was some connection, a mad passion or something of the sort, if he was going to kill her in his office. I don't imagine they suppose he went off his head all of a sudden, and stabbed her in the middle of one of her more interesting free associations.''

"She was very beautiful," Nicola said. She dropped the sentence, like an awkward gift from a child, into their laps. Both Emanuel and Kate started to say "How do you know?" Neither of them said it. Could Nicki have noticed the girl was beautiful in the moment when she saw her dead? With a shock, Kate remembered the girl's beauty. It had not been of the flamboyant sort toward which men turned their heads on the street, around which they clustered at a party. That sort of beauty, as like as not, is the result of startling coloring, and a certain pleasing symmetry of the face. Janet Harrison had had what Kate called beauty in the bones. The finely chiseled features, the planes of the face, the deep-set eyes, the broad, clear forehead—these made her beauty which, at the second or third look, suddenly presented itself as though it had been in hiding. *My God*, Kate thought, remembering, *it needed only that.* "The point I was going to make," she went on after a moment, "is that I feel a responsibility for all this, a guilt if you will, and if nothing else you will certainly be helping me if you allow me to get everything that happened, as far as you know it, straight in my mind. I see fairly clearly how the day went. At ten-thirty Nicola had left, and Emanuel was in his office with the ten o'clock patient when the phone light flashed to indicate a call. Did it flash once, I mean for just one call, or twice?''

"Twice. Obviously, even if it was the same person—shall we say the murderer—calling to cancel, falsely, for both of them, he would take the trouble to call twice. It would immediately be suspicious if one person called to cancel two patients. The patients don't even know each other.''

"Do you know that they don't?''

"Let me put it this way. They may have met casually in the waiting room; it does sometimes happen. But if they knew each other at all well, I would probably know it.''

"It would come up in the analysis?" Emanuel nodded, obviously unwilling to discuss this in detail. "But," Kate asked, "if the twelve o'clock patient, who was a man, wanted, for some reason, to keep her attraction for him, her connection with him secret, wouldn't he do so?''

"It would be unexpected."

"And," Kate added, "might indicate that he had been planning to murder her." No one had any answer to that. "Well, to continue, at ten to eleven you called the service, and they told you of the two cancellations. So you immediately left the office and went to run around the reservoir."

"You see," Nicola interrupted, "you believe that's what he did, and yet it sounds crazy even when you say it."

Emanuel smiled, that half-smile of his which indicated his acceptance of the inevitable. It occurred to Kate that Emanuel was able, more than anyone she knew, to accept the inevitable. It was something, perhaps, for which psychiatry trained you, a profession of few surprises to one well and long trained in it. Could Janet Harrison's murder possibly be considered a professional surprise? Kate tucked that bone away, to be gnawed on later. "I didn't leap from the chair out to the reservoir," Emanuel said. "I may want exercise, but not that impetuously. I went to the back of the apartment and changed my clothes. Then I wandered out in what I think could be called a leisurely fashion."

"Did anyone see you go? Did you meet anyone?"

"No one who can swear to it. The hall was empty."

Nicola sat up. "Perhaps one of Dr. Barrister's patients saw him go by the window, toward Fifth Avenue. I'm sure if we asked him, he'd be willing to ask them, in a matter of this importance. Or he might have seen you from his office."

"It's unlikely; anyway, even if they had, or he had, there's no reason, from the police's point of view, why I couldn't have doubled back. And I didn't meet anyone going around the reservoir. At least, I passed some people, but I can't remember *them*. How could they identify a man in dirty pants and an old jacket, walking fast?"

"You were wearing those clothes when you came back," Nicola said. "Surely you wouldn't have been wearing them during her analysis. Doesn't that prove you didn't murder her?"

"He could have changed them after he stabbed her," Kate said. "But wait a minute. If you're supposed to have planned your own alibi, if you can call trotting around the reservoir an alibi, who is supposed to have made the two calls canceling the patients? You said the answering service records the time. If you were with a patient, and you were, you couldn't have made the calls. Even if the patient didn't see the flashing lights—and the murderer may have known that—the answering service would know when the calls were received.''

''I've thought of that,'' Emanuel said. ''I even went so far as to point it out to the police, though that may not have been very wise of me. They made no comment, but undoubtedly their point will be that I could have paid someone to make the calls for me, or got Nicki to, or you.''

''It's still a weak point in their case. Personally, I intend to clasp it firmly to my bosom. Why, by the way, do you suppose the murderer made the calls then, and not while you were in your office alone? Then there really would be no one's word for it but yours.''

''Perhaps he was unable to make them at another time. More likely, though, he wanted to be sure that I *would not* answer the phone and take the messages. I might recognize that these were not my patients' voices, or—though this seems unlikely—I might have recognized the voice on the phone.''

''There's another possibility too,'' Nicola said. ''If he called earlier, even you, with your great drive to go run around, *might* have had time to plan something else. You might, for instance, have mentioned it to me, and I might have said: Goody, now we can both sit down and figure out the budget, or make love—that is, of course, if I canceled *my* analytic hour, I know it's unlikely, but anyone who knows us as well as this murderer does might know I was just the sort to do something like that. With Pandora out, I might have decided how nice, for a change, to go to bed together in the morning—I don't think he or she wanted to give Emanuel time to think, and he wanted to make sure I was gone.''

''All the same,'' Kate said, ''it may be a slip, and a bad one. Let's hope so. When you came home, Emanuel, the curtain, so to speak, had gone up?''

''Chaos had come would be a better way to describe it. If one weren't concerned oneself, it might even have been interesting.''

''Dr. Barrister told me I had better call the police,'' Nicola said. ''He even seemed to know the number, Spring something, but I couldn't seem to dial, I just picked up the phone to dial operator, so he took the phone and dialed the number. Then he handed it back to me. A man's voice said 'Police Department,' and I thought, This is all a fantasy. I shall tell Dr. Sanders about it tomorrow. I wonder what it indicates. It couldn't have been even a minute later, I suppose, they radioed to one of those cars policemen are always riding around in—do you remember when we were children, policemen used to walk?''

"When we were children," Emanuel put in, "policemen used to be old men. What is it someone said? They're old enough to be your father, and suddenly, one day, they're young enough to be your son.''

"Anyway," Nicola continued, "these ordinary policemen just looked at the body, as though to make sure we weren't pulling their leg, though it seems an odd sort of joke to me, and then *they* called in, and the next thing we knew, the parade had started; men with all kinds of equipment, and detectives, and someone called a deputy inspector, people taking photographs, a funny little man they all greeted with great joy as the 'M. E.' I really lost track of all of them. We were sitting here in the living room. I don't remember when Emanuel came back, but it seemed a long time before they carried her out.

"The only thing I really noticed was that an ambulance came, with some men in white, and one of them said to one of the policemen, 'It's D.O.A., all right.' I saw a movie once called *D.O.A.* It means Dead on Arrival. Whose arrival?''

"They seemed very interested to see me when I returned, needless to say," Emanuel went on. "But I had to sit down and cancel my afternoon patients. I couldn't reach all of them, and one of them was turned away by a policeman, which I didn't care for, but perhaps it was better than if I had come out in the middle of all that and told her to go. At any rate, 'chaos' is the word. How efficient the police are, and how little they understand!''

Later that night the words echoed in Kate's mind: *How little they understand!* Shortly after Emanuel had uttered the words, a detective had come again to talk to them. He had let Kate go, after a long look. Yet, Kate thought, putting herself wearily to bed, the facts, if they were facts, on Emanuel's side were not the sort the police, who must all have stanch lower-middle-class backgrounds, could understand: that a psychiatrist, though he might be more driven than other men, would never commit a crime in his office, on the grounds, so to speak, of his profession; that Emanuel would never entangle himself with a woman patient, however beautiful; that Emanuel could never murder anyone, certainly not stab them with a knife; that a man and woman who had been lovers, she and Emanuel, could now be friends. What could the police make of that, the police who knew, probably, only sex on one hand, and marriage on the other. What of

Nicola? "She was very beautiful," Nicola had said. But surely Nicola was at her analysis, the perfect alibi.

As the two sleeping pills which Kate had taken—and she had not taken sleeping pills since a horrible case of poison ivy, seven years ago—began to pull her under, she concentrated her weakening attention on the doctor across the hall. Obviously, the murderer. The fact, and it was a fact, that he was without the smallest connection with anyone in the case, seemed, as consciousness faded, to be of very little importance.

4

REED Amhearst was an Assistant District Attorney, though exactly what functions were encompassed by that title, Kate had never understood. Apparently he was frequently in court, and found his work exciting and consuming. He and Kate had stumbled across each other years before, in the short period of political activity in Kate's life, when she had worked for a reform political club. Politics had been for Reed a more continuous affair, but after Kate had retired, exhausted from her first and only primary fight, she and Reed continued to see each other in a friendly sort of way. They had dinner together, or went to the theater from time to time, and laughed together a good deal. When either of them needed a partner for a social evening, and did not wish for some reason to plunge in with any other attachment, Reed or Kate, as the case might be, would go along. Since neither of them had married, since neither of them could have considered, for a single moment, the completely outrageous idea of marrying each other, their casual acquaintance became a constant amid all the variables of their social lives.

So they might have continued indefinitely, eventually tottering, occasionally together, into benign old age, if Reed, through a series of impulses and bad judgments, had not landed himself in a most magnificent muddle. The details of this Kate had long since forgotten, believing that the ability to forget was one of the most important requirements of a friendship, but neither of them could ever forget that it was Kate who had got him out of the muddle, rescued him on the brink of disaster. By doing so, she had put him forever in her debt, but Reed was a nice enough person to accept a service without holding it against the giver. To ask for a repayment of the debt was an abhorrent idea, to Kate, and to call on him now would, she could not but realize, put her in the position of seeming to do exactly that. For this reason, despite her resolutions of the day before, she brooded a full two hours the next morning before calling him.

On the other hand, however, and equally imperious, was the need to help Emanuel. No one, Kate was convinced, could help Emanuel, unless he combined her belief in Emanuel's innocence with the knowledge of the police. The only possible way to get that knowledge seemed to be through Reed. Cursing her mind, too finely tuned to moral dilemmas which more sensible people happily ignored, cursing Reed for having ever needed her help, she decided, after two aspirins, eight cups of coffee and much pacing of the living room, to ask his help. It was, at least, a Thursday, thus a classless day. With a lingering thought for her innocent Tuesday morning in the stacks— would she ever return to Thomas Carlyle, abandoned in the midst of one of his older perorations?—she picked up the phone.

She caught Reed just as he was leaving on some pressing mission. He had, of course, heard of the "body on the couch," as they appeared to be calling it (Kate suppressed a groan). When he gathered what she wanted—the complete dossier (if they used that word) on the case—he was absolutely silent for perhaps twenty seconds; it seemed an hour. "Good friend of yours?" he asked.

"Yes," Kate answered, "and in a hell of an unfair mess," and then cursed herself for appearing to be reminding him. But what the hell, she thought, I am reminding him; it does no good to pussyfoot around it.

"I'll do what I can," he said. (Obviously he was not alone.) "It looks like a bad day, but I'll look into the matter for you and report to your apartment about seven-thirty tonight. Will that do?" Well, after all, Kate thought, he works for a living. Did you expect him to come dashing up the minute he replaced the receiver? He's probably making a huge effort as it is.

"I'll be waiting for you, Reed; thanks a lot." She hung up the phone.

For the first time in years, Kate found herself at loose ends, not delightful loose ends, at which one says: If I look at another student theme I shall be ill, and sneaks off, surreptitiously, to a movie; this rather was the horrible kind of loose ends, to which Kate had heard applied (always with a shudder) the cure of "killing time." Her life was full enough of varied activity to make leisure seem a blessing, not a burden, but now she found herself wondering what in the world

to do until seven-thirty. She nobly fought the urge to call Emanuel
and Nicola; it seemed best to wait until she had something construc-
tive to say. Work was impossible—she found she could neither prepare a class nor correct papers. After a certain amount of aimless
wandering about the apartment—and she felt, irrationally, that it was
a fort she was holding, which she must not on any account leave—
she applied the remedy her mother had used under stress, when Kate
was a child: she cleaned closets.

This task, combining as it did dirt, hard work and amazed discovery, lasted her nicely until two o'clock. Exhausted, she then abandoned the hall closet to dust and unaccountable accumulation, and
collapsed in a chair with Freud's *Studies in Hysteria*, a Christmas
present from Nicola several years back. She could not concentrate,
but one sentence caught her eye, a comment of Freud's to a patient:
"Much will be gained if we succeed in transforming your hysterical
misery into common unhappiness." She wished she had had it to
quote to Emanuel when they had still been free to argue, aimlessly,
about Freud. No wonder they had such a hard row to hoe, these
modern psychoanalysts: they saw little enough hysterical misery, and
were left to cope with common unhappiness, for which, as Freud
clearly knew, there is no clinical cure. It occurred to her that her aim
now was to assist, if she could, in restoring Emanuel to common
unhappiness from the catastrophic fate which seemed to face him. A
disquieting thought, from which she passed into idle daydreams.

How the rest of the afternoon passed she never, afterward, could
tell. She straightened up the house, took a shower—guiltily lifting
the phone off the hook first so that a possible caller (Nicola, Reed,
the police?) would get a busy signal and try again—ordered some
groceries in case Reed should be hungry, and paced back and forth.
Several telephone conversations with people who never mentioned
murders or had anything to do with them helped considerably.

At twenty-five of eight Reed came. Kate had to restrain herself
from greeting him like the long-lost heir from overseas. He collapsed
into a chair and gladly accepted Scotch and water.

"I suppose your idea is that the psychiatrist didn't do it?"

"Of course he didn't do it," Kate said; "the idea is preposterous."

"My dear, the idea that a friend of yours could commit murder
may be preposterous; I'll be the first to admit that it is, or to take
your word for it in any case. But to the minds of the police, beautifully unsullied with any personal preconceptions, he looks as guilty

as a sinner in hell. All right, all right, don't argue with me yet; I'll give you the facts, and then you can tell me what a lovely soul he has, and who the real criminal is, if any."

"Reed! Is there a chance she could have done it herself?"

"Not a chance, really, though I'll admit a good defense lawyer might make something of the idea in court, just to confuse the minds of the jury. People who thrust a knife deep into their innards don't thrust upward, and certainly don't do it on their backs; they throw themselves on the blade, like Dido. If they do thrust a knife into themselves, they bare that portion of their body—don't ask me why, they always do, or so it says in the textbook—and, a less debatable point, they inevitably leave fingerprints on the knife."

"Perhaps she was wearing gloves."

"Then she removed them after death."

"Maybe someone else removed them."

"Kate, dear, I think I had better make you a drink; possibly you should take it with several tranquilizers. They are said, together with alcohol, to have a stultifying effect on one's reactions. Shall we stick for the moment to the facts?" Kate, fetching herself the drink and a cigarette, but not the tranquilizers, nodded obediently. "Good. She was killed between ten of eleven, when the ten o'clock patient left, and twelve thirty-five, when she was discovered by Mrs. Bauer, and the discovery noted, more or less, by Dr. Michael Barrister, Pandora Jackson and Frederick Sparks, the twelve o'clock patient. The Medical Examiner won't estimate the death any closer than that—they never estimate closer than within two hours—but he has said, strictly unofficially, which means he won't testify to it in court, that she was probably killed almost an hour before she was found. There was no external bleeding, because the hilt of the knife, where it joins the blade, pressed her clothing into the wound, preventing the escape of any blood. This is unfortunate, since a bloodstained criminal, with bloodstained clothes, is that much easier to find." Reed's voice was colorless and totally without emotion, like the voice of a stenographer reading back from notes. Kate was grateful to him.

"She was killed," he continued, "with a long, thin carving knife from the Bauer kitchen, one of a set that hangs in a wooden holder on the wall. The Bauers do not deny their ownership of the knife, which is just as well, since it bears both their fingerprints." Involuntarily, Kate gasped. Reed paused to look at her. "I can see," he said wryly, "that your ability to differentiate between sorts of evidence is not very developed. That's the chief evidence on their side.

Since every tot today knows about fingerprints, the chances are that, using the knife as a weapon, they would have had the brains to remove them. Of course, a trained psychiatrist of admitted brilliance might have been smart enough to figure that the police would figure that way. Don't interrupt. Dr. and Mrs. Bauer say their prints got on the knife the previous night when they had a small argument about how to carve a silver-tip roast, and both gave it a try. Being sensible people, they don't submerge knives in water, but wipe off the blade with a damp cloth and then a dry one. The prints, if anything, are evidence in their favor, since they have been partially obliterated, as they might have been if someone had held the knife with gloves. This, however, is inconclusive.

"Now we come to the more damning part. She was stabbed while she was lying down, according to the medical evidence, by someone who leaned over the end of the couch and over her head, and thrust the knife upward between her ribs. This seems, incidentally, to have been done by someone with a fairly developed knowledge of anatomy, *id est*, a doctor, but here again we are on shaky ground. This particular upward thrust of the knife from behind (though not with the victim lying down) was commonly taught to all resistance units during World War II in France and elsewhere. The important question is, Who could have got the girl to lie down, Who could have got behind her, Who could have finally stabbed her without at any point inspiring any resistance whatever? You can see that the police are saying to themselves: 'Where does a psychoanalyst sit? In a chair behind the head of a patient.' Detective: 'Why does the psychoanalyst sit there, Dr. Bauer?' Dr. Bauer: 'So that the patient cannot see the doctor.' Detective: 'Why shouldn't the patient see the doctor?' Dr. Bauer: 'That's a very interesting question; there are many possible explanations, such as helping the patient to maintain the anonymity of the doctor, thus increasing the possibilities for transference; but the real reason seems to be that Freud invented the position because he could not bear to have the patients looking at him all day long.' Detective: 'Do all your patients lie on the couch?' Dr. Bauer: 'Only those in analysis; patients in therapy sit in a chair on the other side of the desk.' Detective: 'Do you sit behind them?' Dr. Bauer: 'No.' Shrug of detective's shoulders not reported here."

"Reed, do you mean the police are basing their whole case on the fact that no one else could have got behind her while she was lying on the couch?"

"Not quite, but it is a sticky point, all the same. If Dr. Bauer wasn't there, why was she lying down on the couch in the first place? And, assuming for the moment that she wandered into the room and lay down when there was no one there—and Dr. Bauer has assured the detective that no patient would do any such thing, they wait until they are summoned into the office by the analyst—would she continue to lie there if someone other than the analyst walked in, sat down behind her, and then leaned over her with a knife?''

''Supposedly she didn't see the knife when he leaned over?''

''Even so. And if the analyst wasn't there, why did she lie down on the couch? Why do women lie down on couches? All right, you needn't answer that.''

''Wait a minute, Reed. Perhaps she wanted to take a nap.''

''Come off it, Kate.''

''All right, but suppose she was in love with one of the patients before or after her—we don't really know anything about them—and she, or one of them, let's say one of them, got rid of Emanuel so that he and the girl could make love on the couch. After all, the ten o'clock patient would simply stay, and the twelve o'clock patient *did* come rather early . . .''

''Those two cancellations were made during the ten o'clock patient's hour, so he could hardly have made them himself.''

''Exactly. He got someone else to do it. It gave him an alibi, and since he was there at the time himself, he could make sure that the calls came through, or at least that *some* calls came through.''

''Then why cancel *for* the twelve o'clock patient, and not cancel the twelve o'clock patient as well? All right, perhaps he didn't know his phone number. But then why try to get rid of Dr. Bauer, when you will have the twelve o'clock patient walking in on you anyway?''

''To lovers an hour alone together is an eternity,'' said Kate in sepulchral tones. ''Besides, he really didn't want to make love; he wanted to murder her.''

''I'll say this, you have an answer for everything. Might I point out, however, that you have created this whole plot out of thin air? There isn't the smallest evidence for anything you've said, though the police will, I'm sure, try to collect the evidence wherever possible.''

''If only I were as sure of that as you are. There isn't a shred of evidence against Emanuel either.''

''Kate, my dear, I admire your loyalty to Emanuel, but do exercise your extraordinary ability to face the facts: the girl was murdered in Emanuel's office, with Emanuel's knife, in a position that would have given Emanuel every opportunity to commit the crime. He can provide no alibi; while the phone calls canceling the patients were undoubtedly made, he as well as anyone else could have paid someone to make them. The murder was done when no one else was in the apartment, but who except Emanuel and his wife *knew* that no one else would be in the apartment? Despite your delightful flights of fancy, we don't *know* that the girl knew a single other person connected with that office. In fact, one of the strangest things about this case is how little they seem able to find out about that girl.''

"Was she a virgin?''

"No idea; she never had a child, at any rate.''

"Reed! Do you mean to tell me that when they do one of these autopsies they can't tell whether or not a girl's a virgin? I thought that was one of the first things they reported on.''

"It is remarkable, the old wives' tales that continue to be believed by otherwise quite intelligent people. The point of this tale, I suppose, is to keep girls good. How did you suppose one could tell? If you are thinking of what the Elizabethans alluded to so feelingly as 'maiden-head,' I am sad to report that the number of modern girls who survive their athletic girlhoods with that intact is tiny enough to make your grandmother blush. Otherwise, what evidence did you suppose there was? If semen is present, we know a woman has had sexual relations; if she is bruised or torn, we suspect rape, or attempted rape. Nothing like this, of course, was in evidence here. But, as to whether or not she was a virgin, you would do better asking the people who knew her, if you can find them.''

"I cannot remember when I have been so shocked. The world as I knew it is fast passing away.''

"Your friend Emanuel can probably tell you if she has had sexual relations, that is, if you can get him to tell you anything.''

"Since the police, completely ignoring Emanuel's character, are convinced he did it, what do they suppose was his motive?''

"The police are not so interested in motive; good sound circumstantial evidence is much more their cup of tea. They pay it due attention, of course, and if one of those two patients turns out to inherit a million dollars under Janet Harrison's will, they'll prick up their ears. But a doctor who has become entangled with a beautiful patient and decided in a rash moment to get rid of her is motive enough for them.''

"But they have no evidence that he was 'entangled' with her; that's probably why they haven't arrested him yet. Whereas I have loads of evidence that he couldn't have become entangled with her, couldn't have murdered her, and certainly not on his couch.''

"All right, I want to hear it all. First, let me give you the rest. The thrust of the knife which killed her was delivered with a good deal of strength, but not with more than a strongish woman might have mustered—you for instance, or Mrs. Bauer. Let me finish. The body was not moved after being stabbed, but I've already told you that. No signs of a struggle. No fingerprints, other than those one would expect. The rest is a lot of technical jargon, including photographs of a particularly sickening nature. We come now to the only real point of interest.

"The murderer—we assume it was the murderer—went through her purse, presumably after she was dead. He was wearing rubber gloves, which leave their own peculiar sort of print, in this case on the gold-colored clasp of her pocketbook. The supposition is that if he found something, he took it out. The girl was not very well known to those who lived near her in the Graduate Women's Dormitory at the university, but one of them, questioned by the police, had noticed that Janet Harrison always carried a notebook in her purse; no notebook was found there. Also, she appeared to have no photographs in her purse or wallet, though almost every woman does carry photographs of someone or other. That is all conjecture. But there *was* a picture which the murderer apparently missed. In her wallet she had a New York driver's license, not the new card sort, but the old paper kind which folded, and folded inside it was a small picture of a young man. The police are of course going to try to discover who he was; I'll get a copy of it shortly and let you see it, just in case it rings a bell. The important point is that she had carefully concealed the picture. Why?''

"It sounds as though she thought someone might go through her pocketbook, and she didn't want the picture found. Some people, of course, are naturally secretive.''

"Apparently Miss Harrison was *un*naturally secretive. Nobody seems to have known her very well. There is some information from the university, but it's pretty thin. Oddly enough, her room in the Graduate Women's Hall was robbed the night before her death, though whether this is a coincidence or not we may never know. Someone apparently had a key, rifled through everything, and departed with a 35-millimeter camera worth about seventy dollars. A brand new Royal portable typewriter, worth more, was left, whether because it was too conspicuous to carry out, or the robber was collecting only cameras, it is impossible to determine. All her drawers, and her desk, were thoroughly rifled, but apparently nothing else was taken. It was reported to the local precinct, but, though they conscientiously made out a report, this sort of thing is pretty hopeless. By the time she had been murdered, the room had been straightened out, so any evidence that may have been left is gone.

"The information on Janet Harrison is surprisingly meager, though we haven't traced her back home yet; the police in North Dakota, where she turns out, surprisingly enough, to come from, are finding what they can. All the university can tell us is that she is thirty years of age . . ."

"*Really?*" Kate said. "She didn't look it."

"Apparently not. She's a U.S. citizen, and went to college at some place called Collins. The university noticed that the 'person to notify in case of emergency' section was not filled out, and the omission apparently went unnoticed in the rush of registration. That's about it, I think," Reed finished up, "except for one little matter I've saved, with my well known flair for the dramatic, till the end: Nicola Bauer wasn't at her analyst's the morning of the murder. She called up at the last minute to cancel the appointment. The police have just managed to reach her analyst. She claims to have spent the morning wandering in the park, not around the reservoir, but near something she calls the old castle. People do, of course, spend a remarkable amount of innocent time wandering about, but that *both* of the Bauers should have ambled separately around Central Park while someone was being murdered in their apartment is difficult for the Deputy Inspector wholly to believe. With all the good will in the world, I can't help seeing his point."

Reed got up, and very kindly poured Kate another drink. "Just keep in mind, please, Kate, that they may have done it. I don't say they did; I don't say I shan't sympathize with your conviction that they didn't; I'll help you any way I can. But, please, as a favor to me, keep in the back of your mind an awareness of the possibility that they may be guilty. Janet Harrison was a very beautiful girl."

5

KATE had met Emanuel at a time when they had both gone stale, when the world seemed to each flat and unprofitable, if not out of joint. They happened, in fact, to meet at that identical point in their lives when each was committed to a career, but had not yet admitted the commitment. Their meeting had been the one romantic (in the movie sense) moment in both their lives, and though Kate may have been what Emanuel was later to call "projecting," it seemed to her even then that they both realized they had met dramatically, because destined to meet, that they were further destined never to marry, never wholly to part.

They had crashed into each other, literally, on an exit road from the Merritt Parkway. Kate, as she was soon to point out to him, was exiting in the proper fashion, as anyone might be expected to do. Emanuel, quite on the contrary, was backing up the exit road toward the Parkway from which he had just mistakenly emerged. It was dusk; Kate's mind was on the directions she had to follow, Emanuel's, still seething, was apparently not functioning at all. It was a very pretty crash.

They ended up, after a certain amount of expostulation which soon turned to laughter, driving to a restaurant in Emanuel's car, from which they telephoned for aid for Kate's car. They both forgot that they were expected elsewhere, Emanuel because, as Nicola was later to say, forgetting was his favorite sport, and Kate deliberately because she did not want her hosts to come for her. She had not "fallen in love" with Emanuel; she would never be "in love" with him. But she wanted to stay with him that evening.

Walking now to Emanuel's home, with Reed's warning of the

night before still ringing in her ears, Kate thought how difficult it would be (might turn out to be) to explain their relationship to a policeman. She was walking from Riverside Drive to Fifth Avenue in the hope that the exercise and air might clear her head, and it occurred to her that even this act might seem, to certain people, inexplicable. Suppose someone were murdered now in her apartment; what sort of alibi would it be, the simple statement that she had decided to walk halfway across the city? True, Emanuel and Nicola, whose alibis were similar to this, had not had a destination, but had been seized with an unaccountable desire to wander; true, it was difficult to get into her apartment and it was impossible to think of anyone capable of being murdered there. The fact still remained that she and the Bauers lived their lives in a way for which nothing in a policeman's training prepared him.

The support which she and Emanuel had found in each other in the year following their meeting grew from a relationship for which the English language itself lacked a defining word. Not a friendship, because they were man and woman, not a love affair, because theirs was far more a meeting of minds than of passions, their relationship (an inexact and lifeless term) had given each a vantage point from which to view his life, had given them for a time the gift of laughter and intense discussion whose confidence would be held forever inviolable. They had been lovers for a time—they had no one but themselves to consider—yet this had been far from central to their mutual need. After that first year, they would no more have considered making love than of opening a mink ranch together, yet were there more than a handful of people in the world who could have understood this?

When she reached Nicola's room, Kate, physically exhausted and proportionately less perturbed, found that Nicola's thoughts had been running along the same lines. She had been thinking, that is, not about Emanuel and Kate, but of how few people there were who understood morality apart from convention.

"We have spent this morning and the greater part of yesterday with the police," Nicola said, "being questioned separately, and a bit together, and though they are not actually offensive, as a Berlitz teacher will not actually speak English in teaching you French, they indicate in a thousand little ways that we are both liars, or at least one of us is, and if we would just break down and admit it we would be saving the state and them endless amounts of trouble. Of course, Emanuel has gone stubborn, and won't tell them anything about Janet

Harrison. He claims he's not just being noble, guarding the secrets of the confessional and all that; he simply doesn't see what good it would do, for it would probably just get us in deeper. Don't *you* know anything devastating about her, from that college of yours? Why, by the way, aren't you there? It's Friday, isn't it?" Nicola's ability to remember the details of everyone's schedule ("I called because I knew you'd just have gotten in from walking the dog," she had said once to an astonished and recent acquaintance) was one of the most notable things about her.

"I got someone else to take my classes," Kate said. "I didn't feel up to it." She was, in fact, extremely guilty about this, remembering someone's definition of the professional as the man who could perform even when he didn't feel like it.

"The horrible thing is," Nicola continued, "none of them understands in the least what we're like; they all think we're some special species of madmen who have taken to psychiatry because all sane pursuits are beyond us. I don't mean that they don't know all about psychiatry in a theoretical sort of way—I suppose they are used to the testimony of psychiatrists and all that—but people like us who take unscheduled walks, and talk frankly about jealousy and feelings of aggression, and yet insist that because we talk about them we are not likely to act them out, well, the only thing about me that seemed to make sense to one detective was that my father had gone to Yale Law School. They got out of me that you and Emanuel had once been lovers, by the way, and then concluded, I am certain, that we must all be living in some fantastic Noel Cowardish sort of way because we are all friends now and I allow you into my house. You know, Kate, they could understand a man's cheating on his expense account, or going out with call girls when his wife thinks he's on a business trip, but I think we frighten them because we claim to be honest underneath, though a bit casual on the surface, whereas they understand dishonesty, but not the abandonment of surface rectitude. Probably they are convinced there's something indecent about a man's taking twenty dollars from a woman so that she can lie on a couch and talk to him."

"I think," Kate said, "that the police are rather like the English as Mrs. Patrick Campbell saw them. She said the English didn't care what people did as long as they didn't do it in the street and frighten the horses. I don't suppose the police are actively opposed to anything about Emanuel or you or me or psychiatry. It's just that all this has frightened the horses, and unfortunately the police do not suffi-

ciently understand the integrity of psychiatry—where it is practiced
with integrity, and we might as well admit it isn't always—to know
that Emanuel is the last person who could have murdered the girl.
Where *were* you, yesterday morning, by the way, and why the hell
didn't you mention that you hadn't been to your analyst's when you
were outlining the day?''

"How did you learn I hadn't been there?"

"I have my methods; answer the questions."

"I don't know why I didn't tell you, Kate. I meant to, every time
it came up, but one dislikes behaving like a coward, and dislikes
even more talking about it. Believe it or not—and the police don't—I
was walking around in the park, by the castle and the lake there,
where the Japanese cherry blossoms are. It's always been my favorite
place, ever since I was very little and held my breath and turned blue
if the nurse tried to go somewhere else."

"But *why, why* did you have to pick this one morning to revive
childhood memories, when you could have been doing it on Dr. Sanders' couch, and giving yourself a magnificent alibi at the same
time?"

"Nobody told me Janet Harrison was going to be murdered on
Emanuel's couch. At any rate, I think it's better this way; if I had an
alibi, that would leave Emanuel the chief and only suspect. This way,
the police aren't quite ready to arrest him. After all, they've got just
as much against me as against Emanuel."

"Does the psychiatrist's wife usually come in, in a natural sort
of way, and sit down behind the patient? Never mind; I still want to
know why you didn't go to your appointment with Dr. Sanders."

"Kate, you're getting like the police, wanting neat, reasonable
answers to everything. There are some people who keep every appointment with their analyst, and always arrive promptly—I'm sure
there are—but more people like me turn cowardly. There are several
common defenses: arriving late, saying nothing, talking about other
matters and avoiding the troublesome problem—in which case, of
course, one just keeps coming back to it until one does face it. Mostly
I use the system of intellectualizing, but on *the* day I just felt it was
spring and I couldn't manage it. I got as far as Madison Avenue and
decided, so I went to the park instead. Needless to say, I had no idea
Emanuel would be wandering around the park at the same time."

"Did you call Dr. Sanders and say you weren't coming?"

"Of course; it would be most unfair to keep him sitting there,
instead of letting him have the hour free. Possibly *he* likes to run

around the reservoir; it's a pity he didn't; he might have met Emanuel.''

"Would Emanuel know him?''

"Well, they're both at the institute.''

"Nicki, did anybody see you leave for what you thought would be an appointment with your psychiatrist? Did anyone see you make the telephone call at Madison Avenue?''

"No one saw me make the phone call. But Dr. Barrister saw me leave. Almost always he's busy with patients at that time, but today, for some reason, he was at the door, showing a patient out or something. *He* saw me leave, but what does that prove? I could easily have come back and stabbed the girl.''

"What sort of doctor is he?''

"Woman. I mean, he treats women.''

"Gynecology? Obstetrics?''

"No, he doesn't seem to operate very much, and he certainly doesn't do obstetrics; he doesn't strike me as the sort who would want to be dragged out of the theater or out of bed to deliver babies. Emanuel looked him up, actually, on my insistence, and he's got excellent credentials. Emanuel doesn't like him.''

"Why not?''

"Well, partly because Emanuel doesn't *like* most people, particularly not people who are smooth, but mostly, I gather, because Barrister and he met once in the hall, and Barrister mentioned something to the effect that they were both doing the same sort of work, and at least neither of them ever buried any patients. A turn, I guess, on the old joke about the dermatologist who never cures anyone and never kills anyone, but it annoyed Emanuel, who said Barrister sounded like a doctor in the movies.''

"Well, nature does imitate art; Oscar Wilde was quite right.''

"I told Emanuel it was plain envy. Dr. Barrister is very good-looking.''

"He sounds more suspicious by the minute; I just about decided, the other night, that he must have done it.''

"I know. I've been searching madly for suspects myself and one of the problems is that we aren't exactly seething with suspects. Apart from you and me, and Emanuel, who are innocent by definition, so to speak, we have only the elevator man, Dr. Barrister or his patients or nurse, the patients on either side of Janet Harrison or the homicidal maniac. Not very encouraging. Actually, this whole thing is horrible for Dr. Barrister, though he's been quite nice about it. Police questioning him, and a policeman in the hall outside his office—his patients may not care for that—and then being dragged in by me to look at a body. The fact is, if he were going to murder someone he'd want to murder her as far from himself as possible.''

"We've left out one other possible suspect: someone Janet Harrison met here by arrangement. He canceled the patients, saw that everyone had left, enticed her into the office and killed her.''

"Kate, you're a genius! That's exactly how it must have happened.''

"No doubt. All we've got to do is find this man, *if* he exists.''

It was, however, with this probably nonexistent man in mind, that Kate tracked Emanuel down in his office some time later. She had, of course, determined that he was free, and, knocking first, had gone in and shut the door behind her.

"Emanuel, I am sorry, or have I said that already? I keep thinking of all this as like Greek drama; that from the moment of that collision off the Merritt Parkway, we have been heading for this crisis. I suppose there is some comfort in thinking, however literarily, that fate concerns itself with our destinies.''

"I've thought much the same thing myself; you weren't sure you wanted to be a college teacher, and I had all sorts of ambivalences about psychiatry. Yet here we are, you as a teacher having sent me, a psychiatrist, one of your students as a patient. It seems to have a pattern, yet of course it can't. If we could just show that it hasn't a pattern, or that we're seeing the pattern the wrong way, we'd be clear of all this.''

"Emanuel! I think you've just said something very important and profound.''

"Have I? It doesn't seem to make any sense at all.''

"Well, never mind; I'm sure the reason for its profundity will occur to me later. What I want now is to have you sit down at your desk and tell me everything you know about Janet Harrison. Perhaps what you say will remind me of something I know, and have forgotten. I'm convinced of one thing: if we find the murderer, always supposing he isn't a homicidal maniac casually in off the streets, we will find him through some knowledge we get about that girl. Will you try to be helpful?''

Rather to Kate's surprise he didn't flatly refuse, he merely shrugged, and continued to gaze out of the window onto a courtyard in which there was almost certainly nothing to see. Kate, with a certain studied carelessness, sat down on the couch. One of the chairs would have been more comfortable, but not to sit on the couch was to avoid it.

"What can I tell you? The tape recording of an analysis, for example, would be meaningless, in any important sense, to someone not trained to interpret. It's not full of clues like a Sherlock Holmes detective story, at least not the sort of clues that would be any use to a policeman. She didn't tell me one day that she would probably be murdered, and that if she were, such-and-such a person would probably have done it. Believe me, had she said something definite of that sort, I would not hesitate to reveal it, certainly not from any misguided sense of idealism. The other vital thing to remember is that, to the analyst, it is unimportant whether something actually happened, or whether the occurrence was merely a fantasy on the part of the patient. To the analyst, there is no essential difference; to the policeman there is, of course, all the difference in the world."

"I should think it would matter very much to a patient whether something had really happened or not. I should think that would be the whole point."

"Exactly. But you would be wrong. And I can't explain all this simply, without grossly falsifying it, and by making it too simple, making it false. But if you want, I'll give you, reluctantly, an example. When Freud began on his treatment of patients, he was astonished to discover how many women in Vienna had had, as children, sexual relations with their fathers. It appeared for a time that at least a handful of Viennese fathers had been sexual maniacs. Then Freud realized that none of these sexual experiences had ever taken place, that they had been fantasies. But his important realization came with the understanding that, for the purposes of the patients' psychological development (though not of course for the purposes of sexual morality in Vienna) it did not matter at all whether the incidents had taken place actually or not. The fantasy had an immense importance of its own. Kate, have you ever tried to explain *Ulysses* to a self-satisfied person whose idea of a great novelist was Lloyd Douglas?"

"All right, all right, I see your point, really I do. But let me go on being a nuisance, will you? I never knew, for example, why she thought she needed an analyst. What did she say the first time she came to see you?"

"The beginning is always rather routine. I ask, of course, what the trouble is. Her answer was not unusual. She slept badly, had a work problem, was unable to read for more than a short period, and had difficulty, as she put it in regrettable social-worker jargon, in relating to people. Her use of that term was the most significant thing she said that day; it indicated how the problem was intellectualized, to what degree emotion had unconsciously been withdrawn from it. Most of this policemen could discover; the rest they would find useless to their purpose. I asked her to tell me something about herself; that's routine also. The facts are usually not important, but the omissions may be greatly so. She was the only child of strict, compulsive parents, both now dead. They were quite old when she was born—if you want the details I can look them up. She neglected to mention at that time any love affairs, even of the most casual nature, though it emerged later that she had had one love affair in which she was deeply involved. Occasionally associations would bring her to this, break through her resistance, but she always immediately moved away from the subject. We had just begun to touch on some real material when this happened.''

"Emanuel, don't you see how important that is? By the way, had she—was she a virgin?'' He turned to her with surprise, at the question, at Kate's asking it. Kate shrugged. "Possibly my salacious mind, but I have an odd feeling it may be important.''

"I don't know the answer, as a fact, for certain. If you want my professional guess, I would say that the love affair had been consummated. But it's a guess.''

"Do patients in the beginning talk mostly about the past or present?''

"About the present; the past of course comes in, more and more as you continue. I had a hunch—though do try not to overestimate its importance—that there was something in the present she was *not* mentioning, something connected, though perhaps only in the sense of the same guilt, with the love affair. Ah, I particularly admire you when you get that gleam in your eye like a hawk about to dive. Do you think she was a key figure in a drug ring?''

"You can laugh later; one other question. You mentioned the other evening that she had become angry, that transference had begun. What is transference when it's at home, as Molly Bloom would say?''

"I loathe simplified explanations of psychiatry. Let's say merely that the anger inherent in some situation becomes directed at the analyst, who becomes the object of those emotions.''

"Don't you see, Emanuel? That's good enough. Put together two things you've casually told me. One, possibly connected with her past, which she was hiding. Two, emotion had begun to be generated in her relationship with you. Conclusion: she might have told you, or might have revealed to your sensitive professional ear something which someone didn't want anyone to know. Perhaps there was someone to whom she talked—*she* thought casually—about her analysis—people do talk *somewhat* about their analyses; I know, I've heard them—and whoever that person was knew she had to die. It was easy enough to discover from her the routine around here, and he came in and killed her, leaving you with the body. Q.E.D."

"Kate, Kate, I have never heard such drastic oversimplification."

"Nonsense, Emanuel. What you lack, what all psychiatrists lack, if you'll forgive my saying so, is a firm grip on the obvious. Well, I won't keep you. But promise me, at any rate, that you'll answer any idiotic questions that I want to ask."

"I promise to cooperate in your gallant attempt to save me from disaster. But you know, my dear, speaking of the obvious, the police have quite a case."

"They don't know you; that's the advantage I have over them. They don't know the sort you are."

"Or the sort Nicola is?"

"No," Kate said. "Not that either. It'll come out all right; you'll see."

She felt, nonetheless, as she stood indecisively in the hall, like a knight who has set off to slay the dragon but has neglected to ask in what part of the world the dragon may be found. It was all very well to decide upon action, but what action, after all, was she to take? As was her habit, she extracted notebook and pen and began to make a list: see Janet Harrison's room, and talk to people who knew her in dormitory; find out about ten and twelve o'clock patients; find out who person in picture Janet Harrison had was (lists always had a devastating effect on Kate's syntax).

"I'm sorry to intrude. Is Mrs. Bauer in?" Kate, who had been writing with the notebook balanced against her purse, dropped notebook, pen and purse. The man stooped with her to help her retrieve the articles, and as they straightened up Kate became aware of that peculiar quality of masculine beauty to which no woman can help reacting, however superficially. It did not really attract Kate, yet she felt herself become somehow more girlish in its presence. She remembered once having met at a dinner party a beautiful, modest young Swedish man. He had perfect manners, there was not anything even suggestive of flirtation in his manner, yet Kate had been horrified to notice that every woman in the room seemed aware of him; her horror had turned to amusement as later, when he had spoken to her, she had found herself simpering.

This man was not that young; his hair was flecked with gray at the temples. "You're Dr. Barrister, aren't you?" Kate said. With difficulty she kept herself from adding, "our favorite suspect." "I'm Kate Fansler, a friend of Mrs. Bauer's; I'll call her."

As Kate walked to the back of the apartment for Nicola, she realized how great, in fact, was the connection between appearance and reality. Considered in the abstract, good looks seemed sinister; yet, in the presence of good looks, Kate found them innocent. It was, of course, no accident that in Western literature, certainly in Western folklore, beauty and innocence were usually joined.

The three of them ended by standing, on this patientless day, in the living room. Not that Nicola had asked them to sit down; it was not so much that Nicola ignored the social amenities—she seemed never to have known that they existed.

"I stopped in to see how you were bearing up," Dr. Barrister said to Nicola. "I know there's nothing I can do, but I find it difficult to resist the impulse to be neighborly, even in New York where neighbors are not supposed to know one another."

"Aren't you from New York?" Kate asked, to say something.

"Are any New Yorkers?" he asked.

"I am," said Nicola, "and my father before me. *His* father, however, came from Cincinnati. Where are you from?"

"One of those highbrow critics has discovered, I understand, a new sort of novel about the young man from the provinces. I was a young man from the provinces. But you haven't told me how it's all going."

"Emanuel has had to call off the patients for today. We hope in a day or two he can get back to having patients."

"I hope so too. Do let me know, won't you, if there's anything I can do? I'm full of good will, but rather lacking in ideas."

"I know," Nicola said. "For a death in the family or illness, one sends flowers or food. In this case I suppose all you can do is to keep telling everyone that Emanuel and I didn't do it. Kate is full of ideas and is going to find the murderer." Dr. Barrister looked at Kate with interest.

"Where I'm going," said Kate, "is home."

"I'm going east," Dr. Barrister said. "Can I drop you any-where?"

"That's very kind of you," Kate said, "but I'm going west."

It was as Kate was sitting in the taxi going home that she thought of Jerry.

6

IT was true, of course, that Kate still had the weekend, before Monday should again bring the need to teach her classes. But some preparation for those classes was necessary, particularly since, in the last two days, she had got completely out of touch with the academic world, as though she had been absent for a year. One had, after all, a commitment to one's profession, in spite of any murders, however demanding of investigation.

And what, when she came right down to it, was she to investigate? Something, certainly, could be gleaned by a little recondite questioning around the dormitory where Janet Harrison had lived; examination of the university records might reveal some clue of interest. All that Kate could, without undue interference with her professional duties, undertake. But the police had more or less covered the ground, and what seemed now most fruitful of examination was the other suspects whom the police seemed inclined to treat with little more than superficial interest: the patients before and after Janet Harrison, both men; the elevator man; and any stray men who might, hopefully, turn up and turn out to have known Janet Harrison, however slightly.

It seemed to Kate that, the question of time apart, what was clearly needed was a male investigator, preferably unattached and footloose, able to appear either the worldly young college graduate, possessed of that patina which only the more elegant colleges provide, or the young workingman, who has labored by day and who, in the proper clothes, can hang around discussing ball clubs and whatever else workingmen discuss, without appearing to be slumming.

The description fit Jerry to a fare-thee-well, and indicated, once again, the occasional benefits of a large family.

Not that Jerry was in any way related to Kate; not, that is, as yet. But he would one day soon be a nephew by marriage. Kate did not remember his exact age, but he was old enough to vote and young enough to believe that life still held infinite possibilities. "No young man thinks that he shall ever die." Hazlitt had certainly described Jerry.

Kate, coming from a large family, had also been an only child, a unique combination of benefits. Her parents, in the normal course of events—in the normal course, that is, of a sophisticated, well-to-do, New York City life (with summers in Nantucket)—had produced three sons in the first eight years of their marriage. They had departed from convention, or perhaps from what Kate had come to think of as a planned economy, only far enough to find themselves, when the youngest of their sons was fourteen, with an infant daughter. They had provided Kate with a nurse, and subsequently, a governess, loved her to distraction, indulged her recklessly, and stood by hopelessly as she turned her back on society and became, not only an "intellectual," but a Ph.D. This was blamed, somewhat unfairly, on the fact that she had been named Kate, because all her mother remembered of college English was that this had been Shakespeare's favorite female name. The brothers had all pursued more respected and orderly careers. Sarah Fansler, the daughter of the oldest brother, was engaged to Jerry.

Jerry, of course, was moderately unsuitable. Had he been magnificently unsuitable, say a garage mechanic, the engagement would probably at any cost have been stopped. But to have absolutely put the family foot down on Jerry would have been to have turned one's back—the family was very given to bodily metaphors, usually mixed—on the American dream. Jerry's father was dead; his mother managed a small gift shop in New Jersey, and had, by devotion and hard work, sent her son through college; she would also help to send Jerry through law school beginning next fall. Jerry had won scholarships, had worked summers and after school, had helped in the gift shop, and had an air of understanding the world and conjuring it into releasing its gifts. Jerry, just finished with his six months in the Army, was driving a truck for a frozen-foods distributor until the fall. Kate thought he might be willing to do something a bit more adventurous for an equal amount of money.

A call to Jerry at his mother's home in Jersey found him just returned from work, and quite willing (rather to Kate's surprise) to drive in that very evening and talk to her; it appeared that a friend's car was available. Kate managed to suggest that he keep his destination, and the phone call, secret, without sounding, she hoped, as conspiratorial as she felt. It was odd, she realized, that she should be prepared to trust in this way a young man she had met only a few times at those family celebrations of the engagement she had consented to attend. They had been attracted to each other by the amused air of detachment which, alone of those present, they had both radiated. What are *we* doing here? they seemed, smilingly, to ask each other. Kate was there because she admitted some, though not many, family obligations, and Jerry was there because Sarah was very pretty and very proper. Kate had always thought her rather dull, but Jerry was, perhaps, just smart enough in the ways of the world to prefer a dull, conventional, though pretty, wife.

When he arrived, Kate offered him a beer and plunged right into the matter at hand: "I'm going to offer you a job," she said. "The same pay as you're getting now. Can you take a leave, and go back when you want to?"

"Probably. But I get time and a half on this job for working extra hours." He was relaxed, prepared to be enlightened and, Kate suspected, entertained.

"I'll pay you only the regular amount. This job will be much more interesting, and require more of your talents. But if you succeed, I'll give you a bonus at the end."

"What's the job?"

"Before I tell you that, I want a solemn promise of secrecy. No one is to be told about this—not your family, or your friends; not by the slightest hint are they to know what you're involved in. Not even Sarah is to suspect."

"Agreed. Like Hamlet's friends, I won't even indicate that I might tell if I would. I swear on the sword. Very good play, I thought," he added, before Kate could control her look of surprise. "I promise not to murmur a word to Sarah." It seemed to Kate that his willingness to keep things from Sarah did not bode well for their marriage, but she was past having scruples about any good fortune that came her way.

"Very well, then. I want you to help me solve a murder. No, I have not taken leave of my senses, nor have I developed paranoia or megalomania. Have you read anything about this girl who was murdered on the psychoanalyst's couch? You could scarcely have helped it, I suppose. They think the psychoanalyst did it; he's a very good friend of mine, and I want to prove that he didn't do it, nor did his wife, who is the suspect they're holding in abeyance. But I'm convinced the only way to prove Emanuel didn't do it is to find out who did. A young man like you can talk naturally to a lot of people, can ask questions I can't ask. Also, by the end of spring term the work at college reaches monumental proportions. Get the picture?''

"What about the police?''

"The police are very conscientious, in their unimaginative way. Perhaps I'm prejudiced; probably I am. But they have such a nice suspect, they are so certain that no one else *could* have done it, that their searches in other directions are bound to be somewhat lacking in vigor, or so it seems to me. However, if we find a nice fat clue leading to someone else, I imagine they can be persuaded to follow it up.''

"Have *you* a favorite suspect?''

"Unfortunately, no. We're not only lacking in suspects; we're delightfully free of information of any kind.''

"Perhaps the girl was drugged. Then anyone could have put her on the couch and murdered her, having got rid of the analyst first.''

"You sound very promising. As a matter of fact, though, we do have some information about the murder, if not about other suspects or the girl. She wasn't drugged. If you want the job, I'll tell you all about it. It won't take long.''

It took, however, longer than Kate would have thought. She told Jerry the whole thing from the beginning, starting with her recommendation of the girl to Emanuel. He listened closely, and asked a number of intelligent questions. Kate realized that she was offering him adventure with the pay of security, and it might well warp his whole view of life. The younger generation, so all the journalists said—and it was generally true enough to be frightening—opted always for security, for the sure job, the sure pension, the sure way of life. They might have liked adventure, but they didn't want to pay the price for it; better to read *Kon-Tiki* in an air-conditioned study in Westchester. Jerry was getting adventure, and a salary check determined by a union. It might not be the best training for a young man, but when you came right down to it, finding bodies on the couch was not the best training for a psychoanalyst either.

In any case, there was nothing for Jerry to do until Monday. He promised to come for orders then, late afternoon, by which time he hoped to have disentangled himself from frozen food, and thought up a plausible story, should one be required. Jerry's departure was speeded by a telephone. The call was from Reed. No, he had no other news, but he did have a copy of the picture. Two copies? Yes, she could have two copies. He would bring them up tonight, if that was all right. How about a movie to get their minds off things? Danny Kaye? Heartlessly, Kate agreed.

After the movie, Reed and Kate went out for a meal. Kate took from her purse the picture of the young man. She had looked at the face so steadily that it seemed almost as though the picture might be induced to speak. "The question is," Kate said, "is this the young man of the love affair?" She told Reed about her conversation with Emanuel. "How old would you say this young man is?" Kate asked.

"Perhaps thirty, perhaps twenty-five. He looks very young; at the same time he looks like someone who looks young for his age, if you follow me."

"I follow you. He keeps reminding me of someone."

"Probably of himself; you keep staring at the picture."

"No doubt you are right." Kate put the young man firmly away.

"A conscientious young detective trotted all over the dormitory with that picture," Reed said. "He is a very attractive young man, and the girls and women were delighted to chat with him about anything. They would gladly have said they saw this young man of the picture every day of their lives, to make the detective happy, but the truth was no one had ever laid eyes on him. One older woman thought she recognized him, but it turned out she was thinking of Cary Grant in his younger days. If that young man, or his picture, has ever been around that dormitory, he managed to avoid being seen by anyone, including, incidentally, the service people, who were also questioned. Kate, you realize he is probably a perfectly ordinary young man who jilted her, or, to be less cynical, got himself killed in a war or an accident, leaving her forever bereft."

"He's not as good-looking as Cary Grant. He doesn't look movie-actorish at all."

"Kate, you're beginning to worry me. Are you . . . does this man, this Emanuel Bauer mean so much to you?"

"Reed, if I can't make you understand this, how are the police ever to understand Emanuel? He's the last married man in the world likely to become involved with a woman, let alone a patient. But even if all that were possible, which I don't for a minute grant, don't you see that his office, his couch—these are the setting of his profession? Can't you see that no genuine psychoanalyst with Emanuel's training would be overcome by maniacal passion in his office hours? Even admitting (which I do not) that he might commit any crime as a man, he could not commit one as a psychiatrist.''

"Have psychiatrists so much more integrity than other people?''

"No, of course not. Many psychiatrists I know of are the scum of the earth. They discuss their patients at parties. They grow rich, and brag about the fees they charge; they are paid $150 for their signature on a piece of paper releasing a patient from some institution. The signature means that the patient will be under their care, but they sign and are paid, and hear no more of it. Even one signature a day is a nice yearly income. There are psychiatrists who entertain doctors, so that the doctors will refer patients to them. All charged up to the expense account, of course. But Emanuel, and others like him, love their work; and if you want my recipe for integrity, find the man who loves his work and loves the cause he serves by doing it. How's that for pomposity?''

"What is the cause? Helping people?''

"Oddly enough, no. I don't think so—not for Emanuel at any rate. He is interested in discovering something about the workings of the human mind. If you were to ask him, he would probably say that analysis is most important for research, that therapy is more or less a by-product. What would the D.A.'s office make of that?''

"Kate, forgive me, but you were lovers; that came out in the testimony of the wife, though she did not in any sense offer it. I think the detectives were looking around generally for motives.''

"Then Nicola should have murdered me, or I should have murdered Nicola. Except that we all understand it was a long, long time ago, and never were any embers colder.''

"Where did you and Emanuel meet, back in the days when the embers weren't so cold?''

"I had an apartment back in those days, too. Are you trying to make me out a scarlet woman? Reed, why do I keep forgetting you're a policeman?''

"Because I'm not a policeman. At the moment, I'm the lawyer for the prosecution. Did Emanuel have an office in those days?''

"He shared a little office with another analyst.''

"Did you ever meet him there?''

"Yes, I guess so, once or twice.''

"Were you ever—together—on the couch?''

"Reed, I've underestimated you. You'll make an excellent, quite diabolic prosecutor, able not only to elicit half-guessed-at facts, but able also to distort them and avoid the truth. On the witness stand, of course, I wouldn't be able to explain. The truth, nonetheless, is that Emanuel had just begun in those days. He was doing therapy, so he didn't use the couch, which happened to be part of the furniture—for future use, perhaps. And I was never there in office hours.''

''Kate, my dear, I'm trying to show you what you're up against, plunging into this thing without any idea of what you're getting into. I know, fools rush in where angels fear to tread; but I've never discovered what, if anything, the fools accomplished. No, I'm not calling you a fool. I'm trying to say that you've set out, gallantly, God knows, to save Emanuel, and you may end up only muddying the waters and ruining yourself. And if there is no longer anything between you, as they say in the worst sort of magazines, why are you doing it? From a disinterested love of truth?''

''I'm not ready to admit that that's the worst motive in the world. I'm too old to be newly shocked by the fact that everyone can be bought, that corruption is the only way of existence; every graduation speech, and I have heard many, moans on about corruption. The only thing I know is that here and there one finds someone interested in truth, in goodness, if you insist, for its own sake. How many policemen are there in New York who have never received a dollar outside their salary? All right, perhaps I'm rambling. Look at it in the cold-blooded way you prefer. Emanuel had four years of college, four years' of medical school, one year's general internship, two years' residence in psychiatry, three years' training at the institute, and many, many valuable years of experience. Is all this to go down the drain because some clever murderer killed a girl in his office?''

''I was always under the impression that you had relatively little faith in psychiatry.''

''As a therapeutic tool it is, I think, very clumsy, to say the best that can be said about it. I have many other objections to it. But what has that to do with seeing an able psychiatrist condemned for something he didn't do? There are many things I don't admire about Emanuel, but I feel about him as Emerson felt about Carlyle: 'If genius were cheap,' Emerson said, 'we might do without Carlyle, but in the existing population he cannot be spared.' ''

''May I ask where you intend to begin?''

''It would be less embarrassing if you didn't. Have you found out anything about the other patients?''

''The ten o'clock patient is named Richard Horan. Twenty-eight, unmarried, works for an advertising firm. Was planning to switch his hour as soon as possible, since it was convenient neither for him nor Emanuel, though I gather, *entre nous*, that advertising firms are used to having their personnel in analysis. We live in a fascinating time; there's no getting away from that. The twelve o'clock patient teaches English, I'm sure you'll be delighted to hear, at one of the city colleges. I can't remember which one, but a long subway ride is involved. Also unmarried, and not likely to marry, if the impression of the detective is worth anything; it may not be. Your Emanuel, as usual, is mum, though here I rather respect his point of view. Obviously he can't talk about the patients who haven't been murdered. This patient's name is Frederick Sparks, as you know, but I'll send you a copy of the notes; you will then be in a position to blackmail *me*. Do I make my trust and confidence clear?"

"Can I have their home addresses?"

"You can have anything it is in my power to give you. Just let me know what you're doing, will you, in a general sort of way? And if you get a note to meet a mysterious man with interesting information on some dark street, don't go."

"Flippancy," Kate said flippantly, "will get you nowhere. May I have another cup of coffee?"

7

BY Monday morning life had become, not normal certainly, but with the appearance of being normal. Emanuel returned—minus his eleven o'clock patient—to the practice of psychiatry. Nicola attended her own psychoanalytic hour. Kate, who had disciplined herself to the preparation of work over the weekend, returned to teaching. Saturday evening she had spent with a painter who read only French newspapers, was interested in murder, and had theories about nothing but art. This helped considerably.

But the chief factor in removing the Bauers from the center of attention and the glare of publicity was a horrible crime in Chelsea: some madman had enticed away, raped and murdered a four-year-old girl. The police and newspapers, for the time being at least, switched their main forces elsewhere. (The madman was captured, quite easily, a week later, which brought some comfort to Kate. Madmen, she reasoned, were usually caught. Therefore Janet Harrison could not have been killed by a madman. She found this magnificent piece of illogic quite consoling.)

At ten o'clock on Monday morning Kate lectured on *Middlemarch*. Did anything, after all, matter beside the fact that imagination might create worlds like *Middlemarch*, that one might learn to perceive these worlds and the structures that sustained them? Looking through the novel the night before, Kate had come upon a sentence which seemed oddly applicable: "Strange that some of us, with quick alternate vision, see beyond our infatuations, and even while we rave on the heights, behold the wide plain where our persistent self pauses and awaits us." Really, the sentence had nothing to do with the present case: a murder was not an infatuation. Yet, after the lecture,

Kate realized that while she had discussed *Middlemarch*, she had been incapable of thinking of anything else. The persistent self lived, she thought, in that work where one's attention was wholly caught. Emanuel, listening behind the couch, knew perhaps the same thing. It occurred to Kate that few people possessed "persistent selves," and that Emanuel, as one of them, had to be saved.

She therefore turned her steps, after the lecture, to the Graduate Women's Dormitory, where Janet Harrison had lived. Not many of the students, as Kate had told Detective Stern, lived on the campus, but the university maintained a dormitory for women who wanted to live, or whose parents insisted that they live, under more proper and controlled circumstances. The dormitory was a benefit also to students who did not want to be burdened with any domestic concerns, and it seemed likely that Janet Harrison had chosen to live there for that reason.

Kate had worked out an extremely complicated plan of attack upon the dormitory, which involved a certain amount of strolling around corridors, conferences with porters and maids, perhaps the exchange of muted confidences with the woman in charge of the dormitory; but the need for all this was obviated by Kate's colliding, on the doorstep, with Miss Lindsay. Last year Miss Lindsay had been a student of Kate's in a course in advanced writing which Kate had taken over for a professor on leave and abandoned upon his return with greater relief than she had ever felt before. The course, nonetheless, had had its moments, and Miss Lindsay, whose main subjects were Latin and Greek, had provided most of them. Kate still cherished, in fact, a Latin translation of "Twinkle, Twinkle, Little Star," beginning *Mica, mica, parva stella, Micor quae nam sis, tam bella*, with which Miss Lindsay had presented her on some now quite forgotten occasion. Kate's own Latin, despite a fascinated reading, some years ago, of Virgil's *Aeneid*, was still of the *hic, haec, hoc* variety.

Miss Lindsay was that rare student who can talk informally with a professor without ever crossing the line into familiarity. She followed Kate now, willingly enough, into the lounge, abandoning her destination without a pang. Kate, who needed her, did not argue very strenuously. It occurred to her, not for the first time, that in the solution of a murder Kant's categorical imperative had continually to be ignored. Kate asked Miss Lindsay if she had known Janet Harrison.

"Slightly," Miss Lindsay said. If she was surprised at the question she did not show it. "We have, of course, been talking of nothing else for days. As a matter of fact, the only time I spoke to her, we spoke of you. You are the only teacher who seemed to arouse her out of her usual academic lassitude. Something to do with moral obligations struck her particularly, as I remember.''

''Doesn't she seem to you an odd sort of person to have been murdered? Not, of course, that one exactly expects anyone to be murdered, but she seemed so, I think 'uninvolved' is the word I want, so unlikely, despite her beauty, to inspire passion.''

''I don't agree. In the town I came from there was a girl like that, distant, you know, and rather above it all; but it came out finally that she had been living, ever since she was fifteen, with a grocer whom everyone thought to be happily married. Not so much still waters, but calm waters with a lethal current underneath. Of course, I could be quite wrong about Janet Harrison. The person you want to talk to is Jackie Miller. She has a room near Janet's. Jackie is the sort who talks all the time and never seems to listen, yet she punctuates the flow with pointed questions one somehow can't avoid answering. She knows more about everyone than anybody else. Perhaps you know the type?'' Kate merely groaned. She knew the type all too well. ''Why not come up and see her now? She's probably just getting up, and if you can once start her talking, she'll tell you everything anyone could know. I believe,'' Miss Lindsay added, leading the way upstairs, ''that it was she who told the detective that Janet had always carried a notebook. No one else had noticed.''

Jackie responded to their knock by flinging open the door and waving them gleefully into the messiest room Kate had seen since her college days. Jackie, dressed in a sleeping outfit of very short pants and a lacy, sleeveless top that seemed quite wasted in a woman's dormitory, was making herself a cup of instant coffee with water from the tap. She offered them some; Miss Lindsay refused with commendable firmness, but Kate meekly accepted hers in the hope that this would lead them sooner to the point. She might, however, have saved herself from the agony of drinking the concoction.

''So you're Professor Fansler,'' Jackie began. She was clearly the sort who a hundred years ago would have tossed aside her parasol and said, ''So you're President Lincoln.'' ''I keep hearing about you from all the students, but I just can't seem to work one of your courses into my schedule. All my credits from Boston University were in literature—I just love reading novels—so I have to spend all my time here taking courses in other ghastly things. But I must fit in one of your courses because they all say you're one of the few professors who manage to be entertaining and profound; and let's admit it, most women professors are dreadfully dull old maids.'' It did not apparently occur to Jackie that there was anything infelicitous about this statement. Kate fought down the outrage which such a generalization always aroused in her.

"Janet Harrison was a student of mine,'' she said, without too much finesse. But finesse would undoubtedly be wasted on Jackie.

"Yes, I know. She mentioned it once at lunch, and usually you know she never so much as uttered—the strong silent type, not at all attractive, I think, in a woman. Anyway, this day at lunch (you must have had your mouth full, Kate thought maliciously) she said that you said that Henry James had said that morality depended—the morality of one's actions, that is—depended, or should depend, on the moral quality of the person who was going to do the action and not on the moral quality of the person one was doing the action to. Of course,'' Jackie added, with the first sign of insight Kate had seen in her, "she put it better. But the point was, she didn't agree. She thought if someone was morally bad, you should do something about it because of their morality, not because of yours.'' Kate, gallantly allowing herself and Henry James to be so traduced, wondered if Janet Harrison had indeed said something of the sort. *Could* she have gotten wind of a drug ring?

"Of course,'' Jackie continued, "she was frigid, poor thing, and completely unable to relate to people. I told her so and she practically admitted it. I guessed, of course, that she was being analyzed. She used to leave here promptly every morning at the same time, and I found out she wasn't going to a class, and a very good thing for her. If you want to know, I think the analyst stabbed her out of sheer frustration. She probably lay there hour after hour not opening her mouth. Have you been analyzed?''

It was nearly a quarter of a century since Kate had felt the impulse to stick out her tongue at someone. "Were any other rooms robbed except hers?'' she asked.

"No, it was really very peculiar. I told her she had probably aroused some sort of fetishism in some poor frustrated man. If you ask me, he took the camera as a cover, but he was really looking for something personal; but there really wasn't anything in her room worth looking for''—Jackie slid rather hastily over the unfortunate implications of this remark—"and, of course, she dressed like the matron of a girls' school. I used to tell her she was really very good-looking, if she would only cut her hair instead of just wearing it pulled back, and you know—showed herself off a little. I was fascinated by that picture the detective was showing around here, apparently of someone connected with Janet. Perhaps she did go out to meet a man, after all, though it seems unlikely. If so, she certainly kept him well hidden.''

"Did she go out often?''

"Well, not often, but fairly regularly. She went out to dinner, or she would just disappear, and obviously she wasn't going to the library. I think someone saw her with a man once.''

"Who?'' Kate asked. "Was it someone who saw the picture?''

"The detective asked me that,'' Jackie said in her maddening way, "and, you know, I can't remember. It was someone I was talking to by the fountain, because I remember that someone had put soap in the fountain, and this girl and I were commenting on that; but I can't remember how the question came up—something like my saying one doesn't expect to find soap in a fountain, and she said, speaking of the unexpected, etcetera. But, you know, I just can't remember who it was. Perhaps I dreamed it all. Of course, she— Janet, I mean—was an only child, and I always think that the reciprocal rivalry of the sibling relationship does a great deal to develop the personality, don't you?''

It was likely that she did not expect an answer, but Kate rose to her feet, with a frank look at her watch. Even for the solution of a murder, there was a point beyond which she would not go. Miss Lindsay joined her in a movement toward the door. "You will let me know, won't you,'' Kate said, striving for a casual tone, "if you remember who the person was who saw Janet and the man?''

"Why are you so interested?'' Jackie asked.

"Thank you for the coffee,'' Kate flung back, and, closing the door, sped down the corridor with Miss Lindsay.

"It's a pity no one murdered *her*,'' said Miss Lindsay, echoing Kate's thoughts. "I think even the police would gladly leave it as one of the unsolved cases.''

With an intense feeling of frustration, Kate made her way to the office of university records. Here, with a certain amount of what Jerry would probably have called "throwing her weight around,'' she managed to obtain Janet Harrison's records. For the first and undoubtedly the last time in her life, Kate was grateful to the modern mania for forms. She began with Janet's record at the university; her marks had been B minuses, with an occasional B. To Kate's professional eye, this indicated that her instructors had found her clearly capable of A work, but performing, probably, on the C level. There was a strong tendency among professors, including herself, to save C's for the strictly C students, of whom, God knows, there were enough.

Janet Harrison's college credits were all in order; she had majored in history, with a minor in economics. Then why had she chosen to come to graduate school to study English literature? Well, the fields were not, of course, precisely unrelated. She had apparently applied for, and received, several college loans, and she had also applied for a fellowship. For the details of this application one had to consult the fellowship office.

Cursing, Kate went to consult the fellowship office. Janet had probably gotten the fellowship, but it would be interesting to know. Her marks in college had been almost all A's, though the college, supposedly near her home (Kate was somewhat shaky on the geography of the Midwest) had been too undistinguished to have Phi Beta Kappa. Yet why had a girl who had got A's in her college, however small, fallen to the B-minus level in graduate school? It was almost always the other way around. Probably she had had something else on her mind. In fact, everyone seemed impressed with the fact—now that Kate thought of it—that Janet Harrison had had something on her mind. But what? What?

The fellowship forms were even more demanding than the university forms has been. Where, the fellowship forms wanted to know, had she spent every year of her life? (Leave no gaps! the form stated sternly.) After college, Janet Harrison had gone to the nursing school at the University of Michigan. Nursing school! Now that was certainly odd. History, Nursing school, English literature. Well, young American females did have a way, if they were not early married, of searching about for possible processions, but surely this search was a trifle wide in scope. Perhaps her parents had been of the old-fashioned sort who might send a girl to college, but insisted that she be rained to earn a living. To such people, Kate knew, there were only three ways a girl could be trained to earn a living: by becoming a secretary, a nurse, or a school-teacher.

But Janet Harrison had not persisted with her nursing. Her father had died a year after she began training, and she had gone home to live with her mother. It was apparently at her mother's death that the girl had come to New York to study English literature. But why come to New York? The damned form raised more questions than answered. According to the financial statement appended, Janet had been left, on the death of her mother, with some income, but not enough to pay the large fees of the university, unless she also took a job, and the university preferred to lend students money rather than have them try to carry jobs and graduate work at the same time. She had, Kate noticed, got the fellowship, which was not very large.

Kate walked back to the office with questions whirling on her mind. Had Janet Harrison left a will, and if so—or if not—who got her money? Was it possibly worth murdering her for? Reed would have to find that out. Perhaps the police, whom Kate had a regrettable habit of forgetting, had already looked into this. It seemed obvious enough. Why had Janet Harrison come to New York? The University of Michigan had a perfectly good graduate school. Well, perhaps she had wanted to get away from home, but did it have to be so *far* from home? Why had she chosen so varied a program of study? Why, if it came to that, had she never married? Jackie Miller, blast her loquacious imbecility, might think Janet frigid, or "unable to relate to people" (the girl had, of course, used that very phrase to Emanuel); but she was certainly beautiful and had had, so Emanuel thought, a love affair.

At her office Kate found waiting students and, feeling rather like a trapeze artist, plunged once again into academia.

Exhausted, she reached home later in the afternoon to find Jerry camping on the doorstep. He had the gleam in his eye of the prospector who has found gold. She consoled him for his wait with a beer.

"I have been on the job," he said. "I couldn't reach you this morning, after handing in my temporary resignation, and since I assumed my pay started today, I honorably determined to get to work. You had not, however, left any directions, so I decided to mosey around on my own. I couldn't think of anything else to do, so I went over to that dormitory where Janet Harrison had lived."

"Really," Kate said. "I was there myself. Did you meet Jackie Miller too?"

"I was not concerning myself with females; that, obviously, is your department. I went down to the basement and talked to the porter. Naturally, I didn't ask him a lot of questions about Janet Harrison; that is not, in my opinion, the way to elicit information. I was just a nice eager boy who wanted to know how I could get a porter's job at the university, where I wanted to work, because then I wouldn't have to pay for the courses I wanted to take. Employees don't, you know. We mentioned that the Tigers had a good chance for the pennant, we talked about how much money everything costs, and thus, gradually, did I come into possession of the fact that will save Emanuel, if I may call him that.''

"For God's sake, stop being dramatic and get to the point.''

"The point, my dear Kate, is that the porter's uniform was stolen on the morning that Janet Harrison's room was robbed. The porter was very exercised about the whole thing, because the university is being stubborn about buying him another one; you know the sort of uniform they wear—blue shirt and trousers, with 'Building and Grounds' stitched on the pocket. All right, all right, don't get hysterical. Obviously, you see, a man stole that uniform to get into Janet Harrison's room. A man can't usually go wandering around female dormitories, as I know to my cost, but no one ever notices a porter; he's obviously on his way to fix something, and no one gives him a second glance.

"Now, the beautiful part of all this is that the porter came on duty at noon, when he noticed the uniform had been stolen, and the room wasn't robbed before ten-thirty, because the maid went in then to straighten up. Therefore the uniform was stolen and the room robbed when Emanuel had a beautiful alibi: he was with a patient, and the patient, ladies and gentlemen, was Janet Harrison, who therefore could not have been in the room either. Therefore the room was *not* robbed by Emanuel, and since I don't see why we shouldn't leap to the conclusion that whoever robbed the room murdered the girl, it wasn't Emanuel.''

"He could have hired someone, the police will say.''

"But we know he didn't, and we will prove it. Furthermore, I couldn't check on any of the others, but I went around to Emanuel's house for another buddy-buddy chat with the employees—the Tigers really have a good chance of winning the pennant this year—and discovered that the elevator man is off on Friday. Dr. Michael Barrister does not hold office hours on Friday, and if you will give me the names of the ten o'clock and twelve o'clock patients, we will discover shortly what they do on Fridays. I'll bet you my salary, double or nothing, that whoever robbed that room murdered the girl. And I don't think whoever it was relegated the task to anyone. My reasons for thinking that are that it would be too damn inconvenient if he, or she, had. Speaking of shes, Mrs. Bauer—may I call her Nicola?—was probably at her analytic hour with an alibi. But of course it was a man who stole the uniform, so that doesn't get us very much further.''

"Jerry, you're wonderful.''

"I think perhaps after law school I will join the F.B.I. Do they look for murderers, or only Communists and drug dispensers? I'm rather enjoying this."

"We shall have to map out a plan," Kate said, with a certain amount of primness, to control his exuberant spirits.

"That's simple. Tomorrow morning you return to Thomas Carlyle—if that is the man with whom you were carrying on an affair in the stacks—and I will follow the trail of the ten o'clock patient in the advertising business. You see before you a young man burning with the desire to go into the advertising business. Will you have a thinking man's cigarette?"

8

JERRY arrived at Kate's apartment the next morning at a quarter to nine. They had decided that he would thus arrive each morning for a conference. Kate assumed, though she did not actually ask him, that his mother, friends, and fiancée still imagined him to be driving the truck.

"One thing's been worrying me," Kate said. "Why didn't the man, whoever he was, return the uniform? If he returned it before twelve the porter would never have known it was gone. Why didn't the porter tell the police it had been stolen, by the way?"

"To answer the second question first, the porter didn't tell the police because he doesn't like the police, and they might have 'pulled him in' or thought he was implicated. The theft of the uniform might well make it look like an inside job."

"How easily you slip into the jargon."

"To answer the first question," said Jerry, ignoring this, "he didn't return the uniform because it was risky enough stealing it. Why risk returning it, and double the chance of getting caught? Also, I imagine, it made it much easier for him to get out of the place unnoticed. A man in a porter's uniform isn't really looked at, but a man in a business suit emerging from a women's dormitory might very well be noticed. Easier to use the uniform for a quick getaway, and then drop it down an incinerator someplace."

"What did he do with his own clothes when he put on the uniform?"

"Really, Kate, you don't seem to have much of a flair for this sort of thing, if you don't mind my mentioning it. He put it on over his own clothes, naturally; the porter is, unfortunately, on the large side, so it's no good looking for a tiny murderer. Those uniforms are, of course, handed around, and are not expected to be more than approximate fits.''

''Well,'' Kate said, ''I have, for the moment, decided to abandon Thomas Carlyle. Delightful enough man, in his way, but not exactly restful, and dreadfully time-consuming. I had better take on Frederick Sparks. He is, after all, in my field—I know several people in his English Department, and if there is a motive there, I am likelier than you to smell it out. That leaves you with the advertising business. Perhaps, by tonight, we shall, one or the other, have a suspect bulging with motive. We may, of course, find that our investigations take several days. Perhaps we should keep notes, and when we are finished we can write a manual of do-it-yourself detection. Are you actually going to apply for a job?''

''I haven't really decided yet. You know, I think I'll try to work in Dr. Michael Barrister's nurse. I got a glimpse of her yesterday— very young, very attractive, and, I would guess, very eager to talk, if encouraged immediately after work when she has just spent hours listening to the ailments of aging women. We might as well find out all we can about the sinister doctor across the hall.''

''You haven't met him yet. When you do, you will discover that he is, unfortunately, not sinister at all. However, we must search out every avenue of possibility, if that is the correct phrase. Don't, by the way, get so involved with the young, attractive nurse that you forget my investigation and your fiancée.''

''I only came to work on the case because all detectives have such a fascinating sex life. Have you read Raymond Chandler?''

''I have read Raymond Chandler, and his detective was not engaged to be married.''

''Nor did he have a nice safe job driving around the countryside with frozen food. Nor, now I think of it, did he spend six months in the Army as a cook.''

''A *cook!* Why on earth?''

''Because I've never cooked a thing in my life, and had a great deal of experience driving trucks. But they didn't have any room in the transport section because it was all full up with cooks. Do not, in any case, worry about my morals, which, to the extent they are not already corrupted, are incorruptible. I knew a guy who got involved with a redhead after he was engaged to a fetching brunette. He met the redhead in a village nightclub where he had a temporary job playing the bass fiddle. The two women, between them, wore him down to such a state that he joined a ship's orchestra, even though he once got seasick on the boat ride to the Statue of Liberty, and was last heard of in ragged clothes, playing the violin under a balcony in Rome, waiting for Tennessee Williams to work him into his latest play."

He departed, having acquired from Kate a copy of the picture found in Janet Harrison's purse, money, and a key to Kate's apartment, should he require to return to home base when she was gone.

About Frederick Sparks, whose appointment came after Janet Harrison's, and who had been present at the finding of the body, Kate was prepared to indulge the profoundest suspicions. For a few minutes after Jerry's departure she considered calling Emanuel to beg a few minutes in which to discuss Mr. Sparks. It might be Emanuel whose whole professional career—indeed, whose life was in danger—but in Kate's eyes his professional stature had not diminished by one millimeter, and she found this extraordinarily encouraging, even though it meant she begged for, rather than demanded, time. Kate felt certain that Emanuel's patients would think of him in the same way. She would wait till she had met Frederick Sparks, or at least had garnered some impressions of him, before attempting to extricate something from Emanuel.

She was interrupted in these ruminations by a telephone call from Reed, who sounded exactly as Jerry had the night before.

"We have finally discovered something," Reed said, "that, I have a hunch, will break the case, one way or another."

"I know all about the uniform," Kate said primly.

"What uniform?"

"Sorry, I must have been thinking of one of my other cases. What have you found?"

"Janet Harrison left a will."

"Did she indeed? I hope she was murdered for her money; what we badly need in this case is a motive."

"She had $25,000 invested in some family business which paid her 6 percent (preferred stock) or, to save you the embarrassment of higher mathematics, $1,500 dollars a year."

"Perhaps the family in the business murdered her for her stock."

"Scarcely. I'm trying to tell you that she left a will. She didn't leave the stock to the family. Who do you think she left it to? Forgive me, whom?"

"If she left it to Emanuel, I shall shoot myself."

"Messy. And people unacquainted with guns usually miss, shatter the walls and frighten the neighbors. She left it to a Daniel Messenger, M.D."

"Who's he? Reed! Could he be the youngish man in the picture?"

"Two minds with but a single thought. Or rather, twenty minds. We have already acquired a description of Dr. Daniel Messenger, who practices medical research—does one practice research? I'm sure not—in Chicago. It's obvious he's older than our man, and couldn't be more unlike the picture if he'd planned it that way, the unspeakable blackguard."

"Perhaps he's disguised—dyed his hair or had plastic surgery."

"Kate, my girl, I get more worried about you every time we have a conversation. We are about to receive a picture of the chap, and I think it will convince even you. I gather no one could mistake him for a young Cary Grant; a young Lon Chaney, in full makeup, would apparently be nearer the mark. His hair grows low on his forehead, he has a long, rather fleshy nose, and his ears stick out. Undoubtedly he has a beautiful personality; he certainly must have character, to go into research, with the money lying around for doctors these days."

"What was he to Janet Harrison, and where did you find the will?"

"What he was to Janet Harrison is the question of the hour. He was interrogated by a Chicago detective who swears that the good doctor had never heard the name, and certainly didn't recognize her picture. There is something about that girl which is beginning to fascinate me. How we got the will is a demonstration of the benefits of publicity. The lawyer with whom she had left it called us, and turned over the will. No, you need not ask: the lawyer did not know her. She apparently picked his name out of the phone book. He wrote out the will, a perfectly simple one, and charged her fifty dollars. He had been away on some beastly business trip, and the name registered only when his wife talked on about the case after he got home. He seems perfectly genuine. But there *must* be a connection with this Daniel Messenger, though as far as we can figure out he and Janet Harrison have never even been in the same place at the same time."

"Deposit ten cents for the next five minutes, please."

"Reed, you're in a phone booth."

"With practice, my dear, you will make a great detective. I could hardly spill out all these secrets from a phone in the D.A.'s office.

Kate, I'm beginning to get interested in your case. This probably proves that insanity is catching. I haven't got a dime." He hung up.

Daniel Messenger. For a few hectic moments Kate toyed with the idea of hopping a plane for Chicago. But, however brutal one might be with Thomas Carlyle, George Eliot had to be coped with tomorrow. And of course, one did not "hop" a plane. One took a long slow ride to an airport, and argued for hours with ticket agents who seemed to have been hired five minutes ago for what they supposed to be another job; and if one survived that, one got to Chicago only to join a "stack" over the airfield there, and then either died of boredom or crashed into a plane that thought it was in the stack over Newark. With an effort, Kate brought her wandering mind back to Frederick Sparks. Reed's call, however, apart from distracting her and thickening the plot, had reminded her of the uses of the telephone. She dialed the number of a professor of sixteenth century literature with whom she had studied for the orals, lo, these many years ago.

"Lillian. This is Kate Fansler."

"Kate! How's everything in the university on the hill?"

"Hideous, as always in the spring." April is the cruelest month. That was how it had begun. For a few moments they chatted about personal things. "I'm calling," Kate continued, "to ask about a colleague of yours. Frederick Sparks."

"If you're thinking of hiring him, don't. In the first place he's got tenure and wouldn't dream of leaving, and in the second place he's a great admirer of closet drama, and thinks *The Cenci* is better than *Macbeth*."

"Nothing was further from my mind than hiring him. I'll tell you another time what this is all about. What's he like?"

"Rather tedious. Good scholar. Lives alone, having recently broken away from mother, at least to that extent. Has a French poodle named Gustave."

"*Gustave?*"

"After Flaubert. Although his favorite French author is Proust. Gustave's, that is."

"I take it he does not care for women. Sparks, that is."

"Most people take it. Me, I've given up labels. So many incorrect ones have been attached to me that I've abandoned them entirely. Besides, he's being analyzed."

This was a lead which Kate had no wish at the moment to follow.

"Lillian, is there some way I could meet Sparks, socially perhaps, or at least casually? Soon, that is."

"You fascinate me. No one's been anxious to meet Sparks since the P. and B. committee considered him for tenure."

"What on earth is the P. and B. committee?"

"Oh, you innocents who do not work for city colleges. No one has the faintest idea what the initials stand for, but it's all-powerful. As a matter of fact, I am going to a party tonight for a colleague who just got a Fulbright to India, and Sparks will undoubtedly be there. I've got a date, but I will drag you along as a cousin of his we couldn't dump. The date's that is. Will that do?"

"That will do gloriously. But the fewer lies, the better, I always think. Let's just say I dropped in on you."

"Very well, you mysterious creature. Drop in on me about eight. Bring a bottle for the festivities, and you will be triply welcomed. See you then."

Which left Kate with nothing to do but get back to work and wonder what Jerry was up to. Richard Horan, of the advertising business, must by now be settled down on Emanuel's couch. Dr. Barrister's pretty nurse must be involved with the women patients. Jerry, for all his detective pose, was probably taking in a double feature. Kate put Daniel Messenger firmly from her mind, and turned to *Daniel Deronda*.

9

JERRY was not at a double feature. It would have annoyed him to
know that Kate thought he might be; but his annoyance would have
been nothing to Kate's had she known what he was up to. He was,
in fact, lying in wait for Emanuel.

It was not precisely that Jerry doubted Kate's assurances of
Emanuel's innocence. The two of them, Jerry knew, had been friends,
and, Jerry suspected, something more—though Kate had been rather
vague on this point—and this said a good deal for Emanuel's innocence, since women, Jerry believed, did not automatically have a high
opinion of men they had loved but not married. Nonetheless, to
Jerry's masculine, therefore objective, intelligence, Emanuel was still
Number One as a suspect, and the fact that Kate was convinced of
his innocence did not weigh as much with Jerry as he had pretended.
Although he was prepared to follow Kate's instructions—she was,
after all, paying him—he could carry them out with a greater sense
of single purpose if he had met, and talked with, Emanuel. Jerry had,
at almost twenty-two, great faith in his ability to size people up.

It was not possible, of course, simply to go in and present himself
to Emanuel as Kate's assistant and nephew-to-be. In the first place,
Kate had not told Emanuel about his, Jerry's, part in the investigations; and in the second place, it was important to catch Emanuel off
his guard. For one thing, he wanted to know if Emanuel, with the
eleven o'clock hour now free, would simply wander out, as Kate and
Nicola had been sure he would.

Jerry therefore provided himself with a chamois from a Madison
Avenue store—he righteously did not enter this on his expense account—and stood across the street from the entrance to Emanuel's

office polishing a car. This gave him a fine view of anyone who went out or in, and also a reason for loitering on an elegant street where people were not encouraged to loiter. It would be inconvenient if the owner of the car appeared, but Jerry was prepared to cope with this.

At five to eleven a young man emerged from the building. Richard Horan, in all probability. Jerry, ducking behind the car to wipe the fender, got a long look at him. Mr. Horan would have to be encountered later in the day. Rather to Jerry's surprise, Mr. Horan looked like Hollywood's idea of a "young Madison Avenue executive on his way up"; because Horan was in analysis, Jerry realized that he had expected him to look a bit more harried and uncertain, the Brooks Brothers suit perhaps askew. But here was assurance personified. Jerry felt a surge of relief, the origin of which he did not question; in fact, he was, without knowing it, glad that he did not have to pity Mr. Horan.

Once the object of his scrutiny had disappeared, appropriately enough, in the direction of Madison Avenue, Jerry continued to polish the car, though less assiduously, pausing to smoke a cigarette. He saw one woman enter, and one woman leave, presumably on their way to and from Dr. Barrister's office. To his surprise, neither of the women could be described as "aged." One of them, in fact, was considerably younger than Kate, whom Jerry thought of, though he would have died rather than admit it to her, as middle-aged. (Kate, of course, had had far too much experience with students of Jerry's age not to know precisely how he thought of her.) He forced himself to wipe the entire side of the car carefully, and to smoke a cigarette in an exaggeratedly leisurely fashion, before facing the fact of what was to be done next. He had just about decided that he had better go in and spin some sort of tale to Emanuel, when Emanuel himself, smoking a cigarette, came out of the doorway and turned toward the park.

Jerry could not, of course, be certain that this was Emanuel, but the man was the right age and was, moreover, wearing extremely shabby clothes, such as were unlikely to be worn by any tenant of so excellent a building except this eccentric man who donned old clothes for the purpose of running around the reservoir. Jerry folded his chamois neatly and left it on the fender as part payment to the owner of the car for the use that had been made of it, and followed the man into the park.

It was by no means clear to Jerry what he intended to do next. Trot around the reservoir after the man, trip him up perhaps, and then slip, amid apologies, into a conversation? Emanuel was certainly no fool; could Jerry get away with that? Perhaps, at the reservoir, something would present itself. One thing was clear: this man walked with urgency, with the physical energy of one who has sat too long, who needs, quite simply, to move. This explained why he would go to the trouble of changing his clothes for scarcely half an hour's run.

But he was destined not to have the run. He slowed down on one of the paths, so that Jerry came dangerously close to him. What had stopped him was a woman—who could tell what age?—over-made-up, appearing, appallingly, on the edge of lunacy. She was weeping, and the mascara ran in black streaks down her aging face, mingling with the rouge. Others saw her, some smirked, most simply turned away and skirted the path to avoid her. Jerry's instinct was to do the same.

But Emanuel stopped. "Can I help you?" he asked the woman. Jerry dropped, unnoticed, onto a bench behind Emanuel. The woman eyed her interlocutor with suspicion.

"I've lost him," she whimpered, "I just dozed off, and he's gone away. I don't sleep well at night."

"Your little boy?" Emanuel asked.

She nodded. "I tied his leash to the bench, but he must have pulled it loose. Cyril darling, come to Mama," she began to call. "Don't you hurt him," she said to Emanuel.

"How big was he?" Emanuel asked. "What color?" The scene, to Jerry, was grotesque. But Emanuel put his hand on the woman's arm. "What color was he?" he asked again. The gesture seemed to calm her.

"Brown," she said. "This big," and she made a movement, as of one who holds a small dog under one arm. She looked at the empty arm with love.

"He won't have gone far," Emanuel said. By this time they had collected a small and interested crowd. Emanuel began to search in the nearby bushes, and a few other men, with a shrug to show they thought this all nonsense, joined him. Jerry forced himself to keep his seat. It was one of the other men who, perhaps five minutes later, found the dog, not far off, rolling in some indescribable, to him delightful, mess. A pleasant change after that woman, Jerry thought.

The woman retrieved the dog, scolding him, calling him a naughty, naughty boy, and walking away from Emanuel as though he were a tramp who had accosted her. The man who had found the dog pointed to his forehead meaningfully. Emanuel nodded, and

looked at his watch. No time now for even the quickest run. He has
a patient at twelve, Jerry thought, and he has to change his clothes.
Emanuel began walking slowly back toward the avenue. Jerry did
not follow; he remained on the bench, thinking about Richard Horan.
The need to speak to Emanuel had evaporated, somehow, in the
morning air.

After sitting for half an hour longer in the park, Jerry found
himself viewing the profession of detective with somewhat less in-
souciance than he had felt that morning. In fact, he thought himself
rather a fool. It was all very well to tell Kate, in his most debonair
manner, that he was going down to apply for a job at the advertising
agency where Richard Horan worked, but as an idea, this was several
light-years away from being brilliant. Well, he might not apply for a
job, but obviously the thing to do was to go down to the agency's
offices and look around. It might work out that the best plan would
be to follow Mr. Horan home—Jerry did not linger too long over the
question of where, if anywhere, this would lead—but he might just
as well move now in the general direction of Horan.

Going downtown in the Madison Avenue bus, Jerry pulled out
the picture of the young man and studied it. Could it possibly be a
picture of Horan? Viewing his victim from behind the car fender,
Jerry had had only a general impression; a detailed description of the
man's face had not remained with him. Surely a detective who has
had one look at a man should never again forget the face; Jerry, far
from forgetting it, had really nothing to remember. Still, he felt, swal-
lowing his humility, it was fairly certain that Horan had not looked
like this. Well, one could but make sure.

It is one of the odd tricks of fate that, when we have admitted
ourselves to be foolish, fully to blame for our own mistakes, she will
hand us a piece of good fortune on a platter. The Greeks, of course,
understood all about this, but Jerry had yet to learn it. Years later,
Jerry was to look back on this as the time when he had learned that
though one must do all one can, success is never entirely the result
of one's own efforts. Yet now, emerging from the bus, he knew only
his own inadequacy.

All advertising agencies were named, by Jerry, Bing, Bang, Bilge
and Oblivion. This particular Bing, Bang, etcetera, had its offices on
the eighteenth floor. Jerry stepped from the elevator feeling rather as
though he were going into orbit. Surely there would be a receptionist.
But Jerry was never to know whether there was or not. A hand was

placed on his shoulder; in that moment, Jerry was certain, his hair
began to go gray.

"What are you doing here? Don't tell me Sally's talked you into
going into the advertising racket. Take my advice; stick to the law."

It was Horan. Jerry stared at him open-mouthed, as though he
were an alligator who had appeared suddenly in a suburban bathtub.

"You are the Jerry who's engaged to Sally Fansler, no? I met
you at a party. . . . Anything wrong?" Jerry looked, in fact, as though
he were going to faint.

"Small world," he managed to say. "To coin a phrase," he
added, trying to save himself from the monstrous ineptitude of the
first cliché.

"I think it is, literally. In my opinion, there are only fifty people
in the world, and they keep moving about. Have you had lunch?"

Dear, wonderful, blessed Sally, who really did know everybody.
Jerry had realized, in a vague sort of way, that this might be useful—
he was thinking years ahead to his practice of law—but now he began
to view Sally's connections in an even brighter light. He had often
remarked to Sally, jokingly, that he thought they read different edi-
tions of the *Times* each morning. She never glanced at the sports
page; Africa, the Near East, Russia, the acts of Congress whirled
about somewhere in the outer reaches of her consciousness; if, to
save her life, she had to name the nine justices of the Supreme Court,
she would mention Warren, and die. But for her the *Times* was filled
with small news items of people changing jobs, marrying, divorcing,
supporting causes, and none of these items was ever forgotten. She
not only "knew everybody" through the vast connections of family,
school, college, dates—her social world generally—she also knew
all about them.

"My brother Tom used to date Sally," Horan was saying, as, in
a dream, they stepped back into the elevator. "What are you doing
these days?"

At lunch, Jerry allowed Horan to buy him a Gibson. He was not
used to drinking in the middle of the day, but this, after all, was in
the nature of forcing brandy down the throat of an injured man. Even
through an alcoholic haze, it was brilliantly clear that Horan did not
resemble the man whose picture was now in the inside pocket of
Jerry's jacket. Furthermore, could anyone from Sally's world stab a
girl on a couch? Not in a fit of passion, but in a coolly calculated
crime?

"You in analysis?" Jerry asked. He heard the words with horror.

He had meant, by the most devious circumlocution, to lead up to the subject. He ought not to have had the Gibson. What a detective he was making. Jerry stuffed his mouth with some bread, hoping, not too scientifically, that it would soak up the alcohol.

It was Horan's turn to look shocked. "My God!" he said, "where did you hear that?"

"Oh, I didn't," Jerry said with a wave of his hand. "Just one of these things one says these days, you know, just to throw it on the stoop to see if the cat will sniff it." He smiled encouragingly.

Horan looked like a man who, stooping to pet a dog, discovers it to be a hyena. The arrival of the food provided a fortunate interlude. Jerry began to eat rather rapidly. "Sorry," he finally murmured.

Horan waved a forgiving hand. "I *am* in analysis, as a matter of fact. It's not exactly a secret. As a matter of fact, my analyst is the man who just had a girl murdered on his couch."

"Have you continued with him anyway?" Jerry ingenuously asked.

"Why not? Of course, he didn't do it; at least, I don't think he did. My family thinks I should quit, but what the hell, you can't run out on every sinking ship. To coin a phrase," he added.

"Did you know the girl?" Having begun with direct questions, Jerry thought it best thus to continue.

"No, I didn't, more's the pity. I used to see her in the waiting room when I came out, but I didn't even know her name. Damn good-looking. I told her once that I just happened to have two tickets to a show that night, and would she like to go—as a matter of fact, I'd bought them that morning from a scalper—but she wasn't having any. Cold sort of fish. Odd, just the same, that someone should have murdered her."

It had, hideously, the ring of truth. But surely murderers were good liars.

"Is your analyst a good one?" Jerry asked.

"Highly recommended. He's perfectly willing to sit there for twenty minutes if I don't open my mouth. Apparently I'm resenting him, though. Dream I had." Jerry looked interested. "You're supposed to tell them your dreams, of course; never thought I dreamt much, but you do, if you make yourself remember them. Well, in this dream I was in Brooks Brothers buying a suit. The suit seemed to be damned expensive, but I got it anyway, and when I tried it on at home it didn't fit at all. I took it back to the store, and got into a violent argument with the salesman about how I'd been overcharged, and the goddam suit wasn't worth a nickel. I woke up in a fury, and rushed off to tell Dr. Bauer about it. Well, it seems it was quite a simple dream. I was resenting him, Dr. Bauer, and thought he was cheating me in charging so much for just listening to me talk, but it wasn't a thought I'd wanted to face, so I dreamt about it in that way. Clever, huh?''

It was undoubtedly magnificent as a lesson in analytic technique, but for Jerry's purposes it was worthless. Or could one resent an analyst enough to try to frame him for murder? An interesting thought. Jerry wondered if analysts ever thought of it as one of the risks of their profession. Not a bad motive, now that Jerry came to consider it. He wondered, fleetingly, how Kate was doing with Frederick Sparks.

"Don't misunderstand me," Jerry said, "but did you ever feel you'd like to kill Dr. Bauer?"

"Not *kill* him," Horan answered, apparently unoffended by the question, "though God knows what goes on in one's murky unconscious. One fantasizes about one's analyst of course, but mostly it's picturing oneself running into someone who knows him and finding out all the grisly secrets of his life, or having him drop the professional airs and beg one for help. One of the most maddening things about an analyst is that you tell him a joke, even a damn funny joke, and there's nothing in back of you but silence. I wonder if, that night, he says to his wife—I assume he's married—'Heard a damn funny joke today from one of my patients.' "

"Is he helping you with whatever problem you went to him for?"

"Well, not yet of course, but it's still early. We've uncovered a lot of interesting material. For one thing, even though I don't remember it, it turns out I knew all the time that my mother was pregnant with my brother. Analysis has already helped me with my work."

"Did you have a block of some sort?"

"Not that way. One of our clients makes elegant furniture, and I thought up an ad of a room with just two pieces of furniture in it, the couch and the chair behind it, each of them perfect pieces of furniture, of course. Got quite a nice pat on the head for that."

Horan went on to talk about nonanalytic matters, and it was beyond Jerry's powers even to try to bring him back to the subject for which he had sought him out. He seemed, in any case, most unlikely as a murderer. Perhaps he had hired someone to do the job; but, the world of organized crime apart, was that really possible? And did Horan know anything about the way Emanuel's complicated domestic arrangements worked out? That uncertainty about whether or not Emanuel had a wife might have been a clever blind. Still, could anyone seem, like Horan, so exactly what he was, and not be?

Jerry parted from Horan, who had paid for the lunch, with a feeling of depression and a splitting headache. What could he do between now and the off-duty time of Dr. Barrister's pretty nurse? After a few moments' fruitless contemplation, Jerry went to a double feature.

10

JERRY emerged, like a groundhog, from his place of hibernation into the sunlight. He had seen halves of two movies, and had only the haziest idea of what either was about, but he suspected that the two halves combined made a more interesting movie than either of them whole would have done. His mind, in any case, had been on other things. Why, for example, had he not asked Richard Horan about telephone calls to Emanuel's office? If Horan had arranged for those phone calls canceling the appointments, he might, in his confusion at Jerry's question, have indicated it. On the other hand, if Horan had paid someone to make the calls, Jerry's mentioning them would have put Horan, who seemed at any rate to have no suspicions about Jerry—apart from those about his sanity—on his guard. It seemed to Jerry that being a detective involved, more than any other profession, the constant traveling up dead-end roads. And no one, of course, ever bothered to put up signs on the roads saying Dead End.

Jerry, worried lest he miss Dr. Barrister's nurse, took a taxi from the movie theater to the office where, all unknowingly, she awaited (he hoped) his arrival. He had spent none of Kate's money and an uncomfortably large chunk of his own. He could not, in decency, charge Kate for the chamois, or the movie, or the taxi the movie had necessitated. Well, perhaps he could charge her for the chamois— after all, without that previous glimpse of Horan he would not have recognized him in the advertising office—which would have made, of course, no difference whatever. In the movie, however—and with this Jerry consoled himself—he had worked out a plan for approaching the nurse. That the plan would, had she known of it, have given

Kate the screaming heebie-jeebies, could not, in this moment of desperation, deter Jerry for an instant.

The sign outside Dr. Barrister's office read: Ring and walk in. Jerry did so. The nurse was there, working at a typewriter, alone. "Yes?" she said to Jerry, obviously mystified at his presence, his sex, and his errand. Seen this close, she was neither as young nor as pretty as Jerry had thought.

"It's about my wife," Jerry said. He sounded, to himself, extremely unconvincing, but hoped the nurse would put it down to uxorial nervousness. The nurse seemed undecided whether to laugh or call the police. "She, that is, we, that is—we wanted to have a baby. Is it all right if I sit down?" he added, doing so.

"The doctor isn't here," the nurse said, and then immediately regretted, it was clear from her expression, having admitted the fact to this lunatic. She barricaded herself behind an official attitude. "If your wife cares to call and make an appointment, or if you wish to make one now . . ." She took an appointment book from her desk and hovered over it, pen in hand. "Who recommended you to Dr. Barrister?" she horribly asked.

It was then that Jerry marshaled his by no means negligible reserve of charm. That he looked harried from his afternoon's experiences, he did not doubt. Omitting his usual restraining gesture, he allowed the forelock of his hair to drop forlornly over his forehead. He smiled at her with the smile that no female, since he was four, had been able to resist. The desolate slump of his body, the sorrow in his eyes, the smile, all indicated that here, all unhoped for, was a woman who could understand him. He became, all of him, an appeal from the depths of masculine helplessness to the heights of female competence and comfort. The nurse, though she did not know it, dropped her weapons and retired, joyfully defeated, from the field. She was far from insensitive to masculine attentions, and competent only in dealing with troubled women, whom she cowed. For the first time that day, Jerry was in control of a situation.

"Alice, my wife, was very nervous about coming here. But, of course, she ought to see a doctor. So I had to promise"—his look included the nurse in some all-encompassing understanding of women—"that I would come first and see that the doctor was a sympathetic sort of person. Alice is shy. But I'm sure if I tell her how very nice you are, and that you will of course treat her gently, I'll be able to persuade her to come. I'm sure you must have lots of women with her problem here. That must be mainly what you do, isn't it?''

''Well, we *do* do that, of course. And then there are older women with various—um—problems. . . .'' The nurse seemed to search her mind for the most presentable of these. ''Problems of—well—change of life, and that sort of thing.''

''Of course,'' Jerry said, with a great air of comprehension, though his ignorance of this subject could scarcely have been purer. ''Is there something you can do for that?'' This question was most unnatural for a young husband, a reluctant non-father, to ask, but Jerry hoped it would go down. The nurse, her attention not on the subject of the conversation, but on its quality, swallowed the question easily. ''Oh, there's a great deal you can do,'' she said, twiddling her pen prettily, ''there are hormone injections, and pills, and, of course, the attentions of a competent physician.'' She smiled. ''And then, women have other silly feminine complications.''

Jerry tucked this information neatly away for future reference. ''But you do,'' he earnestly asked, ''treat women who want to have babies?''

''Oh, yes, of course. There are many treatments that help a great deal. And Dr. Barrister is very understanding.''

''I'm glad to hear that,'' Jerry said. ''Because Alice would require an understanding sort of person. Would you call Dr. Barrister 'fatherly'?''

The nurse seemed disconcerted by the word. ''Well, no, not exactly *fatherly*. But he's very competent, and calm and helpful. I'm sure your wife will like him. But you know,'' she mischievously added, ''you'll have to go somewhere to be tested too. I mean, it isn't *always* the woman's fault, you know.''

Jerry decided to allow this to embarrass him. He looked down, ordered the forelock to fall, and coughed. ''Perhaps Alice could come Friday?'' he asked nervously.

''The doctor isn't here on Friday,'' the nurse said. ''Some other day?'' To Jerry, thinking of the porter's stolen uniform, this confirmation was satisfying, but less so than it might have been had it not reminded him that he had forgotten to ask Horan where *he* was last Friday. ''Perhaps I'd better have Alice call,'' he said, rising to his feet. ''You've been very nice. Is—er—I was wondering—is Dr. Barrister very—are his fees very high?''

''Yes, I'm afraid so,'' the nurse said. ''You can't have been married very long," the nurse kindly added. "Perhaps you oughtn't to worry yet."

"You know how women are," Jerry said. "Thank you again."

"Not at all," the nurse said, as he closed the door. Jerry rushed to Fifth Avenue and grabbed another taxi, which he would definitely charge to Kate. Sally expected him. He felt that the interview with the nurse had gone extremely well, but what, in the name of all gynecologic mysteries, had he found out?

As Jerry sped Sally-ward in his taxi, Kate, having seen Daniel Deronda off on his Zionist dream, was also in a taxi, moving toward the building Jerry had just left. She had telephoned Emanuel and Nicola and discovered that the six o'clock patient had canceled, whether because he was retreating from the field or having the usual psychoanalytic misgivings was not altogether clear. "You had better come over," Nicola had said on the phone, "and we will all sit on Emanuel's couch to make sure no one else leaves a body there." Nicola had also, after a good deal of broad hinting from Kate, extended an invitation to dinner.

Kate found them in the living room, where, they had decided, they could watch the entrance to the office and prevent the intrusion of any bodies. Kate put her package, obviously a bottle, down on the table. "Not for you," she said to Nicola. "It's for a party where I am going later to meet Frederick Sparks." She caught Emanuel's eye. "Did Janet Harrison, in her hours with you, ever mention Daniel Messenger?" Kate asked.

"The police have already asked me that," Emanuel said.

"Oh, dear, I keep forgetting about the police. Are they getting restive?"

"Well," Nicola said, "this Daniel Messenger is a help, whoever he is. I got out of one of those detectives that he's a geneticist, at least that's what Emanuel says he sounds like from my rather garbled description; but apparently he's involved in studying some mysterious disease that only Jews get, or that only Jews don't get, in some Italian (I think) places, and apparently if they can find the clue to this evasive tolerance or intolerance they'll know something more about heredity. As to whether they, the police, believe that Emanuel and I never heard of him, who, including the police, can tell?"

Kate looked at Emanuel. "She never mentioned him, I take it, or any theories about genes?" Emanuel shook his head. Kate saw that he was becoming depressed, and her heart went out to him, but there was little, except helping Nicola to babble at him, that she could do. Nicola's mother, Kate learned, had carried the children off to her country home. They had been hearing too much here, and allowing them to go a week after the murder did not seem so much a capitulation before the fates.

"Dr. Barrister doesn't have office hours on Fridays, is that right?" Kate asked Nicola.

"No," Nicola said. "Why?"

"I have come to ask questions," Kate said sententiously, "not to answer them."

"Are there any questions left to ask?" Emanuel said.

"Very many," Kate said firmly. "But you are *not* to repeat any of them to the police. Or to anyone else," she added firmly, looking at Nicola. "Here are some questions: Who stole the porter's uniform on the morning Janet Harrison's room was robbed?" Emanuel and Nicola both stared at her in astonishment, but she hurried on. "Why was her room robbed? Was it merely as some idiot suggested, that a frustrated man wanted one of her more intimate garments?"

"Are you drunk?" Emanuel asked.

"Don't interrupt. If that is so, who is this man? Why did Janet Harrison make a will? It's rather an odd thing for an unmarried young woman to do. Who is Daniel Messenger, that she should will to him, or he to her? Although your erstwhile patient, Emanuel, seems to have led a most circumspect life, to put it mildly, she was seen with a man. Who was he? Who saw her?"

"If you don't know who saw her, how do you know she was seen?" Nicola asked.

"Stop interrupting. You may take notes, or just listen, but let me finish. I am organizing my thoughts. Why did Janet Harrison decide to study English literature when she had started in history, with a bypath into nursing? Why nursing? Why did she come to New York to study English literature?"

"That's easy," Emanuel said. "She knew there was a charming lunatic named Kate Fansler teaching there."

Kate ignored him. "What worried Janet Harrison about the present? What worried her about the past? Who is the young man whose picture she cherished and hid? Did the police show you that? You didn't recognize it. Neither has anyone else. Why? Or rather, why not? What about Richard Horan? What about Frederick Sparks? What about the window cleaner?"

"Window cleaner?"

"Well, it just occurred to me, perhaps a window cleaner, who might have some sort of *thing* about women on couches, who knew her from cleaning the office windows when she was there, or the waiting rooms windows while she was waiting, had observed the routine of your house, and stabbed her one day when he happened to glance in on his way to clean someone else's windows, and had perhaps by now forgotten the whole thing. Who cleans your windows?''

If her object had been to distract Emanuel, she had succeeded. He laughed, and went to get them all a drink. "The office windows aren't ever cleaned when patients are there," Nicola said. "And anyway, we don't have a window cleaner. Pandora does them. There's no danger of falling out, you know, and, in any case, the outside ones are done by the house, because they are a special job owing to the bars across them. But *do* explain all your other fascinating questions. How do you know Frederick Sparks?''

"I don't know him.''

"Then why are you going to a party with him?''

"Because I am Kate Fansler, the great detective,'' she said. Yet suddenly she thought: It's all very well, there are a lot of questions and they add up nicely, but shall we ever find the answers? And why did Emanuel's six o'clock patient cancel? That was, perhaps, the most important question of them all. Having lifted Emanuel from the pit of despair, she was about to tumble into it herself when the telephone rang. "It's for you, Kate,'' Emanuel called from the kitchen.

"But nobody knows I'm here,'' Kate said, taking up the phone.

"I guessed,'' came Reed's voice, "when there was no answer at home. Can you have dinner?''

"I'm having dinner here. Then I'm going to a party to meet Frederick Sparks.''

"Why not take me along? Together, we'll turn him inside out.''

"Nonsense, I'll do better myself. If you're there, and everybody discovers you're an Assistant District Attorney, we'll spend the evening discussing why so many people bribe policemen. You forget, I've been to parties with you before.''

"All right, you ungrateful wretch, then I'll have to give you my great piece of news over the phone. I hope I can conclude that no one but you can hear the sound of my voice.''

"Oh, quite.''

"Good. Dr. Michael Barrister was once sued for malpractice. It had the looks of quite a nasty case, but was apparently settled. Of course, doctors carry malpractice insurance."

"What had he done?"

"Apparently some woman began to grow hair on her chest. Years ago, of course."

"Are you trying to be funny?"

"I couldn't be that funny, even if I tried. Remember, Kate, it probably doesn't mean a thing. The patient in the case had no connection with Janet Harrison. But I thought it might encourage you to know that at least someone in this benighted case has a blot on his escutcheon."

"Reed! Does this mean they're really starting to look elsewhere?"

"Let's say I'm encouraging them. But don't get your hopes up. It's a big step from hormones to a knife plunged home."

"Thanks, Reed. I'm sorry about tonight."

"I should hope so," said Reed, and hung up.

When they sat down to dinner, Kate asked Emanuel to explain to her about hormones. He began by saying he knew very little about it, he hadn't followed developments in the field since his days at medical school, and then he began, as only Emanuel could, to discourse on the subject. At first Kate understood every third word, and then she understood every sixth, and then she caught only a familiar conjunction every dozen words or so, and then she stopped listening. If this case is going to require a detailed knowledge of endocrinology, she thought, I'd better give up right now. Yet, even at that moment, the telephone was ringing in her apartment, peal after unanswered peal, only mildly frustrating to one with a message which was to mark, for the three of them at the dinner table, and for one other, the beginning of the end.

11

FROM the moment when Kate, bottle in hand, arrived at the party, she felt like someone at an amusement park being thrust on one dizzy ride after another. She met her host for only a moment when he seized the bottle, thanked her, and introduced, inaudibly, four or five people standing about. These glanced at Kate, decided she was a specimen of which they already had a sufficient number in their collection, and went on discussing some intramural college fight the central issue of which, if there was one, Kate did not manage to grasp. Lillian had warned her that when members of this department got together, they never discussed anything but department politics, the exigencies of the teaching schedule, the insufficiencies of the administration and the peculiarities—moral, physical, psychological and sexual—of certain absent members. What Kate was not prepared for was the violence with which all these things were discussed, the enthusiasm with which points were made which must certainly, it seemed, have been made before.

Several aspects of the gathering surprised Kate not at all. One was the amount of alcoholic stimulation which members of the academic profession could withstand. They were by no means constant drinkers, but as members of an underpaid profession, they drank whenever they got the chance. This had long since been discovered by text-book publishers, whose habit it was, at any official academic convention, to rent a room and hand round the drinks with a free hand. Nor was Kate surprised that literature was nowhere being discussed. People whose profession was the study of literature did not discuss it when they foregathered, unless the question concerned the constitution of courses or the assignment of them. The reasons for

this were obscure and complex, and Kate had never thoroughly analyzed them. She had been present with enough groups of doctors,
lawyers, economists, sociologists and others to know that it took the
talents of a Svengali to get them to talk about anything at all besides
their subjects.

Yet the people here suffered, apparently, from the fact that they
were employed not by an educational institution, but by a bureau-
cratic system. They were all, to a large extent, clerks, neatly bound
up in red tape, and, like clerks, they gave themselves the illusion of
freedom by discussing and ridiculing the strictures that bound them.
Kate thought lovingly of her own university, where one struggled,
God knew, against the ancient sins of favoritism, flattery and simony,
but where the modern horrors of bureaucracy had not yet strangled
her colleagues or herself.

"My final exam in 3.5," one young man was saying, "was
scheduled for the last day of the exam period, and they wanted the
marks in within twenty-four hours. I pointed out that I could not
possibly read thirty-five examinations with anything approaching fair-
ness, let alone intelligence, and why couldn't I get the grades in three
days later? Do you know what the dean of Utter Confusion said—
actually said—sitting there in his huge office, while the faculty, of
course, far from having an office, can't even find a drawer in which
to place their private belongings? He said, 'But the IBM machines
must begin to operate twenty-four hours after the exam period is
over.' The IBM machines. Why? I ask you, why? But at least I
discovered whom the college is run for. One knew, of course, that it
wasn't run for the students or the faculty; after all, this isn't Oxford
or Cambridge. I had thought it was run for the administration, or the
building and grounds committee. But no! It's run for the IBM machines. Do you know, when I was filling out all those atrocious little
grade cards for the IBM machine, with that revolting little pencil one
has to use, I wanted to write F—— Y—— right across the damn
thing, and see what the IBM machine would make of that, the cy-
bernetic little bastard!"

"That's nothing. The other day I got one of those aptitude exam
results, all figured out by machine, and that idiotic student counselor . . ." Kate moved off in the direction of Fredrick Sparks, slowly,
for she didn't want to appear to have been stalking him. Lillian had
pointed him out to her. He sat back in his chair, glass in hand, observing the room with the pleasant superiority of one who has

emerged successful from the struggle for tenure, and has not yet dropped, screaming, into the pit where promotion is fought for.

Kate sat down on the chair next to him, for most people, the better to make their points, were standing; she asked him, with a regrettable lapse of originality, for a match. He produced an elegant lighter and lit her cigarette with a flourish.

"Are you a friend of Harold's?" he asked. But apparently he accepted the fact that she must be, for he went on to ask if she taught, and where. Kate told him. He expressed envy. Kate, with some dishonesty, asked why she was to be envied. "I'll give you an example," he said, swinging around in his chair to face her. "How many mimeographed communications have you received so far this semester?"

"Mimeographed communications? Oh, I don't know. Four or five, I guess, perhaps more. Announcements of department meetings, and that sort of thing. Why do you ask?"

"Because I have had hundreds, hundreds, thousands, perhaps, by now, and so has everyone else. Not only announcements of committee meetings to discuss every conceivable and inconceivable subject upon the face of the earth, but announcements from the administration: all students wearing shorts or blue jeans must be reported; the faculty is reminded that smoking is *not* permitted on the stairs (this of course is a cozy one, because if a man and woman faculty member want to have five minutes' conversation, and happen to be smokers, they must either retire to the faculty lounge, which is a nest of political intrigue, and in any case is usually given over to some student function, or they can one or the other indulge in transvestism and retire to the men's or ladies' room, as the case might be, because smoking is allowed there, or they can smoke on the stairs, which is what they do). *Or*, there may be an announcement that the pencil sharpener has been moved to Room 804 (if not out of the building altogether). *Or*, there may be an announcement the garbage will now be collected from the courtyard immediately outside the classroom windows every afternoon from one to five. The administration realizes that this will make teaching practically impossible (have you ever heard the noise of a garbage truck close up?), but the faculty must learn which are the important problems in the running of a college. I once got a mimeographed atrocity asking me to come and discuss methods of giving the faculty more time for original work. I wrote back that the best way *I* could think of was not to hold meetings discussing it. As I say, I envy you."

"I hear you're to be congratulated on getting tenure."

"Where did you hear that? I'm not to be congratulated; I'm to be pitied. Gustave is pleased because we now know we shall eat regularly, and retire on a pension; but if I had an ounce of guts I would say: 'You idiots, don't give me tenure; I am already dreadfully inclined to indolence, lassitude, self-indulgence and procrastination. You have enough dead wood in this benighted institution, enough minds which have not been penetrated by a new thought since the possibility of nuclear fission filtered through; but, no, you are a political institution; you must offer me what the masses crave: security.' Of course, it is possible that I shall succeed. That I shall break out from the bounds of faculty life."

"Write a great book?"

"No. Become a member of the administration. Then I shall have a carpet, a whole desk to myself, and perhaps one for my secretary, a larger salary and the right to be nostalgic about teaching. Will you have another drink?"

"That, at least, is the same at my institution," said Kate, declining the drink with a shake of her head. "As somebody said, the reward for teaching well is to stop teaching." Kate was not really fooled by his manner. Beneath the gabble of exaggeration, and the chi-chi reference to his dog (she should really have asked, "But who is Gustave?"), Kate suspected a first-rate brain and a daunted personality. She had no doubt he possessed the guts, the brains and the egoism essential to the stabbing of anyone, but had he done it? Ardent lovers of dogs are frequently those who cannot bear any less than an unquestioning love. He would certainly have had the nerve to make those phone calls. Could he have been attracted to Janet Harrison, largely because she was noncommunicative and withdrawn, and then have offered love, to have it rejected? "How many days a week do you teach?" she asked.

"Four, God help me. And next semester it may well be five. This semester I happen, through the queerest chance of fate, to have Monday off."

"Do you teach in the mornings on all the other days?" Kate hoped the question did not sound as pointed to him as it did to her.

"I will show you my schedule," he said, reaching into an inner pocket. "You might think that this late in the year I would know my schedule. But, in fact, our schedules are so complicated that if I were to commit this to memory it would take up so much space in my

meager brain that I would forget something else, like Anglo-Saxon.''
He handed her the schedule.

It was indeed extraordinary. He taught a course labeled 9.1 at
nine on Tuesday, three on Wednesday, ten on Thursday, and ten (!)
on Friday. Kate asked the reason for this oddity, while thinking, Here
is an alibi, clear and straightforward.

"Oh, but it's very simple, really, provided you have the pecu-
liarly inchoate mind of the man arranging these things. Some students
are on P schedules, or Q, or S or W. This means they must swim at
a certain time one day, and eat at a certain time on another, and on
no condition be on the stairs at a certain time on the third. All this
gets whirred around, and here we are. Sometimes it works out that a
class will meet at one, and then again at three on the same afternoon.
There's a pedagogical challenge, if you want one.''

"Do you ever cut any classes?''

"Never, unless of course one is dying. If one simply *cannot*
teach, one meets the little darlings, and then tells them to run along,
Papa isn't feeling well today. Of course, since the state is paying for
them, and not they or their fond parents, they scamper off overjoyed
and certain they have got away with something. What you must *never*
do is get a friend to take your classes. If the friend is seen (and we
are thick with spies), it will be reported to Big Brother, and both of
you will have something to answer when you come before P. and B.
You look, I am pleased to say, horrified. But the fact is that while
the faculty is the only thing without which you cannot have a first-
rate institution, it is the last element considered here. When, several
years ago, polio shots became compulsory, they were given first to
the administration, then to the kitchen staff, then to building and
grounds, then to the students, and finally (always hoping there would
be some serum left), to the faculty. The IBM machines would have
got it first, had anyone been able to discover where to administer the
injection.''

On an impulse, Kate drew what she now thought of as *the* picture
from her purse and handed it to Sparks. "Have you ever seen him?''
she asked. "I thought perhaps he might have been a student here,''
she glibly lied.

Sparks took the picture and studied it with care. "I never forget
a face,'' he said. "Not a boast, just a fact. But I never remember
voices or names, which is, I am told, not insignificant. Do you know,
I don't think I've met this chap, but I may have passed him on the
stairs, or perhaps only gone up an elevator with him once in an office

building. It's not the whole face though; the eyes are wrong. But the shape of it—well, it's no use, but if I think whom he reminds me of I'll let you know. Did you mislay him somehow?"

"Yes, as a matter of fact. I thought he might be connected with Janet Harrison, a student of mine."

"What! The young lady stabbed on the couch? I was there when they discovered her body, you know. Was she a student of yours?"

"You were *there?*"

"Yes. Bauer happens to be my analyst too. Speaking of faces, hers was extraordinary. I used to come early sometimes, if the damn subway didn't tie me up, just to look at it."

"Did you ever talk to her?"

"Certainly not. As I told you, I'm not much on voices, except my own, which I like to hear going on and on. Besides, suppose that face had turned out to have a squeaky, nasal voice? I could never have enjoyed it again. Tell me, by the way, did she?"

"Have a nasal voice? No. It was a quiet voice, yet nervous. Is Bauer a good analyst?"

"Oh, yes. First-rate. Excellent at hearing what one doesn't say, which with me, of course, is all-important." And suddenly, as though to give Kate the opportunity to hear what he did not say, he leaned back and literally vanished behind a curtain of silence. Kate, who disliked parties, and was tired, felt depressed. Reed had been right. Detective was not a game you played at because you admired Peter Wimsey, and had a friend in a fearful jam. She had crashed a party, cornered this man, bewildered Lillian, and all to what purpose? Did it signify that he was teaching at the hour after ten on the day when the uniform was stolen? He had kept his appointment with Emanuel. Could he possibly have got up to the women's dormitory to rob Janet Harrison's room? It seemed unlikely. Could he have hit out at this quiet girl because he loathed himself for succumbing to an institution he did not respect? You have developed quite a talent for questions, Kate told herself, but you have not found a single answer.

Kate said Good night and Thank you to her host, who clearly did not remember who she was, waved to Lillian, and found herself a taxi. What next? Supposedly Jerry would have got something from Horan, but was he likely to have got more from him than she had from Sparks? So help me, Kate thought, if this case is ever settled, I'll never ask another question apart from literature as long as I live!

Firm in this resolution, Kate paid off the taxi and entered the lobby of her house to find Reed asleep there on a chair. She woke him, none too gently.

"I wanted to see you," he said. "It seems to me that if you're trying to be a detective you ought to stay home and answer the telephone instead of drinking at parties, forcing yourself on people and asking idiotic questions."

"I agree with you," Kate said, leading him into the apartment.

"Let me make some coffee," Reed said.

"Why all this solicitude? I'll make *you* some coffee."

"Sit down. I'll put up the coffee and then I want to talk to you. Two more things have come up—one is fascinating, though I'll be damned if I can make any sense of it, and the other is a little frightening. I'll take the frightening one first." Maddeningly, he vanished into the kitchen, where Kate followed him.

"What is it? I've been sitting down all evening. Is Emanuel in more trouble?"

"No. You are."

"I?"

"How wonderful to be a professor of English! Anyone else would have said 'Me?' The police have received a letter, Kate. Anonymous, of course, and impossible to trace, but they don't pay as little attention to these things as they would like people to think. It's quite coherently written, and accuses you of murdering Janet Harrison."

"Me?"

"It claims, one, that the article you published a month ago in some learned journal or other on James's use of the American heroine was written by, and stolen from, Janet Harrison. You had not published enough, and were concerned about your career. It claims, two, that you and Emanuel were lovers, that you are still in love with him, resented his marriage to Nicola, and planned to get rid of the girl who was a threat, and to ruin Emanuel and incidentally Nicola, whom you loathe. It points out further that you have no alibi, know the Bauer home intimately, and knew the girl well enough to get her confidence and sit behind her. It makes a few other accusations, but those are the main ones. Oh, and it does mention that you robbed her room to rid the place of any notes she might have made toward the article. Now, just calm down and listen to me a minute. It doesn't explain why you should have published the article and only got the wind up after the article had appeared. But it's a pretty cogent case, and the police are taking it with some seriousness. They have also noted that you spend a good deal of time at the Bauer house, possibly covering your tracks, and that you went tonight to meet Frederick Sparks because he may have seen something and you wanted to find out if he had.''

"How do they know where I was tonight? Did you tell them?''

"No, my dear, I did not. They extracted that information, very cleverly, from the Bauers.''

"Is that why you wanted to go to meet him with me?''

"No. I only heard about this later. Since I'm poking my nose into something which isn't my business, I can't get my information hot off the griddle. Let's have some coffee.''

Kate touched his arm. "Reed, do you believe any of this?''

But he had placed the cups, saucers, spoons, sugar, cream and coffeepot on a tray and carried them off into the living room.

12

"Do you believe it, Reed? No, don't pour me any coffee, I couldn't possibly swallow it." Reed poured it, nonetheless, and placed it in front of her.

"I said my news was frightening; I didn't say it was terrifying. And if you ask me again if I believe it, I'll beat you. Quite apart from all other considerations, do you think I would help someone, even someone for whom I felt gratitude and affection, to cover up a murder? What is true is that I know you, and do not know Emanuel, and therefore understand a little better how you felt about wanting to help him. That's something, isn't it? Now, please, drink your coffee. Kate, Kate, please don't. As I shall point out in a minute, this is really the best break you've had so far, in your crusade for Emanuel. You didn't expect to fight dragons and not even scratch your finger, did you? Here, use mine. I have never understood why no woman ever has a handkerchief, except in her purse, which is usually in another room. And I haven't told you my fascinating bit of news yet."

"I'll be all right in a minute. And you know, the girl wasn't found, after all, anywhere near me. How Emanuel must feel—how completely betrayed by circumstances! And do you know the first thing I thought—the first horrible, sniveling, petty thought I had— What will this do to me at the university? Can they possibly want a professor who's been accused of murder? Yet it touches me nowhere as near as it touches Emanuel. Reed, who do you think sent the letter?"

"Ah, the wheels are beginning to go round again, glory be! That's exactly the point. You've frightened someone, my dear, and frightened them badly. Though we may, of course, be leaping to a conclusion in thinking that it's you who frightened them, simply because the anonymous letter concerns you. You may simply be the only available victim, the only one who combines all the necessary qualifications to make the letter stick, even for a moment. But they—I mean, of course, he or she, but the English language is sadly lacking a genderless singular pronoun (do you remember your teacher saying 'everyone will please carry his or her chair into the next room?')— where was I, yes, they-he-she is afraid that some of the threads which are so neatly tangled in our hands will suddenly form themselves into a rope. Now, the question before the house at the moment is, What threads have we, and can we even disentangle them before making them into so much as a piece of string?"

"Reed, you're being very nice. You are very nice, you know, though I may not have mentioned it before. There's something I think I ought to tell you."

"That sounds ominous. You are now going to confess to some incredible folly, after telling me how nice I am. What have you done?"

"Well, the fact is, I've hired Jerry."

"Jerry! Kate, don't tell me you've got involved with a private detective! That would muck things up properly."

"No, Jerry is a sort of Baker Street Irregular, and he's going to be my nephew."

"You can't mean you've hired a little boy! Really, Kate . . ."

"Don't be an idiot. How could a little boy be going to be my nephew?"

"I can't imagine. Perhaps your sister is planning to adopt him."

"Reed, do listen. Of course he isn't a little boy, and I haven't got a sister. But I have got a niece, and she's engaged to Jerry, who happens to be in between things, and could go around seeing people I couldn't see."

"You're not old enough to have a niece about to be married, or are they getting engaged at fourteen these days? And if you needed someone, what's wrong with me? Was being engaged to your niece a major qualification for the job?"

"Reed, do try to understand. You have a job, just as I do, and can't go moseying around all day, even if you would, which, given your job, you couldn't. Anyway, you wouldn't take orders from me; you would just sit around and argue."

"I should hope so. Kate, you aren't fit to be let out alone."

"I'm beginning to believe you. Nevertheless, if you can manage to keep quiet for the length of time it takes you to drink another cup of coffee, I'll tell you where Jerry and I have got so far. That is, I'll tell you what I know; Jerry doesn't report on today's activities till tomorrow morning. Then we can see where we are, and you can tell me your fascinating bit." And, beginning with a description of Jerry, she told him about the porter's uniform, which reminded her of her conversation with Jackie Miller, so she told him that too, and about her investigations among the university records, and about Sparks, and Jerry's plans for meeting Horan and the nurse.

Reed took it, all things considered, rather well. He mulled the facts—if they *were* facts, he assiduously pointed out—over in his mind. "You realize," he said, "that the unspeakable Jackie Miller may hold the key to the whole business, always supposing that someone did see Janet Harrison with a man, and that the man is somehow connected with this case, though that's an awfully large number of supposes. Meanwhile, let me add my information to yours. And don't get all excited when you hear it. It sounds marvelous, but the more you think of it, the less sense it makes. In fact, the more I think about this whole affair, the more disjointed it seems. And, my dear young woman, we will certainly have to discuss this whole Jerry business. How you could for a moment have considered hiring—I suppose that means you are paying him to get himself in trouble, and go about muddying the waters—how you could have considered . . ."

"What's your fascinating fact, Reed? Let's hear it, and consider it, and then, when we've discovered the whole thing is nonsense, we can argue over Jerry at breakfast—I'm assuming it will be breakfast time by then."

"Very well. I told you about Daniel Messenger."

"I know. He's doing something with Jewish genes."

"Kate, that settles it. I am going. You are going to have a good night's sleep, and sometime tomorrow when you are rested . . ."

"Sorry. You told me about Daniel Messenger, and . . ."

"I told you, though you were, as I remember, not prepared to accept the statement, that Dr. Messenger looked nothing like our man of the picture. We had sent a young detective out to interview the good doctor, and it seemed we had wasted the detective's time and the citizens' money. Messenger had never heard of Janet Harrison, had never heard of Emanuel Bauer, had no particular opinions about psychiatry, and had certainly not left Chicago within weeks of the murder. Moreover, he couldn't begin to guess why Janet Harrison should have left him her money, but he suggested that perhaps another Daniel Messenger was meant. This was, of course, nonsense. She had delineated him clearly enough—knew, for example, where and when he had his residency, what sort of work he was doing, and so on. The lawyer had advised her to include the man's address, age, etcetera, which she had done. No doubt in the world that he was the man.

"As you can see, Kate, a pretty problem, though typical of this whole infuriating case—and the young detective was about to call it a day when he thought of something so obvious that he will probably turn out to be a genius and go far in the world—all ideas of genius appearing obvious after the genius has thought of them. Naturally, the detective had a copy of the picture found in Janet Harrison's purse, to be certain that Daniel Messenger did not, by any possible stretch of the imagination, resemble it. And just before he parted from the doctor, on an impulse, though no one had thought to suggest it to him, he showed Messenger the picture. He showed it to him quite casually, apparently, and not expecting anything to come of it. 'You don't happen to know this man, I suppose,' he said, or something of the sort.

"It seems that Messenger stared at the picture for quite a while, so that the detective thought he had gone off into a trance—you know how long seconds can be when you're waiting for a reply—and then Messenger looked at the detective and said 'That's Mike.' "

"Mike?" Kate asked.

"Just what the detective said: 'Mike? Mike who?' And what do you think the doctor said?"

"Oh, goody, guessing games. I just love guessing games. How many guesses may I have, Daddy? What did he say, in heaven's name?"

" 'Mike who?' he said, 'Mike Barrister; we shared a room once, donkey's years ago.' "

"Mike Barrister!" Kate said. "Dr. Michael Barrister. Reed! There's the connection we've been waiting for. I *knew* sooner or later some of our stray facts had to fit together. Janet leaves her money to Messenger, Messenger used to know Michael Barrister, and Michael Barrister has the office across from Emanuel. Reed, it's beautiful."

"I know it's beautiful. For one blinding, flashing, all over moment, it's beautiful. But after the ringing in your ears stops, and you start to think about it a little, it's still beautiful all right, but it doesn't mean a goddam thing."

"Nonsense, she was murdered for her money."

"Even supposing it was enough money to murder someone for—which I don't for a single second grant—who murdered her? Messenger didn't; he didn't leave Chicago. And even if we're prepared to fall back on the hired murderer, which you admit is ridiculous, the result of every investigation in the world proves Messenger is the last person in the world to have done such a thing. He didn't frantically need money, we know that much, with the cooperation of his bank. His wife works as a secretary, and while they aren't rich, they aren't desperate. Far from it, apparently, because they've been quietly saving for the college education of their daughters. They haven't extravagant tastes—their idea of a marvelous vacation is to go camping in the northern reaches of Michigan. They aren't in debt, unless you call a mortgage on their house a debt; in which case you've got several million future murderers in the United States.

"I know, Kate, your mind is moving toward your favorite candidate, Dr. Michael Barrister. We even know he was once sued for malpractice, though I've since learned that the great majority of such suits are quite unjustified, and that every doctor is as likely as not to tangle with some lunatic who resents the fact that he hasn't been given a miracle cure, or who's heard somewhere that this treatment should have been preferred to that. But even if the suit was justified, being sued for malpractice doesn't make you a murderer. And if it did, why should Barrister murder a girl he had never met in order to leave a not very large sum of money to a man he hasn't seen in donkey's years?"

"Maybe Barrister just wanted to get Emanuel into trouble; maybe for some crazy reason he hates Emanuel."

"Maybe he does, though it's hard to imagine why. All we know is that Emanuel didn't particularly take to *him*. But then what has Messenger got to do with it? Why does the fact we are so excited about—that Messenger and Barrister once knew each other—have any bearing on Barrister's feeling for Emanuel? Emanuel and Messenger don't know each other, nor, except for a fortuitous sharing of the same address, do Barrister and Emanuel. It's a lovely fact, Kate, but it gets us nowhere. Absolutely nowhere."

"Wait a minute, Reed, you're confusing me. I'll admit that Messenger, while helpful, isn't exactly clarifying. But we now know who the young man in the picture is. Why didn't *we* recognize him by the way?"

"I didn't recognize him because I've never seen him. And you did, partly. You said the picture reminded you of someone, remember? A man changes a lot in those years between not-yet-thirty and over forty. Remember, Messenger hadn't seen Barrister since, at least we don't think he had. He saw the young man he had shared a room with. If I showed you a picture of a girl you'd known in high school you'd probably say: Oh, yes, that's Sally Jones. She always wore tight sweaters, and lisped. But if I showed you a picture of Sally Jones today, you might very well tell me you didn't know who she was.''

"All right, go on playing the devil's advocate. The fact still remains that Dr. Michael Barrister had the office across the hall, was the one to pronounce the girl dead—at least to Nicola—and all the time his picture was in the purse of the murdered girl.''

"And was left there by the murderer.''

"Who overlooked it; it was folded inside her license.''

"Or who left it there purposely, to lead us to think exactly what you're thinking.''

"Damn. Damn, damn, damn.''

"I couldn't agree more. But something occurs to me. Sparks said the face looked familiar, if you reported correctly. Could Sparks have known who the picture was of, and left it there? He sounds a man who goes in for rather involved circumspection.''

"Perhaps we should show Messenger a picture of Sparks. It might turn out they had played baseball together in the dear, dead days of boyhood. I didn't think to ask where Sparks had come from. Anyway, they might have gone to the same Boy Scout camp when Sparks was visiting a maiden aunt in Messenger's hometown.''

"I don't see why Messenger should recognize everyone in the case, but I agree it might not be a bad idea to show him photographs of all of them, supposing we can get them.''

"At least we are moving away from Emanuel, Reed. Although,'' she added, remembering Reed's first news that night, "we seem to be moving either toward me or toward complete chaos. Still, we are moving. What shall we do next? Of course, we've forgotten Horan; perhaps he killed her as part of some advertising campaign. And the connection between Barrister and Messenger is coincidence. After all, life is full of coincidence, as Hardy knew, though none of us like to admit it. Oh, dear, I am beginning to go round and round. Reed, one question, before I succumb to dizziness and sleep: Where *was* Barrister the morning of the murder? Did the police ever establish that exactly?''

"He was in his office, which was full of patients, some in the waiting room, some in examining rooms. His nurse, of course, was there too. I suppose now the whole thing will have to be gone into more carefully, though the police didn't seem to consider that he had an alibi, that he was, that is, absolutely and unarguably elsewhere. I'm beginning to get a little dizzy myself."

"Well, in the morning I'll hear from Jerry about Horan. And the nurse. Perhaps Jerry . . ."

"Oh, yes, we *must* discuss Jerry. Kate, I want you to promise me . . ."

"It's no good, Reed, I wouldn't remember what I'd promised. And tomorrow is *Daniel Deronda*. Not to mention my other courses. I hope that letter isn't going to get into the newspapers."

"I think I can promise you that."

"Who do you suppose sent it?" But Reed was already at the door. She waved to him sleepily, ignored the remains of their coffee, and dropped her clothes in a heap on the floor. She was certain she would never get to sleep, with Messenger, Barrister, Emanuel, Sparks, Horan whirling in her mind in that kaleidoscopic way, and was still certain of it when Jerry (for she had forgotten to set the alarm) woke her in the morning.

13

"IT's a good thing you gave me a key," Jerry said. "I might have gone on ringing, decided you were murdered, lost my head and called in the police. Are you merely hung over?"

"I am *not* hung over, at least not from drink. Get out of here so I can get up. Make some coffee. Do you know how?"

Jerry chortled happily at this question, and left the room. Too late, Kate remembered that he had been a cook in the Army, and that his coffee ... "Never mind," she called, "I'll make it," But Jerry, who was already running water, did not hear her.

It turned out that Jerry, who gloried in complete ignorance of drip, percolator and filter, had simply dumped some coffee into a saucepan of boiling water; the results were surprisingly good, if one poured with care. Kate, somewhat renovated by her shower and three cups of the brew, cleaned up the shambles of the night before and tried to make up her mind what to do next. Jerry's report of his previous day's activities (considerably edited, and containing no reference to his pursuit of Emanuel) did not seem to make the future course of action any clearer. He ought certainly not to have gone to see Barrister's nurse with that idiotic story; but Kate could not get as exercised over this as she probably should have. It was rapidly being borne in on her that this morning represented a new start. Reed undoubtedly would have insisted that the first step should be to thank Jerry properly and dismiss him. But Kate instinctively knew that when the nebulous plans which were forming in her brain took shape, Jerry would have to be a part of them. There was no one else.

It was eight days since the murder, and already the whole outrageous series of events seemed to be the natural components of

Kate's days. She sat down again across the table from Jerry, and thought that here she was, having morning coffee and evolving plots with a young man with whom, in the normal course of events, she would have had nothing whatever to do. Those people who were, two weeks ago, in the forefront of her life had moved somewhere into the background, out of focus. The various issues, literary and otherwise, which had been at the center of her consciousness, now floated vaguely at its periphery. What she sought, of course, was the return to the more orderly world of a fortnight past. Carlyle (to whom she had not given any attention since a week ago yesterday) was supposed to have said, upon hearing that a young lady had decided to accept the universe, "Egad! She'd better!" All Kate asked, she told herself, was to accept, to restore that universe. It had been shattered, but she could not rid herself of the conviction that, with sustained effort and a prayer, it could be put back together again.

"Any new ideas?" Jerry asked.

"I am not lacking ideas," Kate said, "only the ability to make them meaningful. I am beginning to think that Alice was not in Wonderland at all; she was trying to solve a murder. Beautiful suspects keep disappearing, leaving only their grins behind them; others turn into pigs. We are handed a large ungainly bird and asked to play croquet. And running very fast, we are not staying in the same place: we are positively moving backward. A few days ago we had a number of lovely suspects; now all we have is the heir to the murdered girl, and he doesn't have any connection with the case at all. Well, I'd better tell you about him." She recounted the story of Janet Harrison's will, and told him about Messenger's recognition of the picture. (About the letter accusing herself, she said nothing.) Jerry, of course, was elated to hear that the picture was of Barrister, and Kate had wearily to lead him, as she had been led the night before, to the realization that, exciting as the news was, *it* could not be made to lead anywhere.

"The answer must be Messenger. He's probably a very sinister type, with a good front. After all," Jerry continued, "we don't know he wasn't involved with Janet Harrison. We have only his word for it."

"But he denied having heard of her even before he knew she was murdered."

"After he murdered her, you mean."

"Then why identify the picture, and entangle himself further?"

"He didn't entangle himself; he entangled Barrister. Obviously, he never expected to be connected with the whole business at all. He didn't know she'd made a will."

"If he didn't know she'd made a will, why murder her? The motive is supposed to be her money."

"Perhaps it wasn't her money; perhaps it was, but he hoped the will would never be found."

"Jerry, you are getting weakening of the brain. If the will wasn't found, he wouldn't get the money. But, whatever his motive, he wasn't away from Chicago. And don't start suggesting that he hired someone—I simply could not stand discussing that again."

"I don't think this case is helping your disposition—you're beginning to sound petulant. What you need is a vacation."

"What I need is a solution. Keep quiet a minute, and let me think. While it's not a process of which I expect spectacular results, it's the only form of activity that occurs to me at the moment. By the way, if one can make such good coffee by just throwing the ground-up beans in a pot, why are there so many different expensive kinds of coffee makers on the market?"

"Are you asking for my favorite speech on advertising and the distortion of values in America? I do it very well, and have even been known to talk my future in-laws out of the purchase of an ice-crusher, which some clever ad had actually convinced them that they wanted. Perhaps if I were to begin my speech, it would stimulate your thought processes. Ready? Years ago, the objects of a man's desire were clearly divided into two groups: those things he wanted and needed, and those things he wanted simply because they had caught his fancy. It never occurred to this man to confuse the two, or to convince himself that he needed what he merely fancied. The Puritan . . ."

"Can the police possibly *know* that he did not leave Chicago?"

"I've been wondering the same thing," Jerry said. "His colleagues say, Yes, of course Danny boy was working in his laboratory all day; we heard him talking, or rattling test tubes, or using the typewriter, but of course there are records and tapes. Did you see the movie *Laura?* Speaking of records, don't they keep a record of everyone who flies to New York from Chicago?"

"I rather imagine that they do. They have a passenger list for every plane."

"Then he could give a false name, or take the train. I think our next step is to interview Dr. Daniel Messenger. Even if he turns out to be pure as the driven snow, he may tell us something about Barrister, or life, or genes. What can we lose, except the plane fare to Chicago and several days' time?''

''I haven't got several days' time.''

''I know; and I haven't got the plane fare to Chicago. I suggest we combine my time and your money, and send me off. I promise not to pull any fancy ones this time; let me get an impression of him.''

The idea had already occurred to Kate. She would have dearly loved to talk to Daniel Messenger herself. But if one thing was unarguable, it was that she had to continue in her wonted ways—to be accused of murder is one thing; to abandon one's obligations another. Jerry had more confidence in the value of his impressions than Kate did. This was not precisely personal: as young men went, Jerry had as much sense as could reasonably be expected. The fact was that youngsters cannot judge: she had seen too many half-baked professors popular with students, too many brilliant scholars, a bit on the dull side, scorned. For the student in college there might be a certain rightness in this judgment; but, in this particular instance, Kate was not willing to risk all on the opinion of a twenty-one-year-old who made up in brashness what he lacked in wisdom. Suppose Jerry returned with a definite impression, one way or the other? Would it be worth anything?

Perhaps not. But where was the alternative? Kate vividly remembered arguing once with Emanuel about psychoanalysis as a cure. She had pointed to the length of time it took, its great cost, the lack of control anyone—patient or analyst—had over the process of free association, etcetera, and Emanuel had denied none of it. ''It's a very clumsy tool,'' he had said. ''But it's the best we have.'' Jerry might not be flattered by the analogy, but Kate made it to herself, all the same. A clumsy tool Jerry certainly was, but he was all she had. In any case, apart from Jerry's time and her money, she didn't see what they had to lose—indeed, Jerry, with his frank, youthful masculinity, might well antagonize Messenger less than she.

''The approach, I think,'' Kate said, ''would be to talk to him about Barrister, not about himself. If you're obviously trying to trick him into some dangerous admission, you'll put him off. I know I would be put off. But if you tell him frankly we are in trouble and need his help, you may learn something of value. If he is the murderer, what you learn will not necessarily be worth anything, but then neither would it be if you had a match of wits. Jerry, what I'm saying, bluntly, is that if he's clever enough to have done this, and to have convinced the police of his innocence, you're not going to catch him. On the other hand, if he's as nice as everyone seems to think, he may help us in some way we can't even guess at. Now, I'm not going to let you go out there as Hawkshaw, the great detective, nor do I expect you to pretend to take my advice and then do just what you want." She threw him a piercing glance that made Jerry think of Emanuel and the park. Could she possibly know? In fact, Kate was merely drawing a bow at a venture: she had her suspicions. "Jerry, if you pull any shenanigans this time, that's it. You're back to driving a truck, and no bonus."

"What do I tell Messenger? Who do I say I am?"

"Perhaps we ought to try the truth. Not that I claim any inherent value for it, God forbid; but it has, among our various techniques, the appeal of novelty. Do you need to go home for a suitcase?"

"Well, as a matter of fact . . ." Kate followed Jerry's glance to the foyer; a suitcase stood modestly behind the table.

"Very well, I had better call to see when there is a plane to Chicago." Kate lifted the receiver.

"Eleven-twenty-something. I'll just make it to the airport."

Kate hung up the phone with resignation, and went to get money for Jerry. He was almost out the door before she realized that she had only just told him about Daniel Messenger. How on earth? . . . She got up to ask him.

"The trouble with you," Jerry said, "is that you don't read the newspapers. The police have to give the reporters something, and the contents of the murdered girl's will were just about right. I didn't, of course," he added with becoming modesty, "know about the picture. See you in a few days." He disappeared, closing the door gently behind him, leaving Kate to feel, not for the first time, rather sorry for her niece.

Kate, in her turn, prepared to depart for the university. Reed would undoubtedly have a fit when he learned where Jerry had gone; but the preservation of people's feelings was one of the goods which had vanished with the new state of affairs. Disaster brought ruthlessness in its wake—war had always done so. It was apparently inevitable. She remembered wryly with what difficulty, in the beginning, she had brought herself to use Reed at all. But each ruthless act makes the next one not only possible but inevitable. Perhaps this was how one ended in committing murder.

But what possible series of events, then, had led to this murder?

Janet Harrison had had a picture of the young Michael Barrister in her purse, carefully concealed. This seemed certainly to indicate—if one ignored for the moment the possibility of the picture's having been placed there by the murderer—that there was some connection between Barrister and Janet Harrison. Barrister, of course, had denied it. If he had murdered her, carefully concealing the connection between them (perhaps he had searched her room to determine that no evidence of the relationship existed), what was his motive?

Kate left the apartment and went down to wait for a bus. Suppose he had known Janet Harrison when he was a young man, or suppose he had simply known her, and the only picture of him, which, in her infatuation, she could acquire, had been one of him as a young man. In any case, she had got in his hair and he had killed her. Perhaps she wanted to marry him and he didn't care for her. But surely this was a not uncommon situation; and there are methods of getting rid of importunate young women without killing them, however appealing that solution might appear. Kate had known young women, her own contemporaries, who had become infatuated, had followed the man of their dreams about, spent hours staring up at his bedroom window, telephoned him at outrageous hours of the night. They had appeared desperate enough, yet they were all now married to somebody else, and presumably contented. And if Barrister was the man Janet Harrison had adored, why had she left her money to Messenger, whom she had apparently never seen, whom she certainly had not adored? Or, if it did turn out that she had adored him, why had she carried a picture of Barrister? Jerry suggested that Messenger had put it in her purse, but what would have been the point of that? *No* picture would have been even more confusing than the wrong picture.

Kate arrived at the university in the state of dizziness to which she was becoming fairly accustomed. She sat for a moment in her office, opening her mail in an idle way, and staring at nothing. Her glance fell, inevitably, on the chair where Janet Harrison had sat. "Professor Fansler, do you know a good psychiatrist?" Now, why in the world had the girl asked *her* that question? Was she, Kate, the only older person worthy of respect to whom Janet Harrison had access? It was barely possible. Yet Kate could not help reflecting that the anonymous letter accusing her of the murder had not been as wildly improbable as in her first distress she had thought. Kate stood, somehow, at the center of the enigma. It was she who had sent Janet Harrison to Emanuel; it was there Janet Harrison had been murdered. Had Janet Harrison asked her question of some other professor, for example, she would have ended up, presumably, on some other psychiatrist's couch. Would she have been murdered there? Well, not—Kate forced herself to face this—if Emanuel or Nicola had been the murderer. Otherwise? Well, Barrister had the office across from Emanuel's, and his picture had been recognized by Messenger. Messenger had inherited the money. The farmer takes a wife, the wife takes a child, the child takes a nurse . . . and the cheese stands alone. Who was the cheese?

She was aroused by the telephone from the contemplation of this fascinating question. "Professor Fansler?" Kate admitted it. "This is Miss Lindsay. I'm sorry to disturb you, but you seemed interested enough in the information so that I thought you wouldn't mind. I tried to telephone you at home last night, but there wasn't any answer. I thought you'd rather hear from me than Jackie Miller."

"Yes, of course," Kate said, "it's very nice of you to call. I'm afraid I didn't come away with a very favorable impression of Jackie Miller in her extraordinary pajamas. Are you about to tell me that I am now in her debt?"

"I don't know. But you did seem anxious about the name of the person who had seen Janet Harrison with a man, and the other evening Jackie Miller remembered it. She turned to me and suggested that—um—I might want to tell you what it was." Kate could well imagine what Jackie had said: "You're her pet pigeon, why don't you call her up and tell her?" "Ordinarily," Miss Lindsay went on, "I wouldn't think of bothering you at home, but under the circumstances . . . Of course, as it turned out, I didn't bother you."

"I'm very grateful to you. What's the name? It will all probably turn out to be a mare's nest, but we might as well know."

"Her name is Dribble. Anne Dribble."

"Can anybody possibly be named Dribble?"

"It is unlikely, but that seems to be her name. Jackie thought of it because someone mentioned dribbling. She lived in the dorm here for a short time last semester, but she didn't like it, and moved out soon after. She isn't in the phone book. I'm afraid this isn't very much help."

"On the contrary, I'm very grateful to you. Did you know Miss Dribble at all, well enough, I mean, to decide if she's at all reliable?"

"I didn't know her well, no; barely at all, in fact. But she wasn't—she wasn't Jackie's sort."

"Thank you very much, Miss Lindsay. I expect I can trace her though the university's records. I appreciate your calling." Reed had said that the key to the whole thing might well be here. Probably, however, they would just get another lead that would peter out in some dead end. Kate's class was in fifteen minutes. She called the registrar and requested the address and telephone number of Anne Dribble, who had been registered last semester, possibly this. She was asked to hold on, and did so, not for long. The voice returned to say that Anne Dribble had registered this semester but withdrawn because of illness (this, Kate knew, meant anything from appendicitis to a love affair). Her address was something Waverly Place, and her telephone number . . . Kate wrote it down, and hung up after expressing thanks.

Well, *carpe diem*. She dialed, first for an outside line, then the number. The phone rang at least six times before it was answered by a female clearly aroused from sleep. "May I please speak to Miss Anne Dribble?" Kate asked.

"Speaking." Kate had been certain it would not be this simple. She was going to be late for her lecture.

"Miss Dribble, forgive me for disturbing you, but I think you might be able to help. You know, I'm sure, about the death of Janet Harrison. We have discovered, quite inadvertently, that you saw her in a restaurant some months ago with a man. I wonder if by any chance you know who the man was?"

"Good Lord, I'd forgotten. How in the world . . . ?"

"Miss Dribble, the point is this. Would you recognize that man if you saw him again?"

"Oh, yes, I think so." Kate's heart gave a leap. "They were in a small Czechoslovakian restaurant; I happened to go there because I was visiting a friend who lived down the block from it. Janet Harrison and the man were at the other end, and I had the feeling they didn't want to be approached. But I did look at him. You know, one is curious about the men one's acquaintances go about with, and Janet had always been so mysterious. I think I might recognize him." Kate had not seen Horan; but she thought of Sparks, of Emanuel, of Messenger (who was homely)—could the girl describe the man sufficiently on the phone?

"Miss Dribble, put it this way. If that man were to be lined up with, say, six other men who resembled him superficially, could you pick him out?"

There was a moment's silence. She is going to ask who the hell I am, Kate thought. But all Miss Dribble said was: "I'm not certain.

I *think* I would know him again, but I saw him only from a distance in a restaurant. Who . . . ?''

"Miss Dribble, could you give me a quick description of him? Tall, short, fat, thin, dark, fair?'' (Emanuel's light hair was now mixed with gray, and looked lighter.) "What sort of person was he?''

"He was sitting down, of course. It's probably quite inaccurate, but if you want a general sort of description, he reminded me of Cary Grant. Good-looking, you know, and suave. I remember being rather surprised that Janet Harrison . . . she was attractive, of course, but this man . . .''

"Thank you, thank you,'' Kate muttered, hanging up the phone. Cary Grant!

Yet she managed, just barely, not to be late for the lecture.

14

"COME into my office," Messenger said. Jerry followed him down the hall with a certain sense of giddiness. This morning he had been talking to Kate; now, a ridiculously short time afterward (though the turning back of his watch accounted somewhat for this), he was about to talk with Messenger, although he had not the slightest idea of what he was going to say. Planning that rigmarole for the nurse had been one thing, his fumbling with Horan another, but Messenger made both of these techniques impossible. Jerry could not have named the particular quality that marked Messenger, though he recognized it. Nature had bestowed on Messenger none of her usual frivolous endowments; he had neither looks, nor any sort of physical grace, nor wit, nor superficial cleverness. He was simply himself. Jerry was to try later to explain it to Kate, with no great success. All he could think of to say was that Messenger was *there*. Most people were a collection of mannerisms, but they were not simply *there*, themselves. In any case, Kate's instinct had been right: only the truth was possible.

Jerry explained, therefore, about Emanuel and Kate, about himself and the job he had taken, about the trucks he had driven before and the law school he was planning to attend. "We've come to you for help," Jerry said, "because you seem the one person who might possibly connect some of the odd bits and pieces that we have. Janet Harrison left you her money—that connects you with her, even if she was unknown to you. And you knew Barrister. So far, no two people in this mess connect at all, except, of course, Kate and Emanuel, and neither of them killed Janet Harrison. Perhaps, if you were to tell me something about Barrister . . ."

"I'm afraid the only things I could tell you about him would not be precisely useful to your purpose, which I gather is to cast Mike in the role of chief murderer. Of course, he's probably changed somewhat: most people do. I wouldn't have guessed that Mike would end up with a practice among rich ailing women, but I'm not surprised now that I know it. It's very easy for doctors to make a great deal of money today, and most of them do. I don't mean doctors are more moneygrubbing than anybody else—there are too few doctors, and many opportunites to get rich. And most doctors feel," Messenger smiled, "that they are owed some return for what is an immensely long and expensive training. One of my young daughters thinks now she would like to be a doctor, and I've figured out that it would cost about $32,000 to make her one. All that this means is that the Barrister you are investigating isn't quite the same as the Mike I knew— and I never knew him all that well. He was a reticent sort of person."

"You're not rich." This was not, Jerry realized, to the point, but Messenger interested him.

"No, nor noble either. I don't happen to be interested in most of the things that are expensive, and I'm married to a woman who finds making do a fascinating challenge. She likes to plan, to make clothes, to do things—in the old way. And she likes to have a job. I think that the work I'm doing is the most interesting, important work there is; and, to be frank, I feel sorry for everybody who isn't doing it. But I don't do it because it doesn't pay all that much. I'd be doing the same thing even if it happened that doing this made me rich as Croesus."

"Was Mike like that, when you knew him?"

"Who can tell? I've found that young men have ideas, and theories, but you never know what you are until you become it. Do you read C. P. Snow?" Jerry shook his head. "Interesting writer, to me, anyway; I don't know if your Professor Fansler would agree. In one of his books, he has his narrator say that there's only one test for discovering what you really want: it consists in what you have. But Mike was too young then to make the test; you're too young now.

"I will say this," Messenger continued, "though I'm afraid it won't help you very much—quite the contrary. Mike wasn't the sort who could kill anyone. Not possibly, in my opinion. To carry out a murder requires at least two qualities of personality, I should think. One is what we might call a streak of sadism, for lack of a better word, and the other is the ability to concentrate on what one wants to the exclusion of everything else. To see people, not as people, but as obstacles to be removed.''

"You mean he loved people, and animals, and couldn't bear to see anyone hurt?"

Messenger smiled. "That sounds sentimental. Anyone who wants to be a doctor knows that people have to be hurt, that people suffer. People who never cause pain never cause anything else; and Mike wanted then, at least, to cause a good deal. I don't remember what he felt about animals—certainly he never had one when I knew him. What I mean sounds overblown when you put it into words: he never caused pain for the hell of it—you know, by a triumph of wit or a clever joke. And he never withheld kindness. I don't read poetry, but I had to listen to some in college courses; and I always remember one line which seemed to me very well to describe much of life today, perhaps always: 'greetings where no kindness is.' Mike didn't go in for that sort of greeting. But you mustn't think I'm describing a saint. Mike was very good-looking and attractive to women. He had a good time.''

Jerry looked depressed. It seemed horrible that their chief suspect should turn out to be incapable of murder. But that, after all, was Messenger's opinion, and was Messenger all that smart? He, Jerry, had in college (just to take one instance) been party to a joke that involved an awkward, rather effeminate young man and an exceedingly slick and experienced young woman. He remembered it still with something remarkably close to pleasure. And certainly kindness was nothing to which he had given much thought—and as for this garbage about greetings. . . . Yet he was not capable of murder either. Not even if . . . well, one never really knew; that's what it came down to. If one knew, there would be fewer unsolved murders.

Messenger seemed to read his thoughts. "I'm no authority, you know, no student of human nature. Just my impressions."

"You shared a room when you were residents, you and Barrister. Did you know him before?"

"No. The hospital helped you find rooms, and roommates. When we were on duty, of course, we slept at the hospital, so home was really where we slept when we got the chance, and kept beer in a secondhand icebox.''

"Did you ever meet Barrister's family?"

"He didn't have any, to speak of. Surely the police found out all about that. In fact, the detective who came to see me mentioned it. Mike was an orphan, as he was fond of saying, with a grin. He'd been the only child of an only child, and was brought up by his grandparents; they were both dead when I knew him. I gather he had a happy childhood. You know, I remember something he said once about Lawrence, the writer, I mean. Mike was a great reader.''

"Literature seems to be following me around in this case."

"Odd, isn't it? I've already quoted poetry and Snow, and I don't think I've been guilty of a literary reference in years. Perhaps it's the influence of your Professor Fansler. I don't know why I should think of books in connection with Mike. But the only specific thing he ever told me about his childhood had to do with D. H. Lawrence.''

"Lady Chatterley's Lover?'' Jerry asked.

"I don't think so; were there any children in that?"

"No," Jerry said. "Not born yet, anyway."

"Well, it wasn't that then. In this book there was a little girl, frightened for some reason, and her stepfather carried her about with him while he fed the cows. I don't really know what the connection is, because Mike's grandfather didn't have cows. But something about the way his grandfather comforted him, after his parents were killed—Lawrence had caught that, Mike said. It doesn't sound very important. I don't know why I mention it. Anyway, Mike didn't have much family, though there was some old lady he used to write to."

"Did he have any special woman then?"

"Not that I know of. You're thinking, perhaps, Janet Harrison knew him then, and I didn't know about it. Well, it's not impossible, I suppose. Mike didn't talk about his women, but surely the police know where Janet Harrison was at that time."

"Did he go away much?"

"No. When we had short vacations we slept."

"How long were you together?"

"A year, more or less. For the length of our residency. I came to Chicago. Mike thought he might, too, but he didn't."

"Where did he go?"

"New York. You know that."

"Did you hear from him in New York?"

"No. I don't think he went there right away. He went on a vacation first, camping. We both like camping. I was supposed to go with him, but then, at the last minute, I couldn't. He went on up to Canada—I had a card from him. I told all this to the detective. That's the last I heard of him, except for Christmas cards. We exchanged those for a few years, later on."

"It seems odd you never saw him in New York."

"I've only been there a few times, for medical conventions. I took the family, and any spare time I had I spent with them. Once I saw Mike, but we didn't really have time to get together. Anyway, there wouldn't have been very much point to it."

"It's all clear enough, I guess, except why she left you the money. You didn't save her life once, and forget about it?"

"I don't save lives. I can't, of course, say positively that I never laid eyes on her, but I don't think I did, and certainly not for any length of time. It just doesn't make any sense at all. You don't really know, do you, that Mike ever knew her? So the fact that I once knew Mike isn't really all that conclusive. I'd like to help you; I just can't think of any way I can."

"Are you going to take the money? Perhaps I haven't any business asking you that."

"It's a natural enough question. I don't know that I'll get the money. The girl was murdered, and she has some family who might, I suppose, contest the will. But if I got the money I would take it, provided there was no one with a real claim. I could use the money—couldn't anyone? Besides, there's something odd about a windfall—one never expected it, and then, when one hears of it, one is convinced it was somehow deserved."

"Did Mike know you were going into research?"

"Oh, yes, everyone knew that. Mike used to say if I was going to live the rest of my life on four thousand a year—that's what they paid in those days—I'd better marry a rich wife or one who liked to work. I took his advice, you see—the latter part of it."

Jerry could have spun out the questions—there were many that occurred to him, but he could guess most of the answers, and didn't think them very important, in any case. Messenger could, of course, have been lying. He could have been in league with Barrister for years. But even if they could have concocted this murder for $25,000 between them, Messenger didn't look capable of it. His honesty was so patent that it was, Jerry thought, impossible to be in his presence and even consider the idea of his involvement in a plot. He might be shrewd enough, but he seemed one of those rare persons who say what they mean, and mean what they say—surely the wrong sort to plan some diabolical scheme. Jerry stood up.

"There was one other thing," he said, "though I don't really have to bother you with it. You'll just save me some research. In law, you have to pass the bar exam of the state in which you intend to practice. That's true in the East. There's a certain reciprocity, of course, but if you practice in New York, you have to have passed the New York bar exam. If you've taken the New Jersey bar exam, that won't do. Isn't the same thing true in medicine? Did Barrister have to take the New York exam in order to practice there?''

''No. There's something called the National Board of Medical Examiners—they give a certificate which is accepted as adequate qualification by almost all the states. There are some exceptions, I don't remember what they are, but New York isn't one of them. Other states require some sort of oral or written examination. But Mike had no more exams to take in order to practice in New York—probably he had to register, or something of the sort.''

''Thank you, Dr. Messenger. You've been very kind.''

''Not much help, I'm afraid. Let me know if anything else occurs to you. I think you'll find, you know, that Mike didn't do it. People leave tastes behind them; Mike didn't leave that kind of taste.'' He bowed Jerry out. Jerry, going back to the hotel to put in a long-distance call to Kate, felt that Messenger left a fine taste, no doubt of that; but the case as a whole had by now a taste that could be described only as rancid.

15

KATE rushed away from the lecture room, leaving behind her the students who had come up to ask questions, and ignoring, outside her office, the students gathered there. She put in a call to Reed.

"I've found a Miss Dribble—you know, the one who talked to Jackie-wackie when there was soap in the fountain. She says he looks like Cary Grant. Is it all right to talk now?"

"My dear girl, if we are being overheard, I hope the eavesdropper understands you better than I. Shall we risk a little more clarity? Who dribbled?"

"That's her name. Dribble. Anne Dribble. Remember, you said she would hold the key to the whole thing?"

"I don't remember ever mentioning anyone of that name in my life. Is she someone who knew Janet Harrison? If so, she will go down in history, though it's a pity to immortalize a name like that."

"She knew Janet Harrison slightly; she used to live in the dorm—Dribble, I mean. Jackie Miller remembered that she, still Dribble, was the one who had told her, Jackie, that she had seen her, Janet, with a man. Apparently someone dribbled at breakfast, which reminded Jackie—there are advantages to having a verb for a name—who it was who had spoken to her of seeing Janet with a man; and she, Jackie, told her, Miss Lindsay; and she, Miss Lindsay, called me, Kate. I called her, Miss Dribble, and she said she *thought* she would recognize the man again, but if I wanted a quick description he looked like Cary Grant, good-looking and suave. You have twenty minutes; rewrite that into an acceptable English sentence."

"Kate, I know we need suspects, but do you really think Cary

Grant is likely to have killed her? I could, of course, call Hollywood . . .''

"Reed—which of our suspects looks like Cary Grant?''

"You forget, I haven't seen any of our suspects.''

"You mentioned yourself that the young man in the picture
looked like Cary Grant.''

"Did I?''

"Yes. And Barrister still does, in a general sort of way. I mean,
he's older, but so is Cary Grant.''

"And so am I. Getting older by the minute. What do you want
me to do, offer Barrister a part in pictures?''

"Got it in one. I want some pictures. I want to show them to
Miss Dribble, and if she recognizes Barrister, we've got proof, actual
proof, that Barrister knew her. Of course, it *may* be Sparks or Horan.
Emanuel looks nothing like Cary Grant.''

"Believe it or not, I begin to get your drift. Look, I'll suggest to
them at Homicide that Barrister looks like Cary Grant. I'll probably
be recommended for the vacation I so badly need. Have you got Miss
Dribble's address?''

Kate gave it to him. "And, Kate,'' Reed went on, "don't mention
Miss Dribble or her address to anyone else, there's a good girl.''

"Reed! You *do* think there may be something in it.''

"I'll call you at home this evening. Go home and stay there. I
mean it; that's an order. Don't go dashing off following clues. Promise?''

"Is it all right with you if I hold my office hours and meet my
afternoon class?''

"Go home the minute the class is over. Stay home. Neither walk
nor run to the nearest exit. Sit. You'll hear from me.'' And with this
Kate had to be content.

Following the afternoon class, Kate returned to her office to find
the phone ringing. It was Emanuel.

"Kate, can I see you for a few minutes?'' he asked.

"Has anything happened?''

"That's what I want to talk to you about. Where can we meet
for a cup of coffee?''

"How about Schrafft's? It's a good place for convincing oneself
that life goes on.''

"Very well, then, Schrafft's in twenty minutes.''

But both of them got there in fifteen. The place was quiet, except for a few ladies noisily consuming their afternoon calories at the counter.

"Kate," Emanuel said, "I'm beginning to worry."

"Don't begin now. If they'd had enough evidence, they'd have pulled you in as a material witness. I think it's going to be all right, if we just hold on a little longer."

"*Where* did you learn to talk like that? You sound like one of those authentic precinct novels. It's not me I'm worried about; it's you. I had to go down to see them again today, both Nicola and I did, but it was you they wanted to talk about. In the old days," he added, as the waitress approached, "you used to eat ice cream covered with gooey fudge and nuts. Do you want that now?"

"Just coffee." Emanuel gave the order to the waitress. "Look, Emanuel, I'll tell you this, but I'm not supposed to know it, and you're not supposed to know it, so don't mention it to the police or Nicola. They've got an anonymous letter accusing me. I'm supposed to have murdered her because I'm in love with you and jealous of Nicola. The police have to follow it up. After all, if it turned out in the end I'd done it, they'd look pretty silly if they hadn't followed up a lead like that. And to give them their due, I'm not a bad suspect, as I think I pointed out before."

"This has happened because you tried to help me."

"This has happened because I sent you the girl who was murdered. Emanuel, I've been wondering, why did she come to me for the name of a psychiatrist? I can't help feeling that there's something important about the fact that she did."

"I've been over and over that fact in my mind. But after all, she had to ask someone. You'd be surprised at the abandon with which most people pick a psychiatrist—never bothering to discover if he's properly qualified, a doctor, or anything else. To ask an intelligent, educated person for the name of a psychiatrist is not the worst way to go about finding one."

"But you're thinking that if you'd never backed onto the Merritt Parkway none of this would have happened."

"That's nonsense. The one thing a psychiatrist knows is that things don't 'happen.' "

"Oh, yes, I'd forgotten. If you break your leg it means you wanted to, deep down."

"What's worrying me, Kate, is that the detective's questions about you disturbed me, and I talked a lot more than I've talked up to now. I've been rather reticent about my patients, but I wasn't reticent about you. I tried to explain our relationship. I told them, if they wanted a psychiatrist's opinion, you were incapable of murder, and incapable of stealing pieces on Henry James. I realize now, somewhat too late, that they have probably mistaken my vehemence for personal passion, and will now decide that we planned it together."

"And if we are seen here, they will be certain we are now plotting further."

Emanuel looked horrified. "I hadn't thought of that. I only wanted to . . ."

"It was a joke, Emanuel. When I first heard they were accusing me, I was terrified, with the feeling of panic a small child has when he's lost his parents in a crowd. But I don't feel that way anymore. I didn't do it, and the evidence that I did is nonsense. Actually, I think we may be getting near the end of this horror. I have that feeling of events closing in. But I don't want to say any more yet, in case it doesn't work out."

"Kate. Don't get into trouble."

"At least you'll know that if I do, my inner psyche willed it. That's another joke. Try to smile."

"Nicola's beginning to feel the strain. For a while her natural exuberance kept her afloat, but now she's beginning to sink. And my patients are starting to wonder. If I didn't do it, it seems odd that they can't find the person who did. I feel frightened, genuinely frightened, in a small-boy way. Why can't they look elsewhere? Why do they keep walking round and round us?"

"The police have you, or you and Nicola, or you and me, and that's the case they're trying to prove. To them, the fact that it happened on your couch is a nice, simple, unassailable fact. You can't expect them to look around for evidence that they're wrong. But if we put the evidence right under their noses, they'll have to look at it. That's what I'm trying to do, in my wild and woolly way. Instead of worrying, why don't you try to think of something Janet Harrison said?"

"Freud was interested in puns."

"Was he? I've always agreed with the estimation of them as the lowest form of wit. I remember once, when I was a child, saying 'I'm thirsty,' and some odious friend of my father's said, 'I'm Joe.' Or isn't that a pun?"

"Janet Harrison had, twice, a disturbing dream about a man who was a lawyer."

"A lawyer. The one thing we don't have in this case is a lawyer.

Didn't she have any other dreams? Perhaps the lawyer who made her will . . ."

"You see, the censor works even when you dream. It won't present a thought too disturbing, perhaps because you might wake, or because the unconscious won't let it through."

"Oh, yes, Brooks Brothers, and the awful suit. Sorry, go on."

"We pun in our dreams, as well as when we're awake. Sometimes in several languages."

"Sounds like Joyce."

"Very like Joyce. He understood all about it. I'm wondering if Janet Harrison didn't pun in her dream, not in another language, but in the same language, an ocean away. What a lawyer, in England?"

"They've got two kinds—solicitors and . . . Emanuel! Barrister again!"

"I wondered. Of course, she may just have seen his name outside his door across the hall from me. As evidence, it's worth nothing to a policeman and very little to a psychiatrist, at least by itself. He may just have looked like her father, or someone else; dreams are very involved, and there isn't often a one-to-one relation . . ."

"I think she knew him, I'm sure she did, and before too long I'll prove it. Emanuel, I love you. I hope no policeman can hear me."

"You realize, of course, that Messenger's name is also capable of lots of . . ."

"What did she feel about the lawyer, in her dream?"

"I've looked up my notes; fear, mainly. Fear, and hate."

"Not love?"

"That's very hard to distinguish from hate in a dream, and frequently in life. But speaking of patients' dreams, I'd better get back to the next set."

"She never mentioned Cary Grant, did she?"

"No. Kate, you will be careful, won't you?"

"Psychiatrists are so illogical. They tell you nothing happens by accident, and then they tell you to be careful. No, don't drive me home. It will make you late, and God knows what it would suggest to a lurking detective, if any."

It was Kate's day for walking in on ringing phones. The one in her apartment had the angry sound of a phone that has been ringing for a long time.

"Miss Kate Fansler, please."

"Speaking."

"Chicago calling. One moment, please. Go ahead, please. Here is your party."

"Well, I've seen him," Jerry said, "and I'm afraid we've wasted your money; my time isn't worth much. My impression, for what it's worth, is that he didn't do it. His impression, for what it's worth, is that Barrister didn't do it. Our conversation was full of literary allusions—your influence, he seemed to think—perhaps they are right about E.S.P. Who said 'greetings where no kindness is'?"

"Wordsworth."

"Kate, you should have gone on one of those quiz shows."

"Nope. They wanted me to split with the director, and I refused."

"Do you want me to tell you what he said? It's your money."

"No, don't tell me—write it down. Get down every bit of it you can remember. Somewhere, somehow, there's one little straw of a fact that is going to break the back of this case, and it may be in that interview of yours. All right, I admit it's unlikely; but, as you said, it's my money and your time isn't worth much. Write it all down."

"On little pieces of hotel stationery?"

"Jerry, you must not allow yourself to get discouraged. What did you expect, that Messenger would lock the door and tell you with a glint in his eye that he'd killed Janet Harrison long distance by means of a secret ray gun he'd just developed? We're going to find the answer to this case, but I think the answer will first appear on the horizon as a cloud no bigger than a man's hand. Get the interview written down—rent a typewriter, find a public stenographer, scribble it out on hotel stationery and then get it copied—I don't care. But come home on the first plane you can get out of Chicago. I'll see you in the morning."

Barrister had known Janet Harrison—of this Kate was now convinced. That he had the office across from Emanuel's might be the wildest of coincidences, but it could not be coincidence that he had once known the man to whom Janet Harrison had left her money; it could not be coincidence that he was seen in a restaurant (and Kate was certain he had been) with Janet Harrison; it could not be a coincidence that Janet Harrison had punned so cleverly in her dreams—though she would hate to have to convince Reed, let alone a court of law, of this last one.

Had they met in New York? There was, of course, no evidence at all of this, but the chances were certainly that they had. Probably Barrister had mentioned Messenger, never knowing that Janet Harrison would indulge in the quixotic gesture of making out a will in his favor. Kate didn't remember now where Barrister had come from, but she was fairly certain it was not Michigan—and, of a sudden, something began to root about at the base of Kate's mind. A small disturbing noise it made, like the sound of a mouse behind the wainscoting.

Whatever it was, it evaded her. But wait—if Janet Harrison had met Barrister in New York, she must have met him very soon after his arrival, for the picture she carried was of a younger man. Perhaps it was the only picture Barrister had—perhaps she had stolen it. But why had she hidden it so carefully inside her driver's license? Well, say she had stolen it. I must *not*, Kate thought, starting going round and round again. Let's stick to the one thing I've established—well, established at any rate to my own satisfaction: Barrister knew Janet Harrison. Of course, they would have to confront the Dribble girl with him, but she, Kate, had no doubts of the result of this.

Kate began to make herself supper, wondering when Reed would call. No doubt he would point out that, as a detective, Kate made an excellent literary critic. Although Reed had always been too polite to say so, at least in so many words, Kate knew he thought of literary critics as operating in a rarefied atmosphere far removed from earthly facts. Highbrow critics, he would probably say . . . again Kate was aware of the mouse behind the wainscoting. That same mental disturbance she had just felt when she had thought of . . . what? Of where Barrister had come from.

What had he said then, that day in Nicola's apartment? ''Aren't you from New York?'' Kate had asked him. And he had answered that, as some highbrow critic had said, he was a young man from the provinces. Some highbrow critic who had talked about a certain kind of novel. Well, that highbrow critic had a name: Trilling. But did Barrister know it? Did Barrister read the *Partisan Review*, or a collection of essays called *The Opposing Self?* It was not impossible—yet his tone of voice had been that of one who scorns these matters. Where had he heard Trilling's phrase for a certain kind of novel?

He had heard it from her, Kate Fansler, by way of Kate's student, Janet Harrison. Not a doubt in the world. Again, it was not the kind of evidence of which any policeman could be persuaded to take official notice, but to Kate it was unquestionable. Janet Harrison had listened to that phrase used by Kate, had been struck with it, and had repeated it to Barrister. That meant not only that Barrister had known Janet Harrison, but that he had known her (it seemed likely) when she had still been taking a course of Kate's. So Barrister was a young man from the provinces, was he? Well, one thing that marked the young man from the provinces, in literature at least, had been that he, or someone he had been associated with, had always come to what an English friend of Kate's called a "sticky end." A young man from the provinces indeed!

When Reed called, Kate was ready for him.

"I've got quite a bit to report," Reed said. "I'll be up to see you in a few hours. Is that too late?"

"No. But, Reed, you might as well be prepared—I'm convinced of one thing anyway. And you needn't laugh uproariously. Barrister knew Janet Harrison."

"I'm not laughing," Reed said. "That's one of the things I'm coming to tell you. He's just admitted it."

16

"IT'S a funny thing about the unconscious mind," Kate said to Reed some hours later. "There was no real reason for Barrister to use that phrase about the young man from the provinces when talking to me—I'm certain he had no idea why it came into his head. But he met me, realized who I was, knew about me because Janet Harrison had told him about me, knew he must not on any account reveal that he knew about me, and his unconscious came up with the young man from the provinces."

"Observant chap, Freud. He made a number of suggestions about word tests for suspected criminals—did you know? It's more or less the principle a lie detector works on, or is supposed to work on: the criminal's blood pressure increases when he's faced with a disturbing idea. In Freud's test, he blocks at the disturbing question, or associates in a telling way. Anyhow, Barrister, like a good patient on the couch, decided this afternoon to talk to the point. It's amazing how frightened innocent people can get when faced with investigation."

"Are liars innocent—I mean people who lie about important things that entangle other people in meshes of untruth?"

"The truth's a slippery thing. Perhaps that's why only literary people understand it."

"That's what Emanuel would call a provocative remark."

"And he'd be right. I apologize. Except, of course, that the remark is true. You'd figured out Barrister had known her before we did. And your discovery of Miss Dribble urged me to urge them to put on the pressure sooner than they might have. It was Miss Dribble (since I did not yet know about the young man from the provinces) which encouraged me to go along for the interview, even though I had no official right to do any such thing."

"What did he say? Father, I cannot tell a lie, especially when it looks as though I may be found out?"

"He was quite frank about the whole thing. He didn't think anyone knew they knew each other; and, what with his little trouble about the malpractice suit, he didn't like to risk being entangled with the police. You have to admit he wasn't in an enviable position, the girl killed next door, and he having known her. He quite simply hoped we'd never find out there was any connection between them; and, in fact, if it hadn't been for the will and the picture, we probably never would have. And Miss Dribble, of course."

"Of course. Someone was bound to have seen them, one time or another. If the police had investigated him more, and Emanuel less, they might have found someone else who had seen them by now. Didn't the fact that Miss Dribble had been dug up by me, another suspect, make them suspicious about that evidence?"

"You've more or less been demoted from the list of suspects—the active list, anyway. They did quite a little investigation of you, as you will doubtless be hearing from your friends and associates. Your colleagues considered the idea that you would steal a piece of work from a student ridiculous, and they went on to point out, with some heat, I understand, the various complications of scholarly research. Also—please try not to get upset—the idea that you were still in love with Emanuel, if you ever had been, was proved untenable by the fact that you had been, more recently, in love with someone else."

"I see. Did they discover his name?"

"Oh, yes, they saw him. Kate, this is a murder case. I'm sorry to have to mention it—but I'd rather you heard about it first from me, and were prepared. You're not, I understand, at the moment planning to marry? Sorry—I shouldn't have asked that. Anyway, there didn't seem much reason why you should have done it, and, of course, there were other things apart from motive which made you unlikely. You aren't angry, are you?"

"No, not angry, and not planning to be married. Now, don't get all nervous and fumble with your dispatch case. I appreciate your honesty, and I want to hear more about Barrister. What did he say, exactly? Had they been having a grand passion?"

"He met her at about the time the picture was taken—he needed it for some official reason or other. I think he would have liked to be vague about when he knew her, but we've had a man working on Janet Harrison's history—you *do* underestimate the forces of law, my dear—and he discovered that Janet Harrison had gone on an extended trip to the wilds of Canada I guess Barrister knew that we would soon discover, if we hadn't—and as a matter of fact we hadn't—that he too had been in the same wilds, so he told us they were together there. I gather it was one of those romances, as with people who meet on a cruise or in Italy, lifted out of the daily round of life and unlikely to endure after the return to the daily round. After that Barrister came to New York, and as far as he was concerned it was finished, at least as a serious attachment. But Janet Harrison decided to become a nurse, apparently the better to be a doctor's wife, and then she had to go home when her mother died. After one thing and another, and the passage of years, even though she hadn't heard from him especially, she came to New York. She needed some sort of excuse, so she decided to study English literature at your university. We don't know why she picked that over history, which had been her college major.''

"I can guess at one possible reason, though she may just have thought it was easier to read novels than learn dates. The history department demands that its applicants take something called a Graduate Record Exam; the English department doesn't. Therefore she would have less trouble getting accepted by the graduate English department—her college record would do it.''

"You're probably right. At any rate, there she was. She was naturally a most unconfiding sort, he says—which God knows we've discovered—and he managed to keep the relationship quiet and to see her only occasionally, though she *was* a nuisance. He admits it. Apparently she decided to go to an analyst in order to get over her infatuation, though Barrister didn't call it that, and the fact that she hit on Emanuel was coincidence—though Barrister did know that she admired you very much, which is why she asked you to recommend someone. He hoped she'd be cured, and even offered, he told us, to help pay the fees. He was very frank, Kate, and, I'm afraid, very believable. Like you, he underestimates the police, and thought, if they had a nice motive like that, he'd be for it. The shock when Nicola called him in to look at the body was considerable—I can well believe it. It's to his credit that he called the police immediately. Incidentally, he could have said he had to examine her, shut the door, and looked through her bag, in which case he might have found that picture. He did no such thing.''

"That picture must have given him a jolt."

"No question that the police slipped up there. But of course they thought it was a recent photograph, so I suppose they are to be forgiven. As I say, he told all this quite openly, throwing himself on the mercy of the police. He admitted he was telling it now because the police seemed close to finding it out. He also said that men don't kill women who are inconveniently in love with them, and he hoped we realized it."

"Were they lovers?"

"He was asked that, although the police call it having an intimate relationship. He hesitated over that one—that is, he said 'no' at first, and then said they had been, in the wilds of Canada. He smiled and said he supposed she might have told Emanuel that, so he'd better admit it; he was younger, etcetera, etcetera, but he was emphatic that they had not been 'intimate' in New York. He said openly he had not the slightest intention of marrying her, and to have made love to her would have made him both a cad and a fool. A fool, because what he wanted was for her to go quietly away."

"What about Messenger?"

"He admitted that puzzled him. He *had* spoken to her about Messenger, in Canada, with great admiration apparently, but why she should make a will leaving her money to Messenger years later Barrister didn't know. Messenger is going to have to bear a certain amount of looking into, there's no question of that."

"And Barrister didn't steal the porter's uniform and burgle her room?"

"The police asked him about that, in a roundabout way. He threw up his hands and said that if he would lie to the police in order to avoid a scandal, he was certainly not, as a women's doctor, going to get himself caught wandering around a women's dormitory. He admitted to being relieved as hell that she lived there, since it meant he didn't have to make excuses for not going to her room, and there's no question he avoided the place like the plague."

"It's still odd their relationship was so secret."

"I know that, and so does he. It's one of the things that puts him on the spot. But, Kate, you'd be amazed the queer things that turn up in people's lives, once you start rooting around. I could many a tale unfold. And when the police start asking questions because someone's been connected with a murder case, at least half the time that someone has something he isn't too proud of, or doesn't want known, and he'll lie and muck up the investigation. For example, Nicola once got fed up enough with her husband to fling off and have an affair with another man—did you know that?''

''No.''

''All right, and remember, you don't know it now. Nicola didn't tell us, nor Emanuel. We found it out. Well, Barrister is found out, too. But while it sounds illogical, because he did try to keep the relationship secret after the murder, he still would not necessarily, or even probably, have figured that he could keep it quiet if he were deciding to murder her, at least the way I see it. And the motive just won't do. If you think about it calmly, you'll admit it.''

''I've already admitted it, damn it!''

''When there's a murder, the police lift up a rock that's been in place a long time. And if you've ever lifted up such a rock, you know that there are all sorts of slimy, crawly things underneath. Human beings, by and large, are not a very commendable lot.''

''So we're back with Emanuel?''

''They haven't been able to prove that Emanuel ever saw Janet Harrison outside of the office, but then you see how long they took to establish the connection with Barrister.''

''How many men was she supposed to have been seeing, in her quiet way?''

''You never know, with that type. If the police could get one outside witness, one piece of corroborating evidence, I'd think they'd risk an arrest. Of course, the District Attorney's office is not happy to see arrests if they think they'll lose the case when it comes to trial.''

''But the way I've heard it, they'll push the case if they've got enough evidence, even when they know in their heart of hearts that the accused is innocent.''

''Sometimes. But the police don't have hearts of hearts. They don't work on flair. They work on evidence; the more circumstantial, the better. As it is, between you and me, I think they might risk it with Emanuel. It was *his* couch, *his* knife, *his* patient, and he was the only one likely to be sitting in his chair, with her lying down. There have been cases with no more evidence than that. But his office was, so to speak, wide open, of which a good defense lawyer could make plenty. If they can establish motive, they've got him, though.''

''Is that what you think will happen, Reed?''

''No. I believe you, and I believe your judgment of him. But, Kate, where else are we going to look? The police don't think it's likely that a homicidal maniac was at work, and I agree with them. Of course, Messenger's a possibility, but an awfully farfetched one.''

"Why can't they arrest Barrister as well as Emanuel? Barrister had the motive. I know it's not the world's greatest motive, but, speaking of smart lawyers . . .''

"The motive without the evidence isn't enough. Anyway, not a motive like that. Well, at least things are breaking. At least we've got the detectives started on Sparks and Horan, and something may come from there. What, by the way, has happened to your Jerry?''

"I sent him out to see Messenger.''

"Kate, I really think, after what I said . . .''

"I know—rave on. If Jerry comes up with any startling facts, I promise to tell you. But judging from his report over the phone, Messenger is another innocent babe. You know, Reed, it would be a hell of a blow to psychiatry if they arrested Emanuel. I mean, he's not a fly-by-night crank, or someone who had just taken up psychiatry. He's a member of, and therefore backed by, the most austere institute of psychiatry in the country. Even I, who argue with Emanuel constantly, cannot believe that they would admit as a member, after the extended analysis they require, a man who could murder a patient on a couch. And I'm sure they didn't. Even if he weren't convicted, his arrest would be a hell of a blow. Perhaps there's someone around who loathes psychiatry, and he's going to murder patients at regular, widely spaced intervals, in order to discredit the profession. Maybe you'd better ask all the suspects what they think about psychiatry.''

"I'll make a note of it. Now I must go and get some sleep. *I've* got a trial coming up tomorrow—grand jury, question of pornography. Perhaps we ought to blow ourselves up, all of us, and start again, after the earth has cooled a few hundred years, and try to make a better job of it.''

With which happy thought, Kate went to bed.

In the morning Jerry, looking downcast, arrived with his report. He sat angrily flipping the pages of a magazine while Kate read his notes. Jerry had reported his conversation with Messenger in the form of dialogue; this was followed by an exact, unflattering description of the doctor and completed by an account of Jerry's impressions. He might not have felt there was much substance in the report, but he had taken care with its form. Kate congratulated him on his neatness, but he sneered.

"You *were* literary," she said.

"Weren't we, though? Do you recognize that thing from Lawrence he was gabbing on about?"

"Oh, yes, I think so. It must have made quite an impression on Barrister. It's from the beginning of *The Rainbow*—nobody ever did children better than Lawrence, which is probably because he didn't have any. I take it Messenger was a man you would have felt inclined to trust."

"Yes, he was, if that's worth anything. I'm sure it isn't. In fact, if you want to know, he reminded me of you."

"Of me? Do my ears stick out?"

Jerry flushed. "I didn't mean physically. The impression I have of him was like the impression I have of you. Don't ask me what I mean—it's just that, both of you might be dishonest, but you'd know you were doing it."

"That's a nice compliment, Jerry."

"Is it? It's probably pure, unadulterated crap. What do I do now?"

"He didn't give the impression that he was being dishonest and knowing it?"

"No, he didn't. I'd swear he was honest. Yet people will swear that confidence men are honest."

"I think," Kate said, "that we'll assume he's honest. At least until we have any reason to doubt it. There has to be a constant in every equation—up to now we've had only variables. I think we'll put Messenger in as the constant, and then see what X turns out to equal. Jerry, would you mind awfully much just hanging around? I *think* I may send you to Michigan. The trouble is, if you want to know, we have been approaching this whole problem with fettered imaginations."

She began to pace up and down the room. Jerry groaned.

17

IT had been Thursday morning when Kate had spoken to Jerry. It was now Friday evening. Kate had that day again asked someone to take her lectures. She faced Reed, who sat on her couch, his legs stretched out before him.

"I don't know if I can tell you what happened, properly, from the beginning," she said, "but I can tell you where I began yesterday morning. I began with an idle joke, from one doctor to another, months ago. I began with a dated photograph. I began with one of the great modern novels, and a scene in it, indelibly impressed on the mind of a man because it recalled to him a vital moment of his childhood. I began with a punning association in a dream, an association not of love or infatuation, but hate or fear. I began also with an old lady, and the wilds of Canada.

"I had decided to believe Messenger—you read Jerry's report just now. Messenger said Barrister wasn't capable of murder, and while that statement might be doubted, I decided not, for the moment, to doubt it.

"There were a few other facts whirling around also. A suit for malpractice. Sparks, who never forgets a face. Nicola, and her willingness to tell a sympathetic listener, or even an unsympathetic one, almost anything he may want to know about her life. A window cleaner, who turned out never to exist, but who suggested to me the ease with which anyone, with access to the court outside Emanuel's office and kitchen, could study those rooms. My visits to see Emanuel and Nicola, in the good old days before the crime. A question put to me, 'Professor Fansler, do you know a good psychiatrist?'

"These were all whirling around, as I say, but suddenly on

Thursday morning they seemed to fall into place. I then did, or caused to be done, three things.

"The first involved Nicola. I called her up, and urged her to get herself, as subtly as possible, into a conversation with Barrister. This wasn't hard for Nicola. She simply appeared at his office door after his patients had departed, reminded him that he had said he was eager to do what he could to help, and announced that what she needed was someone to talk to. When I was a kid, we used to play a game I thought rather silly. One person would be given, on a slip of paper, a ridiculous phrase, such as 'My father plays piano with his toes.' The point was to tell a story to your opponent, who, of course, had not seen the slip of paper, and to work your ridiculous sentence into it. Naturally, what you did was to tell a story full of outrageous statements, since your opponent had three challenges to discover which was the one on the slip of paper. Of course, the opponent almost never got it, because all the statements you made were as outrageous as 'My father plays piano with his toes.' This, in effect, was what Nicola had to do. I wanted to know Barrister's opinion of D. H. Lawrence, particularly of *The Rainbow*, and particularly of one incident in *The Rainbow*. Nicola had reread the appropriate section of the novel—fortunately, it came in the first seventy-five pages. She had to introduce this, however, along with lots of other literary discussion, so that it would not stand out from the surrounding material.

"Nicola did it beautifully.

"The second thing I 'did' was done by Nicola also. She fluttered, in her delightful way, around Barrister's office, and managed to discover, partly by asking him, but mostly by telling him—you miss a lot by not knowing Nicola's style—a bit of his routine.

"The third thing cost money. I sent Jerry out to a little town called Bangor, Michigan. He's on his way back now, but I spoke to him on the phone last night. Jerry had quite a time. He was looking for an old lady, but she was dead. Fortunately, it's a small town, and he managed to find the people the old lady had lived with before she died. They weren't related to her; she paid them for her room and meals, and for her care. This arrangement had been made by Michael Barrister, who, of course, comes from Bangor, Michigan.

"It was Michael Barrister who supported the old lady; it was not a great amount of money he paid to the couple in whose house she lived, and as she grew older, and needed more care, he increased the amount. When she died, Michael Barrister made a quite suitable gift of money to the people who had cared for her over the years, and had given her, I suppose, the kind of affection that can't be bought.

"All this was straightforward enough, but I was after something else, and Jerry, with his boyish charm, managed to get it. He asked if the checks had ever stopped. After this build-up, you may perhaps not be overcome with astonishment to hear that they had. Barrister had sent a check every month, all through college, medical school, his internship and his residency. Then they stopped.

"The couple were decent people. They went on caring for her, but finally the financial burden became too great, and the man of the couple made a trip to Chicago. He managed to find that Barrister had gone to New York, and by going to the library and consulting a New York phone book, found his address. The man wrote to Barrister, and received back a letter of apology which explained that Barrister had been in financial difficulties, but was now all right. With the letter was enclosed a check for all the money due for the past months, and for the month to come. The monthly checks never stopped after that, until the old lady's death. But during those checkless months which had elapsed, the old lady had had a birthday, for which Michael Barrister had always sent her a letter and a present. The present was always the same: a small china dog, to add to her collection of china dogs. When the checks didn't come and the birthday was skipped, the old lady refused ever to hear Barrister's name again. She had called him Mickey, which no one else had done, but now she refused to refer to him, or to take anything from him again. The couple with whom she lived had to pretend to be supporting her, while taking Barrister's money, without which, of course, they couldn't get on. They didn't communicate with him any more, and the old lady never received another china dog."

"Touching story," Reed said. "Who was the old lady?"

"Sorry. I shouldn't have left that out. She had lived with Barrister's grandparents, and had cared for him when he was a boy. In the grandparents' will, all they had was left to their grandson, with a note added saying they were certain he would always care for the old lady. He always did.

"We return now to Nicola's conversation. She reported it to me word by word—in the event of all court stenographers being wiped out in a plague, together with all recording machines, I think Nicola would do nicely—but I will give you only the substance. Barrister has read *Lady Chatterley's Lover*. Otherwise, he has read nothing by D. H. Lawrence, whom he seemed, by the way, inclined to confuse with T. E. Lawrence, and gave it as his opinion, furthermore, that modern literature was off on the wrong track. It might be all very fine for professors and critics, but if a man read a book, what he wanted was a good story, not a lot of symbolism and slices of life.

"What Nicola discovered about Barrister's office had, I imagine, already been discovered by the police. He has a waiting room, several examining rooms and an office. Women, in varying stages of readiness, are treated in the examining rooms and talked to in the office. Barrister moves from one to the other, as does the nurse. If he is not in one, it is assumed he is in another. The ladies often have to wait quite a while, and are used to it—a fact, incidentally, which can be confirmed by anyone who has ever consulted a successful gynecologist. In other words, as you have already told me, Barrister did not have an alibi, though that good defense lawyer to whom you are always referring could make a great deal out of the fact that he was certainly having office hours at the time of the murder. Probably all the women who were there that day will have to be questioned closely, though not, thank God, by me.

"I now added to this information something Nicola had suggested the day after the murder, and something Jerry had discovered in an interlude with the nurse which I would, on the whole, rather ignore: that Barrister specialized in women unable to conceive, in women suffering from various 'female' problems, and in women wretched in their change of life. Incidentally, I called up my doctor, a conservative type on the staff of a teaching hospital, who was finally induced to tell me—all doctors, I've discovered, dislike the suggestion that medicine is ever badly practiced—that while many doctors treat women in menopause with weekly injections of hormones, he personally feels that too little is known about the effects of hormones and that they ought to be used only in cases of extreme need. Women, however, like the effects and are given hormones by many doctors. Do you want a drink?"

"Go on," Reed said.

"I'm now going to tell you a story, a story suggested to me by all these facts. Once upon a time there was a young doctor named Michael Barrister. He had passed his boards, and served his year of residency. He liked to camp and hike, particularly in what we seem to be calling the wilds of Canada, where you sleep out, or rent a room from a forester, or stay in an occasional hostel. Mike, if we call him that, went camping and met, in the wilds of Canada, a girl named Janet Harrison. They fell in love . . ."

"But her father was the mightiest man in the whole kingdom, and his but a poor woodsman."

"If you interrupt, Mommy isn't going to finish the story, and you'll have to go right to sleep. After a time the girl had to go home and so, pledging eternal love, they parted. Michael Barrister then met another man, a man who resembled him closely. They went off together on a hike. Mike spoke freely to the man, as one does with strangers; he told him a great deal about himself, but he did not tell him about the girl. One night the stranger killed Mike, and buried his body in the wilds of Canada."

"Kate, for the love of heaven . . ."

"Perhaps it was an accident. Perhaps it was only after Mike died in an accident that the stranger saw the situation he was in—perhaps he thought he would not be too readily believed—in any event, the idea came to him to take over Mike's identity.

"It was an enormous risk; a million things might have gone wrong, but none of them did. Or none of them seemed to. The bit about the old lady was a problem, but that seemed to resolve itself. The difficulty, of course, was that friends of Mike's would show up, but he could snub them—so that they would think that Mike had changed. It seemed as though the angels were on his side. The body was never discovered. When he got letters, he answered them. The real Mike had a first-rate record, and the stranger had no difficulty setting up a practice. The malpractice suit was certainly a storm, but he weathered it.

"And then came the first huge problem: Janet Harrison. Her actual arrival was delayed many years. She had gone to nursing school, with the plan of joining Mike eventually in New York, and her letters spoke of this often. He wrote back trying, without harshness, to let the affair die down. He took longer and longer to answer her letters. When her mother died, she had to go home. But eventually, despite the delay, Janet Harrison, Nemesis, came to New York. She had never stopped loving him, and did not, or could not, believe that he had stopped loving her.

"He could not very well refuse to see her. He considered this, but she might talk, and it seemed better on the whole to know what she was up to. She soon discovered, of course, that he wasn't Mike. With a close-enough resemblance, it is remarkably easy, I imagine, to fool people. It does not occur to people that you are not who you say you are—simply that you have changed. But it is quite another matter to fool a woman who has loved a man and been to bed with him. She was a secretive type—that was a break for him—but she was determined to prove this Michael Barrister an impostor, and to avenge the murder of the man she had loved. She knew she was in danger—and she made a will, leaving her money to the man her Mike had admired, to the man who seemed like Mike. Unfortunately, if she collected any evidence, she didn't place it with the lawyer who made her will. She kept it in her room, or perhaps in a notebook she carried around with her. That is why he had to rob her room, even at tremendous risk, and go through her pocketbook after he killed her.

"She used to stand across the street and watch his office. She wanted to unnerve him, and undoubtedly she succeeded. But eventually she needed an excuse for the daily visits she wanted, and the presence of Emanuel gave it to her. Once, perhaps twice, she saw me emerge after a visit to Emanuel and Nicola. If she went to me, would I suggest Emanuel? She came to me, and I did. Had I not suggested him—well, why should we worry about what might have happened?

"She took no one into her confidence, partly because she wasn't the confiding sort, any more than Mike was, partly because who would have believed her? Even though she is murdered, you are having trouble believing me now. One can imagine how the police would have treated a story like that.

"Dr. Michael Barrister knew he would have to act, certainly once she had started going to a psychoanalyst. On the couch she might say something, might even be believed. In any case, as long as she lived, she was a terrible threat. But he did not want to kill her. He was sure to be in the center of it; the closeness of his office to Emanuel's promised that. No matter where she was killed, the fact that she was in analysis would emerge, and he might be questioned. Perhaps, therefore, he could induce her to love him, could even marry her. He resembled remarkably the man she had loved. He knew women. He knew that they liked to be overpowered, and directed. He began to try to win her love. He must have thought for a time that he was succeeding. She allowed him to make love to her, yet something told him that she, too, was playing a game. She was trying to weaken his defenses.

"He knew the workings of Emanuel's home. Observation, talks with Nicola, glances through the court windows, told him all he needed. He had the rubber gloves of a surgeon. The telephone calls were child's play. He knew that Emanuel, given freedom, would gallop off to the park. If by some perverse chance Emanuel had not gone, Barrister was in no way committed; he could, at any moment, turn back. But Emanuel left, and Janet Harrison came to keep her appointment in an empty office. Barrister appeared. He probably told her some story of Emanuel's being called off, and led her to the couch, where, perhaps making love to her, he got her to lie down. Perhaps he pushed her back before he drove the knife home. No blood got on him, but if it had, he had only to climb in the court window of his office and wash himself. Of course, he took chances. He had to.

"But by killing her in Emanuel's office, he took as few as possible. He would have been involved no matter where she was killed; that is, his existence would have come to the attention of the police as a neighbor of her analyst's. He certainly could not kill her in his apartment—he never took her there. She lived in a woman's dormitory, a place in which people continually come and go. He killed her with Emanuel's knife on Emanuel's couch. This not only made Emanuel suspect, but rendered suspect anything Emanuel might say about what the girl had revealed in analysis. The girl had told him of me and Emanuel and Nicola—he knew we were friends, and he certainly picked up a lot of our past history from Nicola. Later, he sent the anonymous letter accusing me. Again he had a daring plan; he took enormous risks, and he won, or seemed to win. If he hadn't overlooked the picture, if Janet Harrison hadn't made the will, he would have got away with it."

"And if you, my dear Kate, hadn't obviously become a teacher because you were a novelist *manquée* . . . Talk about good stories! You ought to publish this one."

"You don't believe it."

"It isn't a matter of whether I believe it or not. Let's say I not only believe it; let's say it's true. You said the police might laugh at Janet Harrison. That's nothing to the way they'll howl at this. You haven't one shred of proof, Kate, not one—not even the whisper of one. The old lady? Mike was in financial difficulties, and his love affair put the old lady out of his mind. A novel by D. H. Lawrence? I can see myself explaining that to Homicide. An association in a dream related in the course of analysis to the chief suspect? The fact that the man he roomed with for one year didn't think the Mike he knew was likely to commit a murder? Murders are all too often committed by unlikely people—isn't it always the most unlikely person who turns out to have done it in books?"

"All right, Reed, I admit I haven't good evidence. But it's a true story, all the same, and it isn't just that I've become enamored of my invention. I knew you'd laugh. But don't you see that there must be proof somewhere? If the police with all their resources looked, they'd find it. Maybe somewhere there is still something with the real Mike's fingerprints—okay, so that's unlikely. Maybe Mike's body could be found. If the police really tried, they could find evidence. Reed, you've got to make them try. It would take Jerry and me years . . ."

"I should say so, digging up half of Canada."

"But if the police will only look, they'll find something. They might find who this man was, before he became Michael Barrister. Perhaps he was in jail somewhere. You could get his finger-prints . . ."

"Kate. All you've got is a fairy tale, beginning 'Once upon a time.' Find me evidence, one uncontrovertible piece of evidence that this man isn't Michael Barrister, and maybe we can get an investigation under way. We could hire private detectives, if necessary. All you've got now is a theory."

"What sort of evidence do you want? The real Mike wouldn't have forgotten that scene in *The Rainbow*. Am I supposed to find that the real Mike had a strawberry mark on his shoulder, like the long-lost sons from overseas in late Victorian novels? What would you accept as evidence? Tell me that. What?"

"Kate, dear, there can't be any evidence, don't you see? We can get Barrister's fingerprints, but I promise you they're not on record—he'd have known something as basic as that. Suppose we face Messenger with him—all Messenger can say is: He resembles Mike, but Mike has changed. Suppose you even discover that back in his medical school days Mike had a beautiful singing voice, that this Dr. Barrister is a monotone. Voices, I'm certain, can go. Though if you could discover that to be true, it would certainly be better than what you've got."

"I see," Kate said. "I've given you the motive and the means, but it's not enough."

"It's not, my dear. And I honor you too much to pretend respect for a theory that's a castle in the air. You've been worrying too much, and you're under strain. If I told the D.A a story like this, I'd probably lose my job."

"In other words, Barrister has committed the perfect crime. Two perfect crimes."

"Kate, find some way I can help you. I want to. But life isn't fiction."

"You're wrong, Reed. Life isn't evidence."

"You admit you've made up this entire story. Kate, when I was in college, taking freshman English, the professor gave us a paragraph, and we were all to write a story beginning with that paragraph. We were a class of twenty-five, and there were no two stories remotely alike. I'm sure, if you took a little time, you could make up another story, with Sparks or Horan as murderer. Why not try it, just to prove my point?"

"You forget, Reed, I've lots of evidence, though not the sort you find acceptable. The same sort of evidence proved to me that Barrister had known Janet Harrison. It so happens that Barrister got frightened and admitted it. But if he hadn't, I'd be sitting here now still trying unsuccessfully to convince you that those two had known each other."

"Perhaps you can face him with this story, and get him to admit it."

"Perhaps I will. An assistant D.A., I will tell him, knows about this tale, so why don't you kill me and prove to him that I was right?"

"Stop talking foolish. Where's that picture of the 'real Mike,' as we are now calling him? Get it, will you?"

Kate handed it to him. "One gets the feeling sometimes that it could speak. But I'd better not say that, I'll simply confirm you in your conviction that I'm round the bend. What did you want the picture for?"

"Ears. They don't show very well, do they? A good deal of work has been done to identify people by their ears. Too bad Real Mike didn't get his picture taken in profile. Then we could get a picture of Barrister's ear."

"Will you look into that, Reed? And please don't give me up as incurably demented. Perhaps I am just weaving fancies . . ."

"I know that conciliatory tone. It means you're about to do something I don't approve of. Listen, Kate, let's think about it. If we can come up with one piece of evidence that isn't literary, psychological or impressionistic, maybe we can interest the police. I'd rather go after a hormone dispenser, anyway, than a psychiatrist. Shall we go to a movie?"

"No. You may either go home, or you may drive me to the airport."

"Airport! Are *you* going to Bangor, Michigan?"

"Chicago. Now, don't start sputtering. I've been promising myself a visit to Chicago for a long time. They've got Picasso's 'Man with the Blue Guitar' there and I have suddenly developed an uncontrollable desire to see it. While I'm gone you might read Wallace Stevens's poems inspired by the painting. He deals very effectively with the difference between reality and things-as-they-are. Excuse me while I pack a bag."

18

"COME into my office," Messenger said.

"Do you always work on Saturday?"

"If I can. I find it quieter than other days."

"And I have come to destroy the quiet."

"Only to postpone it. How can I help?"

Sitting across from Messenger, Kate confirmed for herself Jerry's impression. Messenger was lovable; there was no other word for this homely, gentle, intelligent man. "I'm going to tell you a story," Kate said. "I've told it once already; I'm becoming quite a storyteller. The first time it was received, if not with screams of hilarity, at least with grunts of disbelief. I'm not going to ask you to believe it. Just listen. Tonight you can tell your wife, 'I didn't get anything done this morning; some madwoman appeared and insisted on telling me some idiotic sort of fairy tale.' It'll make a nice anecdote for your wife."

"Go on," Messenger said.

Kate told him the story, just as she had told it to Reed. Messenger listened, smoking his pipe, disappearing at times behind a cloud of smoke. He emptied the pipe when she had finished.

"You know," he said, "when I went up to Mike in New York, he didn't at first know who I was. Natural enough, I guess; I'm not someone you'd expect to meet in New York. I noticed he'd got very elegant and didn't want to bother with me. There are those who are always ready to think they're being snubbed, and those who don't think anyone will ever snub them. I belong to the first class. Mike told me I'd changed. Well, I thought at the time, It's all in the eyes of the beholder; he's changed. But you know, I hadn't changed. There's one thing about having a face that could stop a clock—it doesn't seem to vary with the years. But I wear glasses now, which I didn't used to do, so it seemed logical enough that it was that.''

"You mean the whole story doesn't strike you as utterly fantastic?''

"Well, you know, it doesn't. The man I met in New York wasn't a beer drinker. I don't mean he told me that; we didn't have a drink, but he didn't look like a beer drinker. Mike didn't like hard liquor, just beer and wine with meals. Still, tastes change. I'm afraid your Reed Amhearst would say we ought to go into business together as writers of science fiction. Maybe we should.''

"It's a deal. You do the science, I'll do the fiction. Reed would say I'm magnificently qualified. What I want now, Mr. Collaborator, is one fact. Like a strawberry mark on Mike's shoulder. Mike wasn't nearsighted, was he, or deaf in one ear?''

"I know what you want. I knew at that moment in your fairy tale when Mike met the stranger. But Mike wasn't nearsighted, or deaf, or a monotone, or an opera singer. The only thing I can think of is that Mike could wiggle his ears, you know, without moving any other part of his head. But that wouldn't do as evidence either. Besides, I'm told anyone can learn to do it, if he practices long enough. I have a lovely picture of your Dr. Barrister sitting at home, night after night, learning to wiggle his ears. You see, I'm rambling on, not being any use at all.''

"I told you a crazy story, yet you didn't ring for the authorities and say, 'Get this woman out of here.' Believe me, that matters more than you know. Mike must have liked you enormously. Janet Harrison knew it; that's why she left you her money. You know, there's a nice crass motive I can hold out. If we can prove this tale, or get the police to prove it for us, you've got a much better claim to that money she left you.''

"Unfortunately, that will make my testimony all the more suspect. The trouble, you see, is that I knew Mike only a year, and we weren't exactly Damon and Pythias. I don't remember when he told me that bit about the Lawrence novel—probably I asked him about his family because he never mentioned having any. For the most part, he didn't talk about himself. We discussed medicine, the advantages of different specialties—that sort of thing. Wait a minute, what about teeth?''

"I thought of teeth. I'm a reader of detective stories. The dentist in Bangor who looked after Mike's teeth died long ago; Jerry couldn't find any trace of his records. Probably the dentist who took over the practice from Mike's dentist kept only the records that were active, and even *he's* gone. It happens that I changed dentists about five years ago when the family dentist retired, and I called the dentist I go to now—you have no idea what a nuisance I've been making of myself—only to discover that all he has is the record of the work *he's* done on my teeth. The dentist who retired sold his practice, but the dentist who bought it hasn't kept records going back to the year one. The only dental record of me is of the work that's been done in the past five years, and that isn't much. Most of my fillings date back to my adolescence. You don't happen to know, for instance, that Mike had all his wisdom teeth extracted. If we could prove that, and this Dr. Barrister turns out to have four very present wisdom teeth . . ."

Messenger shook his head. "At the time, of course, I wasn't looking for anything. Being a resident is a very wearying and demanding business; often we weren't home at the same time. I don't even remember if Mike snored; I don't know if I ever knew. As a matter of fact, I haven't got a very good memory for personal things. My wife complains about this from time to time. I'm always complimenting her on hats she's had three years. I remember looking at my wife one day, and thinking, You're gray. But I hadn't noticed it happening. I'm sorry. You've come all this way and . . ."

"I could have telephoned. I wanted to come. There's a plane back this afternoon. I'll even have time to go to the museum."

"Why not come home to lunch with me? I'd like you to meet Anne. She's the most sensible, down-to-earth human being in the world. Maybe she'll think of something."

Kate was glad to accept the invitation. They were a nice family. After lunch, Kate and the two Messengers sat in the backyard, as the Messengers called it, and Kate told her story once again. Anne was not, like Kate and Messenger, a dreamer. Her reaction was more like Reed's. Yet as Kate was leaving, Anne said: "I'll be honest, Kate; I think this story was just logical enough for you to believe it at first, and since nothing you knew absolutely contradicted it, you allowed yourself to become convinced. I don't believe your story really happened. But it's not impossible that it happened, and if Dan knows something that can prove it, we've got to dig that something out. I'm more systematic than he is about everything except genes. I'll try to help him remember, in a systematic way. But please don't hope too much."

And Kate went to see the "Man with the Blue Guitar."

                                   *   *   *

She was home by ten o'clock. The trip from Kennedy Airport
had taken almost as long as the flight from Chicago, longer if she
counted her wait for luggage, but even so, she was glad she'd gone.
Reed called at ten-thirty.

"I know I met you at a political club," he said, "but I didn't
know you were planning to emulate a political candidate. Do you
think you might stay put now, say, for twenty-four hours? Did you
get anything? Well, hope springs eternal. I, though I have not been
winging through the wild blue yonder, have not been idle. I have
consulted Ear Expert. Ear Expert said picture we have insufficient.
Still, he'll try. We have set a detective, posing as a street photogra-
pher, to get a picture of the ears of Dr. Michael Barrister. It also
occurred to me that there was probably a picture of your Mike in his
college year-book—possibly with ears. Or there may be a picture of
Mike among the old lady's belongings, if we can find them. Ears
don't change, I was fascinated to hear. Even a boyhood picture might
do. Not that it's evidence, of course. The other side gets its own ear
expert, who says 'inconclusive.' That's the trouble with expert evidence—you can usually get plenty for both sides. But I'm trying.
What was Messenger like?"

"I wish I'd met him years ago and persuaded him to marry me."

"Oh, Lord, you *are* in a bad way. Shall I come and cheer you
up? I can tell you about my lovely time with the grand jury. They
decided the books we had gone to such great trouble to capture
weren't pornographic. I don't know what the world's coming to, as
my mother used to say."

"Thanks, Reed. I'm taking a grain and a half of Seconal and
going to bed. Sorry about the trial."

"Never mind. I'm thinking of giving up law and writing pornography."

The ringing phone seemed to pull Kate up from depths far, far
down in the ocean of oblivion. Frantically she fought her way to the
surface. It was midnight.

"Yes," she said.

"Dan Messenger. I've woken you. But I thought you'd want me
to. We've got it. You can thank Anne. Are you there?"

"I'm here."

"Anne told you she was systematic. She made lists, categories;
we kept going over them. She started, in her logical way, with scars,

though of course our present Barrister would have seen them too. I mean, if Mike had had his appendix out, this guy would go and get his appendix out. Always supposing he wanted to be that thorough. No bells went off when she mentioned scars, I'm ashamed to say, so we went on to other categories. Allergies, habits, times we'd gone out together. Are you still there?''

"God, yes!"

"Then she hit on one that seemed ridiculous; the category of clothes. One could hardly say this guy wasn't Mike because he didn't still have the old tweed jacket Mike cherished. Not that Mike did. I mean, I don't remember any tweed jacket. I said I didn't remember his clothes at all. We wore white almost all the time, including shoes. And then, you know, it came to me. Shoes. White shoes. I had only one pair—there wasn't any money in those days, and I'd got huge holes in the sole. It was raining, and the hole in the shoe worked like a pump. My feet were soaked, and so were my only pair of white shoes, and I asked Mike, who was off duty, if I could borrow his. Our feet looked about the same size, and even if Mike's didn't fit too well, at least they were dry. He told me I could borrow them, but that I'd find them a little hard to walk with. I asked him why. 'Because I wear a lift on one heel," he said; 'you probably haven't noticed it, most people don't. It's only five-eights of an inch, but to a man with legs the same length, it will feel as though you're walking with one foot on the curb.' Well, I tried them on—they were too small, in addition, and I didn't wear them. Still there? Grunt once in a while, will you? It's disconcerting with no sound at the other end, like talking into a stage phone. That's better.

"I haven't had much to do with orthopedics since medical school, but I think if a man once wore a lift, he would go on wearing it. Still, you'll have to check that. The great point is, Mike did have a scar, though I never saw it. But if he had an operation we can find a record of it; there's no problem about that. You're going to have to check on all of this, though, with an orthopedist, and the police.

"Mike didn't tell me about his scar at that time. I might have remembered it more readily if he had. Some months later Mike went back to the hospital when I knew he was off duty, and naturally I asked why. We didn't hang around if we didn't have to. He told me he wanted to watch a spinal fusion. He couldn't stay the whole time; it's a very long operation, sometimes eight hours. I think as an operation it's so recent, comparatively speaking, because they didn't have the proper anesthetic until recently. I asked him about the operation when he came back, and he said it wasn't as neat a job as his. 'My scar's like a pencil line,' he said. He told me he'd had a slipped disk, and they'd done the spinal fusion. The operation was successful enough, but when it was over he still had this terrible lower back pain. It was an old general practitioner in Bangor, he said, who cured it. I don't mean the operation hadn't been necessary—there was pressure on the nerve, the muscles in one leg were atrophying—but it was the old guy who cured the pain. He found out Mike's legs weren't the same length. There was seesaw motion in the pelvis. Mike had a lift put on his shoe, and that was it. So it's over to you, lady. I don't know how you're going to get your Dr. Michael Barrister undressed, but when you do, remember, the scar isn't that screamingly visible. I've found out this much for you: it runs up and down, over the lower vertebrae, for three to four inches. At some point, it loops out. That's where they fold the skin back. You might start by noticing if our friend wears a lift on his shoe.

"But remember this—even if your story is true, the murderer may have noticed. He may have tried on Mike's shoes. He may have looked the body over very carefully for scars, and found this one. If he wears a lift on one shoe—and though I've racked my brain, I can't remember which—and if he's got a scar, your story may still be true, but we'll never, never prove it."

When Messenger, roundly thanked, had rung off, Kate called Emanuel. He was not, it turned out, asleep. Never a good sleeper, he was now an insomniac.

"Emanuel. This is Kate. I want you to call up an orthopedist. Well, all right then, the first thing in the morning. I want to know if a man who wears a lift on his shoe because his legs are of uneven length would ever decide to do without the lift. And I want to know if the scar from a spinal fusion could ever disappear. No, I don't want your opinion. I know you're a doctor. Ask an orthopedist. And he better be sure enough to swear in court. Sleep well."

19

SUNDAY night, or, more accurately, Monday morning at two A.M., there was a gathering at Kate's house—whether it was a celebration or a wake depended upon a guest who was not yet there. Emanuel, Nicola, Jerry and Kate were waiting for Reed. Kate had flirted momentarily with the thought of inviting Sparks and Horan, but Emanuel's unwillingness to meet his patients socially argued against the idea, even if it had had anything else to recommend it.

Reed had worked like a yeoman since early Sunday morning. Emanuel had apparently aroused his orthopedist from sleep, and instead of asking him questions, had simply persuaded him to call Kate himself. Kate had in turn reported the conversation to Reed. "You know how doctors are," she had said. "This one was just a shade this side of irritable, but I gather that for Emanuel's sake he didn't like to refuse to talk to me altogether. He probably thought I was writing a novel, and he answered my questions in the most long-winded, technical way possible. But then doctors are always indulging in either incoherence or oversimplification—if you want my opinion, I don't think they even understand each other. However, I did manage to gather one or two things."

"I don't suppose," Reed had answered, "you would care to tell me why you were interrogating an innocent orthopedist at such an ungodly hour Sunday morning?"

"I will tell you in time, and there is no such thing as an innocent orthopedist. They are all as rich as Rockefeller and as arrogant as swans. I know at least two, and am therefore able intelligently to generalize. Anyway, his information, much diluted, is this: Once someone has had a spinal fusion, he is marked for life as a man who has had a spinal fusion. That may sound a little obvious, but it was important to establish it. It's a long operation—which I knew already—and sometimes involves two surgeons, one who works on the spine and disc, and one who works on the nerves. It is unlikely in the extreme that anyone who had been cured of a back pain by the use of a shoe lift would ever abandon its use. I know that's not a *sequitur*, at least not yet, but just listen. What is a spinal fusion? Sorry, I forgot you laymen have such difficulty following a medical man. People get herniated, or get slipped discs—yes, I know they're getting them all the time, even dachshunds get them. In other words, a piece of cartilage between two vertebrae slips out of place so that it is pressing on the nerves in the spinal column. In severe cases, there will be a numbness in one leg. The commonest way of dealing with a disc which continues thusly to slip is to remove it, and fuse the surrounding vertebrae together. The fusion is done by taking bone from another part of the body—nobody else's bone will do, except an identical twin's—grinding it up (all right, I'm almost finished; no, I did not call you up on Sunday morning solely to deliver a disgusting medical lecture), and placing it between the vertebrae to be fused. The vertebrae thus eventually grow together into one solid piece, and the patient is left with a scar over the fused vertebrae. Are you with me?

"Here, my long-suffering Reed, is the point. Mike Barrister— my Mike, you know, not the one now in the office across from Emanuel—had a spinal fusion; also, he wore a lift on one of his shoes because his legs were of unequal length. No, of course he wasn't a freak. It's immensely common. But unless there is an extreme difference in leg lengths (that's rather hard to say) the person usually will compensate for it by an odd sort of rolling walk. However, once there is an injury to the back, the constant movement of the pelvis, because of the uneven length of the legs, causes acute discomfort."

"Kate," Reed had said, "are you trying to tell me, in your own way, which I must say has become exceedingly long-winded and full of unnecessary details, that Janet Harrison's Mike had an operation? When?"

"That, my pet, is what you, please, are going to find out. He probably had it in Detroit, which is, isn't it? the biggest city in Michigan; but that's just a guess. The lift on the shoe you will have to take Messenger's word for. Of course, if you're going to continue to be stubborn, I can call hospitals myself . . ."

"All right, I'll call the hospitals. Then what?"

"Then, my boy, we've got to get Dr. Michael Barrister un-dressed. I would hate to tell you some of the schemes that have been rushing through my fevered brain. I don't suppose you could get a search warrant."

"A search warrant is to examine premises, not persons, and I'll let you in on a horrible secret. You'd be surprised how few search warrants are ever issued. The head of the narcotics division testified the other day in court, and he admitted quite calmly that in thirty years his men had never obtained a search warrant. Citizens are, unhappily, but fortunately for the police, remarkably unaware of their rights. The police have a number of tricks for getting where they want, of which plain bullying is the chief."

"If I could only get in there when he was taking a shower."

"Kate, I'm not even going to listen to you for one more minute unless you promise, your solemn word-of-honor-hope-to-die, that you will not attempt to undress Barrister, see him undressed, lead him into any situation where he is likely to get undressed, or in any way involve . . ."

"Will you help, if I promise?"

"I won't even continue this conversation until you promise. I want your word. All right. Now let me call hospitals. They will tell me none of their clerks works on Sundays. No one works on Sundays, except you and your friends. I will then threaten and cajole. But we may have to wait, even so. I don't know to what degree the New York Police Department is willing to flex its muscles. Now, stop evolving schemes. I'll call if and when I get any news. And remember your promise."

Kate had had to wait until the afternoon, when Reed called again. "Well," he had said then, "I will not tell you what I have been through. I'll save the details till we are old and gray, and our brains have room only for memories. We have established the operation. Now, if I follow you correctly, you want to discover if Emanuel's neighbor, Dr. Michael Barrister, has had an operation for a spinal fusion and if he wears a lift on the heel of one of his shoes."

"You follow me perfectly."

"Good. Now here's a bargain; take it or leave it. I understand your feeling for Emanuel, the importance of this case to psychiatry's popular reputation, etcetera, etcetera, but I still don't like what this case is doing to you. You are giving up your work in the library, cutting classes, spending money like a drunken sailor, taking sleeping pills, flying all over the United States in a most abandoned manner,

getting long-winded and leading young men astray. All this has got
to stop. Therefore my bargain. I will tonight discover for you, provided Dr. Michael Barrister spends tonight at home, whether or not
he has the scar from an operation, whether or not there is a lift on
all his right shoes, or all his left shoes. If there is no scar, and no
lift, I think the police will be very interested. We have, after all,
established the operation. In other words, I'll admit this is your piece
of evidence, and we'll look at Barrister much more closely, as a man
with opportunity, means and motive. But, here's your side of the
bargain. If Dr. Michael Barrister *has* a scar over any of his lower
vertebrae, whether or not he has lifts on his shoes—for we haven't
got any decent evidence that your Mike had lifts on his shoes (don't
argue with me, I haven't finished)—if Dr. Michael Barrister has such
a scar, then you agree to ignore this case, stop hiring Jerry, go back
to your work. In short, you promise generally to return to your
wonted ways. Is it a bargain? Never mind how I intend to undress
Barrister; we'll discuss that after I've done it. Is it a bargain?''

And Kate had promised that it was.

Inviting Jerry and the Bauers to wait for Reed had been her own
idea. They had discussed the case from every angle, up to and including what Kate now called her venture into ''once upon a time.''
She told them of her bargain. She told them Reed would be late. And
as the night wore on, she fed them coffee, which they drank, and
sandwiches, which they did not eat. After a while, they could think
of nothing more to say, and they fell silent. So silent that they heard
the elevator and Reed's steps. Kate was at the door almost before
Reed's hand was off the bell.

For the first time Reed met Emanuel, Nicola and Jerry. He shook
the hand of each, and asked for a cup of coffee.

''I take it,'' he said, ''that you all know what I was up to tonight.
There are many ways the police use to break into an apartment. For
example, they disconnect the lights in a house. The tenants rush out
into the hall to see what the trouble is, and the police slip in through
the open door. Once the police are inside, very few people will forcibly evict them. That scheme occurred to me, but I abandoned it for
various reasons: Barrister lives in a new and elegant house on First
Avenue; throwing the switch there would not be easy; more important, we wanted him undressed. That meant waiting until he had gone
to bed, in which state he was unlikely to notice that the lights were
out. We might simply have woken him and said we were inspecting
a gas leak, but in that case it might be difficult to get him out of his

bathrobe and pajamas. Therefore, I hit on the scheme of waiting till he had gone to bed, ringing the bell until he opened the door, and then demanding that he accompany us to headquarters for questioning. It was undoubtedly an odd hour to question someone, and we were prepared for indignation, but, of course, nothing ventured, nothing gained. So, a little after midnight, we went to call on Dr. Michael Barrister.''

"Who is 'we'?'' Jerry asked.

" 'We' is your humble servant and a uniformed policeman. Uniforms are very useful for convincing people that one is, in fact, the police. Also, they generate a certain atmosphere of emergency which I was eager to have generated. The policeman who came with me did so as a favor. If I succeeded in my errand, as I told him, he would come in for a good deal of commendation; he might even be promoted. If I failed, I promised to see that none of the onus rested on him. I wanted him there, atmosphere apart, to have a witness as yet unconnected with this case. I was afraid that my connection with certain aspects of it''—he glanced at Kate—"should I be called upon to testify, might, in certain hands, be capable of misinterpretation.

"We succeeded in rousing Dr. Barrister from bed. He was, as I feared, wearing pajamas. He had, in addition, thrown on a bathrobe. Had he slept in the nude, and opened the door that way, we would simply have engaged him in conversation, one in front, one in back. As it was, we had to ask him to dress and come down with us to 'Headquarters.' There is, actually, no such place as 'Headquarters,' but I wanted to be both as ominous and as vague as possible. After much shouting and threatening, and references to important men who were, I gather, the husbands of his patients, he consented to get dressed. He said he wanted to call a lawyer, and I told him he would be allowed one call from 'Headquarters,' according to regulations, may be blessed saints forgive me! Finally, he agreed to get dressed, but protested anew when the policeman followed him into the bedroom. I explained that this, too, was regulations, to be certain that he did not telephone or injure himself, or conceal a weapon, or hide anything. He flung into the bedroom, purple with rage, closely followed by the policeman, who had been carefully instructed by me. I had originally thought of telling the policeman to examine Barrister's shoes, but I abandoned the idea. We were going to succeed or fail in this outrageous enterprise depending on the scar, and it seemed as well to concentrate on that.

"The policeman followed his instructions well. Barrister flung off his bathrobe and pajamas, and as he bent over slightly to pull on his underpants, the policeman stepped up for a good look. His instructions, had he any doubt of what he saw, were to trip, falling on Barrister, to examine Barrister's back more closely, and then apologize. This might have been necessary had Barrister turned out to be an exceedingly hairy man; when skin is covered with hair, it is difficult to determine if it is scarred or not. But Barrister wasn't hairy.

"Needless to say, I waited for Barrister and the policeman as I suppose expectant fathers wait for doctors. The two of them came out of the room together, and the three of us went downtown. Eventually we aroused the D.A., who said it was time someone dug up some blasphemous evidence in this unprintable case."

Kate and Emmanuel had risen to their feet. Nicola simply stared. It was Jerry who spoke.

"There wasn't any scar," he said.

"What have I been telling you?" Reed said. "No scar. He was examined again downtown. No sign of any spinal fusion. But the policeman put it best. 'Neatest bit of back I ever saw in my life.' he said. 'Not a mark on it.' "

Epilogue

SIX weeks later Kate sailed for Europe. There was no one to see her off, at her own request. She disliked *bon voyage*, parties, preferring rather to lean on the deck rail waiting for Manhattan to slip away. She had a cabin to herself, second class, ample work to do, and the prospect of a pleasant and productive summer.

The evening newspapers, six weeks before, given the story by Reed (who liked to keep reporters on his side), had blazoned forth the headlines: "New Suspect in Case of Girl on Couch." The *Times*, picking up the news late, had put it more decorously. Emanuel and his patients settled back to the analysis of unconscious motives. The Psychiatric Institute made no comment—it never did—but Kate felt certain she could hear its collective sigh of relief echoing in the night.

Jerry had returned to driving a truck, and to Sally, who was becoming somewhat restive with the lack of attention. He had refused a bonus. Kate had pointed out that it was part of their original agreement, verbal but no less binding for that, but Jerry, adamant, had taken only his salary. Kate put the amount of the bonus in a bank, intending to allow it to collect interest until it should be withdrawn as a wedding present.

As the ship came abreast of Brooklyn, a view which Kate found productive of nothing but thoughts concerning human decadence, she went below. She walked through one of the lounges and was astonished to discover Reed, sitting in a chair, looking as though he had grown there. She stared at him.

"I," Reed said, "am going to Europe."

"Well," Kate said, "I'm relieved to hear you know it. I thought perhaps you imagined yourself in the lobby of the Plaza. Are you on vacation?''

"Vacation and leave. I decided to come at the last minute, and have to share a cabin with two young men who make up in vigor what they lack in virtue, but at least I am here. Protection.''

"Who are you protecting?''

"Whom. For an English teacher, you do have more trouble with your pronouns. I wanted to protect you, so to speak, in the quarantine period, to be sure the fever was gone.''

"What fever?''

"Detective fever. I've known a few people with cases like yours. They invariably sail for Europe and trip over a body on their way to the shower. It was simply no good expecting myself to sit in New York, imagining you following clues and dropping literary allusions.''

Kate fell into the chair beside him. Reed smiled, and then raised his arm to beckon a passing steward.

"Two brandies, please.''

The James Joyce Murder

To the first reader of this—and other things

Contents

Prologue

JAMES Joyce's *Ulysses*, as almost everybody knows by now, is a long book recounting life in Dublin on a single day: June 16, 1904. It was on June 16, 1966, exactly sixty-two years later, that Kate Fansler set out for a meeting of the James Joyce Society, which annually held a "Bloomsday" celebration.

Adopting what she hoped was a properly Joycean attitude, Kate reminded herself that she would be approaching the Gotham Book Mart, home of the James Joyce Society, at almost the same hour in which Leopold Bloom, the hero of *Ulysses*, had walked out upon Sandymount Beach. "And had I any sense at all," Kate thought, "I would be on a beach myself." But having become temporary custodian of the Samuel Lingerwell papers, and thus unexpectedly involved in the literary correspondence of James Joyce, Kate thought it only proper that she attend tonight's celebration.

The Gotham Book Mart, on New York's West Forty-seventh Street, welcomes members of the James Joyce Society into a room at the rear of the shop. Kate was somewhat surprised to discover how many men were present—not only prominent Joyce scholars, but young men, the sort one least expected to encounter at the meetings of a literary society. But the reason was not far to seek. Writing their doctoral dissertations on Joyce, they hoped to come upon some secret, still undiscovered clue in the labyrinth of his works which would make their academic fortunes. For Joyce had by now, in the United States, added to all his other magic powers that of being able to bestow an academic reputation.

Kate was not a member of the James Joyce Society, but the name of Samuel Lingerwell assured her entrance, a welcome, a glass of the

Swiss wine Joyce had especially favored. One thing is bloody certain, Kate thought after a time. When I pick a graduate student to help me with the Lingerwell papers, he will have to be most unJoycean, unLaurentian, unModern altogether. Someone who will not be searching for his own fortune among dear Sam's literary remains. On the whole, a Jane Austen devotee, I should imagine. Someone who calls her "Jane." I shall ask Grace Knole to recommend a likely candidate.

Which explains how Emmet Crawford came to spend the summer at Araby.

1

The Boarding House

"KATE," Reed Amhearst said, disentangling his long legs from the small car, "what on earth are you doing here? If you had decided to embrace the rural life, you might, in decency, have let me know. It's a great shock to return from Europe and find you established on some deserted hilltop in the Berkshires. What is the matter with that cow?"

Before Kate could answer, a red cat tore around the corner of the house with a brown dog in hot pursuit. "More of the local fauna," Kate said, in what she hoped were conciliatory tones. "Come inside and tell me all about New Scotland Yard. The cow is bellowing for her calf."

"Has she lost it?"

"It was taken away from her; she'll forget it in a day or two. How was England?"

Reed followed Kate into the huge vaulted living room, at one end of which chairs were grouped about a large fire. What certainly looked like a bar stood close by. Reed was proceeding toward the fireplace in a decorous manner when, from a nearby stairway he had not noticed, there burst as though catapulted into their midst a smallish boy. Reed pondered the possibilities of catapulting him back, and reluctantly dismissed them.

"See if you can answer this," the smallish male creature said, ignoring Reed. "Which is faster, bleeding to death or suffocating?"

"Suffocating, I should think," Kate ventured. Reed stared in fascination.

"You're wrong, wrong, wrong. I knew you'd be. Just remember this." The boy's gestures at this point indicated that Reed, too, might benefit from his advice. "If one man is drowning, and another is bleeding from a severed artery, work on the bleeding man first. It takes nine minutes longer to die from lack of oxygen than to bleed to death. How'd you like to shoot a few foul shots, Kate?"

"At the moment I'm engaged," Kate said. "Where is William?"

"Arguing with Emmet about some guy called James Joyce."

"Well, tell William to stop arguing about James Joyce and shoot some fouls with you. I take it today's essay is complete?"

"O.K., I'll get William," the boy returned, departing with an alacrity that suggested an unwillingness to dwell upon the subject of today's essay.

"Kate . . ." Reed began.

"Sit you down," Kate said. "Let me get you a drink and try to explain the whole thing."

"I've only come for a few days," Reed told her, accepting the chair. "This sounds as though it might carry us through to next Groundhog Day. Why didn't you tell me you were moving to the country? Who is that boy? Who is William? Who is Emmet? Not to mention the maternally stricken cow, the fiery cat and the pursuing dog. And who is James Joyce?"

"Certainly you know who James Joyce is?"

"If you mean the Irish author of several indecipherable books, I know who he is. But given the extraordinary aspects of this establishment, he might be the gardener. For God's sake, sit down and explain. I return from only six months in England to find you transformed, transported and transfigured."

"You just added that last one to make the series come out right."

"I certainly never expected to see you living in the same house with a small boy. What ages are Emmet and William?" Reed asked, as though suddenly struck with the awful thought that Kate had undertaken the housing of small boys in large numbers.

"In their middle or late twenties, I suppose. William Lenehan is tutoring Leo, he of the various deaths, and Emmet Crawford is going over some papers for me. The cat belongs to Emmet, and the dog belongs to the gardener, whose name is not James Joyce but Mr. Pasquale. The cow belongs to the farmer down the road who uses our land. Leo is my nephew. Cheers."

"Well, despite a three-hour drive I had not anticipated, and sur-roundings I could not have imagined, it's good to see you, Kate."

"And you. In the present circumstances, I might even risk hy-perbole and say you're a sight for sore eyes."

"You're tired of all those cows; I'm not even complimented. I've missed you, Kate. In England I kept thinking . . ."

"Kate," interrupted a young man from the doorway. "If that woman is permitted entrance into this house, I shall have to tender my resignation. Reluctantly, to be sure, since the collection is a fas-cinating one. There's a letter—But I cannot have that woman hanging over me as though I were a pie and some extravagantly exciting news about you were the plum she was in hopes of pulling forth."

"Emmet, you must realize that country people are incurably cu-rious, like cats. It's only urbanites who can ignore their neighbors. Tell Mrs. Bradford Leo is my illegitimate child, that I murdered his father, and that I'm setting up a polyandrous colony here in the hope of starting a new religion. That ought to keep her quiet for a while."

"The only thing that would keep that woman quiet is a bullet in the brain, and even then I'd think her lips would go on moving out of sheer force of habit. Her excuse for being here, incidentally, is to borrow some vinegar."

"Can't Mrs. Monzoni lend her some vinegar?"

"Mrs. Monzoni wouldn't lend Mary Bradford a wet paper towel. You had better go and cope. Why not tell her I've just served ten years for cannibalism, and am not to be trusted when aroused?"

"Oh, very well. Reed, may I introduce Emmet Crawford. Mr. Reed Amhearst." Kate departed with evident reluctance, followed by the palpable sympathy of Emmet.

"Who is Mrs. Monzoni?" Reed asked.

"The cook. Have you read the correspondence Joyce had with his English publishers in 1908? It's enough to make a cat cry. Imag-ine thinking *Dubliners* obscene because it suggested that Edward VII was less than a paragon of virtue, and used the word 'bloody' on two occasions. Of course, Lingerwell changed all that, bless his coura-geous heart. He also did the *Portrait* and the *Rainbow*."

"Do you mean he was a painter?"

"Who?"

"Lingerwell."

"A painter? Why on earth should a painter publish the *Por-trait*?"

"I can't imagine. Mr. Crawford, I have the unhappy sense of not having understood a single circumstance or statement since I first drove up that unduly precipitous hill . . .''

"I bet it's something in winter . . .''

"To be frank, I have no interest in its condition during either the temperate or intemperate seasons. I am trying to understand what you're talking about. How does one *do a Rainbow*?''

"Aren't you from the Library of Congress?''

"Certainly not. I am from the office of the district attorney of the County of New York, if my profession happens to be germane to this extraordinary discussion.''

"Sorry. The Library of Congress people have been rather camping on our doorstep. Have you come to make an arrest?''

"I have come, I had hoped I had come, to pay a visit. I am a friend of Miss Fansler's.''

"That will be nice for Kate. William and I do rather stick to hermeneutics, theological and nontheological, and Leo's conversation alternates between basketball and the grimmer aspects of first aid. Well, perhaps I may assume the departure of Mary Bradford and return to my Odyssean labors. See you at dinner.'' He wandered out to leave Reed balancing the relative advantages of another drink and an immediate departure. With the return of Kate, the scales tilted decidedly toward the drink.

"She's gone,'' Kate said, "though not without collecting a bottle of vinegar, expressing inchoate horror at the use of wine vinegar at twice the price of ordinary, asking if she could borrow the house for her garden club's tea, informing me she was busier than anyone else on earth, and wondering, with barely concealed salaciousness, what were the functions of the two young men in this household. I have become very disillusioned about the rural character. I suspect that Wordsworth, when he took to the country, never spoke to anyone but Dorothy and Coleridge, and perhaps an occasional leech gatherer. Tell me about England.''

"Kate! *What are you doing here*?''

At that moment there arose from outside the cry as of a pack of wolves about to make the kill. "I forbear to ask what that is,'' Reed said wearily.

"I expect,'' Kate said, walking in a leisurely fashion to the window, "that is the Araby Boys' Camp arriving for a wienie roast. Reed, would you like to take me to dinner at a not very reputable hash-joint-cum-bar in a nearby town? I warn you that they play the jukebox constantly, but the surroundings might be more easily ignored."

"I never dreamed," Reed said, leading Kate firmly from the room, "that I would look forward to a jukebox as to the Sirens singing." Reed closed the Volkswagen door on Kate, walked round to the driver's side, and again folded his long legs in place beneath the steering wheel. He turned the tiny car around and burst down the driveway so precipitously that Kate could well imagine the look of admiration directed at their back by numberless awestruck boys.

"Why have you set up a boarding house?" Reed asked, when they were seated in the booth. "When I left you, you were a more or less rational associate professor of English. Have you lost your senses, your money or your grip? I have seldom been so alarmed about anyone."

"It's not *really* a boarding house, of course, it just looks that way at a superficial glance. Actually, my whole summer situation can be summed up as a fortuitous concatenation of improbable events. Which is to say that life has this in common with prizefighting: if you've received a belly blow, it's likely to be followed by a right to the jaw."

"I didn't know you were fond of boys."

"I am *not* fond of boys. If you mean Leo, he is the right to the jaw. The point is, Reed, you simply weren't here when I got around to the thought of consulting you. Surely there's enough crime in New York without your rocketing off to England."

"England has gone a long way toward solving the problem of crime caused by drug addiction. They have *not* gone a long way toward solving the problem of eccentric behavior—in fact, I think they invented it. If Leo is the right to the jaw, may we begin by discussing, according to your exceedingly ill-informed and inappropriate figure from prizefighting, the belly blow?"

"I don't think you knew Sam Lingerwell—I'll have the veal cutlets and spaghetti; I wouldn't exactly *recommend* it, but it's distinctly superior to the chicken pie."

"Two veal cutlets and spaghetti," Reed told the waitress. "I heard of Mr. Lingerwell for the first time this afternoon; he was mentioned by Emmet Crawford in the midst of some extraordinary story about Edinburgh."

"Dublin, surely. James Joyce."

"You're right. Dublin. Curiouser and curiouser."

"Sam Lingerwell died last fall, at the ripe and wonderful age of ninety. He sat down in a chair, lit up a cigar, and started to read a book by Sylvia Townsend Warner. They found him in the morning. I went to school with Lingerwell's daughter, and in some way I continued to be friends with him and his wife long after his daughter joined a convent."

"A convent?"

"I'll come to that part of the story in a moment. Sam, and the Calypso Press which he started—well, you've got to read some of Alfred Knopf's memoirs of publishing in his early days to know what I mean. Sam was one of the grand old men of publishing; there are scarcely any of them left. The sort who knew literature, had guts, and would have thought you were hallucinating had you mentioned the present tribal customs of Madison Avenue. They all went back to a time when it was possible to go into the publishing business without a million dollars, a taste for cocktails, a publicity manager and fourteen computers. All right, I'll spare you the speech about the good old days. Suffice it to say, Sam was the best there was, and in those days that was pretty good. He was the American publisher who had the guts, the taste or whatever it took to publish James Joyce and D. H. Lawrence and lots of others, English and American, whom we now consider classics, but who were just thought to be dirty naturalists back around the First World War."

"Ah, I begin to understand what 'rainbow' Mr. Crawford and I were discussing."

"The *Rainbow* was later, of course, but I'm glad to hear you're getting the idea. At the moment, we're all thinking more about Joyce. Emmet, with occasional grunts of encouragement from me, is trying to sort out Sam's letters by author, so that we can decide whose correspondence ought to go where, which may explain why Dublin keeps coming up in the conversation. *Dubliners* was the first book of Joyce's anybody published. Now don't let me wander on to Joyce; one just keeps going, getting more and more complicated with each sentence and never arriving at any conclusion. Where was I?"

"The good old days of publishing."

"Ah, yes. Well, Sam had been publishing marvelous books and corresponding with now famous authors for something like fifty years, and needless to say he'd accumulated quite a valuable library and collection of papers. In recent years he'd let people use some of the letters he could get his hands on for collections and so forth, but it was clear that something had to be done to organize his papers and library, so—two years ago he purchased the house in which you were so shocked to find me today, moved all his literary and other belongings up here, and prepared to follow in due course. In the meantime, he traveled. I doubt, really, that he would ever have moved up here. Sam liked to joke about what he would do in his 'old age.' ''

"Where was his wife?"

"She died a number of years ago. Sam had a fine life, friends, interesting occasions and good conversation, but his family life was a sad one. He and his wife had two daughters; one died of cancer in her early twenties, and the other, Veronica, the one I went to school with, became a nun. Sam was an agnostic humanist, like most of the intellectuals of his generation, and her conversion and all was a great blow to him. Still he saw her from time to time and they were on good terms. Sam left everything to Veronica in his will, including the house."

"How did *you* get involved in all this?"

"That *is* the point, I do realize that. I'm sorry this explanation is so long, particularly since, once you understand the background to the story, it doesn't become a bit more intelligible, really. As I said, Sam died. He didn't have a funeral, not believing in these matters. The *Times* obituary mentioned Veronica's convent, and I wrote her a note. A short while later I had a reply, and she asked to come and see me."

"Bringing with her an eight-year-old boy named Leo whom she had acquired at the nearest orphanage."

"Reed, you're not paying attention. I told you Leo was my nephew. There is no connection between Leo and Veronica."

"Of course not. Silly of me to have thought it. Do we risk the blueberry pie or just settle for coffee? Good. Veronica, you were saying, came to see you."

"There's no need to tell you this if you're going to be petulant."

"I petulant? I have the world's sweetest disposition, as who knows better than you. It is only that, as I motored up here in my little Volkswagen, I pictured talking to you by the fire in peace and quiet, instead of which I find you in the midst of a positive holocaust of male activity. Do you suppose if we went back now the fireside would be deserted? At least all those dreadful boys may have shrieked their way off into the night, stuffed with wienies."

"Reed, don't you care for children?"

"Not in the least."

"Odd, I never knew that."

"I would have told you, as the maid said when resigning from the house where they kept alligators, but I didn't think the question would come up."

"Well, well. I'm afraid my hearth will not yet be sufficiently deserted. Shall we take a walk?"

"Since I don't appear to have a choice in the matter, I acquiesce with my usual grace." Reed paid the bill, and they walked into the evening. "Do continue," Reed said. "Veronica came to see you . . ."

"Yes. She explained that her father had left all his possessions including his library and papers, and the 'boarding house,' as you call it, to her—and would I help her to determine exactly what *was* in the collection so that it might be best disposed of. I pointed out that someone who knew the market value of these things would be more to the point, but it seems she's not interested in money, but in getting the books and papers to the places where they will do the most good. She had already been besieged by universities, the Library of Congress, and so forth and so on."

"Was there any particular reason why she should come to you?"

"No reason, or—if your mind happens to work that way—every reason. I knew and loved her father, who had gone out of his way to be kind to me on many occasions; I think she understood that I would welcome a chance to serve him, even posthumously. There aren't, I suppose, many people who realize that to provide an opportunity for service may be in itself a service. Do you follow me?"

"Exactly, as you know."

"Also, there weren't really all that many people she could go to. All she suggested, of course, was that I take a couple of days to look through things—families with collections of papers rarely have a clue as to the work involved in sorting them out. You know about the Boswell papers found in a croquet box in an old castle?" Reed shook his head.

"Remind me to tell you, the next conversation but one. It became clear that the collection ought to be sorted, and that it would take more than just me to do it. I began, in the vaguest way, to fool with the idea of spending the summer here instead of dancing off to Europe."

"I begin to see, as through a glass darkly."

"A cloud no bigger than a man's hand. That cloud was soon joined by another, Leo."

"I wait, ears eagerly attuned, for an explanation of Leo. To be

frank, I have never fathomed the mystery of your familial connections.''

"Familial connections are always difficult to explain, and impossible to sever. Not that one really wants to, I suppose. However
trying one's family, there is some call of blood to blood which one
is somehow impelled to answer. I have nothing in common with any
member of my family, and yet in crisis, personal or national, one
always rallies round.''

"What is a national crisis?''

"Christmas.''

"Oh, I see.''

"This crisis, however, was personal. Leo is the middle one of
three children, and apparently all middle children exist precariously
upon the earth, threatened from above and below, so to speak, and
trembling with insecurity, which often takes the form of obstinance,
violence and pure laziness. I don't claim to understand why, if you
can be beautifully secure thinking of yourself as an older child, or a
younger child, you can't say to yourself 'I am the middle child' and
go on to something else, but then child psychology has always been
beyond me. In any event, Leo was doing poorly at school, badly at
home, and indifferently at Group.''

"Group?''

"Reed, I really think you're *trying* to be perverse. Surely you
know what Group is—didn't you go to one on Saturdays when you
were a little boy in New York?''

"I was *not* a little boy in New York. I was a little boy in Bal-
timore, Maryland.''

"Oh. A backward community, obviously. Groups are to knit up
the loose ends of offsprings' hours when parents might otherwise go
mad. For a walloping sum, Group takes your child to the park, ice
skating, or climbing on the Palisades. Leo did not care for Group.
Personally, I see this as a sign of clear intellectual ability, but Leo's
parents, and the child guidance counselor they consulted, looked on
it in a different light.

"All this, of course, would have had nothing in the world to do
with me,'' Kate continued, ''if fate, which the Greeks understood so
well and we so poorly, had not taken a hand. Leo's parents decided
to give a family dinner party to celebrate their wedding anniversary,
and in an unfortunate moment of familial sentimentality, I consented
to attend. All three of my brothers are constantly trying to draw me
into their various social circles, though they have, thank God, rather

given up introducing me to socially acceptable bachelors. I'm getting older, the bachelors are becoming more inveterate in their bachelor-hood, and anyway I can never be trusted to behave properly. Leo's father is the youngest brother. Reed! What an angel you are to listen to all this. The truth is, I guess, I've been rather lacking a sympathetic ear.''

"Is this youngest brother as stuffy as the rest?"

"Stuffier. But he's also the one who invests money for me, and helps me with my income tax, so I've developed more of a modus vivendi with him than with the others. What possessed me, at the night of their anniversary dinner, to mention Sam Lingerwell and his library and his house in the country, I cannot imagine. True, I was graveled for lack of matter in conversation there, as always, but I am still inclined to blame the gods. However, the fact that I might be spending the summer in the country implanted itself in the not par-ticularly fervent imagination of my brother, and a week later I got an invitation to lunch.

"This in itself," Kate said, stopping to light a cigarette, and perching herself uncertainly on a tree stump, "was ominous. He said he had a favor to ask of me, and hoped I would lunch with him at White's, where they serve Beefeater martinis for which, he remem-bered, I had a fondness. It would never occur to my brother to come uptown and have lunch at a place convenient for me. Favor or no favor, he works and I—well, he has never really faced the fact that I work, and anyway, what do professors *do*? With my usual dexterity, I leapt to the conclusion that it was a question of money. It has always bothered my brother that although I inherited exactly as much money as he did, I have been content to live off the income, and let my stocks grow, or divide, or whatever it is stocks are always doing. As long as I never actually touched my capital, my brother couldn't really complain if I wasn't trying as hard as I ought to be to double my portfolio or turn over my investments or any of those obscure financial operations. But I thought, well, probably he's gone and dis-covered he needs a little ready cash, and he's going to try to negotiate some complicated thing. I went, prepared to have two martinis and to extract every ounce of satisfaction from his monetary problems.

"I couldn't have been more wrong." Kate made a little hole in the earth and buried her cigarette end. "My brother is very rich in-deed, and probably would have been startled to death to know I'd even thought he would be interested in my slender funds. He, need-less to say, has doubled *his* inheritance many times over, as well as earning all sorts of money in that Wall Street law firm of his. It transpired, when I was barely through my first martini, that he wanted to talk about Leo.

"What it all came down to was that Leo was behind in school, recalcitrant when he wasn't aggressive, and he needed a summer devoted to being tutored, *not* being sent away to a camp, and living in a household of which he would be a single juvenile member. In short, my brother, putting together Leo's problems, the advice from the guidance counselor, and my unfortunate confidence about my summer plans, suggested that I take Leo for the summer, complete with tutor, give him that sort of 'I take you for granted and like you just as you are' treatment which appears to be my manner with children—the truth is, if forced to talk to children, I talk to them exactly as I talk to anyone else—and see if we might get Leo back on the rails. My brother had promised to take his wife to Europe for the summer, and I gathered, without exactly being told, that any disappointment in this matter would be likely to render my brother's life uncomfortable for a considerable period of time. He offered to pay for the tutor, whom I would hire, to lend me his elegant car, and to bear the expenses of the whole 'boarding house' operation."

"So you agreed?"

"Of course not. I absolutely declined. I told my brother that he and his wife could jolly well take a house themselves and minister to Leo. I finished my two Beefeater martinis, my lunch, capped it off with an excellent brandy, and departed in a cloud of righteous indignation."

"Kate," Reed said, "you are the most maddening woman I have ever met. I can't imagine, for example, why I, who could be happily resting in an air-conditioned apartment in New York, should be walking along a country road with you, being devoured by mosquitoes and uncomfortably aware, from the tickling in my nose, that I am about to begin a prolonged attack of hay fever."

"One doesn't get hay fever in July."

"Well, whatever one gets in July, I'm getting. There! You see." Reed sneezed violently. "Yet here I am, slapping at mosquitoes, hating the country, and an exile from even such house as you have in it. How did you end up with Leo, for God's holy sake?"

"He ran away and came to me. It became quite clear that everyone was trying so hard to understand that he longed to be in the company of someone who didn't understand him and wouldn't even try. I sent him back home, of course, but I promised he might spend the summer with me. My brother, with the mulishness that marks all simple-minded people, was outraged that Leo should have run away to me. Anyhow, that's how the 'boarding house' came so over-whelmingly into existence.''

2

An Encounter

REED, who had fallen into what fitful sleep he could find between the discomforts of mosquito bites, sneezing and confusion, was awakened the next morning by a boy's voice saying, quite distinctly, almost it seemed in his ear: "Hurray! I got the bitch, I'm sure I did!" This was followed by an older voice answering in stern tones: "You must *not* use the word 'bitch.' As I have tried to explain, there is language one uses with one's associates, and language one uses with one's elders, and these overlap only about fifty percent of the time. 'Bitch' is *not* an incidence of overlapping, except when applied to the female of the canine species. But," the voice added, in lower tones, "I do believe you nailed her."

Reed sat up in bed. Probably it was a dream. He found his watch on the night table and consulted it: five forty-five. Impossible. Yet the second hand of his grandfather's excellent watch continued to plod its way round its small dial. This was it, the absolute, unarguable end. He would climb into his car and be gone as soon as he could capture a cup of coffee, Kate or no Kate. However fond he was of Kate, there were experiences he was not prepared to undergo. Kate— Reed lay back for a moment and thought about Kate. A shout from some female in what seemed the throes of a temper tantrum could be heard at a certain distance. Not Kate: an unpleasant voice. Kate's voice . . . Reed was asleep.

When he awoke again his grandfather's watch said ten minutes to ten, and all was golden silence. Perversely, he wondered what had happened to everybody. Dressed, he tiptoed into the living room: deserted. No one burst into the room or catapulted down the steps. Relaxing slightly, Reed moved on into the dining room, where he found a place set, with a sign saying "For you" sitting neatly on the plate. A glass of orange juice stood on the sideboard in a bowl of chopped ice; next to it stood an electric coffeepot, a toaster, some bread and a box of cold cereal. Propped against the cereal was a sign saying "No eggs served after nine-thirty." Grinning, Reed carried his orange juice to the table and picked up the newspaper lying by his plate. A newspaper in the country! Imagine! His astonishment turned to bemusement as he noticed it was yesterday's *Berkshire Eagle*. On it Kate had written: "In case reading a paper at breakfast is a necessity." Reed settled down to the *Berkshire Eagle*.

The silence of the household persisted through breakfast and followed him out onto the lawn. It was one of those days, Reed decided, when even the person most persistently skeptical of rural charms succumbs to the conviction that the creation of the earth was not an absolute nonsense. A hummingbird, apparently motionless in midair, darted from flower to flower. Reed gazed happily about him.

The guest room in which he had spent the night looked out over the back of the house; a fence, with a gate in it, ran perhaps six feet from his window. The voices he had overheard must have been leaning on the gate. Who, Reed wondered, was the bitch they had "got"? Turning from the gate, he followed a path which led to a driveway and thence to a road. He would take a walk. He paused in the road to light his pipe and muse on the peace of rural life. Apart from the telephone poles and electric wires nothing had changed, he was certain, in a hundred years. On a distant hillside, cows moved in the sunlight. Reed decided he quite liked cows forming part of the landscape on a distant hillside. Puffing at his pipe, he thrust his hands in his pockets and started down the road. Any illusions he might have had about a rural universe untouched by the industrial revolution were immediately shattered by four simultaneous uproars. First he heard the roar of jet engines, and, looking up, saw the white trail of what was probably the eleven o'clock jet from Boston to Chicago. On the road an old jalopy roared by, apparently with a souped-up engine, going, Reed was prepared to swear, eighty miles an hour, and driven, to judge from the glimpse he managed to get, by an adolescent whose arrogance, together with his engine's exhaust, floated out behind the car in a general pollution of the atmosphere. On a field to Reed's left, a tractor started up, and down the road from him a giant milk truck performed some mechanized maneuver. Reed retreated into the driveway.

Perhaps on the whole it would be better to go through the gate and down across the fields. He unlatched the gate, walked through it, latched it again (for the field was clearly for cows, though none were presently inhabiting it), and started to stroll. He was immediately joined by the large brown dog, but its aim seemed companionship rather than violence. Reed again lit his pipe, thrust his hands into his pockets, and stepped forward into an enormous mound of fresh cow dung.

His remarks, happily audible to none but the brown dog, were certainly such as might have been heard on the countryside a hundred years ago, perhaps on a similar occasion. Some aspects of rural life were clearly unchanged. These did not, however, include the extraordinary machine which, headed in Reed's direction across a field of hay, seemed to be making the most frightful clatter and flinging huge objects into the air. With a shrug indicating that he would have to throw out the shoes in any case, Reed set off across the fields in the direction of the machine. The dog, who considered that some union had been consummated by the occasion of Reed's swearing, trotted along.

Together man and dog approached the machine, which seemed, with some amazing mechanical awareness, to have seen them coming and to have paused in its flinging operations. As they approached, however, Reed could determine that if mechanization had reached farming, automation had not: the machine was being pulled by a tractor, and the tractor was being driven by a man. He awaited Reed's approach in an attitude of pleasant anticipation.

"Stepped in it, eh?" he asked when Reed was within earshot.

"Could you see all the way from there?"

"Just could tell by the way you hopped about. Visiting Miss Fansler?"

"Temporarily," Reed answered, amused to see that curiosity extended to the males hereabouts. It occurred to him that this might be the husband of the disliked Mary Bradford who came to borrow vinegar.

"My name's Bradford," the man on the tractor said, in confirmation of this thought.

"Amhearst," Reed answered.

"That's the name of the town where I went to college," Bradford said. "U. Mass. Agricultural School. Are you surprised that a farmer went to college?"

"I am," Reed said frankly. "I thought farmers considered book learning nonsense."

"Those that do go broke. Farming's changed more in the last twenty years than in a thousand years before that."

"I can see that." Reed pointed to the baler.

"That is quite a machine," Bradford said. "It picks up the hay, pushes it through that machine there, which binds it into bales and wraps them with string, and then tosses the bales into that wagon. When the wagon's full, I use my other tractor to pull it back to the barn, where the bales are put on an elevator which carries them to the hayloft."

"What do you do if the machine breaks down?"

"Fix it. A farmer who can't fix his own machinery is in trouble. Want to see this thing work? Hop up."

This seemed to Reed, who was absolutely nonathletic, like an invitation to commit suicide. But Bradford pointed to the rod connecting the tractor with the baler, expecting Reed to stand on that. Reed complied.

When they started off, Reed's attention was absorbed, first in holding on, and then in wondering how soon his teeth would be knocked out of his head. It was only after they had traversed the field several times that he managed to watch the baler: the hay had been previously cut and turned over to lie in rows. The baler scooped it up, bound it, tied it up, and spat it out. Amazing. The brown dog trotted alongside, appearing in imminent danger of being run over. But all these rural creatures had adapted to the machine as readily as they had adapted to the other changes in their environment.

"Yet I," Reed thought, "am not adapting. In fact, I'll probably develop a permanent tremor."

Bradford finally stopped the machine as it appeared to be about to penetrate a barbed-wire fence; Reed, shaken into indifference, rather hoped it would. But Bradford handled his machine as though it were a horse whose spirit he admired. As Reed stepped down he greeted the earth, cow dung and all, with a silent prayer of exaltation. He had received and met some challenge during his ride on the baler. Reed lit his pipe.

"What did they use for baling when you were a boy?" he asked.

"Horses, a pitchfork, and three men, I guess," Bradford answered. "But I was a boy in Scarsdale and don't really know."

"Scarsdale!"

"Yes. My father was a lawyer. I like farming. My wife's from around here—her family swam over in front of the Mayflower with the painter in their teeth. Beautiful here, isn't it?" The last phrase bore no shade of sarcasm. Reed followed Bradford's gaze. It was beautiful. "It's most beautiful on a tractor, from the middle of the fields. Come for another ride someday." Bradford waved his hand and started up the tractor. Reed walked back across the field, trying first one muscle and then another, in anticipation of the ache he knew to be inevitable.

When he had shut the gate behind him, he saw Kate, reading in a lounge chair under a tree. "Does the schedule permit of conversation now?" he asked.

"It had better. Mary Bradford is on her way to bring back the vinegar and partake of a cup of coffee."

"I, too," said Reed, collapsing into a chair, "have had an encounter. With Mary Bradford's husband."

"I know that already, you urban innocent. Mary Bradford saw you leap on the machinery, apparently waited to see if your intentions were homicidal, and determining that they weren't, decided to find out what you had said to her husband before he got the chance to tell her himself."

"You make her sound a most attractive lady. Has she no redeeming features—salt of the earth, perhaps, a natural bonhomie, a certain physical vigor?"

"Most of her physical vigor, as you shall soon hear, is in her voice. To hear her tell it, nobody works as hard as she, nobody contributes so much to society and receives so little from it, nobody has so much rectitude, propriety and good old-fashioned morality. Since her golden rule is 'Do unto Mary Bradford as Mary Bradford would like you to do unto her,' it is difficult to see whence her high moral tone. But don't let me prejudice you. What did you talk about with Brad?"

"As it happens, I was so busy having my teeth shaken out of my head, and observing the wonders of mechanized farming, that we didn't say very much. My shoes are covered with cow dung, and my spirit is oppressed."

"Reed. Have we got you down with our noisy ways? As I hope you could see this morning, our household is not really as mad as it seemed yesterday. This *is* peaceful, isn't it?"

"All events have conspired to rob me of my self-respect. I left New York yesterday feeling rested, vigorous and able, in my own way, to cope. Ever since I chugged up your beastly driveway I have been reminded of my ignorance, dipped in cow dung, made to appear effete next to some sunburned monster of masculinity on a tractor, and finally doomed, it seems, to listen to the chatter of the sunburned monster's wife."

"You don't fool me for a minute," Kate said. "Your masculinity and self-respect are no more in danger from today's events than they have ever been. You may be suffering from a surplus of fresh air—I know the feeling. Reed, I think what I cherish most about you is that calm assurance that does not need to prove itself. As to the cow dung, although it may be ruining a good pair of shoes, its price is above rubies and the envy of all gardeners. Pasquale will scrape it off your shoes and put it around a flower."

"Kate, the truth of the matter is, I had rather hoped . . ." But the sudden entrance of a car into the driveway dashed the hope or left it unexpressed. "Do you mean she drove up from just down the road?" Reed asked in amazement.

"No one ever walks in the country, except city folk. Hardworking farmers have no time for such foolishness. Hello, Mary," Kate called, getting to her feet. "May I introduce Mr. Amhearst. Mrs. Bradford."

"I guessed it was you in the guest room this morning when I came to get the cows. You can always tell when there's someone in the guest room because the windows are open then, and the blinds down, which of course they aren't when the room's empty. Ah, I thought, Kate Fansler has another guest. I bet it's a young man, she prefers men guests. I prefer women, who make their beds and don't expect to be waited on hand and foot, but then Kate has all those servants, so that probably isn't a consideration with her—I do envy people with help, but of course they all want to be paid a fortune and not do a thing—that dreadful Mrs. Pasquale down the road came in to help me once, talking, talking all day long, and I ended up doing all the work myself. No point to that."

Reed, who had risen, scarcely knew which part of this diatribe to respond to, if, indeed, any response was necessary.

"I hear you're a district attorney," Mary Bradford said.

Reed now stared at her in total amazement. He caught Kate's eye and saw her shrug, a shrug which said, "I didn't tell her."

"Shall we go in the house and have a cup of coffee?" said Kate, moving firmly toward the door.

"I really shouldn't," Mary Bradford said, following her. "I've baskets of raspberries to make into jam, and these days, of course, I'm my own hired man; then, if I don't get to clean the upstairs soon, we'll simply have to move out of it, and Brad, of course, is worse than the children, throwing his clothes around—I always get a sock right up in the vacuum cleaner. 'Look,' I say, 'I'm not the only person around here capable of picking things up . . .' " Reed paused on the back porch to remove his shoes and socks and entered the house with bare feet. His normal impulse would have been to go to his room for another pair of shoes and socks, but the thought of allowing his naked feet to become grist to Mary Bradford's mill was too strong. He began to understand the effect Mary Bradford had on people. The woman positively tempted one to behave in an improper manner in order to provide her with material. This was an effect of undue propriety, shading off into prurience, which Reed had not personally observed before, and it fascinated him.

They settled themselves around the dining room table: everyone soon had a cup of coffee. Reed had the strange sensation of taking part in some aboriginal ritual. He wiggled his toes quite happily, and wondered what on earth Mary Bradford would find to say next.

"I call it shocking and improper behavior," she said, accepting one of Kate's cigarettes. "I've given up smoking," she added, lighting it. "Naturally, it's nobody's business what a man does in his own house, I suppose, but he rides up the road with them in a convertible, bold as you please, and what goes *on* in a big house like that on a weekend, all those girls. An orgy. I wouldn't be surprised," she added with a significant look, "if there were drugs. Drink of course goes without saying. One morning all those people are going to get up to do something, and find they can't stagger further than the nearest bottle."

"Are we discussing someone I know?" Reed asked in a voice straining so hard for innocence it sounded simpering to his own ears.

"The district attorney's office of Berkshire County ought to know about him," Mary Bradford said with emphasis. "But of course they haven't even got time to pick up these people who speed down the road, going fifty miles an hour right past a sign saying 'Children. Go Slow.' I have to lock my children in the house when the summer people come, I don't mind telling you."

"The boy I saw rocketing by this morning didn't look like 'summer people' to me," Reed said.

"That white trash," Mary Bradford snorted, identifying the car in question with no difficulty. "A new baby every year, and not enough sense or money to care for the ones they have. Who wouldn't have eighteen children if it weren't a question of buying them shoes?"

"How many do you have?" Reed asked. He was curious to discover if Mary Bradford ever stopped talking long enough to answer a question. Kate merely sat back, smiling. Clearly she had been through all this several times before.

"Two," Mary Bradford said. "And they're properly dressed and not allowed to run around picking up whatever they take a fancy to. Of course, once that camp opens and all those lazy parents who send their children to the day camp come rushing up the road, it's impossible to cross over to our barn safely. But then, we're just farmers, and no one worries about farmers. You have to learn how to go on welfare, or get some union to support you, to succeed these days. Well, I must get back and make Brad's lunch. He'll just have to have peanut butter sandwiches. With all those raspberries to do there isn't time to prepare anything." She talked her way out of the house and into her car, pausing to make statements and then to digress from them at extraordinary length until, when she had finally backed the car out, Reed felt that he had survived an air raid, and that someone ought to sound the all clear.

"What sort of meal," Reed asked, "is lunch around here? If you think you catch a note of trepidation in my voice, it is definitely there. Kate, my sweet, I long for you to return to civilization, and I shall hope to commandeer hours of your time when you do, but I am afraid that I'm too frail a being altogether to withstand the rigors of the rural life. I don't know which is more horrifying, really, being bounced about on a tractor, wallowing in manure, or listening to the conversation of that angel of light from down the road. Not only is she malicious and suffering from logorrhea, she doesn't even conclude a thought. Who is that sybaritic chap down the road with the girls and the orgies?"

Kate laughed. "A very amusing character, as it happens, who's coming to dinner tonight. He's stopped in several times with invitations, and I finally proffered one. Just as you insist on trotting around in your bare feet, giving Mary Bradford loads to say when next she shares a cup of coffee with a neighbor, so Mr. Mulligan goes out of his way to act like an inebriated playboy. As a matter of fact, I've talked with him long enough to gather that he's a full professor of English and has published a good many books of literary criticism. Please don't go, Reed. Stay at least until tomorrow, meet Mr. Mulligan, and let us try to restore your faith in the countryside. It has its charms, you know. Open fires, silence, long lonely walks, beauty that sometimes takes one's breath away.''

"I noticed the beauty on my tractor ride. Would you care to take one of those lonely walks? As a matter of fact, I set one foot on the road this morning and was nearly run down by the industrial revolution.''

"Let's take some sandwiches, which I promise will not be peanut butter, and have lunch at the top of that hill. The brown dog will probably accompany us, but otherwise it should be quite peaceful. Of course, Mary Bradford will undoubtedly see us go, and conclude The Worst.''

"I shall look on it as a moral obligation to render one of Mary Bradford's suspicions correct. I feel quite inspired. All right, all right, I'm going to get on some shoes.''

"And I shall get the sandwiches.''

"Well,'' said Reed, "I am prepared to stay until tomorrow morning, reconsidering the possibilities of the rural life. I suppose Leo will join us for dinner?''

"And Emmet and William, but without the rest of the Araby Boys' Camp. Leo will report on The World, as passed by Mr. Artifoni, who runs the A.B.C., but otherwise, it won't be too absolutely terrible. Wait and see. Mr. Mulligan is nice, and Emmet really quite interesting in his effete, and William in his bluff, way.''

"What I look forward to is spending the afternoon on the hills in my way. You don't suppose we'll meet herds of cows do you, or,'' he added, "a bull?''

"No bulls around here.''

"Then whence the calves? Have they developed parthenogenesis?''

"They have developed artificial insemination.''

"There is no doubt about it, country living is decadent, immoral and soul-annihilating. Does the brown dog have a name? We appear to have become friends.''

"Brownie.''

"And what is the name of the red cat?''

"Cassandra. She belongs to Emmet. But she is usually called Pussens."

"What was *that*?" Reed stopped with one foot on the porch.

"Someone shooting woodchucks."

"Do you think they are likely to shoot us by mistake?"

"Well, they have telescopic sights on the guns, and presumably they can tell us from a woodchuck."

"Kate."

"Yes."

"Hurry up and make those damn sandwiches. If we're going to be shot, let us die in one another's arms."

"We are going," Kate said, "for a walk."

"I wonder," Reed mused, "what Mary Bradford thinks goes on in a rural orgy. Well, at least I know that if you're drowning and bleeding to death all at once, I shall apply a tourniquet immediately and wait for the proper moment to begin artificial respiration. I must remember to ask Leo at dinner how long Mr. Artifoni says it takes to die of a bullet wound."

3

Counterparts

REED and Kate sat at opposite ends of the dinner table; from time to time their eyes met, but for the most part they listened to the exchange between those on either side. It had been a good walk, a good afternoon. The cocktail hour had been, if not shattered, at least cracked by the return of Leo, but Reed did not feel inclined to complain. Kate seemed to treat the whole matter of Leo in the light of a fascinating experience, like a safari, or an exploration of one of the poles: difficult, physically exhausting, but educational and replete with possibilities for future anecdotes, should one survive.

Mr. Mulligan had joined them at the cocktail hour. He proved to be a pleasant, if slightly pompous man around forty. "So you've met our Mary Bradford," Mr. Mulligan had said, accepting a martini and settling down, with evident satisfaction, before the fire. "In that case I shan't have to describe her. I'm supposed to be a pleasant, if slightly pompous man around forty. So to my friends, but they always suspect I'm what the Scots call 'havering.' Do allow me to assure you that while the last man to claim rectitude for himself, warranted or otherwise, I do not partake of orgies, alcoholic or sexual."

"I didn't know you were a writer," Kate said. "I thought you were a dreary academic, like me."

"Dreary academics write, haven't you heard? In my case, I write far too many books entitled 'The Future of the Novel,' 'The Novel and Modern Chaos,' 'Form and Function in Modern Fiction'—to be properly alliterative that should have been in French Fiction, but alas,

I don't read French. All my books talk about the decline of the old values and the emptiness of modern life—you get the picture. I suspect that none of them is any good, really, but I've published so many it was bound to be impressive after a while, and I have achieved not only tenure and a full professorship, but invitations to speak at women's clubs and even the possibility of running a sunrise semester on television next fall. What more can any man ask?''

"Who publishes your books?" Kate asked. "The University of Southern Montana Press?"

"No, oddly enough. The Calypso Press."

"Then you must be underestimating the books. If Sam Lingerwell's firm publishes them, they are no doubt first-rate."

"Do me a favor, kind lady, and rest content with that supposition. We may have to publish or perish, but I see no reason for perishing with boredom while we read what one another has published. The irrationalities of the academic world need not, after all, be pushed quite to their logical conclusions. Thank you, I should love another drink."

That had been at cocktails. Now, at dinner, Leo announced: "I got Mary Bradford right between the eyes this morning, I'm certain of it. Well, on the side of the head anyway, didn't I, William?"

"Very likely," William said, his major attention being on the chicken divan.

"It is really extraordinary," Emmet observed, "how we can't stop talking about that beastly woman. What did you 'get' her with, Leo? Something sufficiently deadly, I trust."

"Mary Bradford," Kate said, "is like a threat of war, or a strong suspicion that one is pregnant: it is literally impossible to think of anything else. But with sufficient control, one can at least attempt to converse on other topics. All the same, the woman does fascinate. She is so absolutely certain of her own rightness, and so absolutely, offensively wrong on every possible count. There I go again, you see. Leo, I'm not sure I altogether approve of your rifle practice, if that's what you are supposed to have gotten Mary Bradford with. Certainly I don't think you should talk about it."

"I haven't told anybody," Leo grumbled. "Nobody that counts."

"Just all the boys at the Araby Boys' Camp," Emmet said.

"They don't matter," Leo insisted.

"My dear Leo," Kate said, "you are as incurably urban as the rest of us. Each of those boys has a family simply longing to devour any available morsel of gossip. Last week, Reed, five miserable adolescent boys cracked up in a particularly nasty accident down the road; they must have been going eighty miles an hour, and the car was literally cut in half. Do you know, for two days the locals came from miles around to view the scene of the wreckage. The man whose property it was had to put up 'No Parking' signs, and only the summer people saw anything unusual in this behavior.''

"I agree with you about the rifle all the same,'' Emmet said. "One is always reading about people being shot by accident with innocent rifles. I categorically deny the innocence of rifles.''

"If a rifle has no bullets,'' William, who seemed to take this as a personal challenge, replied, "you might be able to kill someone by hitting him over the head with it, but you certainly can't shoot anyone. It's an excellent outlet for Leo.''

"Shooting with an empty rifle?'' Mr. Mulligan asked.

"It's got a telescopic lens,'' Leo hastened to explain, before William could grab the ball and run with it. "I sight through the lens and learn to hold it steady when I pull the trigger. William's promised he will take me for rifle practice at the end of the summer. Of course, nothing happens when you pull the trigger, but sighting's fun. There's a man down at the farm who shoots woodchucks miles away, and never misses. Well, yards anyway,'' he added, catching Kate's eye.

"How can you be so certain there are no bullets about?'' Reed asked.

"Oh, dear,'' Kate said. "We just found the gun in the barn; the gardener made sure it was quite empty, and I think he oiled it up a bit. Leo has most solemnly sworn *not* to touch a bullet with as much as a fingernail if he finds one, and I have looked pretty thoroughly and there really aren't any bullets around that I can see. Now you've immersed me in the midst of an awful qualm. But I don't really know very much about boys, and it does seem one is being spinsterish and antimasculine to refuse guns altogether; I have insisted that no one can, while under my roof, shoot a living thing, and that's probably ladylike enough.''

"Why practice with a gun if you can't shoot anything, even in the distant future?'' Mr. Mulligan asked.

"Well, Leo and William both assure me it will be rewarding to shoot at targets. I must say I don't approve of shooting at Mary Bradford, all the same. Impossible she no doubt is, as I am the first to admit, but ought you really, Leo, be aiming to kill even with an empty rifle? It does seem a bit in defiance of the spirit of the ruling, if not the letter.''

"You're probably right," William said. "But I get up early with Leo" ("Damn early," Reed muttered) "and he likes to practice aiming in the mornings, and there, right before our eyes, simply begging to be aimed at, so to speak, was Mary Bradford. There she is, you know, every morning, yelling her head off.''

"What on earth is she *doing* at five-thirty in the morning?" Reed asked. "Collecting dew-bespeckled toads?''

"Bringing in the cows to be milked.''

"I do hope she doesn't see you aiming at her," Kate said. "Whatever Mary Bradford may be, we should maintain certain standards of decorum, should we not?''

"But she can't see us, Aunt Kate," Leo assured him. "In the first place, we're well hidden, what you might call ambushed. And then she doesn't expect to see anyone up at that hour, because all city slickers sleep till all hours she always says. And she makes so much *noise* yelling at those cows, you'd never believe. And some of the things she calls them. One morning . . .''

"Leo!" William's voice, together with a glance of the most ferocious aspect, caught Leo and transfixed him.

"My dear Leo," Emmet said. "Should Miss Fansler care to know what Mary Bradford says in the morning, she has recourse to the simple expedient of arising at that hour and listening. Meanwhile, I'm sure you will agree that to report in detail would be neither enlightening nor decorous.''

"If she's that fascinating," Mr. Mulligan remarked, "I shall make a point of getting up to listen to her myself.''

"Perhaps," Emmet said, "we ought to give a cow-catching party, coffee and vituperation, come in your nighties, and prepare to be shocked into a state of total wakefulness.''

"Mr. Artifoni says," Leo remarked, "that shock is one of the most dangerous states following an accident. That's why it is so important to be careful, when there's been an accident, to . . .''

"Mr. Artifoni, I take it," Mr. Mulligan said, "is the local oracle in charge of the camp up the road.''

"He is," Kate answered, "and there are moments when the convenience of having the A.B.C., as it is called, for Leo's sake, is distinctly overbalanced by the impact, not only of Mr. Artifoni's remarks, which are of course intelligent and helpful, if likely to apply to rather special situations"—Kate smiled at Leo—"but by the impact of seventy boys. Whenever I see a group of boys together I fear for the future of humanity. That no doubt proves why I am an old maid, and doing nothing about the future of humanity personally. Shall we have coffee in the living room?''

Reed was surprised but pleased to see Leo, Emmet and William disappear in one direction, while Kate led Mr. Mulligan and Reed himself back into the living room.

"Black, please," said Mr. Mulligan. "Say what you like about *my* orgies, Miss Fansler, and all you like about your own spinster-hood, I'm afraid if you continue to run so masculine and efficient a household, you are bound to be accused of having orgies yourself. Do you think," he asked, sipping the coffee with pleasure and accepting brandy, "we might join households and have an orgy, just to say we'd done it? Isn't one under some sort of obligation to offer grist to Mary Bradford's mill?''

"Exactly what I was thinking this afternoon," Reed said. "She positively bullies people into forcing her disdain. If I were her husband, which heaven forfend, I would shove my socks up her vacuum cleaner personally. What a nasty remark that sounds. Do you see what I mean?''

"Perfectly," Kate said. "You must get Emmet and William to join you in some suitably diabolical plan. But do please leave Leo and me out of it. Frankly, the woman terrifies me and horrifies me in equal proportions, and I *am* responsible for Leo.''

"One doesn't, of course, care to sound in the least like our nosy neighbor," Mr. Mulligan remarked, "but might I ask, without appearing ghoulish, just who Emmet and William *are*? You do see, fair lady, that the very formation of the question anticipates an innocent and reasonable answer.''

"You feel quite certain I am not going to tell you they are my lovers, my illegitimate children or my gang?''

"Quite so. I take it their duties revolve around Leo, who is your nephew.''

"William's do. And Leo really is my nephew, by the way. No doubt it has already been suggested that he is a small misstep I am passing off in this manner. Is there, by the way, a word for auntly, counterpart to avuncular?''

"I doubt it," Mr. Mulligan said. "Perhaps we can invent one. I've always felt certain the major reason Joyce wrote *Finnegans Wake* was to have the fun of making up words. How about auntilary?''

"Not bad. Well, in my auntilary capacity I hired William as

buddy-cum-tutor to Leo: a companion, one might say, for the young Telemachus. He, William, happens to be a graduate student in the university where I teach. One great difficulty in hiring male graduate students as summer companions for a nephew is that, as Evelyn Waugh said, they like small boys either too little or too much, but William is doing well with Leo. Since Leo attends the A.B.C., William's duties are not onerous; he has the use of this excellent library, his keep and the stimulating companionship of Emmet.''

"As well as a well-run house and the services of your excellent Mrs. Monzoni.''

"You know Mrs. Monzoni, Mr. Mulligan?''

"Not really. But I have heard tell, needless to say, of that outrageous young woman, Miss Fansler, who can't do her own cooking, cleaning or housework, or even look after her own nephew. You are new to this life, Miss Fansler. I have been summering here now for nigh on a dozen summers, and I have learned that the reason rural people imagine so much obscene behavior is because they themselves, to a large extent, indulge in it. Do you, by any chance, know the commonest crime on the police blotters of Vermont, to pick a New England rural state?''

"Bootlegging?'' Kate suggested.

"Perhaps,'' Mr. Mulligan said, turning to Reed, "Mr. District Attorney can tell us.''

"Incest, I imagine,'' Reed answered.

Mr. Mulligan nodded. "Father and daughter is the commonest, though there are other forms.''

"You horrify me.''

"Naturally I do, dear lady. But if you stop and think a minute, you'll see why the rural character, however sanctimonious his background, can imagine situations which we urban types consider within the grasp only of geniuses like Faulkner; your rural citizen is, so to speak, to the manner born.''

"I'm certain Mary Bradford, whatever her iniquities, has never committed incest, nor had it committed in her family.''

"You may be right. But I make some claims to being a judge of character, and there aren't all that many sins I would put past the ability of that lady, whose name I solemnly swear will not cross my lips again tonight, to perform. May I ask what Emmet is doing?''

"He's looking over Sam Lingerwell's papers and attempting to arrange them into some order which will make possible their ultimate disposal. Right now he's getting together the stuff on Joyce, and rather to my surprise, because Jane Austen is his idea of the only novelist worth mentioning, he's become very much interested, particularly in *Dubliners*. Emmet keeps muttering about Lingerwell's appreciation of Joyce's appreciation of the short-story form. Jane Austen, of course, did not write short stories. Did you know Mr. Lingerwell, since he was your publisher?''

''He had retired from active publishing before I came along. I heard he had bought this house, but I never saw him here.''

''Well, Emmet is doing very well, all things considered. It's only this new excitement over Joyce's *Dubliners* that keeps him here, because he loathes the country, is terrified of snakes, shivers literally from head to foot at the thought of walking across an open field, and goes to the nearby town where we shop, population three thousand, for the sheer pleasure of walking on pavement and seeing a pigeon. He's very good for Leo too, even though Emmet's the sort who, if he feels like exercising, lies down till the feeling passes. But he talks to Leo as though they had both recently been members of the Jet Set and given it up out of boredom. It's a good experience for Leo, who has always been treated like a boy scout who had let down his troop.''

''William and Emmet appear to be quite delightful counterparts,'' Reed said, ''but do you think they are—perhaps 'wholesome' is the word I want—wholesome enough for Leo?''

''What wholesomeness they lack, Mr. Artifoni and his camp provide in ample doses; personally I find Emmet's effeteness considerably more wholesome than the robustness of the camp, but perhaps I ought not to admit it. Leo may begin the day here aiming idle rifles with William and discussing Joyce with Emmet, but he is then transported to camp, where, following the pledge of allegiance to the flag, and the Lord's Prayer, he learns the more abstruse aspects of the push shot, as developed by Bob Cousy.''

''Kate,'' Reed said, ''you are a remarkable woman. Bob Cousy indeed.''

''My respects, dear lady,'' Mr. Mulligan said, rising, ''and my farewells. This weekend I am having a cocktail party, and I would be delighted, Miss Fansler, if you and Mr. Amhearst, as well as Emmet and William, provided you can leave Leo with Mrs. Monzoni, will come by on Saturday afternoon. I hope I can promise you that nobody will so much as mention Mary Bradford.''

Kate accepted the invitation for herself and promised to extend it to Emmet and William. Reed's response was a touch provisional. He did not know, he told Mulligan, from one moment to the next, whether he could stand the country any longer, not having, as Emmet did, the attractions of James Joyce. But should he be there . . .

"I am expecting two friends to arrive sometime tomorrow afternoon," Kate said. "You will be relieved to know that they are both female. Perhaps our household will quite overweight your party, should we all appear; on the other hand, I can certainly promise you that Grace Knole will add to any gathering."

"*The* Grace Knole. She *is* your colleague, isn't she?"

"No longer, alas. She has retired. But she is still very much *the* Grace Knole. She is coming with a young colleague of mine who is also a friend of William's."

"I shall be delighted to see all of you on Saturday, dear lady," Mr. Mulligan said, extending his hands with a ceremonious bow. "Until Saturday then, my special salutations to the illustrious Professor Knole. I am very pleased to have met you, Mr. Amhearst, and hope you choose to remain."

"Who *is* the illustrious Professor Knole?" Reed asked when Mr. Mulligan had bowed himself from the room. "Is she that illustrious?"

"In the academic world," Kate answered, "just about as illustrious as they come."

4

Grace

THE illustrious Professor Grace Knole regarded, with a sense of loving desperation, the landscaped Taconic Parkway as it swept past her,
or she along it, at seventy miles an hour. Eveline Chisana, who was
driving the car, certainly knew her business; moreover, she, Grace
Knole, was nearly seventy herself, like the miles per hour they were
traveling, and ought not, rationally, to fear death. Eveline was not
yet thirty and certainly demonstrated, so far, no suicidal tendencies.
Old ladies should, if possible, not act like old ladies, particularly
when they were outraged at being retired at the height of their powers. And damn good powers they were too, Grace thought, though I
says it as shouldn't. "I suppose the car is in absolutely tip-top condition?" she asked, lightly, she hoped.

Lina, as everyone called her, grinned and slowed down to a decorous fifty-five. "Sorry," she said. "I expect I was thinking. Not a
revolution over sixty miles an hour, I solemnly promise."

Grace stared at the young woman with interest. How different,
she thought, from the young women of my day, who had, of course,
to choose. Most young ladies today chose a house complete with
husband and babies in suburbia, but even those like Lina who got
Ph.D.'s and did brilliant scholarship, seemed to find time to drive,
dance, cook and make love, all with equal expertise.

Lina had not made love, not really, a fact of which she was
thinking as the speedometer climbed high into the seventies; she had
not really made love, nor, which was more to the point, had William.

She planned to confront him, once and for all this weekend, across a constantly widening chasm of virginity. What a figure of speech! She could imagine her horror should it appear in a student paper. Chasms do not widen, she might write on such a student paper, at least not before one's eyes, to pick only the most obvious infelicity. Damn William. Damn. Damn. Damn.

"As a matter of fact," Grace said, "I shouldn't in the least mind walking. I *am* sorry to be such a nuisance, but I once had a misadventure in a Stanley Steamer, and you were going eighty. Perhaps it only looked like eighty from here."

Lina again slowed down, grinning her apologies. Dear Professor Knole. A frump, there was no other word for it, brilliant as she was. William said that the first time she entered the room to lecture, he thought the cleaning woman had taken leave of her senses and was about to make a speech. Until she opened her mouth, of course. A somewhat untidy, square person she was, with uneven hems dipping between calves and ankles, sensible walking shoes, hair which looked as though she had chopped it off herself with a paring knife. Yet at seventy she had turned down an offer of twenty-five thousand dollars to conduct one seminar on Chaucer, turned it down because she had other fish to fry. The right kind of frump to be, Lina thought. How much of life has she missed?

"From Kate's description," Grace said, "I gather her household is a rather unstable emulsion of small boys and James Joyce. I understand neither, of course, but I feel one should hold oneself open to new experiences. I read *Lady Chatterley's Lover* recently when it was legally reissued. It seemed to me that poor Constance simply didn't have enough to occupy her time."

"Should she have taken a course in medieval symbolism?" Lina mischievously asked.

"She might have done worse; in fact, in my opinion, she did."

"There's no real connection between Joyce and Lawrence," Lina said, amused. "Quite the contrary, in fact. I understand they loathed each other's work." Professor Knole might be the greatest living medieval scholar, but to her all novels written since the industrial revolution were infantile distractions of which the children, given sufficient time, would tire. "From what William writes, Emmet has found some exciting letters about *Dubliners*. William, of course, is very circumspect; his letters are always written with one eye on the jury box."

"Which is *Dubliners*? That hasn't got Leopold Bloom in it, has it?"

"No. That's just the point about *Dubliners*. The stories are about different people in Dublin, all in varying states of physical and spiritual paralysis." Lina thought of the last story of *Dubliners*, "The Dead," of Gabriel Conroy's lust for his wife, and Michael Furey, dead from standing in the rain, dead for love. She thought of Bloom on Sandymount Beach in *Ulysses*, dreaming of love, and the crippled girl, dreaming of love. Oh, God.

"I expect it only *looks* like eighty from here," Grace said.

"Professor Knole," Lina asked. "Have you ever noticed how when you've something on your mind, you seem always to engage in conversations about it, and passages about it leap at you from books. It happens, I think, with hungry men in prison camps and people who've just given up smoking."

"And sex," Grace said, her eyes on the speedometer. "I used to notice that. Years ago, of course."

"We are nearly at the turning anyway," Lina said, slowing down.

Grace unfolded Kate's directions and began to read them aloud.

Despite the threatening rain, Reed and Kate walked across a field in which the hay had only just been cut. The brown dog, who gave every sign of having enlisted under Reed's banner, accompanied them. They walked on one edge of the fifty-acre field, and could see the baler drive in and begin to work on the other.

"He's got to gather it in," Kate said, "even though it probably isn't dry yet. If hay is rained on, after it's been cut and lying on the ground, it's finished. So much farm lore have I acquired." Together they regarded the baler as it scooped up the hay, transformed it, by some unseen process, into neat, rectangular bundles, and then shot the bundles into the wagon. "I never tire of watching it," Kate said.

"Let's cross the brook and climb the hill," Reed said. "I want to talk to you. I don't know why I should mind having my privacy invaded by distant machines, but I do. Shall we leap over this barbed-wire fence?"

"Of course not. You'll do something irreparable to your trousers. One lies humbly on the ground and rolls under. Thus." Kate accomplished the movement with a grace that bespoke practice. "One must be careful," she added, "to pick a place free of cow dung."

"Perhaps," Reed wistfully said, "if I had taken up tennis and kept leaping over tennis nets . . ."

"Vigorous people are so exhausting," Kate said. "This summer has been rather full of vigorous young people. All the young men who are counselors at Leo's camp, after they've finished eight long hours with the boys, begin to play heated games of basketball exactly when any sane person, it seems to me, would lie down with a cool drink. De gustibus, as they say."

"Kate?"

"Mmm."

"Will you marry me?"

Kate stared at Reed a moment, and then patted his shoulder. "That's very kind of you, Reed, it really is, but no thanks."

"I didn't ask you if you'd like to go out to tea. Good grief, I've heard proposals that one eat in a certain restaurant treated to more profound consideration."

"But there's probably an active choice between two restaurants. What William James called a forced option. I don't intend to marry."

"Meaning: there have been men you wanted to marry, and men who wanted to marry you, but they have never been the same men? Who said that?"

"Barrie. That's not what I mean, Reed. It's a matter of world enough and time."

"I didn't realize I was addressing my coy mistress."

"You know, never, until recently, have I stopped to consider what those words mean. The young lover says them, and we tend to think they mean only that life is short, youth but an instant, days fleeting. But it's more profound than that. Haven't you ever noticed how everyone you know has either world or time, but never both? People who have a world, a job, work, a place to put their lives— they are always short of time. It's the condition of having a world. But people with time: widows on park benches, old men, women with their children at school, even children at a loose end—these have time enough, but no world. Either world or time, never both. I've decided that I would rather have the world."

"And marriage, you are certain, provides only time."

"Time or, if you like, a different world for which I do not happen to be suited. This summer has been a revelation, Reed. I have experienced the world of domesticity for which I don't care, even with all the assistance provided by my brother, and I've also experienced time, unformed, filling the day. I think—well, I'll read a book, but then I think, really, I ought to work first, and then I don't get to work and in the end, like the ship-wrecked sailor in the poem by Milne, I shamefully lie about and do nothing at all.''

"What happened to the sailor in the end?''

"All right, he got rescued. But I'm not shipwrecked, only momentarily becalmed. Reed, I am certain you don't realize what a selfish unwomanly, undomestic creature I am. I don't want to take care of anybody, really, or be the angel in the house. I'd rather ague about medieval symbolism with Grace Knole. Try explaining that in a woman's magazine.''

"My dear, I don't want to be taken care of, and I can't say that your angelic qualities are the ones which, above all others, have overwhelmed me. Couldn't we share a world, and a certain amount of time?''

"The first thing you know, you'd want to have your boss to dinner, or he'd invite you to a party that couldn't be refused, and I'd find myself planning menus, and picking up a new evening dress because all your associates had seen the old one, and having my hair done, and making conversations with lawyers at dinner parties. As it is, we can be together now when the fancy takes us—and I prefer you that way, not hog-tied, hag-hidden. Just Reed; not *my* husband, *my* house, *my* drapes—rather two circles, as Rilke said, which touch each other. You know, you never told me, even that day on the hills, how England was.''

"I had other things on my mind on the hills, as I have now. England was chiefly notable for the fact that you were not there.''

William and Emmet emerged from the house and proceeded, with a certain amount of preparation, to occupy lounge chairs in the sun. Emmet applied suntan lotion, and William some idiotically named concoction which promised to, and astonishingly did, keep off insects.

"It may give you skin cancer," William cheerfully observed, "but it does prevent bites. Have some.''

"Thank you, no. For some reason insects do not find me overwhelmingly attractive. In fact, they bite me only in the absence of all other sentient life, and then only as the final alternative to starvation. It's supposed to have something to do with the nearness of the blood to the surface of the skin. But there are multitudinous theories.''

"I shouldn't think you'd worry about sunburn, then.''

"I don't *worry*," Emmet said. "Not brood, that is, or tremble with anxiety. But I find it rather more satisfactory to get evenly tan all over than to look as though I'd been tipped in boiling water and had a layer of skin removed, in flakes."

"It's none of my business . . ." William began.

"Always a sure sign that one is certain it is."

"You're probably right. Please omit the introductory syllables. Why, then, do you affect these effete mannerisms, positively inviting everyone within earshot or reach of gossip to consider you limp of wrist?"

"How do you know I'm not limp of wrist, as you so coarsely put it—if you'll forgive my saying so."

"For one thing, you visibly restrain a shudder every time you look at Leo."

"Oh dear, is it that obvious? I am sorry. I don't mind some little boys, about five perhaps, with short pants and Prince Charles haircuts, bless their well-bred little hearts; Leo's a shade on the hearty side, don't you find?"

"Leo's all right, as long as someone takes him seriously, and treats him with dignity. You haven't answered my question."

"Which question, dear William, was that?"

"Oh, hell, Emmet, I admit you're entertaining, very entertaining, and I particularly admire the way you hold your liquor."

"Your own capacity is quite beyond praise."

"Not like yours. You simply get cleverer as the evening progresses. Do you think your tolerance for liquor is correlated with your nonattraction for mosquitoes?"

"It's not so much mosquitoes, Kate tells me, as deer flies and a kind of flying ant. Whatever it is you're obviously panting to say, why not *say* it?"

"I've nothing against fags, as it happens, though they do seem to have been swarming over the landscape recently, but you've been carrying on a passionate love affair for three years with a married woman. Why do you insist on suggesting that you couldn't be aroused to passion by anything more feminine than a choirboy?"

"May I respectfully inquire how . . ."

"Don't worry. It's far from common knowledge. Lina Chisana, who's coming up this weekend, went to school with your—ah—mistress. They're close friends. So are Lina and I. Neither of us gossips, as you can probably gather since your—ah—mistress told Lina. Let me, however, get this off my chest by admitting that I've told Kate. She, not unnaturally, was concerned about you and Leo. I've known *her* three years also, by the way, and she is reputed to be as sea-green incorruptible as Carlyle and as discreet as the tomb.''

" 'Mistress,' '' Emmet said, examining his legs for signs of sunburn, "has always seemed to me a word which might be used with more precision. Ought we not, etymologically, to reserve it for a woman financially supported by a man, usually maintained by him in some establishment, clothed by him, and expected to lie with him whenever he should choose to present himself?''

"I don't quite see . . .''

"Today we use the word for any woman to whom a man has made love. But, after all, why should she be his mistress? They are more properly one another's lovers, are they not?''

"Try telling that to Mary Bradford.''

"Oh, screw Mary Bradford, if you can stand the idea. Which reminds me, since we're exchanging confidence in this charming, not to say girlish fashion, how long is it since you, in your devout way, have had a woman, even in your dreams?''

William stood up. "I'm sorry, Emmet. Clearly, I've offended you. Please accept my apologies. I merely thought . . .''

"Oh, for Pete's sake, sit down. What so infuriates me about people committed to a life of chastity is that they seem to think its purity will be impugned if they discuss it. I wasn't trying to give you tit for tat, only to serve you, humbly, as you, I gathered, wished to serve me. Never mind. I'm damnably in love with a married woman who can't get a divorce, and who's married to a brute. The reason this summer's work is enticing me into a serious consideration of modern fiction is because I find the earlier, more melodramatic works a little too close to the bone.''

"I'm sorry. Where is she this summer?''

"With her husband. Sailing about on a blasted yacht. Would you mind frightfully if we talked about something else?''

"All right; James Joyce. How does it go with the early letters?''

"I humbly thank you, well, well, well. Sam Lingerwell was truly a great man. When the effects of your bug-away wear away, come in and let me show you a few letters. That is, if Leo and his athletic cohorts have not descended upon us. Do you know, I think I've met your Lina. Italian-looking, with an enormous vitality and an infatuation with eighteenth-century poetry. So she arrives with Grace Knole, does she? Imagine a household with three such distinguished and brilliant women in it, none of them married, and all existing in some emphatic attitude toward virginity.''

''What in hell does that mean?''

''Elementary, my dear boy. One is now confirmed in her virginity, which only the grave is left to try. One is already regretting her virginity, which will soon, I would guess, be gladly sacrificed to the first man who presents himself in the right light amidst the properly alcoholic ambiance; and the third . . .''

''That's a goddamn offensive thing to say!'' William stood up, upsetting the bottle of bug-away, which leaked onto the ground to the great distress of such ants as happened to find themselves in its path.

''And the third . . .''

''Emmet, for Christ's sake.''

''Ah, I see that the vigorous Leo has returned, accompanied by Mr. Artifoni himself.''

''Perhaps,'' William said, ''I ought to apologize. I thought I meant well.''

''No apologies in order, anywhere around, as far as I can see. Only a warning, or shall we say, a suggestion. I very much liked Miss Lina Chisana when I met her, and so does the woman I love. I hope you weren't offended by my evident assumption of Kate Fansler's non-virginity; I'm sure she wouldn't be.''

''Oh, damn virginity,'' William said.

''My point exactly,'' Emmet said, arising slowly and with dignity. ''I quite look forward to the feminine injection into our household, particularly Grace Knole. What time are they expected, do you know?''

Mr. Mulligan, meanwhile, conferred with his cleaning woman-cum-cook about tomorrow's cocktail party. ''It better not rain,'' he said, ''because I've invited the whole town of Araby, and if we can't overflow on to the lawn, we shall have to overflow upward, toward the bedrooms. Offer up obeisance, Mrs. Pasquale, to whatever gods there be.''

5

Araby

WHETHER due to the ineffectiveness of Mrs. Pasquale's prayers, or her gods, or merely to meteorological conditions, the weather on Saturday could scarcely have been worse. A steady downpour drenched the lawn and trees, leaving treacherous puddles on all the chairs and tables. "However," Mr. Mulligan remarked to Mrs. Pasquale, "one can never tell. They do, after all, say about Berkshire weather, if you don't like it, wait ten minutes. Have we dusted the bedrooms, Mrs. Pasquale?" Mrs. Pasquale, who was doing something with hard-boiled eggs, ignored him. He wandered off to stare from the living-room window.

The whole town of Araby was not, of course, coming—only the summer residents, and only such of these as were in their houses that weekend, and whom Mr. Mulligan found invitable. The year-round people would not be invited, nor expect to be. Mary Bradford, since her ancestors had apparently sustained some connection with the Mayflower, and her husband with Scarsdale, might have been invited on general social grounds, but her personality made such an invitation better ungiven. It was tacitly assumed by the summer people that the Bradfords could not attend cocktail parties which were given inevitably, if not consequently, at milking time.

The town of Araby, to quote from the standard picture book on the Berkshires, is situated north of Pittsfield, and owes its continuing rural character to the fact that it was bypassed by the railroads. Certainly it is outstanding, if not unique, in western Massachusetts for being totally without any commercial establishment whatever. Mail is delivered by Rural Free Delivery, and Araby's inhabitants learn to live with the fact that the nearest pack of cigarettes to be bought is eight miles away. Taxes are high, since only homes can be assessed to raise the money for roads and schools. The summer people are taxed, in fact though not in principle, at twice the rate of the year-round people, which, since the summer people are all clearly rich as Croesus, strikes the board of assessors as only equitable. Mr. Mulligan had been known to observe that his barn, a modest-sized building originally designed to house horses, in which he now kept his car, was assessed at nearly twice the value of the Bradford barn, which contained a fortune in milking equipment and hay elevators. But somehow the summer people never found the time or energy for a thorough investigation into these matters.

Araby's name was often commented upon, since almost alone among New England towns it was called after neither an English dukedom nor an Indian phrase. Tales of how this odd nomenclature originated were widespread and of equal dubiety. The commonest of these relates how an early settler had fancied himself a sheik, and liked to say he was "of Araby." How he transferred this strange inclination into the town's name was never properly explained, nor likely to be.

By the second weekend in July nearly all the summer people were "up," and of these, nearly all crowded into Mr. Mulligan's living room. The contingent from Kate's house, six strong, arrived halfway through the proceedings, when the casual acquaintances were about to take their leave, and the hilarity was about to ascend to its highest decibel count. Mr. Mulligan greeted them with the greatest possible enthusiasm, and immediately announced that he intended to monopolize Grace Knole, because she was so distinguished and fascinating, and Lina, because she was fascinating and unknown to him.

"And the young man is well cared for, I trust," he called to Emmet and William as they helped themselves to martinis.

"Gone visiting," William said.

"A chum from that jolly day camp," Emmet said. "His turn to invite the chaps for wienies and marshmallows. What a round of social activity country living is, to be sure."

"Martini or scotch?" Reed asked Kate.

"What would you say if I asked for a Manhattan?"

"Whiskey and sweet vermouth? I'd know you'd changed so

you'd probably consent to marry me, and I'd feel if you'd changed that much, I probably wouldn't want you after all.''

"I've heard more gallant statements.''

"I am not feeling gallant. Only old, foolish and oddly apprehensive.''

"Of what, Reed? How unlike you. Whenever I get vague feelings of apprehension, you always accuse me of some particularly feminine idiocy.''

"If you must know, our walks on the hills are the only part of this whole rural interlude I view with entire satisfaction. What was Mr. Artifoni, of the physical fitness and first-aid routine, going on about when we returned home from the hills yesterday?''

"Mary Bradford.''

"That woman again? It seems scarcely believable.''

"I couldn't agree more. It seems all the cars of parents delivering or calling for their offspring at the A.B.C. pass along our road, frighten Mary Bradford's chickens, and threaten her children, so she insists, with imminent extinction. She's taken to arriving at the camp, as it's dispersing and making loud, threatening remarks and talking of suing Mr. Artifoni. I believe she actually bullied a state trooper into giving speeding tickets to parents. Anyway, Mr. Artifoni has murder in his eye.''

"So of course the first thing he did was to come around and talk to you.''

"Well, I'm new around here, and therefore supposed to have a higher tolerance for local gossip and complaints. Also, he was delivering Leo home, which was nice of him. What are you eying, in your most district-attorney way?''

"Mr. Mulligan,'' Reed said. "He may not have orgies, but he's clearly the fastest worker since Don Giovanni, and with somewhat the same tastes, if I remember correctly the confidence of Leporello.''

"I see,'' Kate said, "and so, blast him, has William. But after all, she's well up in her twenties, and supposedly knows what she's doing.''

"I doubt very much,'' Reed said moodily, "if any of us knows that. Have another drink.''

"I must say your glooming-about is scarcely flattering to me.''

Reed looked at her. "The simple fact,'' he said, "is that I love you, and I wish you'd come back to New York and be properly sinful with me in an air-conditioned apartment. If you want my opinion, most city dwellers, one rung beneath the Jet Set and the writers of nasty articles for *Esquire*, are as innocent as a lamb unborn.''

"Speaking of lambs," Kate said.

"I know, that's why the phrase came into my head, no doubt. Do you think he means to seduce her during the cocktail party, or immediately afterward, or will he first tell her all about Form and Function in French . . .''

"We had better go and talk to William."

"Emmet is talking to William."

"And clearly he's sunk twice, and is likely to go down a third time. Can you run interference?"

"Kate," Reed said, beginning to shoulder his way, not too gently, through the crowd, "you must explain to me about William."

"I can't explain William," Kate said. "I can't explain Emmet or Leo, or anybody. Emmet was explaining James Joyce to me this morning in agonizing detail, and I've decided I can't explain him either. William!" Kate called, having now edged within earshot.

William obediently swam the short distance toward her through the currents of people.

"Where is Grace Knole?" Kate asked.

"Being told about artificial insemination by the Osterhoffs."

"Ye gods, we had better go and rescue her. Would you have any great objection to leaving now, if we should be able to disentangle her from the details of a cow's personal life?"

"Nothing could please me more," William said fiercely, with a glance toward Mr. Mulligan and Lina, "than to leave this instant."

"I find, don't you know," Emmet said, joining them, "that my interest in artificial insemination is scarcely breathless with fervency. And let's admit it, nonartificial insemination is much more interesting, and nonartificial, noninsemination is better still . . .''

"Oh, shut up," William ungraciously said.

"Though, of course," Emmet went on in a small voice, bringing up the rear in their pilgrimage to Grace Knole, "a nondiscussion of nonartificial noninsemination is best of all."

"Don't go," Mr. Mulligan said to Lina.

"But they're all leaving."

"Let them. I'll see you home. You can't desert me now. I always tire of cocktail parties about this time, and when they're your own you can't get up and leave, the great inconvenience of giving cocktail parties as opposed to going to them. What are you drinking?"

"I think I had better stop drinking."

"Never stop drinking when you're still able to think you had better stop drinking, the first rule of a successful life of indulgence. And of course a life of indulgence is the only possible life to be lived in summer houses in the country during the torrid months. Drinking is one of the few simple pleasures left in modern life, drinking and love."

"Is love really a simple pleasure?"

"To the complex, haven't you noticed? Norman Mailer has made a small fortune trying to transform love into a simple pleasure. But the only one who succeeds is James Bond, because he's so simple himself his pleasure can scarcely be otherwise. You puncture a girl's tires with a little gadget developed for 00 personnel, and then enjoy her in the grass dodging gunfire the while. The great mistake is unnecessarily to complicate life."

"I'm afraid I'm a rather complex person."

"Exactly. And as Oscar Wilde has told us, simple pleasures are the last refuge of the complex."

Kate and William walked home together. William having declared a frantic need for fresh air and Kate, downing all her civilized impulses, having decided to accompany him. Reed drove Grace Knole home, together with Emmet, whose eagerness to return to the Lingerwell papers was barely disguised. Kate had very mixed feelings about William, which were in no way simplified by the conviction that her determination not to interfere in his affairs was going, finally, to be over-borne by the necessity of interfering in them. She ought not, of course, to have let Lina Chisana visit. But she had too late realized the intensity of the relationship between Lina and William. No doubt that relationship was such that only Henry James could have done it justice. Either William would have to let down the bars, or Lina, if she stuck with him, would have to dedicate herself to a life of placid friendships on the order of Grace Knole's, and between these two extremes Kate was hard put to decide which was the most unsatisfactory. Still, whether dalliance with Mr. Mulligan . . .

"What is that unspeakable blackguard's first name?" William asked. Kate dearly wanted to say "What blackguard?" but, never very good at sudden assumptions of naïveté, she merely said, "Padraic, spelled in transliterated Gaelic. I believe," she added, "he is known to his friends as Paddy."

"Where did he find his friends," William asked, "in the nearest seraglio?"

"The nearest seraglio is probably in Istanbul."

"I expect he's got one upstairs, the . . ."

"Now look here, William, I don't wish to sound middle-aged and assume any auntilary attitudes, but you have got to choose, you know, between a life of absolute celibacy and the love of a young woman. You simply can't have both, and the sooner you stop fooling yourself, the better."

"I know there are no standards left anywhere," William said, "but surely fornication is not yet the only way of life possible, even on the part of older women who are widely assumed to be models of virtue while seething with lust."

"All right," Kate said, standing quite still. "I myself admit a perhaps distasteful disinclination for either continence or matrimony, which doubtless makes me a criminal in your eyes. Don't interrupt. There *are*, however, crimes of omission, you know. If you spend hours and days and weeks with a young woman without even kissing her, you're asking for trouble and ought to take your lumps when trouble comes. I might add," Kate said, viciously kicking a stone from her path, "that since we are exchanging *ad hominem* remarks in this shameless fashion, let me suggest that if you want to be a priest, by all means go and be one. I'll give you all the support I can. But if you choose a life of noncelibacy, then try noncelibacing. Now, if you want to take the first train out of here, I'll try to find someone for Leo."

"There's a train from Pittsfield tomorrow morning. I'll call a taxi and take the train, since that seems to be what you wish."

"Oh, come off it, William, I wish nothing of the sort. What would Leo do without you, particularly at five-thirty in the morning? Of course, I'd like you to stay."

"I can't have you thinking I meant to accuse you, I mean, it never occurred to me to suggest that you were . . ."

"A fornicator? Never mind. All relationships are changing, William, and rather to my surprise, for I have a great many old-fashioned tendencies, I think they're changing for the better. I still like courtesy, perhaps even formality of sorts. But I also think, as some pundit said, that the only crime sex can commit is to be joyless."

"I wish I could explain to you how I feel."

"Never mind. Concentrate on explaining the finer points of Hopkins' prosody, since that's the subject of your dissertation and you must, you know, get past your dissertation block. Remember, as C. S. Lewis so wisely said, it is easier to describe the threshold of divine revelation than the working of a pair of scissors."

Later that night, when Kate, having pleaded total exhaustion, had gone to bed with a stiff nightcap and fallen, not without much tossing and turning, into a troubled sleep, she was awakened by someone calling her name and knocking on her door. She thought at first that the house was on fire, and then that Leo had been kidnaped, these being the worries uppermost in her mind. But it was Lina, clearly on the verge of hysterics and prepared, Kate realized at a glance, to fly over the edge in the absolutely next moment. When Lina's sobs had subsided, however, and Kate had braced herself for another heart-to-heart with the younger generation about the perils of fornication on which she was prepared, with Lina, to take a decidedly spinsterish view, Lina sobbed out the name of Mary Bradford.

"Mary Bradford! What now, what possibly now?"

"She *said* she didn't think there was anyone home except just him. And naturally she leapt to the conclusion—there was a positive light in her eye, and nothing had happened, I mean, nothing really, but Padraic said he thought someone would probably slit the bitch's throat if she didn't watch out, so naturally, she won't waste any time spreading the story . . ."

"He said that *to* her?"

"Yes. When she walked into the house to see him, after the party. Kate, would you mind if I asked you about something?"

"Let's go down to the kitchen. I'm going to make some cocoa."

"Cocoa?"

"Why not? It's a soothing drink, isn't it? Now listen to me, Lina, I don't want to hear a lot of confessions you're going to loathe me in the morning for knowing. If Mary Bradford walked in before you met a fate worse than death, it may have been her best act in what has clearly been a misspent life. Padraic Mulligan isn't all that bad, even if I suspect him of not having a clue about either form or func-tion in fiction of any nationality, but if you want to go off on a fling, I'm sure you could wait for a moment a little more spontaneous, if not affectionate. Coming down?"

"But," Lina said, when they were in the kitchen, "virginity can become a burden."

"Everything is a burden, especially nephews, students and the early letters of James Joyce. But remember, my dear, as Keats so wisely said, life is a vale of soul making. Do you know, I haven't the faintest clue how to go about making cocoa? Let's have a hot scotch sling.''

6

The Dead

"DAMN, blast and to bloody hell," Reed said. "Operator. *Operator.* We live in an age of automation, but Araby, of course, does not have dials. Moronic operators apparently hired from the nearest institution for retarded baboons. If I *knew* the number in Boston, my dear young woman, I would scarcely be troubling you. I *know* there are probably eighteen John Cunninghams in the Boston telephone book, we are simply going to have to try them all until we find the right one. Yes, it's Sunday, I do know the days of the week. No, I do not want to receive another call at this number, I want to find the right Mr. John Cunningham. Do you know," he said to Kate, covering the receiver with his hand, "I do believe I have gotten through to some functioning part of the child's brain."

"They're going to put dials in next year," Kate said.

"By next year," Reed said, hanging grimly on to the receiver, "I humbly trust that whatever happens in the town of Araby will be a matter of the most supreme indifference to all of us. Hello, hello, is this Mr. John Cunningham? I am sorry to be bothering you so early, but did you by any chance attend Harvard Law School, class of '44? Believe me, sir, it is not my idea of a joke—an official of the electricians' union; I see. I'm sorry, but it is a matter of the greatest importance, I do assure you. Operator. *Operator.* On to the next John Cunningham, my child. From the list that Information has given us. The area code, like the city of Boston, remains unchanged."

"Reed," Kate said. "Couldn't you get his address from the Harvard Alumni Office, or some index of lawyers or something?"

"If they functioned on Sunday, no doubt I could. The police will be here in about five minutes, and we need a Massachusetts lawyer. Yes, Operator, well, let it ring. It was considerate of you," Reed said, turning to Kate, "since you were intent on opening a boardinghouse in the midst of rural iniquities, to open it in Massachusetts. As I went to Harvard Law School, I can at least draw upon some acquaintances and not throw myself on the mercies of just any lawyer. Very well, Operator, they have no doubt gone away for the weekend. Let's try the next John Cunningham. Kate, for God's sake, don't start crying. The woman isn't worth a tear, not a sigh. Miss Knole, take her off and see if you can talk some sense into her. Yes, Operator, I'm still here, though gladly would I be in city pent. Mr. Cunningham? Jack? Thank God. Reed Amhearst here. Fine, until an hour ago. Listen, do you happen to remember that night in Scollay Square when you said if there was ever anything you could do for me? Well, I hope when you said anything, you meant anything. I'm in Araby, and a woman has just been murdered. Araby. Near Tanglewood. Berkshire County. I think you'd better, if you don't mind. We'll arrange the details later. Good. If you can find Pittsfield, I'll tell you how to get here from there. By all means stop for a cup of coffee; I'm reasonably sure they can't arraign us for homicide in under four hours, particularly on a Sunday. Perhaps my being from the district attorney's office of New York will help some—anyway, I'm certainly going to try it. Someone I cared for? That's the whole trouble, Jack, she was someone no one cared for. Righto. Hello, Operator. Thank you, my child, and bless you, we have come through." Reed hung up. "Come on, Emmet, let's see how our lady professors are doing."

It had seemed to Kate that someone was calling to her, and she was trying to answer the call, but William was marrying Lina and quarreling with Emmet over the ring, which Leo, dressed oddly in velvet doublet and hose, was insisting had to be used as a prize for push shots. Someone in the back of the church was calling. Her unconscious mind struggled vainly to incorporate this sound, which was threatening sleep, into her dream. Kate awoke, to find Grace Knole calling her name.

"What time is it?" Kate said.

"About six-thirty, I think. Are you awake, or do you need time to pull yourself together?"

"What's happened? Leo? Lina and Mr. Mulligan . . ."

"Apparently one of the routine maneuvers in this household included rifle practice at five-thirty in the morning?"

"Has something happened to Leo?"

"Leo is fine, I think. But William has shot some woman who was fetching the cows. Some woman named Bradford. Shot her right through the head. I never did care for guns."

"There were no bullets in the gun. No one ever knew what kind of bullet went in the gun. Oh, my God. Is she dead? Are you sure?"

"I have seldom been as sure of anything. I took the trouble to go out and look at her, since everyone else seemed to be on the edge, if not in the midst, of hysteria."

"Is everyone up?"

"Everyone but Lina. Your Mr. Amhearst says we will have to call the police. Emmet wanted to go down and get her husband, but it was decided to wake you first. I hope you can wake up fast enough to formulate some plan, because except for Mr. Amhearst, who says we have to have a Massachusetts lawyer, nobody seems to have a clue what to do next."

"Emmet *had* better go tell the husband. No, I'll go. It isn't really properly anyone else's job. It'll take me one minute to get dressed."

But when Kate got downstairs she found Reed on the telephone, and the others—all but Lina, who apparently was sleeping the sleep of the troubled young—huddled about in the dining room, where the telephone was, looking, Kate could not help thinking through her fears, like a group of stockholders meeting to dissolve a corporation. Leo was in the kitchen receiving the ministrations of Mrs. Monzoni. When Kate looked in, she had decided that, in the circumstances, Mrs. Monzoni was coping as well as anybody else could, probably better.

Now Reed, finding Kate recovering over her second cup of coffee, turned to walk out the door.

"Where are you going?" Kate asked.

"To inform Mr. Bradford that his wife is dead. I take it I shall find him in the barn, milking."

"Do you think," Emmet asked, "the cows made their own way back, led by the thought of food, and driven by the pressure of their swollen udders?"

"That's a point," Reed said. "Are the cows out there now?"

"By no means," Grace said. "They weren't even there when I went to look at her."

"I gather," Kate said, "from what Leo has told me, that she never actually followed them all the way home. They needed some urging from the rear, but once started, they kept going. I think Bradford waits for them in the barn, where each cow goes to her own stanchion and is then locked in."

"Well," said Reed, "I'm on my way, so we will soon know."

"I'm going with you," Kate said.

"You're staying here." Reed's eyes met hers. "If Cunningham calls back, by any chance, or if the police arrive, tell them I'll return shortly. I think you'd better get Miss Chisana up, and make sure Mrs. Monzoni doesn't leave the house. Of course, no one is to touch the body or go outside."

"Well," Emmet said. "The sleuth at work."

When Kate returned from her errands Emmet was still talking. "William," he said, "hadn't you better say something—anything, really, just so I know you're quite all right: shocked of course, but basically sound. William!"

Kate walked up to William, who finally turned and looked at her. "Don't worry," he said, "I'm not hysterical. Just horrified and mystified in equal parts. It wasn't my fault. I didn't know there was a bullet in the gun; I didn't know there was a bullet in the house."

"William," Kate said, "who was shooting the gun, you or . . . ?"

"I was. I had taken it from Leo to sight through the telescopic lens, and I said, 'Here goes,' and pulled the trigger. I didn't think even with a telescopic lens I could hit anything. But of course I had the two lines crossed exactly at her temple. The trigger . . ."

"You could scarcely have missed at that distance," Grace said, "if you'd been cross-eyed and suffering from astigmatism into the bargain. I used to shoot," she said surprisingly, "when I was a girl in Montana. We didn't have telescopic lenses, of course, but I could have hit that woman at that distance in my shooting days with one good eye. Why were they shooting guns, Kate? This may seem an odd time to ask the question, but I didn't know about this morning target practice until just now."

"Now that the woman's dead," Kate said, "I can't imagine how I ever allowed such a thing. But when it was a boyish sport, it seemed somehow defensible. I remember defending it at dinner with Mr. Mulligan."

"So Mr. Mulligan knew about the target practice. Did anybody else?"

"Everybody," Emmet said. "Let's face it, Kate, there's nobody in the whole shining Araby valley who didn't know, and most of them probably wrote and told their friends and relations. Mr. Pasquale knew, I'm absolutely dead certain Leo told him, and Mrs. Monzoni, and all the boys at the camp and Mr. Artifoni and the counselors."

"Did Mr. Bradford know?" Grace asked.

"I'll jolly well bet he knew."

"Emmet!" said Kate. "Surely he would have said something."

"Said something? He probably jumped for joy and slipped a bullet in the gun himself."

"Emmet!"

"All right. And if either of you starts going *nil nisi bonum* etc., to me about that woman, I'll scream, I promise you. She was a scourge and a menace, and I can't see that her being dead means we have to lie to one another." Emmet bent down to pick up his red cat and held it to him, stroking it. "I'm not saying her husband shot her. Had I been her husband, I would have beaten her to death slowly with wet ropes. What I am saying is that William didn't really shoot her, and I think we should be determined that the police are going to know that."

"He shot her in fact," Reed said, coming into the room. "Kate, should we send Mrs. Monzoni down to help Bradford for a while?"

"How did he take it?" Grace asked, as Kate went off to the kitchen.

"He's stunned. He went right on milking his cows. Hello, there are the state police."

"Reed," said Kate, returning, "the police."

"All right, I'll talk to them. Now let's remember one thing. Ah, the sleeping Miss Chisana at last. Sit down, Miss Chisana, Kate will tell you all about it. For God's sake, tell the truth, all of you. Don't try to lie, or be heroic, or hide some idiocy because it sounds suspicious."

"Is William going to be charged with having shot her?" Kate asked.

"I'm not certain of the legalities in Massachusetts. He's certainly committed technical murder, probably in the third degree. But of course, as I believe I mentioned to you on another occasion, in another place, the police tend to regard the most obvious man with a certain interest."

"William had no reason to kill her," Lina said. "It isn't as though he'd shot me." William went over to stand beside her.

"O.K., everybody," Reed said. "Here we go."

*   *   *

"What have the police done so far?" John Cunningham asked. He was sitting at the table with Kate and Reed, gratefully consuming a large lunch. The others had gone upstairs except for William and Leo, who were shooting baskets outside.

"Not much," Reed said. "They haven't even removed the body, though they've covered it. The two state troopers who arrived can't have been, either of them, a day over twenty-four, and though I guess people had been accidentally shot before, it had never been a question of murder. They have notified the sheriff, and he or his representative will be along shortly, supposedly with photographers and a medical examiner, if that's what you call him in Massachusetts. It took all my persuasive powers to keep them from taking William away with them."

"I take it," Cunningham asked, "you've decided there's no point in maintaining it was an accidental death?"

"Someone accidentally dropped a bullet into a gun?"

"It's possible, you know. Every day of the week some kid loads a gun, or shoots one off accidentally. Perhaps someone was fooling around, heard someone coming, and left the gun loaded?"

"Who, for example?"

"What about the boy?" Cunningham asked.

"He swears he didn't load it, didn't even have a bullet for it or ever see one. I believe him, but I realize the sheriff might not," Kate said. "Frankly, however, I'd rather believe in murder than try to hang an accidental death on Leo."

"The gun was in the house always, except when those two morons were playing at target practice, is that right?" Cunningham asked.

"Yes."

"Had they had their target practice on Saturday morning?"

"Yes."

"Good. Then sometime during Saturday, or in the very early hours of Sunday, someone slipped a bullet into that gun. Someone who lived in the house is the most likely then."

"Not at all," Reed said. "We were all gone on Saturday afternoon. Anyone could have walked in. These country houses are never locked."

"It's really great," Cunningham said, helping himself to more strawberries. "Nobody can have an alibi, because we can't know when the bullet was put in, or for what time an alibi is needed.

Nobody had to be within miles of the gun when it actually went off to have been the murderer. If I understand correctly your rather incoherent explanation of the prevailing situation, anyone, just about, from the families of the boys at that Araby Boys' Camp sanitarium right down to Miss Fansler herself, had ample opportunity and knowledge to put the bullet in the gun. Furthermore—These are delicious strawberries, by the way; grown locally, I assume. I am glad to discover that the natives do something besides laying nefarious plots for one another.''

"I am happy to allow you your little joke,'' Reed said, "and able, with extraordinary broadmindedness, not to envy the disinterest with which you sit there guzzling strawberries and cream. However, I do object to having my explanation called incoherent. The household may be somewhat lacking in, shall we say, the ordinary components of normal domesticity, but my account of it was, I think, exact to the point of crystalline clarity, don't you agree, Kate?''

"I don't think this incident can be helping your disposition,'' John Cunningham said, "or perhaps you've become sensitive over the years, sinking into pampered bachelorhood. Sensitivity is not allowed to us married men with four children, and swarms of in-laws who agree among themselves only in disapproving of the way we raise our progeny.''

"Reed is the least sensitive, in a pejorative way, person I know,'' Kate said, with a vigor that surprised her. "Perhaps a practice of criminal law in Boston has accustomed you to the regular appearance of the bodies of neighbors, scattered about. You may not be aware of it, but I am in the delightful position of having either my nephew or his tutor arrested for murder or manslaughter, unless I or one of my guests is arrested instead. I am beginning to think the only solution, as Lord Peter Wimsey would have suggested, is poison for three in the library. In any case, I see no reason for berating poor Reed. He seems to me the only thoroughly sensible person in the whole dismal situation . . .''

"Who will, no doubt,'' Cunningham said, picking up her sentence and concluding it for her, "be able to prove that he is neither the murderer nor likely to perjure himself in defense of the murderer, should that person turn out to be a woman he loves or any member of her household. All right, sit down, both of you, and stop thinking you can behave like characters in a Henry James novel with the sheriff and very possibly the district attorney on his way. I am, as you point out, a criminal lawyer. I assume that that, together with an incident in Reed's and my past, is the reason you called on me at this juncture. Let us, therefore, try to see this whole situation as the police are going to see it, and not as we would like to have it represented in a beautifully wrought novel by a writer of exquisite sensibility. Keep quiet, both of you.

"Now." Cunningham pushed away, with evident reluctance, the bowl of strawberries. "Assuming that this murder was not the result of any long-seated grudge, and consummated at this moment by an extraordinary stroke of ill-luck because this household had at last provided the opportunity—and I need hardly add that we shall do everything in our power to prove that exactly that is the case—the murder must have been committed by one of a given number of people. To start with those nearest to the victim, her husband or, I should think from what you tell me of her, practically any other member of her family. Does she have any other family hereabouts?"

"Not that I know of," Kate said.

"Well," Cunningham went on, "it does sound as though we ought to call the woman's removal an act of sanitation and let it go at that. Still, a state that can blink at one murder, however desirable, will soon find itself blinking at thousands."

"If you believe that," Kate asked, "how can you be a criminal lawyer?"

"I don't blink at murder. I defend men accused of it. Isn't that rather a naïve question for a big, grown-up girl like you?"

"There is no need," Reed said, "to be offensive."

"Nor any intention, I assure you. Still, you're a district attorney, and when you find yourself with a body on your hands, you call a lawyer."

"I was thinking of our friendship in law school."

"Come off it, Amhearst. You two might as well accustom yourselves to a lot of straight talk, because that's what you're going to hear."

"My apologies," Reed said.

"And mine," Kate added. "Though my remark was, believe it or not, inspired more by curiosity than malice. No offense in the world."

"And none taken. Now, in addition to the husband, we have all the members of this household, each of whom loathed the victim, many for personal reasons, the other perhaps for personal reasons we are not aware of. I gather the delightful lady was not above a spot of moral blackmail, and in fact took particular pleasure in walking in on people in awkward situations, which reaches beyond this household to Miss Chisana and to Mr. Padraic Mulligan.''

"You're not going to have to tell anybody that!'' Kate said. "You swore when we were frank about these things that—Look, I have betrayed a solemn trust because of the seriousness of the circumstances, but I did so only on the understanding . . .''

"Of the seriousness of the circumstances. There you go again, all purity and righteous indignation. Remember, the police are going to find out a good deal, and we have got to know more. Whether or not we use our information is a decision which can and must wait for a later time. It's no good sweeping dirt under the carpet, if the first thing the police are going to do is lift up the carpet and inspect the floor beneath it with a microscope. What was I talking about?''

"Mr. Mulligan?''

"Ah yes, and Miss Chisana. Then we have Mr. Artifoni, according to my list, he of the A.B.C., who appears to have a pretty motive . . .''

"Hardly a motive for murder.''

"Perhaps a motive for a murder that was supposed to be, for all intents and purposes, undetectable. Then there are the Pasquales, of whom Mr. works in your garden, and Mrs. works for Mr. Mulligan. Then there is Mrs. Monzoni, whose loathing of the victim was expressed to every possible person on every possible occasion. These named, we have remaining, apart from person or persons unknown to us, only the members of this, you must pardon me, my dear lady, eccentric establishment. A small boy; his tutor, who seems vowed to a life of celibacy while passionately in love, and suffering from a block in his dissertation. Another doctoral candidate, acting as scholar and researcher, who seems to combine the manner of Oscar Wilde with the sex life of Frank Harris. He is in need of a shot in the arm, academically speaking, and who knows—do you, dear lady?—what he may have found among the late Mr. Lingerwell's papers—all right, make a note and tell me later. Then we have the two female guests—Lina Chisana, apparently a brilliant young woman of enormous vitality and charm, temporarily encumbered with the weighty burden of virginity, and Professor Grace Knole . . .''

"She is completely without either motive or opportunity.''

"And therefore deserving of special attention.''

"She is seventy and extremely illustrious with no conceivable . . .''

"No doubt you are right. At the same time I could enlighten you with tales of seventy-year-olds of illustrious reputation who went beautifully off the rails in a last, desperate bid for power or experience.''

"Surely," Reed said, "that occurs somewhat earlier in life."

"In most cases. Exceptions, while statistically small, may be numerically staggering. To these we add you two, but let's for the moment assume your innocence established. After all, you're hiring me."

"Yes," Kate said, "about your fee."

John Cunningham waved a dismissive hand. "Don't worry about that now," he said grandly. "We have more important things to discuss. Besides," he added, "I stopped long enough this morning in my pursuit of relevant information to determine that you are related to the Wall Street Fanslers, half a dozen of whom are, I understand, your brothers."

"Cunningham," Reed said, "I hope it is clearly understood that any debts to be incurred by this investigation or defense . . ."

"Reed," Kate said. "This is my eccentric establishment, as Mr. Cunningham calls it, and it was my maniacal permission which allowed the gun to be shot off, neither of which did you approve of for a single instant. You included, if memory serves, the entire rural ambiance of your condemnation. So I will not have you assuming any financial responsibility . . ."

"Ladies and gentlemen." Mr. Cunningham stood up. "Perhaps my joking is on the heavy-handed side, though if you get the idea that I'm a crude bastard, we will get along in this investigation rather faster. Let's talk about fees when we know if there's any case here at all, and whether this will ever go to court. In the event that either of you turns out to have murdered the loathsome lady in a fit of misspent passion, I shall gracefully retire from the scene, and you can call in Louis Nizer. Ah, a car. The gentlemen, I doubt me not, from the Commonwealth of Massachusetts, Berkshire County, or do you think they've called in an assist from the Boston Police Department? Now, let me do the talking at first, except when a question is asked directly of you, and answer then as simply as possible. Remember, the abilities of the police to appreciate the complexities of a novel by Henry James, or even Jane Austen, if it comes to that, are considerably less than mine, and I suppose you've gathered by now that mine would hardly win me a bachelor's degree from a backward agricultural college."

Reed, coming up to stand behind Kate, put his hands on her shoulders as John Cunningham went forward to greet the authorities.

7

Two Gallants

THE two men who entered seemed courteous enough. Kate realized, a bit guiltily, that she had built them up in her mind as ogres. John Cunningham stepped forward to introduce himself and, having introduced Reed as an assistant district attorney of New York County, indicated his own position as counselor to Miss Fansler. The two Berkshire County officials, while greeting with definite cordiality a professional peer, seemed to Kate's perhaps oversensitized perceptions, to fear his allowing their camaraderie to lead to unorthodox, unwelcome familiarities. But Reed continued to efface himself, to their relief, and they addressed their questions, mostly to Cunningham, but partly to the room at large. Kate had the impression that should she insist on speaking for herself, she would meet with distinct, if veiled encouragement.

"Your colleagues, I gather," John Cunningham said, walking to the window, "are proceeding with their accustomed rituals out of doors. They have located the body?"

"Yes, thank you. They'll be busy for quite a while outside. Then, with your permission, they will come inside. Might I ask to see the murder weapon and the young man who fired it named"—here he consulted a note—"William Lenehan? The men can then get started with the ballistic and fingerprint problems."

Cunningham turned questioningly to Kate. "The gun is on the back porch," she said. "I'm certain it will be fraught with fingerprints, if that's the right phrase. William is outside playing basketball with Leo. About Leo . . .''

"I'm certain," John Cunningham interceded, "that we need have no fears about Leo. The gentlemen here will talk to Leo, a minor, only in your presence, and with your permission. Perhaps he ought to come in so as not to witness the removal of the body."

One of the men, at a nod from the other, disappeared to direct the fingerprinting of William and the gun, and the return indoors of Leo. He reappeared shortly.

"Who exactly is the owner of this house?" the first man, who in his companion's absence had reminded Kate that his name was Stratton, inquired. He had the air of one who begins with simple matters.

"Miss Fansler," Cunningham suddenly said. "Who does own this house?"

"Miss, or perhaps Sister, or would it be Mother, Lingerwell."

"I beg your pardon," Mr. Stratton said.

"She means a religious, no doubt," his companion added.

"Ah, of course; and how is she related to you?"

"Perhaps," Kate said, "we could sit down. Might I offer you something to eat or drink? Mr. Cunningham found the strawberries exceedingly . . ."

"No thank you," Mr. Stratton said. "Let's sit down by all means. Go on, Miss Fansler."

"Miss Lingerwell—perhaps I might just call her that—is no relation to me at all. In fact, I don't know her very well anymore."

"Then she is merely the landlord, from whom you are renting the house?"

"Well, you see," Kate said, feeling like a doubtful swimmer who has just leapt into the midst of a very deep, very cold, quarry pool, "I'm not renting the house. Could we, Mr. Cunningham, begin at the beginning?"

"And where is the beginning, my dear woman?" Cunningham asked. "With Adam and Eve, or the discovery of America, or the settlement of New England, or the founding of the town of Araby . . ."

"Mr. Cunningham." Mr. Stratton's voice indicated that he was coming to grips with fundamental matters. "Am I to understand that the members of this household have been instructed by you to answer questions only in your presence, and with your permission?"

"That is within the letter and meaning of the law, is it not?"

"Certainly. On the other hand . . ."

"On the other hand, I quite see your point of view. You would rather pursue your investigations undeterred by me. Well, proceed, my two gallants. I shall return to Boston and to my own affairs, from which this unfortunate occurrence diverted me. Perhaps you will be good enough to indicate whether you intend to take legal action against William Lenehan."

"He will be arraigned, certainly and then, in all probability, released in the custody of—you if you should choose, Mr. Cunningham."

"Not however today, I gather."

"I think not. Tomorrow."

"Very good. I shall return or, more likely, meet you in the courthouse. Good-bye, Miss Fansler, for now. Thank you for those truly excellent strawberries. Reed, might I have a word with you on my way out?" Kate watched him go, accompanied by Reed, and began to feel, for the first time that day, a rising sense of panic.

"You were telling me, Miss Fansler, that you do not rent this house?"

"Perhaps I do rent it technically. I don't know. I'm here trying to bring some order into the papers of the late Samuel Lingerwell. Mr. Emmet Crawford is helping me."

"Mr. Crawford is no relation to you."

"No. He is a graduate student in the university where I teach."

"I see. And Mr. Lenehan's duties are in connection with the boy? Is that correct?"

"Yes."

"Is Mr. Lenehan any relation to you?"

"No. He is a graduate student also. I am really afraid, Mr. Stratton, that I have an unfortunate talent for unconventional situations. I can never decide whether odd things happen to me or, as Shaw suggested about himself, I happen to them. I fear you must find all this dreadfully strange."

"Then apart from the boy, who is your nephew, no one in the household is related to you at all, or even very well known to you?"

"I cannot think," Kate, who had been priding herself on the remarkable degree of calm she was maintaining, burst out, "why the matter of relationships is one which strikes you as of such overwhelming importance. True, I am not living in the bosom of my family. However, since my parents are dead, my family is, so to speak, without a bosom—though I have to admit I should not have the slightest desire to throw myself on it, should one be discoverable. I can quite see that from the police point of view, this household must appear a dreadful strain on your descriptive powers, but perhaps if you look at it in the light of a summer study group, complete with casual nephew, it will appear a more orderly phenomenon.''

"Is Mr. Reed Amhearst any relation?''

"I shall go mad, round the bend, completely and absolutely crackers. Reed Amhearst, if you must know, Mr. Stratton, is a man with whom I happen to be . . .''

"Spending what was supposed to be a quiet weekend,'' Reed said, walking into the room. "You've no objection to my listening in, silently, have you, Mr. Stratton?''

"Perhaps,'' Mr. Stratton said, in a voice which admitted no possibility of irritation, "I can conclude my questions on this household. Present here also are, according to my notes, a Miss Eveline Chisana, and a Miss Grace Knole, as well as . . .''

"Both ladies should be referred to as Professor,'' Kate said, with some asperity. Reed might have saved her from God knew what ghastly admission, but she was not about to let Mr. Stratton get away with anything. She had taken quite a dislike to Mr. Stratton, who appeared, insofar as one could perceive anything through his bland manner, to be returning the sentiment in spades.

"Professors of what?''

"English and comparative literature. Professor Knole is a specialist in medieval literature, Professor Chisana in the eighteenth century.''

" 'Be not the first by whom the new is tried/Nor yet the last to lay the old aside,' '' Mr. Stratton surprisingly said.

"Exactly,'' Kate agreed.

"And what are you a specialist in, Miss Fansler?''

"Victorian literature. 'Ring out, wild bells.' 'Oh, love, let us be true to one another.' ''

"I prefer the eighteenth century. Order.''

"Professor Chisana's views exactly. I'm sure you'll get on very well.''

"She and Professor Knole are guests here?''

"Yes.''

"Were they previously acquainted with any members of the household besides yourself?''

"Professor Chisana is a friend of Mr. Lenehan's. Professor Knole may, before her retirement, have known both of them—I'm not certain. She certainly knew Emmet Crawford, since she recommended him to me. She was head of the department in which both men are graduate students.''

"Mr. Amhearst and the boy are also your guests?"

"Yes. Though Leo might be called a member of the household."

"In what exactly do Mr. Lenehan's duties consist?"

"He offers companionship and instruction to Leo. Leo had fallen rather behind in his schoolwork. Under William's direction, Leo writes essays, does problems in arithmetic, and learns to relate coherently his experiences, at camp and elsewhere." Mr. Stratton looked as though he thought Kate too could profit from lessons in relating her experiences coherently.

"I wonder," he said, "if you would have any objection to my questioning the other members of your household? I believe we have determined who all of them are, except for the help, indoors and out."

"Whether they talk to you seems to be their decision, or the law's, not mine."

"Very well. And is there a room in which I might question them quietly."

"There's the library, where Emmet works."

"That will do very nicely, thank you. Only one more question, Miss Fansler, for now. How well did you know the dead woman?"

"Not very well. On the other hand, I'm not sure there was much to know. As you will no doubt gather if you pursue your investigations, she was not widely loved."

"Had you any reason to dislike her?"

"Apart from the fact that she had all the endearing characteristics of a bobcat, no. Whom do you wish to see first?"

"Since Mr. Crawford is supposedly in the library, we might as well start with him." They all stood up. "I hope, Mr. Amhearst," Mr. Stratton said, "that you will not mind answering a few questions later on."

"Certainly not. Might I, at the moment, usurp the privilege of making a suggestion? After you have questioned everyone in this house, you might turn your attention to the rural community outside. I strongly suspect that you'll find the cause of your crime there. Mary Bradford was hated by many, and it seems to me likely that this household, with its lack of surface conventionalities, appeared a likely agent for the carrying out of the murderer's plans."

"We have every intention, Mr. Amhearst, of pursuing that line of inquiry. Will you be kind enough, Miss Fansler, to show us to the library?''

"What's the other fellow for?" Kate asked Reed, as they walked out onto the lawn. " 'I have a little shadow that goes in and out with me,/And what can be the use of him is more than I can see;/He's just exactly like me from my toes up to my head . . .' I hope the rest of it isn't appropriate. Do you really think the answer is in the rural community outside, as you so stuffily put it?''

"The other fellow—to take your questions in the order in which they were presented—is note taker and witness, should one be required.''

"And protector of Mr. Stratton, should any of us go beserk and try throttling the pompous son of a . . .''

"Kate, he's only doing his job, though I do admit his manner is a trifle unrelaxed.''

"Unrelaxed! He makes a stuffed shirt look like a crumpled nightgown. It occurs to me, not for the first time, that you are something special in the way of a district attorney: you're neither familiar nor pompous with people you meet, and that's not only commendable, it's extraordinary.''

"To answer your second question . . .''

"I take it back; perhaps you're pompous after all.''

"I don't know if the crime is really outside this household. I'm reserving judgment, but I thought it well to direct Mr. Stratton's attention in that direction. Kate, will you please behave yourself? You were allowing him to annoy you into admissions you would not ordinarily make, and that is exactly his intention. Whatever were you about to say when I came in?''

"None of your business. If you wanted to find out, you should have stayed outside and listened. Reed, you're not really worried that I'm going to land us in some frightful situation by letting my tongue run away with me? I've nothing to hide, really, and you yourself said we weren't to withhold . . .''

"Do you know why I want to marry you? Because if it's not exactly legal to beat your wife, it's less illegal than to beat a woman to whom you're not related in any way. Shall we get married?''

"You just want to marry me so I can't testify against you in court. You're afraid I'm going to tell Mr. Stratton that you wanted to marry Mary Bradford in order to stuff your socks up her vacuum cleaner. Reed, Reed, where is this going to end?''

"Do you know, I'm frightfully worried about where it's going to end, and I think, far from being a mare's nest, this whole situation may well be a hornets' nest about to explode. But though I'm certain I ought to be lecturing you about the proprieties, and brooding about what all those innocents are saying in there, and feeling mournful over the death of Mary Bradford, who met, God help her, a mean and violent death, I'm aware of only one desire . . ."

"Which had better, according to your own precepts, be unexpressed. Do you know, you're beginning to talk like me, full of subordinate clauses, and penultimate climaxes, interspersed with periodic sentences. We can't possibly disappear, can we?"

"Not possibly."

"Why did Cunningham disappear? Do you think he's given us up as a bad job, or were we taking too much of his time?"

"He felt that for all of us to talk only in the presence of a lawyer would not give the tone of innocence it is so important to convey. Cunningham's clever as hell, and he knows the police know it. If he walks off leaving us to their tender mercies, it's as good as saying he doesn't even think they've got a case."

"Doesn't he?"

"All Cunningham's clients are innocent by definition, didn't he tell you?"

"I hope we are innocent. But if we don't find the murderer, and I don't see, really, how we can, won't it be a dreadful cloud hanging over us all?"

"Oddly enough, I don't believe the innocent need fear the clouds, not in this case. Hello, speaking of innocents, we appear to be about to entertain Mr. Mulligan."

"The news must be all over the valley. You see before you a man making straight for the horse's mouth."

"Ah, Miss Fansler," Mr. Mulligan said, approaching. "What sad news."

"You refer to the death of Mary Bradford?"

"Death is always sad. But I referred, actually, to the inconvenience to your household. Might I offer any assistance?"

"Come in and have some lunch. If the police should join us, you can help me to behave myself in their austere presence. If not, we can exchange gossip. Had any orgies lately?"

"Kate," Reed said between his teeth, "I have definitely decided not to wait for marriage. I tell you what, Mr. Mulligan," he said, raising his voice to its normal range, "perhaps Miss Fansler will allow us a little sherry before lunch, since the circumstances are, shall we say, a bit exceptional."

Kate stuck out her tongue at him.

8

Ivy Day in the
Committee Room

BY four o'clock Mr. Stratton had finally worked his way through the household, including the cook and gardener. Mr. Pasquale, indeed, was never there on Sunday, but aware of the presence of the police, he had arrived and begun weeding an already weeded flower bed, making it manifest that he hadn't the smallest intention of leaving until the fall of night or the departure of the police, whichever should occur first. The news of Mary Bradford's gruesome death had spread far and wide, beyond the bounds of Araby, and the sightseers were already beginning to converge. The police were coping with these, but Kate was heard to mutter that they had better get some "No Parking" signs, as in the case of the automobile accident, to which Reed answered that there were always, in any community, rural or urban, people to whom a murder was an experience invigorating in the extreme, and the scene of a murder fascinating beyond description. He supposed these were the sort who attended hangings in the eighteenth century, and drawing and quarterings in Tudor times.

Mr. Stratton consented, since it was four o'clock, to partake together with his cohort, of a sandwich and a glass of milk. He consented reluctantly, overborne apparently by the obvious hunger pangs of his associate and the information that the nearest restaurant was sixteen miles away, coming and going. Following this repast, he requested to see the three "lady professors" in the library. Food had clearly not improved his disposition, which had in addition been tried to the uttermost by his attempts to grapple with James Joyce.

"Perhaps," he said when they had all forgathered, "you three, since you are all professors of literature, can explain James Joyce to me."

"I am reminded, Mr. Stratton," Grace Knole said, "of a novel by Thomas Hardy, a minor novel I believe, though the name escapes me. In this particular work, a man, courting a young woman, is forced to admit to her that he has also proposed in the past to her mother and grandmother."

Mr. Stratton looked as though he was already regretting his decision to consult them. "But how," he began, "could one man . . ."

"I suggest that you not get bogged down in the mathematics of it now," Grace said. "Turn it over in your mind when you're trying to get to sleep tonight, remembering that women in those days married and had children at sixteen, and a good thing too, you are doubtless thinking, forced into confabulation with three spinsters of varying ages." The look on Mr. Stratton's face indicated that that was exactly what he had been thinking or, to be more exact, had been about to think, for Grace Knole's mind, working more rapidly than that of any other brilliant scholar, was bound to be several steps ahead of a mere policeman's.

"About James Joyce," Mr. Stratton said.

The three looked inquiringly at him.

"There's a story here, now, called 'Ivy Day in the Committee Room.' While eating the lunch Miss Fansler was kind enough to offer me, I read that story in a book Mr. Emmet Crawford in his turn was kind enough to offer me. I had asked him, since he seemed to keep mentioning this writer James Joyce, if there was anything short of his that I might read. The story was eighteen pages long, and I didn't understand a word of it. Neither," he added, "did my associate."

"Yes," Kate said. "It's always been a difficult story, as a matter of fact. Do you mean, Mr. Stratton, that nothing seems to happen in it?"

"That's exactly what I mean."

"But that, you see, is the whole point. Nothing is happening in Ireland at all. All the people are dead, actually; incapable of love."

"Like Mary Bradford," Lina said.

"Now that you mention it," Kate said, "exactly like Mary Bradford."

"Is that," Grace asked, "why Forster said of Joyce that he was throwing mud on the universe?"

"Forster was speaking of *Ulysses*, and in any case I think he's retracted the statement since. He said that when everyone thought of Joyce as immoral."

"There's a story I heard," Grace said, "of someone's dining with Joyce, and raising a glass of wine with a toast of immorality. 'I won't drink to that,' Joyce is supposed to have said, turning down his wineglass."

"It was white wine," Kate said.

"Does it matter," Mr. Stratton asked, in tones of one who has suffered long and silently, "what color the wine was?"

"Of course it matters," Kate said. "That's the whole point about Joyce's work. In 'Ivy Day in the Committee Room' the most important thing that happens is a bottle goes 'Pop.' "

Mr. Stratton looked as though he would soon go "Pop" himself.

"What's Ivy Day, to begin with?" he asked.

"There's a book, paperback, I believe, called *A Reader's Guide to James Joyce*," Grace said, "by William York Tindall. You must allow me to present you with a copy. I get a faculty discount, a privilege extended even to emeritus professors. Tindall says, if I remember correctly, that everything in the story acquires meaning by reference to Parnell. Do I understand you to be suggesting, Mr. Stratton, that everything in this case acquires meaning by reference to James Joyce?"

"Is Ivy Day Parnell's birthday then?"

"That's funny," Kate said. "I'm not certain if it's his birthday, or the day he died, or something to do with the divorce. But on that day, October 6, everyone in Dublin who wishes to bask in remembrance of Parnell wears ivy in his buttonhole. They are all paralyzed of course."

"Of course," said Mr. Stratton.

"Why do you supose Emmet showed Mr. Stratton 'Ivy Day in the Committee Room'?" Lina asked.

"It was Joyce's favorite story," Kate said. "Everyone else's favorite, of course, is 'The Dead,' one of the great stories in the English language."

"What's that about?" Mr. Stratton asked.

"About a man named Gabriel Conroy who has never learned to love," Kate said. "About the truth that everyone in Ireland is dead, except perhaps the dead."

"Cheerful sort of chap he sounds," Mr. Stratton's associate surprisingly put in.

"*Ulysses* is more cheerful," Kate said.

"Isn't that supposed to be an immoral book?" Mr. Stratton asked.

"Neither legally nor actually," Kate said. "In point of fact, it's one of the most moral books in the language. Bloom is bringer of love to a dead city, and to a not-yet-artist who has not yet learned to love. Light to the gentiles."

"I thought there was a lot of sex in it," Mr. Stratton bravely said.

"There's a lot of sex in life," Kate answered.

"In some lives," Grace Knole said. Kate avoided Lina's eyes.

"Would you say," Mr. Stratton asked, "that Joyce is important?"

"Of course he's important," Grace said. "Read Richard Ellmann's biography. Brilliant. Not, I believe, in paperback. Too expensive for me to offer you a copy, even with a faculty discount. Perhaps," she suggested, "you could put it on your expense account."

"I never know what people mean by important," Lina said.

"All these letters of his lying around here," Mr. Stratton said, before a literary argument could ensue. "Mr. Crawford tells me the Library of Congress and lots of universities have been after them."

"Ah," said Grace Knole.

"Odd that a woman should be killed at a house with a collection of letters from an Irishman."

"There was probably no connection at all. Now Mary Bradford was the sort," Kate added, "who would have found *Ulysses* a dirty book, and Bloom a dirty man. Of course," she added, "Joyce didn't have much use for WASPS."

"Wasps?" Mr. Stratton asked, with the air of one prepared to hear anything.

"White Anglo-Saxon Protestant; Puritan; Calvinist."

"I'm a Calvinist," Grace Knole said.

"I am sure he would have made exceptions." Kate smiled. "In fact, we know he did. But his vision encompassed mainly the world of Catholics and Jews. There was a time, you know, when he thought of being a priest. 'I have given up the Society of Jesus for the society of Jewses,' he's supposed to have said."

Mr. Stratton and his associate looked rather shocked. "You seem to know a great deal about Joyce, Miss Fansler," Mr. Stratton said.

"Very little, I assure you."

"I thought you said your specialty was Victorian."

"So it is, but we are not all allowed to stay sheltered and unmolested within our periods, however vast. I give a course in the history of the English novel, under which title we include the Irish."

"Well," said Mr. Stratton, rising, "I think I had better speak to Mr. Mulligan now. I understand he was here. Is he still, do you know?"

"Talking to Emmet, I believe," Kate said, rising also. "Shall I send him in?"

"If you would be so kind," Mr. Stratton said. "Thank you for your literary help, all of you."

"*Our* pleasure," Grace Knole said, leading the way from the room. "But what," she asked when the door had shut behind them, "is the name of that other man, the one who's always with Stratton but barely utters?"

"I haven't a clue," Kate said, "but I call him M'Intosh."

"Why?" Lina asked.

"Read *Ulysses*," Kate maddeningly said.

"I shall make a note of it," Grace said, "and of all the other interesting information just received. *White* wine." She took a notebook from her pocket and wrote in it.

"Do you make a note of everything?" Lina asked in amazement. "Is that how you remember everything?"

"Absolutely. Even the frightful things."

"I have no trouble remembering them," Lina laughed.

"Oh, yes you do. When Alice picks the Red King out of the grate he says, 'I shall never forget the horror of that moment,' and the Red Queen says, 'You will, though, unless you make a memorandum of it.' Since," Grace went on, returning the notebook to her pocket, "we have been ushered from the committee room, shall we take a walk? I wonder if it is milking time, by any chance."

"They're probably just finishing up," Kate said, "to go by what Leo has told me. But of course I did *not* make a memorandum of it."

"Do you think Mr. Bradford would mind our intruding on him, especially today?"

"He's rather patient about it, actually. It seems to me Leo and William used to spend every afternoon down there at milking time, till they knew more about it than he did. Anyway, maybe we ought to be detectives and see how he's reacting. Shall we go? Across the fields, or down the road?''

"The road, I think," Grace said. "I understand how to cope with cars better than those dangers I know not of. With which, incidentally, the rural life seems to be replete. I have known many raging passions in my time, from naked ambition to naked lust, but no one has ended shooting anyone else, though a few to be sure have ended their own lives. I blame it not on the greater inherent violence of rural life, but on the greater familiarity with guns and violent death. I expect after you have many times seen a deer or woodchuck blown to bits, the thought of a human being blown to bits is that much less impossible to conceive."

"Bradford once told me," Kate said, "that there are no thefts around here precisely because everyone knows that everyone has a gun, knows how to use it, and will use it."

"It does then, doesn't it," Grace asked, "sound rather as though someone would be likelier to grab a gun and shoot Mary Bradford out of sheer annoyance, rather than slip a bullet into someone else's gun? I mean, do you think this really sounds like a rural crime? It seems to me more the crime of a metaphoric mind."

"A Joycean mind, you mean?" Lina asked.

"Literary, anyway."

"I don't follow that," Kate said. "It seems to me some rural type who hated her saw the chance of getting rid of her and took it. The fact that it would be involving a pack of nuts from the city in a hell of a lot of trouble simply added to the attractions of the method. Here comes a car."

The three of them stepped to the side of the road as the car, driven too fast by the inevitable adolescent male, slowed only enough to permit the yelling back of some invitation seething with sarcasm. As the three of them returned to the road, Grace chuckled.

"Now in a piece of mystery fiction, that car would contain not howling adolescents, but adventure. Do you read mystery stories?"

"Certainly," Kate said. "And do Double-Crostics. It's either that, I've found, or bridge, boats and skiing. Why?"

"It is interesting," Grace said, "how unlike life those stories really are. Their whole point is that so much *happens*. I don't mean those Ian Fleming books. Even nice little English mysteries, of what Auden calls the body in the vicarage type, they're so full of *events*. We have had a murder, now, but all we do, of course, is talk about it, and walk down a road together, three odd ladies in tennis shoes, to watch the husband of the deceased milk some cows.''

"I know what you mean," Kate said. "The English mystery begins with someone reading one of those advertisements in the *Times*, on the front page where they used to be so eccentric as to put them, and it says, 'Peter, if you are wondering about me, go and see Henry. Colin.' So Peter rushes off to see Henry, who turns out to be an old nanny aged eighty, and the next thing you know he's trapped in some house behind the Iron Curtain, climbing out by hammering a piece of metal into the brickwork over and over again. If anybody locked me into a house, which is of course highly unlikely, I'd stay until I was rescued or, more likely, die of starvation.''

"That was a very good book all the same.''

"Of course it was a good book. Then there was the one I read recently of a thirty-fiveish spinster who goes to Europe for a vacation, has her car used for smuggling something or other into France, ends up locked in a cellar with some marvelous Frenchman, and takes the opportunity to learn what sleeping with men is all about, while the criminals are dropping bodies into the ocean the while.''

"That was a very good book too.''

"Excellent. But the point, I think, is that things don't happen to people who've lived thirty-five years or more without their happening.''

"You're right," Grace said. "If I'd been locked in the cellar at age thirty-five with a Frenchman, however fascinating, I would have ended discussing some abstruse point of medieval culture if he was educated, or letting him tell me about the perils of the French economy and Gallic bravery in wars if he wasn't. Either one is the sort to whom adventure happens, or one isn't. And if one is the sort, I suspect one doesn't think or talk or read very much, one just adventures.''

"One is certainly not likely to be locked in the cellar with a fascinating Frenchman," Lina said.

"And if we were, we would be so distressed at the thought of all those bodies being dropped into the ocean, we would not be thinking about having experiences.''

"I would," Lina said.

"The whole point about mysteries," Grace said, "is that it is so nice to read about other people's doing things without having to do that sort of thing oneself.''

"We are the sort who read mysteries and make memoranda," Kate said, smiling.

They had arrived at the barn. Bradford was milking, helped by the farmer from down the road.

"Do you mean they milk with machines?" Lina said, looking about her.

"They do everything with machines," Grace said. "I've gathered that much."

"Do the cows like standing with their heads caught that way?" Lina asked, after the visiting ladies, properly introduced, had, together with Kate, offered their condolences.

"Since they're fed that way, they like it," Bradford said, "but the new theory is that they're better off in open-pen barns, with a milking room and no stanchions. Watch out now." He reached above their heads and opened a trapdoor in the ceiling. A bale of hay came tumbling down from the hayloft above. He untied it and began raking the hay out to the cows.

"Mr. Bradford," Kate said. "Is there any way we can help with your children? We'll be glad to take them home with us for supper, and to sleep, if that would help you in any way."

"Thank you," Bradford said. "That's very kind. But a young lady from the village, friend of the family, has come out to look after things."

"Well," Kate said, "let me know if there's anything at all we can do."

The three ladies watched as Bradford fed the calves with powdered milk dissolved in water, removed the milking machine from each cow, fed each cow varying amounts of grain, and listened with a practiced ear to the machinery in his milk house. There a large, stainless steel tank, he explained to them, cooled the milk in three minutes from the cow's body temperature, about a hundred degrees, to less than sixty degrees. Three times a week the milk truck siphoned the milk out of the tank directly into the truck and drove away with it.

"Amazing," Grace said. "Is the whole top of the barn filled with hay?"

"It will have to be full soon, for the winter," Bradford said. "The hay we just fed the cows is the last of last summer's crop. There are over four thousand bales of hay in there already, and more to come. Would you like to see the hay elevator work?" he asked.

"Well," Grace Knole said, "if you would be so good."

"Please don't trouble," Kate said at the same time.

"No trouble," Bradford seemed glad to take his time explaining. "Those bales in the wagon," he said, "were thrown up there by the baling machine. We take each bale out of the wagon and put it on this elevator, which lifts it up to the hayloft. Watch out now." He started the machinery, and the elevator lifted the bale of hay up to the second story of the barn. Bradford, leaping to the hayloft before the bale, lifted it from the elevator and threw it back in the hayloft. "Come up and see," he said.

The three ladies eyed the perpendicular ladder leading to the hayloft with varying concern. Lina and Kate, without much hesitation, scrambled up it. Grace Knole remained on the ground. "I no longer admit," she said, "the possibilities of *either* cellars or haylofts. Look around, and tell me about it." Kate and Lina were astonished at the size of the barn's second floor. There was not a support or column visible; only open space and thousands of bales of hay. "It's a beautiful building," Kate said to Bradford.

"Designed it myself. Mary thought I was crazy, but I said it was possible to design an absolutely open hayloft. Poor Mary," he said, remembering. The three of them climbed solemnly down.

"One man," Grace said, as they started back up the road, "can run a farm, provided he is a mechanical genius, an architect, an agronomist, and a veterinarian rolled into one."

"What an extraordinary amount of hay," Lina said.

"On the whole," Kate said, "should one run into a Frenchman, I think a cellar would be preferable. Less irritating to the nasal passages, and less likely to induce acrophobia."

Reed was waiting for them halfway up the road. "Where have you been?" he asked. "You're not supposed to wander off from the scene of a murder without permission."

"Do you mean we're under house arrest?" Grace asked.

"We were exploring haylofts," Kate said.

"Find anything?"

"I should hate," Kate said, "to have to find anything in a hayloft. Bradford seems something less than inconsolable."

"I couldn't help wondering," Lina said, "about the girl from the village."

"Has Mr. Stratton asked Mr. Mulligan about Joyce?" Kate asked.

"What in God's name," Reed said, "is 'Ivy Day in the Committee Room'?"

"He *has* been asking about Joyce. What about 'Ivy Day'?"

"It seems Mr. Mulligan didn't know about something going 'Pop.' But then, of course, neither did I."

"But you haven't written several books on form and function in modern fiction."

"It's odd about Mr. Mulligan," Grace said.

9

Clay

By Sunday night, the police squads had finished. The mortal remains of Mary Bradford had been removed. "And where her immortal remains may be, I scarcely dare to think," Emmet observed. Mr. Stratton departed, together with his associate now dubbed M'Intosh.

On Monday, William was due for arraignment in the county court. Reed offered to drive him down, and Lina, for whose company William now manifested an almost childlike need, went along. They were to be met in court by John Cunningham, who would bring, Reed astonished everyone by saying, five thousand dollars in cash or certified check. "Cunningham's certain that's absolutely the highest bail they can set," Reed told Kate. "In fact," he continued, "if it's that high, it doesn't bode well for William if the police fail to find the murderer."

"But William hasn't committed murder," Kate said.

"He has, my dear. Accidental murder, but murder nonetheless."

"No more than if I ran over someone in my car, and killed her."

"In both cases, you see, the victim would be dead at the hand, so to speak, of another."

"Reed. Where is Cunningham getting the five thousand dollars? Does he provide it as part of his legal services?"

"May I live to see the day. The money is put up by the prisoner, or his friends, who will get it back if he doesn't vanish."

"I'm certain William doesn't have five thousand dollars."

"William doesn't have five thousand cents; not, that is, to spare."

"Reed, it's clearly my responsibility . . ."

"Which I, temporarily, am assuming."

"I can't see why you should come all over gallant."

"Neither can I. If you insist on immuring yourself in the woods, setting up a household which startles even the most hardened criminal lawyer in Boston, and then strewing the countryside with bodies, there is no good reason under the sun why I shouldn't let you find bail for your unfortunate employees, or leave them to battle their own way out of this predicament. After all, they must have known what they were letting themselves in for when they went to work for you. However, since I am not only as besotted as you are, but entangled into the bargain as a prime witness, if not a suspect, you must let me take upon my manly shoulders what responsibilities I can. In short, be of good cheer, have a drink waiting, should we return, and pray that the judge lets our William off with bail. This news, and more, will I bring upon my return; now, I to county courthouse, and thee to Araby, as they insist on saying in those dreary Shakespearean histories."

"They are *not* dreary."

"Good. Let us hope we get out of this mess soon enough to go and see one in Central Park. Odds bodkins!"

It was, therefore, a diminished group which settled down to lunch. Leo was off at camp, receiving the instruction of Mr. Artifoni. "Doubtless," Kate said, passing around the salad, "he will lecture the boys on the finer points of treating gunshot wounds. With luck, we will learn tonight whether one dies faster of a bullet in the head or the heart."

"I thought it was a sports camp," Grace said. "Is treating gunshot wounds a sport?"

"Every American boy should know first aid, my dear lady," Emmet said. "Surely you can grasp that. If, like me, he faints at the sight of blood, and doesn't know artificial respiration from Cheyne-Stokes breathing, he is clearly going to be of no use in emergencies, or so Leo informs me. I pointed out that boys are by definition no use in emergencies, but Leo said you never can tell. That's it, you see, Mr. Artifoni has all those little creatures positively longing for a calamity. Had Mary Bradford bled to death, I should have suspected half the camp of doing it to provide tourniquet practice. I'm virtually certain Leo's nightly prayer is that William or I will sever an artery and he can save us. Our dinner conversation is of the goriest, isn't it, Kate? Were it up to me, I would forbid the child to mention so much as a corpuscle. Does that answer your question?''

Grace grinned at him. ''Mr. Crawford, I must arrange for you to address the master's students on Jane Austen, just so that I can come and listen to you.''

''James Joyce, please, or someone equally modern. I've been reading through such scads of material, all of it marvelous, that I'm thinking of throwing over dear old Jane and writing on the importance of editors to modern literature. With Kate's permission, of course.''

''Someone *ought* to do a book on Sam Lingerwell. How far have you got now?'' Kate asked.

''It's scandalously slow going. Lingerwell did at least arrange the letters chronologically, which is to say each September he took out another huge file box and as he answered them, started throwing in all the letters he received. It would have been much easier, needless to say, for me to arrange the stuff by date rather than correspondents, but that would scarcely be of as much use to scholars. The Lawrence letters are fascinating, but the Joyce letters are the ones which really show up Lingerwell. Particularly the letters about *Dubliners*. After the *Portrait*, and with *Ulysses* under way, he wrote Lingerwell rather less. But the trouble they gave him over *Dubliners*, you wouldn't believe it. What the printers particularly objected to, apparently, was the fact that he mentioned real places in Dublin. Can you imagine? Today, if an author doesn't mention real places, he might just as well be writing for the funny papers. All he has to do is say 'any similarity to an actual person or place is purely coincidental' and everyone knows it's a *roman à clef*.''

''Wasn't there something there shouldn't have been about Edward VII?'' Grace asked.

''How you do pick up information,'' Kate said.

''Well, why shouldn't he have something to say about that fat voluptuary?'' Emmet asked. ''I know, I know, you are going to tell me Edward brought about the *entente* with France, whatever that was. But he just managed it because he spoke perfect French. The French, who are devoid of any moral sense, can't help admiring a man who speaks their precious language well. He still spent all his time enjoying himself in a childish way.''

''I have always liked him,'' Grace said. ''Admittedly he hated abstract ideas or intelligent conversation, and apparently threw a fit if one was dressed a shade less than impeccably. But he had great tact. He was once visited by an Indian prince who, after eating asparagus, threw the stalks over his shoulder onto the carpet. The other guests all stared at him in hopeless fascination, but old Tum-tum just started throwing *his* stalks over his shoulder, as though it were the most natural thing in the world, and soon all the guests were doing it. I like tact on that scale."

"Better than his mother, anyway," Kate said, "who is supposed to have been unreasonably upset when some visiting potentate sacrificed a sheep on one of the best rugs in Buckingham Palace."

"Tum-tum?" Emmet asked.

"That, I understand, is what his mistresses called him," Grace said. "I have to admit, you know, that in addition to being fond of Edward VII, I think *Dubliners* exceedingly overrated. I was looking at it last night, after our particularly fascinating session with Mr. Stratton. If half the Ph.D.'s in the country hadn't taken it upon themselves to write endlessly about the book, I don't think anyone would have paid it more than passing attention."

"That's what I've always felt about Milton," Kate said. "Once you've read *Paradise Lost* fourteen times, you damn well *have* to find it interesting."

"I don't agree, as you know," Grace said. "But I do not mean to disparage Joyce. I'm only suggesting that *Dubliners* is of real interest only because it led to *Ulysses*."

"To put it another way," Emmet said, "*Dubliners*, being Dublin without Bloom, never quite finds real life, as opposed to real death."

"We were saying something like that yesterday afternoon to those two gallants. Isn't it rather heartless," Kate went on, "speaking of how awful Dublin was, for us to be sitting around gossiping about Joyce with a woman recently dead on our doorstep?"

"Some," Emmet said, "we know to be dead though they walk among us; some are not yet born though they go through the forms of life; others are hundreds of years old though they call themselves thirty-six. I can't think why they should occur to me in connection with Mary Bradford; perhaps it's only in connection with you."

"That quote's never from Joyce."

"No," Emmet said. "I prefer lady authors, really; their wisdom is somehow distilled by the purity of their perceptions."

"Wow!"

"Do you like it? I thought it up for a beginning sentence of an essay."

"And where did you find that about some we know to be dead though they walk among us?"

"Virginia Woolf. Pity Lingerwell never corresponded with her. Now if you had any Woolf letters, you wouldn't see me for the dust."

"Emmet, don't joke about such things. The question is, what are we going to do about Mary Bradford?"

"You're not suggesting first aid after all this time?"

"I'm suggesting, not to put too fine a point on it, that if we don't find out who put the bullet in that gun, William's life is not going to be very easy, and I gather it isn't a bed of roses even now."

"Nobly spoken," Emmet said. "I, too, though you may not think it, have grown fond of William, and indeed have suggested that he apply to you for permission to desert Gerard Manley Hopkins, magnificent poet that he is, and write his dissertation on some of Lingerwell's material. But I'm afraid his block is psychological if not sexual; his whole life, really, is one long orgy of continence. Having committed murder, however unintentional, does not appear to me precisely the method one would choose above all others to help him over the double hurdle of dissertation block and rigid chastity. But what can we do? You are not, I trust, suggesting that we find a rural type and frame him?"

"I am suggesting," Kate said, "if I'm to be brutally honest, that we at least allow ourselves to assume it is a rural murder, and look for a rural murderer. I hope—indeed, I trust—that we shall be able to keep an open mind in the face of any evidence. At the same time I would rather like to find some evidence. The police, with a single-mindedness that is rather typical of them, appear to be concentrating their powers, on which I am not inclined to place too high a value, on our own poor selves."

"Well," Emmet said, "looking on what we know of this rural community as so much clay, let us see if we can design ourselves something of particularly clever construction."

"To continue your figure, it's rather a small amount of clay we have."

"Araby is a small town."

"Can we be certain the murderer is from Araby?"

"I rather think so. Of course, someone may have told someone, who told someone, who told someone in Detroit, who came all the way east to do the murder, but I can't help feeling that the neatness of the whole plan involved a particularly local familiarity with the conditions.''

"Might I,'' Grace said, "ask a thoroughly tactless question?''

"By all means,'' Kate said. "But while we're mentioning tact, let me grasp the opportunity to say that there isn't the smallest reason why you should stay here. I'm delighted you agreed to come for a visit, and should I ever again take a house, which is about as likely as that I will allow myself to be launched in a spaceship, I should be delighted if you would honor me by being my guest. Meantime, however, I shouldn't blame you if you decided to get the hell out of here. If Lina wants to hold William's hand . . .''

"And I'd be surprised if he lets her go that far,'' Emmet said.

"Someone,'' Kate continued, ignoring Emmet, "will be glad to drive you home. I love you, I love having you, but please don't feel you have to stay, on the same theory which induced King Edward to throw the asparagus over his shoulder.''

"Nothing could induce me to go. Unless you feel you can no longer bear my company, or find my presence, under the circumstances, the proverbial straw.''

"Nonsense.''

"Then let us say no more about it. I accepted your invitation, you know, not only because I like going places since I retired, and because dear Lina was driving up anyway, but also to serve my own ends. Should you ever become extricated from this preposterous situation, Kate, I would like to talk to you about something rather special.''

"How enticing. Let's go to it immediately after lunch.''

"Certainly not. First things first. I insist, since I'm to remain, on asking my thoroughly tactless question.''

"Ask away.''

"Are we certain that it was William who shot the woman? Or was it, possibly, Leo, for whom William is assuming the blame or, more exactly, shouldering the burden of inevitable guilt.''

"Naturally,'' Kate said, staring into her coffee cup, "that occurred to me, right off like a shot, to be perfectly frank. I taxed William with being a chivalrous idiot, and suggested, with more forcefulness than delicacy, that I had never noticed lying to be a help, however gallant the lie, however compromising the circumstances. William agreed with me most sweetly, and assured me that he, in fact, had taken the gun from Leo and fired it. Leo, whom naturally I didn't want to interrogate too closely, seemed to agree with this account. My own suspicion, for what it's worth, is that William convinced Leo that he, William, had shot the lethal weapon when Leo had actually done so. A case, you might say, of brainwashing. Leo thinks the world of William, and would gladly accept William's word, forcefully enough presented, against the evidence of his own senses. But whether William is actually telling the truth, or protecting Leo, we may never know. Clearly, it's impossible, at this point, to pursue the matter any further.''

"For some reason," Grace said, "I think it's important."

"Of course it's important. Apart from everything else, I have assumed, albeit unwillingly, summer custody of my nephew, only to involve him in a murder case, if not in the actual murder. What I shall say to my brother I scarcely dare to think."

"You haven't, I take it, heard from him."

"Fortunately, he is in Europe, and it is to be hoped that the European edition of the *Times*, which he is almost certainly reading, will not carry the story of our relatively minor rural murder. But a day of reckoning will come. I shall have to arm myself with a stiff brandy and say 'I told you so.' I don't know what I told him, but I always find that statement leaves the opposition searching for the retort glorious, during which hiatus one departs from the scene of combat. I'm worried about Leo, naturally, but that's mostly because it seems a worrying sort of situation. In point of fact, he's done wonderfully well this summer, though whether due to the presence of William, the absence of his parents or the simple transformations of time I couldn't say."

"Thank you for letting me get that off my mind," Grace said. "Let us return then to our clay, as Emmet called it. Araby. How small is it?"

"About four hundred, including babes in arms. About one hundred and forty odd households, I think, pay taxes. Of these, well over half are summer people with large, highly taxed establishments, who do not use the schools, the nursing service or the library—which, incidentally, I have discovered to be a fancy name for a few tattered volumes available between the hours of two on Thursday."

"What made Sam Lingerwell ever decide to buy a house here?"

"A good question it only recently occurred to me to ask. I've written a letter to his daughter, and with luck may get answers to a number of things. The reason, however, is probably simply that he visited here and liked the country. *We* know that the rural community is not exactly to the taste of the urban devotee, but that was hardly likely to emerge on a casual weekend. The views are beautiful, the air cool, and somehow country life seems so simple when one is contemplating it from a New York office in the middle of a frantic afternoon. He certainly couldn't have known, for instance, that Mary Bradford would be a neighbor.''

"Well, then," said Emmet, getting down to it, "who have we in Araby who might have put the bullet in William Lenehan's gun? There's us, the Bradfords, Mr. Mulligan, Mr. Artifoni and his camp—who else can we mold into a suspect nearer to the heart's desire?''

"North of us, all summer people whom, alas, I am inclined to exonerate. They haven't 'called,' as the country people say; they certainly wouldn't know anything about the household—anyway, not enough to slip a bullet into the gun. Doubtless they've heard gossip about us from some of the natives, but that's always wildly off the mark—certainly impossible for all murder-planning purposes. That leaves the local people on the road, who of course include the Pasquales and the Monzonis, both of which families know all about us and are prime suspects. But did they hate Mary Bradford, really hate her? Make a note, Emmet, we must find out. Of course there are other farmers, and one or two Italian families to whom Mary Bradford always referred as 'white trash,' but apart from the fact that they are cheerful and improvident, like the Flopsy bunnies, I know little about them. I'm beginning to find this conversation depressing. More and more suspicion on poor us.''

"Not necessarily," Emmet said. "Personally, I'm counting heavily on Mr. Mulligan. Who knows how close Mary Bradford was to the truth in her talk of orgies. And while Mr. Mulligan clearly has tenure, and is a full professor at a relatively young age, because he's published so much, one can be fired from a tenure position for moral turpitude.''

"Surely that means raping a student in the halls, at the very least.''

"Running orgies might do in a pinch. Or seducing your assistant professors. Even if Mr. Mulligan only thought Mary Bradford was a threat, won't that do? Then there's Artifoni, into whose affairs I would dearly love to look. Oh, stop worrying about Leo, Kate, I'm sure he's righteous as all get-out with small boys, but how much was the woman affecting his camp? Also, I don't want to cast aspersions in these matters, if they are aspersions, but Americans might do well to wake up to the fact that homosexual men who deeply resent women are not absolutely always those who go about prancing like little fawns. My suspicions, were I inclined to have any, would certainly be directed at men who spend their whole working time directing boys' activities, their whole playtime at games for boys, their spectator time watching male sports, and if they marry, always have five little crew-cut sons. I bet they drown the girls at birth. Mary Bradford may not have figured all this out, but who knows what her suspicions were. That woman had a nose for scandal, you have to give her that."

"Emmet, are you suggesting that I have not only exposed my nephew to murder, but have placed him in a camp filled with queers?"

"Relax. In point of fact, if Artifoni killed Mary Bradford, it was probably something to do with his precious camp. I'm merely trying to suggest that the most wholesome people may in fact have the personality for murder, which we ought to keep in mind should it be impossible to pin the murder on Artifoni for other reasons."

"Your language leaves much to be desired."

"Why not look at it the other way?" Grace said. "What possible motive could anyone in this house have for killing her? For one thing, the body would be unmistakably on their doorstep. For another, however huge a nuisance she was, and I gather that can scarcely be exaggerated, no one here had to kill her to keep her out of his life. At the worst, this summer's end would conclude any conceivable reason for further relationship. For a third, would anyone among us so stage a murder that a child or his tutor would become the instrument of death? It speaks of a lack of imagination for which I find no evidence here."

"None of this applies if it was Mrs. Monzoni or Mr. Pasquale."

"True. Clearly that needs following up. But this discussion does mean we must look at Mr. Mulligan, I agree with that. Orgies or no orgies, Lina's evidence, should she give it, certainly indicates some lack of imagination on Mr. Mulligan's part."

"How do both of you know so much about Lina and Mr. Mulligan?" Kate asked.

"The Lord hath given us eyes; should we see not?" Grace said. "There were moments when those pleasant summer people were telling me about artificial insemination, and the marvelous indications of the proper time for insemination established by the cows' mounting one another—you may well look amazed, my dear, but I have noticed people often rejoice in discussing sex under the aegis of agriculture—there were moments during this enlightening discourse when I really thought Mr. Mulligan was going to do a little mounting himself, right there in his living room.''

''Professor Knole, I'm shocked,'' Kate said.

''I too,'' said Emmet.

''The trouble with you two,'' Grace said, ''is that like all young people, you wish to restrict the benefits of what I believe is called frank language to your own cohorts. I have often thought we who are more mature should let you hear how it sounds on the lips of another generation. More coffee, anyone?''

10

Eveline

THE courthouse contingent returned just before dinner, sore-footed and world-weary, calling loudly for drink and sustenance.

"I thought perhaps you would bring John Cunningham back with you?" Kate said to Reed.

"Frankly," Reed said, "we can't afford it."

"Doesn't he have any nonbusiness hours he just gives away?"

"Not he. At least, not when he's got any cases pending, and I guess that's constantly, to all intents and purposes. Don't be hard on him, Kate. He took a lot more time to turn up in court in Pittsfield today than he would have done for many clients paying double the fee. And a jolly good thing too. I've brought you a present, by the way."

"Why was it a jolly good thing? You're terrifying me."

"I better have a martini on the rocks. Our only meal was a soggy sandwich and Coca-Cola, neither my favorite forms of food. I am either too old or too degenerate to get a lift from Coke. Thank you. Do serve Lina and William too; their need is greater than mine. Take my advice, dear girl, and don't play around with guns. We had, of course, to pull a judge whose grandson had just shot off his own foot."

"Reed, how frightful!"

"It's not supposed to be anything else. Guns are the devil and all, I've always thought so. But poor William was feeling bad enough in all conscience, without having the judge lecture him at great

length, holding up an already overcrowded court calendar into the
bargain. I thought he would make William write a hundred times
over 'I never again will touch a gun.' "

"It's I who should write something over and over," Kate said.
"I've always loathed and detested guns. But I was afraid of imping-
ing upon a masculine prerogative. Also, I'd read *Hedda Gabler* at
perhaps too impressionable an age. Let's face it, modern Freudian
lingo has got us so frightened of appearing to be castrating women
that we won't even take a gun away from a boy. And I do not want
to hear a chuckle out of you, Emmet Crawford."

"I haven't so much as uttered, dear lady. Proud enough am I to
be drinking cocktails with the grownups."

"Well, this is a special day."

"May I have something with my tomato juice, Aunt Kate?" Leo
asked, pleased at the break in routine which permitted William and
Emmet and himself a place at the cocktail hour.

"I'll give you something in your tomato juice you won't like,"
Kate viciously said.

"Mr. Artifoni says . . ."

"I don't care if Mr. Artifoni forces gin down the throats of his
gurgling charges, you cannot have anything in your tomato juice."

"Aunt Kate! To eat, I meant. Mr. Artifoni says that no good
athlete ever drinks or smokes or . . ." Leo interrupted himself to reach
for a handful of nuts.

"Or what, for the sake of the blessed saints?" Emmet asked.

"Or stays up past ten o'clock," Leo concluded. "Good athletes
never see 'The Late Late Show.' "

"What else happened in court?" Grace asked.

"I'll spare you the technicalities and the long, dreary hours, the
spirit-defeating atmosphere. William was arraigned and released on
payment of bail." Reed paused as Emmet, at a sign from Kate, led
Leo from the room. William and Lina had already departed. "Let us
pray," Reed continued, "that William does not consider pulling a
Lord Jim and fleeing his conscience all over the tropics, because
riding on that lad is more money than I'd care to lose. I must say,
Eveline was a great support in time of need. She even cheered me
up, which was well beyond the call of duty."

"What will happen if William is found guilty of murder in whatever degree it properly is?"

"Who knows? Perhaps a suspended sentence. Let's hope it
doesn't come to that."

"The simple fact is," Kate said, "we have to find the real murderer."

"Kate," Reed said. "I cannot bear to have you hatching some plot that would give the Hardy boys pause. Let's face the fact that it's almost impossible to find out who put the bullet in that gun. All we can do is stir up a peck of trouble and probably get the lot of us run out of the country. Not that I'd mind."

"Reed, believe it or not, I haven't a clue as to how to put a bullet in a gun. Maybe there are others with similar alibis, and by a process of elimination . . ."

"We'll have no one left in Berkshire County who isn't aiming a rifle at *your* head. Kate, I beg of you, behave."

"Won't the policemen do anything?"

"Everything, as is the dull lot of policemen. But what you've got to recognize is that, unless the police are absolutely overwhelmed with evidence to the contrary, they're inclined to assume that the man who pulled the trigger is the murderer. They are certainly not going to run around like one of your favorite detectives proving by some esoteric mumbo jumbo that would never stand up in court—which is why the culprit always commits suicide—that so-and-so must have done it because the gun, by some miraculous idiosyncrasy known only to two people, will shoot a bullet only if the Lord's Prayer is murmured over it in Sanskrit on three successive rainy nights. If you absolutely forced another martini on me, I might acquiesce with a fair grace. Speaking of grace, you never asked me what was the present I brought you."

"I hope it's a proper clue which will lead inevitably to the solution of all our problems."

"That remains to be seen. What I brought you is the collected works, or at least as many as I could collect on short notice, of our Mr. Mulligan. It transpired, during one of those soggy-sandwich repasts about which I was wringing your withers a while back, that Pittsfield, bless its up-to-date little heart, has a community college and a bookstore. So while the court was recessed, Cunningham was on the phone, and William and Eveline seemed capable, under pressure, of getting along without me, I wandered round to the bookstore and discovered that many of Mr. Mulligan's books are available in paperback. The clerk told me they were very popular with students, mainly, he intimated, because they were such good 'cram stuff'—his phrase, not mine. Anyway, since you and Grace Knole keep saying you're interested in Mr. Mulligan, I thought you might want to cast a professional eye on whatever it is has got him a promotion to full professor and all the rest of it. Considering, I mean, that he didn't know what went 'Pop' in the committee room.''

"Who's hatching plots now, my little Hardy boy?"

"That's the thanks I get for bearing gifts. Another? I couldn't possibly. Force it down my throat."

"Dibs on *Form and Function in Modern Fiction*," Grace said, looking over the package of books.

"By all means," Kate said. "I shall confine myself to *The Novel: Tension and Technique*. Much more my cup of tea anyway."

"Dinner, dinner, dinner," Leo called, "Mrs. Monzoni said so."

"And what of interest did Mr. Artifoni say today, my little man?" Emmet asked as they were seated at the table.

"Mr. Artifoni said that guard is the most important position in basketball, even if he doesn't get to shoot baskets and it doesn't seem so important at first. He said," Leo went on, helping himself generously to mashed potatoes, "that the guard doesn't talk of how many baskets *he* got, but of how many baskets his man got."

"How many baskets did your man get?" Kate asked.

"He didn't," Leo said. "We never play basketball on Mondays. Please pass the pickles."

William and Eveline, after suitable apologies, had departed for supper in town, doubtless to consume the same sort of veal cutlets with which Kate had entertained Reed on his first night in the country. They returned at something after ten o'clock, apparently having undone whatever bonds of sympathy they had woven since the murder. William went upstairs to bed, pleading a fatigue which certainly was likely enough, while Lina threw herself in front of the fire and began guzzling brandy in an ominous manner. Reed, too, had retired, Emmet was at work, as ever, on the letters which were becoming something close to a passion with him, Grace Knole was upstairs, presumably settling down for the night, and Kate resigned herself to a discussion of the perils of womanhood.

"I expect you're damn sick of the lot of us," Lina said. "And small reward I am to you, for inviting me for a visit, or rather, permitting me to invite myself. I'd better take myself off in the morning. I cannot image," she viciously added, "where the idea that men are the aggressors in sex ever arose from. Shrinking violets are nothing to it."

"So Shaw always insisted. At the same time, there *is* Mr. Mulligan."

"How horribly, hideously true. Can it be that men merely object to the entanglements of love, not to sex itself?"

"Dylan Thomas, as I remember, propounded some such theory. But then he was clearly not the best example of monogamous manhood, however good a poet."

"William's monogamous. He loves one only: himself."

"What exactly is William's problem? Sin?"

"I think so. And the fact that he thinks he can't possibly marry, financially speaking. I don't think he really minds that I have a Ph.D. and he doesn't yet, but he does mind not being able to get to work on his dissertation, and finding it all grind when he does get down to it, and not very likely to be interesting in the end."

"In the Victorian period, of course, when muscular Christianity was popular, people like Carlyle would recommend work and cold baths."

"Exactly William's theory, evidently. He keeps plodding at Hopkins' inscapes, and takes long cold swims in the ocean when he's home. I am not Victorian, thank the lord. My feeling is, if a man has so much energy he wants to swim halfway to Europe, why not put the energy to good use and go to bed with someone? What *has* he been doing here to sublimate, now he's so far from the ocean, besides pretending to shoot guns?"

"He plays with Leo, climbs mountains, swims in the pool. He's even been known to play tennis with me once or twice. Lina, is there some reason why it has to be William? Can't you, according to the old bromide, be friends and find your love life somewhere else?"

"I could, of course. As you know, to my shame, I've even considered being seduced, if not actually attacked. But in the end, it's always William, blast him. I mean, we seem to be right together about so many things. And in all the years I've known him, he's never found anyone else either. And one thing about William, he sticks to his principles. I mean, he isn't one of those with pure girls on one hand and loose women on the other, which is so often, I fear, supposed to be a failing of religious young men. I mean, he really *believes* in chastity."

"If that's so, then why not stop brooding and put your mind to something else—writing a book, perhaps, or taking a trip around the world, if you prefer that. You're wonderfully free, you know. Does it frighten you to look at it in that light?"

"I'm not independent like you, Kate. I like doing things with people I know."

"Then stop having fantasies about sleeping with people you don't know—the masterful Italian, á la Mastroianni, met one dark night in Naples or on the Riviera."

"That's a low blow."

"Look, Lina. Life isn't replete with possibilities. For women who don't just naturally move into a house in the suburbs with husband and children and community activities, there are only three possible lives. You can marry and continue to function professionally, even with children. The number of this sort increaseth. Or, you can not marry, seeing a clear choice and choosing to work. This sort belongs, usually, to an earlier generation, like Grace Knole. Their number decreaseth. Or you can be one of that third group, much less publicized, which requires and enjoys the love of men, usually more than one man in a lifetime, and scorns the role of homemaker. There used to be lots of Frenchwomen of that sort who pined away when forced to spend any time at their chateaux."

"Like George Sand, you mean, or Madame de Staël?"

"If you insist on rather extreme examples. Or Madame du Châtelet—do you know Nancy Mitford's book on her? Or in this century, Doris Lessing. Simone de Beauvoir, Colette. As Doris Lessing put it in an interview, marriage is not one of the things she's good at."

"Are you in the third group?"

"It would appear so. Certainly running a house this summer has not improved my temper. The point, however, is that you are in one of the first two groups, probably the one who marries and continues with a profession. You wouldn't be a virgin in your late twenties otherwise, frankly, but who knows. Now don't open your little mouth to ask any questions about me, because I don't intend to answer them. Why not forget dreams of William, on the one hand, and dreams of wild nights with unknown lovers of infinite experience on the other, and settle down to work? Meeting the man with whom you could spend your life is as much serendipity as anything: it usually happens when you're worrying about something else. As to your taking yourself off in the morning, don't. Now, before you become absolutely blotto on brandy, would you mind telling me, in all the detail you can muster, what happened in court today?"

When, several hours later, Kate staggered upstairs with Lina in tow, and saw her headed in the general direction of bed and oblivion, she reached her own room with a sense of infinite relief, and a long-ing for solitude. But life appears to offer solitude only to those al-ready burdened with too much of it. There was a knock on the door, and Grace Knole came in.

"You look exhausted," Grace said. "I've only poked my nose in to say good night, and to tell you that Mr. Mulligan has all the literary mastery of a preengineering student. But we can talk about that tomorrow."

"By all means. But do come in and tell me what that matter was you were hinting at so beguilingly at lunch."

"I'm afraid that's rather a long conversation, Kate. Tomorrow will do for that, too."

"Oh, come in and sit down, for heaven's sake. I told you all we do is talk—or were you telling me?—on the way to see the cows. Talk, talk and more talk, and some of it actually conversation. I do intersperse it, of course, with tennis and walks, and an occasional swim—but let's face it, if you want to know what a man likes, watch what he does. I talk."

"Interspersed also with a little lovemaking now and then?"

"Grace, I will not discuss sex with one other person this summer, and maybe not even next. What in God's name has got into you? Lina I can excuse—she's very twixt and tween, and simply brimful of indecisions. But what possible reason you can have . . ."

"Keep your shirt on. I do not intend to lay at your feet my personal burdens, if any. I merely wished to point out, somewhere along the way, that the president of Jay College probably wouldn't be able to have a lover. A husband, yes. Don't you think you smoke too much?"

"Certainly I smoke too much. I comfort myself with the thought that there's nothing like knowing what *kind* of cancer you're going to die from. Light up a cigarette and be *sure*. Grace, have you gone completely, ninety-nine point forty-four percent mad?"

"Very likely. Believe it or not, there's a shortage of really com-petent women around, let alone women who aren't married to men whose careers or egos foreclose any possibilities of their having a college president for a wife. Let's face it, Bunting may be the most prominent woman president around, she was even on the Atomic Energy Commission, but if her husband hadn't, most unhappily, died, she'd still probably be tutoring in chemistry somewhere. As for the unmarrieds, those who can hold their own in the world of college and university administration—as I said, you're probably too tired."

"I'm certainly too tired to be president of Jay College for Women. This is the first indication I've ever had that your powers were failing. Or have you simply developed an odd sense of humor? Jay College may be one of the oldest women's colleges in the country, and with a great reputation, but not even two hundred years of respectable history could survive me."

"Rave on. Just think about it. The trustees are, I happen to know, prepared to make you an offer. They've done a lot of research on you, sat in on your classes, read your books . . ."

"You're positively making me blush. I haven't gone crimson like that . . ."

"Since the last person paid you a heartfelt compliment. You have many drawbacks, I don't mind telling you, and your inability to accept a compliment is certainly one of them. Also, you're somewhat less than a mountain of tact, you're impatient with brainlessness and the throwing around of weight, and while you have the greatest respect for manners and courtesy, you have none at all for the proprieties as such."

"I wonder you ever thought of me."

"Well, you know what Henry James wrote to a young acquaintance who had just met Edith Wharton: 'Ah my dear young man,' he wrote, 'you have made friends with Edith Wharton. I congratulate you; you may find her difficult, but you will never find her stupid, and you will never find her mean.' "

"That's nice, Grace. But hardly the qualifications for a college president, which, incidentally, I definitely don't want to be. Did you suggest me?"

"It might surprise you to know how many people suggested you. I've already given you the bit about the scarcity of capable women. I'm here this weekend, really, to sound you out—and to add to the soundings all the persuasions I can personally bring to bear which, as you know, I profoundly feel."

"Thank you. I'll try to take that compliment properly. But you know, were I asked for suggestions of people to be president, I'd suggest you. You'd be perfect, Grace."

"I agree with you, actually. And unlike you, I accept compliments with the greatest self-satisfaction and not the shade of a blush. But people these days want their college presidents young. To be frank, I can't imagine why. It seems to me that college presidents, like popes, ought to be old when appointed: they can then afford to take risks, and they can't live on too long and get set in their ways.

That, however, is not the American way. They did ask me to serve pro tem, but I refused. All the headaches, and no power. Don't try to answer now. Perhaps I shouldn't have let this come up, with all this other problem hanging over your head—but I thought I'd give you another bone to gnaw on.''

"Many thanks. Are you suggesting I marry in order to qualify for the job?''

"I'm suggesting nothing. Only trying to hint at the problems. But before you turn it down, Kate, remember, it's a position of power, and power is one of the most remarkable experiences there is.''

"I've never wanted power.''

"I know that. Exactly why you should take it, rather than someone who has always wanted it. Good night, Professor Fansler.''

11

The Sisters

KATE had written, the day of the murder, to Sam Lingerwell's daughter, informing her of the catastrophe and asking as many questions as she could think of. Kate was not clear really whether she was apologizing or howling for help, but after writing the letter over four times—few letter-writing manuals include models for informing someone of murder—she finally sent the fifth version off without even bothering to reread it. Sister Veronica had answered by return:

Dear Kate:

I was saddened by your letter, with its frightful news, and your kindness in underestimating the enormous burden to yourself. I have taken the liberty of mentioning the matter to the Mother Superior, and she has agreed that all the sisters shall say a special prayer for you. I trust we will not offend you with our prayers: I know that my father did not care for them. Poor Mr. Lenehan, who must bear the dreadful burden of having fired the gun, is most constantly in our prayers as in our hearts.

I feel myself enormously to blame. I ought not to have asked you to undertake so great a responsibility. If there is any way now in which I can proffer practical help, do please let me know of it. You will, I am certain, understand how impossible it was for me to cope with my father's papers, particularly since, to judge from the offers being urged on me at every turn, they could be the source of a good deal of scholarly work. But perhaps by now the greater work is fin-

*ished, or will you merely smile that I should so underestimate the
magnitude of the job?* [Kate smiled.]

*To answer your question, I am not certain why my father bought
a house precisely where he did. In fact, I asked him that question the
last time I saw him. It seems that some partner in his publishing firm,
from which he had, as you know, more or less retired, had been used
to visit a Mr. Mulligan in that part of the country. He was informed
by Mr. Mulligan, and subsequently informed my father, of the house
which was for sale, and which my father found attractive and subsequently bought. I am not certain, however, but I rather doubt, that
Mr. Mulligan knew my father.*

[Here followed some points about Kate's actual "renting" of the
house.]

*The other sister here join me in my prayers for you. There is no
way to thank you. But should you be enabled to stand up under this
trial, it can but increase the gratitude I, as my father before me, must
always feel toward you.*

Dominus vobiscum

"So Mulligan knew Lingerwell was coming here," Reed said,
when Kate had shown him the letter.

"She doesn't say that exactly. Sam Lingerwell did get here
through Mr. Mulligan, but only indirectly."

"Interesting, just the same, that there was a connection."

"Interesting in more ways than one. Did it ever occur to you,
Reed, to wonder how Mr. Mulligan manages to afford that house,
and Mrs. Pasquale, and all, even on his income from his books and
his salary as a professor—full, admittedly, but still, a professor?"

"In the first place he's a bachelor, and in the second place most
teachers of literature have incomes additional to their salaries, or so
you often tell me."

"True enough. But Mr. Mulligan happens to have mentioned to
Lina, who told me, that he started as a very poor boy, and is still
supporting his parents. So much for his bachelor freedom and his
inherited income. He drives a Jaguar, has a swimming pool, together
with all the filter machinery thereto, and it is no cheap matter to
entertain houseguests, as I know to my cost, and Mr. Mulligan does
it constantly."

"Kate, if you are trying to cast Mr. Mulligan in the role of the
first murderer, I positively forbid it. At least, cast away, but don't *do*
anything about it. He may have the morals of a billy goat and the

literary qualifications of General Eisenhower, but there is no reason . . .''

"Reed. Did you *read The Novel: Tension and Technique* before presenting it to me with all the airs of a man serving mangoes in January?"

"Naturally I didn't read it. Do I expect you to read the *Harvard Law Review*? Talk sense."

"Very well. Let me tell you then that Mr. Mulligan has contended himself with collecting a lot of tired clichés, if a cliché may ever be said to be without fatigue, and has simply written them all down in a most inept manner."

"You mean he can't write?"

"On the contrary, he writes with a certain felicity. He can't think."

"The man in the bookstore in Pittsfield said, as I'm sure I told you but you probably weren't listening, that they are very popular with students."

"For purposes of cramming, or, likelier still, plagiarizing papers. They sound undergraduate enough to be genuine, don't you get the point? Grace Knole found the same with the book she was reading."

"Look, Kate, I know you consider book publishing a profession second only in purity of soul to the Little Sisters of Charity, but surely they are as happy to make money as anybody else. If the books sell, there's your answer."

"They sell only in cheap paperbacks, and then to college students. Furthermore, they sell in paperbacks not published by the Calypso Press."

"What's your point?"

"That it's really extraordinary that Calypso ever published these books in the first place, and in hard cover into the bargain. They have a college list that has the respect of every faculty and is the envy of every other college department in the publishing field. What's Mulligan doing on it?"

"I'm sure I don't know. Don't you think perhaps you're exaggerating the ineptitude of the books? After all, you don't read everything that's being published today."

"Heaven forfend."

"Well, there you are."

"Reed, I think I'll take a day or two off and drive down to New York, maybe have a talk with the people at Calypso. Being in charge of the Lingerwell papers should provide an excuse. Anyway, I can't stay around here very much longer without a small interlude, and this looks as good a chance as any. Will you lend me your Volkswagen?''

"What's the matter with your car, or rather your brother's? It's bigger and safer."

"Now don't come all over the protective male. I have to leave my car here for William or Emmet to drive and fetch Mrs. Monzoni, among other things. Of course, if you're feeling possessive about your beastly little bug, I'll rent a car, or have Emmet drive me to the train."

"Why not let me come with you?"

"Thank you, Reed, but would you rally round here and keep things afloat?"

"Meaning, as you always mean when you start talking like an ad agency, that you want to be alone to think, or some such nefarious activity."

"What an understanding man you are."

"I am not in the least understanding. I simply lack forcefulness and manly overbearance. Besides, if I go back to New York, the office will certainly develop a crisis, and I'll have to cut my vacation short."

"I'm sorry it hasn't been a better vacation."

"It has had its moments. When are you leaving?"

"This evening, I think, after dinner. Do you want to walk down to the vegetable garden with me? I want to ask Mr. Pasquale to take some zucchini over to Mrs. Pasquale to cook for supper for Mr. Mulligan."

"You may suspect him of murder, but you send around vegetables?"

"Naturally; one must be neighborly."

"Why not take them yourself and be really neighborly?"

"Because if I ask Mr. Pasquale to take them to Mrs. Pasquale, he will take enough for them to eat at home."

"Ah, you're catching on, I see, to rural life."

"There is no life, my dear Reed," Kate said in ponderous tones, "least of all the rural, without its mysterious rites and rituals. I will also send some corn and cucumbers."

12

After the Race

In point of fact, Kate greatly enjoyed driving the beastly little bug, as she had called it. True, one bounced about as though on a motorcycle, and the protection to be afforded, in a crash, by its beetle body, was certainly minimal; yet driving it, she felt that she and the car were working together, whereas with the huge automobile lent her by her brother, she seemed to be steering on gracious sufferance from the car itself.

Feeling, not without guilt, lighthearted, she turned onto the main route leading to the Taconic Parkway. She had decided to eschew the shortcuts in the interest of saving time: it would certainly be preferable to reach New York in time to call Ed Farrell, the present editor-in-chief at Calypso, and possibly even see him tonight. She had been unable to reach him on the phone before leaving Araby; the hope was that he would have returned, by eleven, should he have been out, as he so often was, at dinner with an author. Kate smiled in anticipation as she began to mount Smith Hill. The natives claimed this was a hill so high the wagons had to be emptied, in the old days, before the horses could pull them to the top, and it was the test of any old car to see if it could make the hill in third. A signal light was at the top of the hill, and Kate found an idiotic (and secret) delight in racing the car to see if she could get through the light before it changed to red. She began now to race. I ought not to speed in cars, she sternly told herself since, like Alice, she was in the habit of talking to herself with a certain severity. But the race against the light, which she barely sneaked through, exhilarated her. I expect I'll be driving a motorcycle next, she said, but not even this frightful thought could dampen her spirits. She remembered that Mr. Mulligan, who had stopped by late in the afternoon to thank her for the vegetables (nominally; in fact, he was on the lookout for tasty bits of news, or perhaps the chance to take a walk with Lina), had remarked that he always tried not to stop at the light at the top of Smith Hill, because if you got through that, and didn't meet up with an accident or the need for gas, you could make it all the way to the Saw Mill River without stopping, and on one glorious occasion he had made both lights on the Saw Mill and had got to the Henry Hudson Bridge without falling below thirty-five, except for tolls.

The country was more beautiful than ever in the evening light. The farms seemed set out on the hills, neatly plowed fields contrasting in shades of green with their adjoining meadows. Kate felt certain that the good life might somehow be possible here, yet knew this to be only a dream. A short time after the race for the light, she turned on the car's lights, seeing that many of the vehicles coming toward her had already done so. Night was approaching. The little bug trundled along in high. There was very little traffic on the Taconic Parkway. She had a feeling that she would be able to tell Mr. Mulligan she had matched his record. Suddenly a car shot out of a side road. Kate slammed on her brakes, and her car jerked to a halt. Cursing, Kate heard the car stall. She turned the starter. Silence. The motor was not turning over. The battery was dead. Damn, hell and corruption.

A car soon stopped, offering help. Kate asked only to be pushed to the side of the road, which the man gingerly did, the bumper of his large car not really meeting the bumper of the Volkswagen. "Sorry I can't be more help lady," he said. "I'm afraid I don't know anything about cars, particularly those little foreign ones. I'm the sort who calls a repairman if the television set becomes unplugged. *You* know."

"To be frank," Kate said, "I have frequently doubted whether anyone understands the internal combustion engine. Perhaps you would be kind enough to call for help, however, when you pass a phone?"

"Gladly," the man said. "Maybe you got a flat tire?"

"I don't think that would affect the battery, do you?"

"No, I guess not. Noticed your lights are very dim. You seem to know a lot about cars."

"Only what I learned from leaving the ignition on one long, sad night. But surely the battery ought to have been recharging all this time." The man waved an amiable hand and departed. Kate sat down on the roadside to wait. She was joined, before very long, by the state police.

"Anything wrong, lady?" they asked in tones which, if not discourteous, were certainly not brimming with graciousness either. Kate restrained an impulse to say she had given way to a desire to sit on the roadside and meditate.

"My battery appears to have gone dead," she said. "The motor won't turn over."

They greeted this analysis of the situation with all the skepticism due any woman who calls by name any of a car's inner accouterment.

They lifted the hood (I wonder if it's called a hood, Kate thought) at the back of the car, and gazed meaningfully into the engine. "Water in the fuel line?" one said. The other reached into the back seat and lifted the rear seat out. "Plenty of water in the battery," he said. "What about the gas filter?"

"That would scarcely affect the battery," Kate said, for the second time that evening. It was by now quite dark. The state troopers did not appear to appreciate her contributions to the discussion.

"Let's see your license and registration," one of them said. At that moment a repair truck, apparently summoned by the man who had pushed her to the side of the road, appeared.

"Hey, Mac," the trooper said. "See if you can figure out what's the matter here."

The repairman turned on the ignition and tried to start the car. Nothing happened. "Battery's dead," he said.

"My battery," Kate said, feeling more and more like someone who has been given only one line in a play and must keep repeating it in rehearsal after rehearsal, "should have recharged while I was driving."

"Your generator's probably gone," the repairman said. He extracted a long wire, with clips on either end, and began placing the tips mysteriously. "The minute you put on your lights you drew all your juice out of the battery. In most cars, there's an indicator on the dash to tell you. Not these babies."

"I wouldn't have noticed it anyway," Kate said.

"Your brushes are probably gone. Have to tow you in."

"My brushes?" Kate said.

"I've been patrolling this road a year now," the state trooper said. "No one ever had trouble with brushes."

"It's unusual to have the generator go in these cars. Particularly"—the repairman flashed a light at the speedometer—"in one that's gone only nine thousand miles. Very strange. These cars don't break down much. Have to tow you in."

"Just a minute," the state trooper said. "Your license and registration."

"Have I done anything wrong?" Kate asked. The state trooper, with his companion, waited stolidly, not deigning to answer. Kate reached into the car for her purse, into the purse for her wallet, into her wallet for her driver's license. It wasn't there.

"It must be," she said. "A New York State driver's license, quite up to date, with no convictions on it." From her wallet she carefully removed her faculty identification card, her university bookstore card, her faculty club card, her social security card, her Blue Cross card, a small calendar and three five-cent stamps. "It's always there," she said.

"It's an offense to drive without an operator's license. Let's see the registration."

Kate remembered Reed's voice: "The registration's here, in a plastic folder, in the map compartment. I keep it underneath. You'll have to show it," he had added with a frivolity which now seemed prophetic, "when they pick you up for reckless driving." She slid into the car and looked in the map compartment. The plastic folder was there, but no registration form was inside it.

"No registration," one state trooper told the other. Kate wondered, not for the first time, why all state policemen either are or appear eight feet tall and devoid of all human feelings. Probably their boots, she thought. And goggles.

"You'll have to come with us," they said.

"Do you mean in your police car?" She was ignored. The trooper turned to the repairman. "Can you haul that in?"

"Right. I could recharge the battery," he said, shrugging his shoulders, "and she might get started, but with the lights on, she wouldn't go far." He handed Kate a card.

"Get in," the trooper said. Kate got into the back of the police car, and one of the troopers got in the back with her, apparently to make certain she did not try to throttle the driver. "Is it a very bad offense to drive without a license?" she asked the trooper next to her. He did not answer. Evidently it was not his custom to converse with criminals.

At the state police station, Kate was told to wait. She asked if she might telephone, but was again ignored. Then she was called to talk with an officer behind a desk.

"Why were you driving without a license?" he asked.

"Someone must have taken it out of my wallet."

"The same person who took the car's registration?"

"Apparently."

"Why should anyone do that?"

"I can't imagine. They couldn't have known I would have to stop, and if I hadn't stopped, you wouldn't have found out. So it can't have been a desire to cause trouble."

"Know anyone who'd want to cause you trouble?"

Kate shook her head.

"Got any identification with you?"

"All the identification cards from the university where I teach."

"Which university's that?"

Kate told him. It was clear his opinion of it, if any, had declined on learning of her association with it.

"Do you own the car you were driving?"

"No."

"Who does?"

There was a long, palpable pause while Kate did not answer the question. Should she give them Reed's name? On the surface of it, it seemed logical enough. They would call him in Araby and straighten out this whole dreadful mess. But Reed, after all, was an assistant district attorney, and reporters did look at police blotters. Anyway, if two people recently connected with a murder should now be in the hands of the police again, however innocently, would it not be one of those tangles which somehow, as time passes, become inexplicable in simple words? In any case, it certainly couldn't *help* Reed to be tied up in all this.

"Who owns it?" the officer asked again.

"I don't know," Kate said.

"You don't know. Do you mean you borrowed it, but you don't know from whom?"

"I didn't steal it," Kate said.

"Are you acquainted with the person you borrowed it from?"

"It's not that I don't know," Kate said, shifting her ground. "It's that I won't say."

"Take her inside," the officer said.

"Haven't I a constitutional right to make a phone call before you lock me up?" Kate asked.

"Everybody knows all about his constitutional rights today," the officer said. "Rights, rights, rights, for everybody but the police. You can make one phone call. In there."

One of the troopers led Kate into another room where a telephone stood on a table. She put in the call to Araby. It was answered, against her most fervent hopes by Leo. "Leo. This is Aunt Kate."

"Hi, Aunt Kate. You in New York already?"

"No, dear. Leo, will you let me speak to—" she glanced up at the trooper, who was watching her—"let me speak to the oldest man there." To the trooper, this sounded like just what he expected from a woman who had probably never had a driver's license, had eaten the registration, and done something hideous to the generator. So his looks implied.

"Mr. Pasquale's gone home."

"Not Mr. Pasquale, Leo. Staying in the house."

"I don't know who's older, William or Emmet. Wait, I'll ask."

"Leo!" But before Kate could stop him, he had dumped down the receiver in the way of small boys, and could be heard shouting in the distance.

"Hurry up," the trooper said.

"I'm having a little trouble finding him," Kate said. The trooper's look suggested that it wouldn't surprise him if she had trouble finding the Empire State Building on Thirty-fourth Street and Fifth Avenue in the blaze of the noonday sun.

"William's older," a breathless Leo reported. "Funny your wanting to know their ages now you're gone. Emmet's birthday . . ."

"Leo. Please. Let me speak to the man who isn't William or Emmet."

"Is this a game? Mr. Artifoni says . . ."

"Leo. Please."

"O.K., O.K." The receiver crashed down again. After what seemed only a little longer than forever, while Kate resolutely refused to meet the eyes of the trooper, Reed's voice could be heard.

"Kate? Where on earth are you?" No voice, Kate thought to herself, no voice sounded so beautiful.

"I'm in a police station. State police. The car registration's gone, along with my driver's license, and something ghastly's happened to the generator." She realized her voice sounded as panicky as she felt.

Ridiculously, she recalled a *New Yorker* cartoon of long ago in which a woman is telephoning from a police station: "Henry," she is saying, "I did something wrong on the George Washington Bridge."

"Where are you?"

"Where am I?" Kate asked the trooper. He told her.

"All right, I'm coming, in your brother's scorned limousine. Let me talk to someone there."

"I didn't give them your name. I was afraid . . ."

"I respect your noble silence. Let me talk to the officer in charge, if possible."

"I don't know if they'll let you. They were going to put me in a cell." Kate looked up at the trooper. "He wants to talk to you," she said. The trooper looked dubious, but he took the phone.

So Kate, only slightly to her disappointment, didn't wait in a cell after all. She waited in the waiting room for Reed's arrival which, she decided, could not be in less than an hour.

He arrived in forty-five minutes, however, having driven the limousine, one supposed, at close to eighty. Kate hoped to remember in calmer times to ask him if he had made the Smith Hill light.

"Here I am in the clink," Kate said. "Oh, frabjous day. The question is, as I figured out while waiting for you, what am I accomplishing by being here, or, more exactly, what am I not accomplishing by not being somewhere else?"

"Meaning: who took your driver's license and my registration? A fascinating question. But I think we had better get out of here first."

The man behind the desk, while managing to convey that he was in no way mitigating the severity of Kate's misdemeanor, spoke to Reed as though he was now assured of not having an escaped, if harmless, lunatic on his hands. "Very well," he said, "we'll release Miss Fansler, provided she does *not* drive. You, I trust, have both an operator's license and a registration for the automobile you are driving?"

"Certainly," Reed said, reaching for them.

"All right." His glance was perfunctory. "You'll want to drive round to the garage that has the other car. Perkins, tell this gentleman where it is."

"I have a card," Kate said. "Is there a fine?"

"There will be. And you'll have to send your license in to have the convictions recorded, if and when you find it. In case you don't find it, you'll have to apply for another, and be certain to report the convictions. Goodbye."

"Oh, Reed, was I ever glad to see anyone? You may not feel in your element treading through cow dung or clinging to tractors, but in a police station, you're the man of my dreams."

At the garage, the mechanic, waving the generator, greeted Kate. "Someone pulled the wires out," he said. "Disconnected it. A kid's trick. I thought the brushes couldn't be gone after nine thousand miles. Look"—he waved the generator at Reed—"not even any corrosion on the armature."

"What would have happened," Kate asked, "if I hadn't had to slam on the brakes for that car?"

"Sooner or later, after you turned on your lights, the engine would just have died on you."

"But those wires must have been pulled out before I started. How could I have got this far?"

"There was enough juice in your battery to start her up. With just the engine running, you'd go O.K. But your lights draw on your battery."

"Clever; very clever. I'm sorry about your generator, Reed."

"It's all fixed," the mechanic said. "I'll just screw it back in. Shouldn't give you any more trouble. Lucky I happened to be here."

"How much do I owe you?" Reed said.

"Six dollars, three for the labor, three for the towing."

Reed handed over the money. "The question is," he said, "how are we going to get this bug home? It will almost go in the back of your brother's car, but not quite."

"I could drive it, Reed. I'd be really careful, and now, with the generator back . . ."

"Perhaps I should have left you in jail. We'll just have to come back for it. Would it be possible," he asked the mechanic, "for me to leave it in your lot over there?"

"Help yourself. But I'll be glad to sell you a towline if you want to pull her home."

"Is that legal?" Reed asked.

"Not on the Taconic. Take 22."

"I guess it'll be cheaper in the long run," Reed said.

So it was rather with the air of being a procession that they arrived home in Araby. The household, including Leo, who had refused to go to bed, and who was suspected of hoping to see his aunt in jail, all came out on the lawn to greet them.

"And you said we never had adventures," Grace said.

"Some adventure. I was made to look like a perfect fool, never got to New York, and have exposed poor, much-beset Reed to even more Galahad-like endeavors."

"He always seems to be hauling one of us out of jail," William said, "but I still don't see what you did wrong."

So they all went inside to discuss it over refreshments, Kate, like Pooh, feeling the need of a little something.

"It's all very funny," Kate said to Reed later, when the others had finally gone to bed, "and doubtless it will make a lovely story in several years' time, like all those dreadful things that happen to Cornelia Otis Skinner that she manages to be so hilarious about, but what I want to know right now is . . ."

"Who was interested enough in your not getting to New York to go to all that trouble?"

"Suppose the state police hadn't come along? They might never have found out I was driving without a license."

"If you stopped anywhere along a parkway, they were bound to find you. But if by some chance you'd ended in a garage, even if you found someone who understood a car's electric system—and at that hour most gas stations have only boys who fill tanks and wipe windshields—all of that would have delayed you sufficiently. Why?"

"It can't have been too serious a reason. I mean, the person clearly wasn't prepared to take life-and-death measures. He didn't fiddle with the steering mechanism, or the brakes."

"Kate, my darling."

"Oh, it would probably have been better if he had. I'd have landed in a ditch and gone on to take the train. I suppose everyone in Araby knew I was going to New York?"

"Did they know you were going to talk to someone at Lingerwell's firm?"

"Everyone in the household knew, I suppose. Somehow, in the country, everyone *does* know everything. Or maybe it's just that I'm not used to living in a household."

"Everyone in the house and Mr. Mulligan."

"Blimey, yes. And Calypso's his publisher. Reed, do you think . . ."

"I think we had better sleep on it. Tomorrow I'm going to drive to New York, in brother's limousine, without telling anyone about it, and see Ed Farrell at Calypso myself. Of course, it may all have been sheer malevolence.''

"Let me go with you."

"Certainly not. You must wait here to come and rescue me when I get picked up for vagrancy. Anyhow, I hope to go and come in a day. You'll just have to drive Mrs. Monzoni in the bug without registration.''

"Don't you think Ed Farrell is likelier to talk to me than you?''

"My title, such as it is, may go further toward convincing him this is a matter of great importance.''

"Meaning, you can bully better.''

"Meaning, whatever it is he has to tell, it may be betraying a confidence. There is, somehow, something more palatable about doing that to a lawyer whose interests are strictly professional.''

Early in the morning, Kate heard Reed's car pull out. Deciding to get up and dress, she was not unbearably surprised to find, on opening her underwear drawer, her driver's license and the Volkswagen's registration reclining neatly on top of a pile of bras.

13

A Mother

AFTER breakfast on Wednesday, Kate decided that, whatever the rites and rituals of rural life, simple kindness urged a call upon the young lady now holding up, so to speak, the pillars of the Bradford household. Undoubtedly, Kate thought, there was something she could do; if no act of neighborliness were discoverable, she could at least provide sympathy and an assurance of help at any future time, should it be needed.

Emmet, instead of immuring himself in the library, as was his inevitable wont, had taken himself off on a hike across the fields, an undertaking so atypical as to suggest an aberration. Still, there was no doubt, no one, since the murder, was really behaving a bit like himself. William, having taken Leo to camp, had continued, with Kate's permission, to Williamstown, where he intended to consult some books in the Williams College library, the nearest respectable collection of literary and scholarly works. From time to time Kate thought, rather desperately, of Reed's money, subject to forfeiture should William disappear altogether. Yet it did not seem either possible or desirable to restrict his movements. He knew the situation, and if his own sense of honor would not keep him from fleeing, certainly no external restraints were likely to.

Lina and Grace Knole were supposedly at work or, at the least, at thought. Lina, with her career yet to make, was working on a book to do with the proper names in eighteenth-century novels—an abstruse enough topic, yet not quite as firmly in the "how many angels can stand on the head of a pin?'' category as the ordinary mocking layman might think. Lina was a brilliant teacher, alive, interesting and interested, deeply devoted to her work and respecting herself for doing it; but these qualifications were, these days, insufficient without publication. That no one but other scholars would ever read about proper names in the eighteenth century was not held to be an argument against the book, nor should it be. Still, how far had the subject chosen Lina, as subjects should choose those whom they overmaster, and how far had Lina arbitrarily decided on the subject since a book there had to be? Soon the whole profession would be swamped in an avalanche of published, unreadable works, neither conceived with excitement, nor nurtured with love, nor welcomed with gratitude.

Which recalled, of course, Grace's proposition of the night before. Might a college president actually reverse the trend, or at least run counter to it, making teaching, rather than research, again an honorable profession? Walking down the road, kicking at the gravel, Kate willed herself into a refusal to consider the offer of the presidency. Not yet, at any rate, was she ready to consider it. The brown dog trotted up. Kate greeted him, pulling his soft ears affectionately. ''Reed's gone today, old chap,'' she said. As to Reed . . .

Kate had at least learned enough about rural ways to know that one never knocked at the front door unless one had been invited formally, and not always then. She walked around to the kitchen door and tapped on the pane. A young, pretty girl opened the door. Neither her age nor her looks seemed of first importance in any consideration of her because of a quality which was so clearly hers in amplitude: sweetness. It occurred to Kate, stepping into the neat kitchen, how rare a quality it was, how often its appearance was merely a cover for passions of an unusually hostile sort.

''How nice you've made the kitchen look,'' Kate said. Mary Bradford had talked constantly about how hard she worked, how none of her family ever put anything away, but her kitchen, her house, had always looked like Pandora's box, constantly pouring forth its unattractive contents. Now the working space in the kitchen had been cleared off; flowers, which Mary Bradford had never had time to gather, stood on the table. The girl had been about to make a cake using, Kate noticed, real ingredients—butter, sugar, flour, eggs—not a prepared mix, as Mary had done.

''I'm Kate Fansler from up the road,'' Kate said. ''I should have come along sooner to offer my help, but somehow . . .''

"It must have been very hard," the girl said, "having all the confusion and nastiness of a shooting. Are the police gone?"

"Quite gone, I think, at least for now. The autopsy held no surprises; the arraignment of the young man who fired the gun, while disagreeable, was not surprising either. Wouldn't you like to send the children up to us and have a few hours to yourself? You must have been working very hard."

"It's mostly been the visitors. Today at least they haven't started coming in the morning. But I do expect them this afternoon. I like people, really, but . . ."

"But not when they ooze four parts maliciousness to one part curiosity. And now I've come and ruined your one free morning. Why not let some of us sit with the children tonight, and you can go to a movie. Perhaps Mr. Bradford would like to go too. Let's take it as settled then. Don't let me keep you any more, now. If you should decide you want a few hours . . ."

"Please don't go, Professor Fansler."

"Goodness, no one calls me that, except a few students and book salesmen."

"Dr. Fansler, then."

"Absolutely *no one* calls me that, if I can help it. I'm always afraid of being asked to set a leg. Just Kate will do, or Miss Fansler, if informality makes you uncomfortable."

"Miss Fansler, a lot of people who have stopped in have had a good deal to say about you, as I suppose you realize. That's how I knew you were a professor, of course: gossip. But Mrs. Monzoni says you're one of the few people she's ever worked for who trusts other people to go about their own jobs, and I imagine you've had a great deal of experience with people as a teacher."

"Some," Kate said, since this seemed to require an answer. "But I'm not very good at ladling out sympathy. I try to respond as sensibly and forthrightly as I can, but to tell you the truth, I'm not the motherly type. Of the students who don't like me, and their numbers are legion, half say I'm as hard as nails and the other half that I'm cold as a fish. They're probably right."

"You seem to me to be kind, and intelligent and sensible and able to keep things to yourself, and I simply don't know what to do," the girl said, and burst into tears.

"Blast," Kate said. "I am sorry. Can I offer you my handkerchief, only slightly used to get something out of my nephew's eye? The great advantage of country clothes is that they contain pockets, which city clothes, of course, never do—unless some dress designer has undergone an inspiration, and then the chances are ten to one he's put the pocket in such a place you can't put anything in it without looking as though you were starting a tumor—look here, Miss, I don't even know your name, but whatever the problem is, I'm certain it can't be as terrible as you think. Certain things, incurable diseases, are terrible—but most things only need to be expressed and they start getting into proportion. 'Troubles told are troubles halved,' as someone said, and if his little aphorism does sound simpering, it's nonetheless true for that. What *is* your name?''

"Molly."

"Look, Molly, if you've had the perception to see that I have an honest face, you've obviously got powers above the ordinary, and might as well take advantage of it. I don't gossip, or care especially about making trouble—my sins lie in quite other directions—so if talking will help, allow me to offer my ear. Don't you, by the way, think you ought to do something with that lovely mixture there? I've never made a cake in my life, but ought the milk to be soaking into the flour in those funny little channels?"

Molly smiled and turned on the electric mixer. "It will sound awfully foolish to you," she said.

"Probably. You'd be amazed how few human deeds don't sound foolish. My own follies are innumerable. With a girl as young and lovely as you it must be either a man or money; which is it? And you may not realize it, but if you plan to tell me you'd better hurry up about it or I'll begin sounding like a character in a bad play."

"I'm going to have a baby."

"I see. Mr. Bradford's baby?"

"Yes. How did you know?"

"People often make the mistake, Molly, of thinking that one learns nothing from books. One learns a great deal, actually. You're obviously in love with him. How pregnant are you?"

"Oh, I don't want an abortion, if that's what you mean?"

"That is not what I mean. I was simply wondering, as they say in bad plays, how long this has been going on."

"I met Brad first at auctions—my father is one of the main auctioneers in the county, and I used to go with him. Farmers' auctions, I mean. At first we only talked, but then—well, we knew we cared for each other."

"You must have met somewhere besides auctions, though admittedly my only experience of auctions is Parke-Bernet, where. . . ."

"We did go out for meals sometimes, or for a drive. But we didn't, nothing happened, of course. He was married."

"And continued to be until he became a widower, what is it, four days ago? You can't have discovered you're pregnant in that amount of time. Now you know what is meant by 'hard as nails.'"

"You're right. If a man's married, it doesn't make any difference how he feels about his wife, or what she does."

"I wouldn't go that far. Frankly, Molly, I met his wife, and I should think that even the archangel Gabriel would forgive her husband for taking love anywhere he could find it, let alone with anyone as sweet as you. If I sounded harsh, it's because I've become a little sensitive about self-righteousness this summer. I'm sorry."

"You've just about said it, the way we felt. The reason we—it happened, finally, was because Brad said—he said she'd been unfaithful to him."

"Mary Bradford! I don't believe she could have stopped talking long enough. Is it possible?"

"He said—I'm afraid this sounds terrible. Brad said she'd only have done it if she was certain she could make two men absolutely miserable while she was at it. Him and the other one."

"I see. Incidentally, didn't all the years Brad has spent inseminating cows teach him anything about where babies come from?"

"That was my fault. Brad got me pills. But . . ."

"But you forgot to take them, one or two days." Molly hung her head. "You know, my dear, there's nothing like wanting to get pregnant by a man to whom you're not married to increase fertility. I wonder it hasn't been looked into more. It's the same principle by which married women who can't conceive always manage it the minute they take a job, return to school, or plan a trip to Europe. Well, marry Brad and have the baby. I'm morally certain you'll be a better mother to his other two than the late departed."

"Don't you see," Molly said, pouring the batter into cake tins, and then putting the tins in the oven, "everyone is sure to say he murdered his wife. They won't be able to prove it, I guess, but why shouldn't Brad have put the bullet in the gun? He knew all about guns, and he knew all about their pretending to shoot."

"How did he know that?"

"The little boy told him."

"Leo?"

"Yes. He and the young man who takes care of him, they used to come down to see Brad, and ride on the baler, or in the hay wagon.

Brad told me the boy loved riding in the hay wagon and dodging the bales as they were thrown in. I'm sure the boy—Leo—didn't mean to say it was Mary they were shooting at, but I'm sure he did. Anyway, Brad told me about it.''

"I must be a very inattentive aunt. I didn't even know Leo was riding in the hay wagon. It sounds rather dangerous, dodging bales of hay. But then, William was supposed to . . ."

"We can't go on living here if everyone thinks Brad killed his wife. And he didn't, Miss Fansler. You've got to believe that. Brad wouldn't.''

"Molly, let me give you one piece of ponderous advice. Never worry about what people think—people, that is, whom you don't care for and whose opinions you don't respect. And the odd thing is, once you stop caring what people say, they largely stop saying it. I don't deny it may be hard on the children if you stay here with this murder over your heads—but anywhere Brad farms, the story is bound to turn up, so why not face it out here? There is, you know, always the chance that they will find out who really put the bullet in the gun. Live your life. Marry Brad, love his children, all of them, and stop paying attention to people who aren't worth ten seconds' thought.''

"I feel better. You won't tell anyone what I've told you.''

"I don't promise that. I will almost certainly tell Mr. Amhearst, who is, so to speak, working on the case. But trust me not to tell anyone who isn't capable of keeping a confidence. Mr. Amhearst, by the way, is as likely to start gossiping with the neighbors as I am to become Shah of Persia, so don't brood about it.''

"Will you have a cup of coffee?''

"Thank you. And then I must get back and join my guests for lunch.''

"Please wait till the cake's finished and take it with you.''

"I mustn't wait that long," Kate said, glancing at her watch, "but if you really want to make Leo madly happy, and send us all off our diets, we'll pick the cake up when we come to sit with the children, say at seven?''

"I'll send the cake up this afternoon. Don't think about sitting with the children, Miss Fansler. I like it here. I don't really want to go out anywhere at all.''

"That's so obviously true, I won't urge you. When Leo comes home, I'll send him down for the cake. Will you promise to let me know if there's any practical way I can be of help?''

"Miss Fansler, do all your students burst into tears at the sight of you and tell you all their troubles."

"Only the few who notice my heart of gold beneath the rough exterior. Don't fret, Molly, it's not good for the baby. I'll stop in again in a few mornings, and we'll confine our conversation to the weather, if that happens to be all you feel like talking about. Thank you for the coffee."

It's all very well, Kate thought, scuffing her way back up the road, but what a motive! And who, after all, knew more about guns than Brad? His one defense might have been that he didn't know those two idiots were shooting at his wife, but Molly's now told me he did know. Can anyone be as innocent as she is and not be innocent? It would require a kind of doublethink I refuse to believe her capable of. What a ghastly mess. If Brad did do it, we can never prove it. It'll hang over his head all his life, and over William's head as well. But what way out is there? We are scarcely likely to find any hot clues now. If this were happening in one of those marvelous books by Ngaio Marsh, we would reenact the whole thing, starting with Saturday morning, and in the course of it the guilty one would give himself away. But I fear that's beyond our powers. Inspector Alleyn's methods are no doubt fine for Scotland Yard, but here in Araby it would merely seem as though we'd all gone crackers. Damn Reed. Why isn't he here to discuss this with me?

Reed, at the moment, was walking the pavements of New York musing, astonishingly, upon the breeze-swept meadows of Araby. The pavements seemed actually to absorb the heat and send it forth, many times increased. But the offices in which dwelt Calypso Publishing were air-conditioned. The receptionist who greeted Reed added her own coolness to the atmosphere, as though she suspected him of trying to offer her a lengthy, handwritten, unsolicited manuscript. When she learned that he wanted to see Mr. Farrell, her general suspicion of authors became visibly transmuted into a particular suspicion of salesmen.

"Do you have an appointment?" she asked.

"No. Will you be good enough to take in my card, and tell Mr. Farrell I would like to see him on a matter of some importance?"

"Have a seat," she said. "I'll see." She returned shortly to announce that Mr. Farrell was on the long-distance telephone, but would be out shortly.

Ed Farrell, when he appeared, turned out to be a tall, handsome graying man of troubled mien. Reed got the impression that he spent many hours sitting up with authors, and was glad to see someone not large with book. "You haven't *written* something, have you?" he asked, as though unwilling to take Reed's nonwriting status on faith.

"I haven't even written a letter since my mother died five years ago," Reed said. "Thank you for seeing me. I'll try to be as quick as I can."

"What's the district attorney's office investigating now? Salacious literature? We don't print it."

"As it happens, Mr. Farrell, I'm here under false pretenses, and I had better tell you that straightaway."

"You're not an assistant district attorney?"

"I am, yes. But there's nothing official about my visit to you. In fact, I'm on vacation, and was on an assignment in England before that, so I haven't been near the office in months. On the other hand, this is not entirely a private matter either. It concerns a murder."

"You fascinate me. I don't read mysteries, though we publish, I am told, some of the best. In fact, I agree with that brainy critic who didn't care who killed Robert Ackroyd. But none of us, I imagine, is above the thrill of murder in real life, particularly if we don't know the victim."

"I'm staying in the country with Kate Fansler. A woman was accidentally shot near the house, by one of her houseguests. We have reason to think that the shooting may not have been as accidental as it looked—that is, that someone loaded the gun, knowing that it would be aimed in the belief that it was not loaded."

"How extraordinary. I know Kate, of course. Sam Lingerwell left all his papers to his daughter, and Kate's helping her look over them. Don't tell me you think she shot this woman. Kate's incapable of killing anything but a mosquito. She's even a great defender of spiders, whom she insists on calling our friends. Kate's all right, isn't she?"

"Fine, at least, as far I know. But interestingly enough, she set out last night on her way to see you."

"Really? I never heard from her."

"Not unnaturally, since she didn't get to call you. Her car was tampered with, and the license stolen; she ended up in a police station."

"She's not in jail?"

"No. We prevailed on the officer in charge to be merciful. I want to ask you this, Mr. Farrell. Did anyone call you last night and urge you not to reveal something or other to anyone, under any circumstances?''

Mr. Farrell looked at Reed as though he had at last been granted a vision of the Delphic oracle. ''Did you tap the telephone line?'' he asked.

''Of course not. Can I persuade you to answer my question?''

''In a general sort of way, yes, considering your position and that you're a friend of Kate's. Someone did call last night, though not until rather late. I wasn't within reach of a phone till I got home about eleven. Maybe a little before.''

''And he reached you then?''

''Yes. Always accepting 'he' as a pronoun applying to both sexes.''

''Did he mention that he had been unable to reach you in the afternoon?''

''Yes.''

''What I want to know, Mr. Farrell, is what that man, for I think it was indeed a man, said to you. I give you my word, as a lawyer, a district attorney, a man, and incidentally a friend of Miss Fansler's, that the information will not be used, or made public, unless it becomes essential to the solution of the murder. And in that case, I feel certain you would not consider it proper to keep silent after all.''

''You put me in a very difficult situation, Mr. Amhearst.''

''I'm aware of that, and believe me, I'm sorry. Kate seems to think a lot of you, and of course, as you know, she thought the world of Sam Lingerwell, whose firm you are now the head of.''

''Only editor-in-chief of the trade department.''

''Kate seems to think that you're the one who matters.''

Mr. Farrell stood up. ''Will you excuse me a moment, Mr. Amhearst? I'll be right back.'' He went out, shutting the door behind him, leaving Reed to look at the bookshelves, filled with books published by the Calypso Press. It occurred to him, not for the first time, what an extraordinary human endeavor a book was. Mr. Farrell returned in fifteen minutes.

''All right, Mr. Amhearst, I'll talk, as they used to say in the movies when I was a boy. I've told them not to interrupt me with any calls, and to put off my appointment. Oh, never mind, just some hungry young idea man with a book that will sell in the thousands and not add one cubit to human stature. I went out to check on you. Anyone, after all, can have a card made up, or steal one, and know

Kate Fansler, or say he does. Also any sort of man could be an assistant district attorney. We have a book of memoirs being done for us now by Justice Standard White, who used to be on the Federal Court of Appeals.''

"I worked for him at one time.''

"So he informed me, though I had only hoped he would have heard of you sufficiently to give you a recommendation. I've always thought it a great pity that he was never appointed to the Supreme Court, but no doubt we can discuss the vagaries of American justice on another occasion. He said he would trust you with his most treasured secret, should he have one. I also asked him to describe you. I may not read spy stories for pleasure, but one need only read the newspapers to know the odd things that happen every day, including impersonations.''

"How did he describe me?''

"He said your clothes were Brooks Brothers, your manners Groton, your ideas Stevensonian (Adlai, that is), and that you looked like an extremely attenuated Trevor Howard with glasses.''

Reed laughed. "It ought to be a very good book when he gets it written.''

"So we believe and hope. Now, as to our problem.''

"Perhaps I can simplify your unwelcome task by saying that I'm virtually certain the man who called you was Padraic Mulligan. What we can't imagine, frankly, is what he's got to conceal. I gather, from what Kate tells me, that he isn't the greatest writer of literary criticism since Matthew Arnold, but supposedly anyone could find that out by reading his books.''

"That's the understatement of the century. He pours out books on modern fiction—'modern' being for him an elastic term to cover any work since Shakespeare he feels like mentioning—and makes a great many generalities about modern chaos together with plot summaries.''

"Kate says he writes with some felicity.''

"Ah,'' said Mr. Farrell.

"Do you mean he doesn't write his own books? You'd think he'd find someone at least competent to write them for him.''

"Oh, he writes them, all right. At least, nobody else does.''

"Mr. Farrell, you intrigue me. Has he blackmailed someone in the firm? Not you, I hope.''

"It's hard these days to blackmail anyone who's heterosexual and hasn't actually left evidence of a major crime. That is, if that's what you mean by blackmail. Actually, he has blackmailed me, though the word is perhaps a trifle harsh. Book publishing *is* a business. Tell me, Mr. Amhearst, Justice White described you as a man of few frivolities. I gather that you read every word in the *Times*, enjoy an occasional decorous evening at the Plaza, and go to the movies and theater from time to time. Have you heard of Frank Held?''

"You don't have to be wildly frivolous to have heard of him. Like having heard of the Beatles; one can't help it. I've seen some of the movies about him—all naked women and complicated gadgets. I particularly enjoyed the one where the girl . . .''

"I see we're on the same wavelength. Perhaps you know what those books bring in, what the reprint rights bring in, what the movie rights bring in? Publishers make a fair amount of best sellers like the Frank Held books, but that just makes up for all the good books they publish that barely make their getout. The money really begins to come in, Mr. Amhearst, with subsidiary rights—movies, and so on.''

"Interesting. But what has this to do with Mr. Mulligan?''

"He writes the Frank Held books.''

Reed's surprise brought him to his feet.

"A *very* attenuated Trevor Howard,'' Ed Farrell said.

"The Frank Held books are written by an Englishman, what's his name. I know he hates publicity, and there aren't supposed to be any photographs of him, but the facts are plentiful enough. Why, I thought everyone knew he was related to . . .''

"Padraic Mulligan writes the Frank Held books. Believe me, Mr. Amhearst. And he was especially anxious that Kate not know it, and especially that someone named Knole not know it. I don't know when he began to realize he could make us publish his 'academic' books, and so get him a fast promotion in the crazy publish-or-perish academic world. What I can tell you is that everyone in the academic world is so busy publishing, no one reads anyone else unless he's in exactly the same line of country, and then only to be certain he hasn't been anticipated.''

"But why should Mulligan want to go on being an academic? What an extraordinary thing. With what he's making he could, he could . . .''

"The ways of men are strange, Mr. Amhearst. No one knows that better than an editor. Whether he has a deep longing to be part of the academic world, whether he really likes to teach, whether his whole delight consists in mocking for his own benefit the standard of academic judgments, whether he secretly thinks his books are good—who knows? All I can tell you is that if we hadn't agreed to publish his academic stuff, he'd have taken Frank Held elsewhere. And we could not bear, Mr. Amhearst, to see Frank Held go elsewhere. I know what you're thinking. Sam Lingerwell could have borne it. Sam Lingerwell wouldn't have published Frank Held in the first place, and that's the bloody truth. But he lived in different times. What with mergers, the gigantic cash payments to authors—don't get me started. I console myself with the thought that one Frank Held, and one dreadful academic book by Padraic Mulligan, support any amount of first-rate stuff, some of it even poetry—stuff that doesn't sell in ten years what a Frank Held novel sells in ten minutes.''

"Mr. Farrell, I won't waste your time with euphemisms and subtleties. Do you think Padraic Mulligan would kill to keep his secret from being made public, or to stop himself having to pay for silence?''

"Naturally, the question in my own mind. We can never say with assurance, but I should doubt it. In the end there would be too much at stake. He treasures his secretive role, and he never spends a fraction of the money he makes, or rather has left after the government gets through with him; he's a bachelor, of course, and our tax laws really do make true the old saw about two living cheaper than one.''

"I know," Reed said. "I'm a bachelor myself.''

"But Mulligan likes just having all that money. He's not a bad egg, you know. He likes giving people things, he likes to know that he could walk into any store in the country that sold anything, and buy it. The knowledge is more important than the purchase. In my experience, there are two general attitudes toward money: the one that wants to have a million dollars, and the one that wants to spend a million dollars. Mulligan is in the first class. He wouldn't risk all that, I think, even if his secret were in peril.''

"Yet suppose, as happens to be the case, that he didn't actually have to *commit* the murder. There's the beauty of it. You drop a little bullet into a gun, and then leave it up to chance. You don't pull the trigger, you can't even be certain the trigger will be pulled.''

"I don't believe it of Mulligan, though you can't trust me; I may be simply protecting a valuable property. But whoever dropped the bullet in that gun was taking a long chance—not only that the gun wouldn't be fired, but that it might be fired at the wrong person. It might have killed a stranger, a child—I think Mulligan would have shied away from that. He's got more imagination than your criminal seemed to require.''

''Thank you, Mr. Farrell. You've been kind and more helpful than you can guess. I promise to preserve Mr. Mulligan's secret if it's at all possible. It was he who tried to stop Kate on her way to you, or so we think.''

''It would appear so. When he reached me on the phone he complained of not being able to get to me all afternoon and evening, and he swore me again to secrecy as though he knew I would be questioned shortly.''

''He did his best to stop Kate without injuring her, and he succeeded. I wondered that Mr. Mulligan would know enough to disconnect a generator in that way, and know exactly the effects of the disconnection, but of course, that's the sort of thing Frank Held has to know.''

Mr. Farrell shook hands. ''My best to Kate,'' he said. ''Tell her to come and see me when she gets tired of cows.''

After lunch, Kate poked her head in the library to see how Emmet was getting on. He seemed sunk in thought, and when she spoke his name, he leapt to his feet like one suddenly possessed. ''I don't know what's the matter with everyone today,'' Kate said.

''I was thinking.''

''No kidding. About whose problems, yours, mine or Joyce's?''

''All of them, I guess. Kate, would you mind shutting the door?''

''Only,'' Kate said, ''if you promise not to confide in me.''

''I'm saving that for when I'm a good deal drunker. I'm always more amusing when I'm drunk.''

''As someone pointed out, you only *think* you're more amusing.''

''I've got through the 1930s. Lingerwell's letters, I mean. I've been going through each year trying to collect the letters by author— I've explained all that, but this time around I've been paying particular attention to the Joyce letters, which are only beginning to be organized. Of course, the folders are just lying here—I mean, this isn't a guarded room or anything . . .''

''Emmet, I have never heard you so incoherent. And I thought that there was no situation which would find you without the right words, the light words . . .''

''You should like an advertisement for beer.''

''Ah, that's better. You'd got through the 1930s letters—''

''I was reading each letter, you know, trying to give future students a rough idea of the contents—my excuse, of course, since they're fascinating and I couldn't bear not to read them. Toward the end they get easier to decipher because Joyce dictated them, his eyesight was failing. The one I read yesterday was an ordinary, pleasant letter to Lingerwell—they hadn't been writing as frequently, but suddenly, in the middle of the letter is a sentence. Let me read it to you." Emmet picked up the letter and began to read with difficulty. He cleared his throat several times. Kate suddenly knew how he must appear to the woman he loved. She had never seen the mask drop before. " 'Watch out carefully, my dear Lingerwell, for the next letter I write you. There will be a long envelope—we can only seem to find a small one today—and in it an attempt to thank you for your help.' "

"Is that all?"

"That's all. The letter goes on to say he's fine, delighted with his grandson, and so forth."

"What was in the next letter?"

"That's it. It's gone."

"It may have been something valuable. Sam Lingerwell took it out and put it somewhere else."

"I wonder. A lot of these letters are valuable, in a monetary sense. But he left them all together, intending, I suppose, to go over them someday. Kate, I've been reading all I could get about Joyce, and you know, in order to thank that woman who supported him in Switzerland, he offered her the original manuscript of *Ulysses*. She declined it. Do you think . . ."

"That could hardly be contained in what Joyce calls 'a long envelope.' Besides, I seem to remember it was bought by some famous collector for a handsome sum. It can't be that. Emmet, are you suggesting that the envelope has been stolen?"

"I don't know."

"If someone stole it, why not steal this letter too, which gives the show away?"

"That's just it. Someone was looking through here, and happened on the valuable envelope, but didn't have time to check through for other references."

"I think you're imagining things. Perhaps whatever it was, was too valuable to accept as a gift, and Lingerwell sent it back."

"That's what I thought. But there's a reference in a letter years later, which seems to argue against that. Apparently Lingerwell had sent some money to the Joyces, whether his own or money he'd collected isn't certain, because we don't have Lingerwell's letters. But this last one from Joyce, dictated of course, refers obliquely to Joyce's past gift; it says: 'If you do as I have requested, and I trust you as much as anyone, it will be thirty years before you can consider yourself repaid.' Sounds rather as though someone else worded it for him. Joyce was very sick at the end, wasn't he, and then there was the war.''

"What idiocy to have come to Araby at all. I should have persuaded Veronica to present the whole mess to the Library of Congress and let it go at that. What could this gift possibly have been?''

"Have you read Harry Levin? I think I'll go for another walk. Kate, you might as well know, I've searched the house.''

"Emmet!''

"I had to, every room, dodging people, sneaking into guest rooms—illicit nocturnal pussyfooting between bedrooms is nothing to it. I think I'll take up being a sort of Raffles; if only I looked more like Cary Grant, and less like Little Lord Fauntleroy. I found your driver's license, by the way.''

"Thank you, dear boy, but I had already discovered it. You *were* thorough. Emmet, what are you suggesting?''

"Walking in the fields isn't *so* frightful,'' Emmet said, "if you sidestep the cow dung and refuse resolutely to think about snakes. Brad is out baling again—enormous amounts of hay those cows eat.''

When Leo came home, Kate sent him down for the cake. "Try not to drop it,'' she said, "and walk carefully. Watch out for cars.'' Why is it, she thought, that we cannot restrain ourselves from flinging advice at children, though we must all know in our heart of hearts that they are incapable of paying the smallest attention to it. Perhaps it's the modern way of fending off evil spirits. "Leo,'' Kate said, suddenly reminding herself of something, "I understand you enjoyed riding in the hay wagon when the baler was flinging the bales in?''

"Now, Aunt Kate. It's not dangerous. I showed William. An *inchworm* could have gotten out of the way.''

"Where was William when you were riding in the wagon?''

"He was there, most of the time. Sometimes that Mrs. Bradford, you know, asked him to help her with something. She was a real— I won't say it, now she's dead.''

"And, Leo. Do you think you could carry this bottle of wine down to the young lady who made the cake without dropping it either, or drinking any?''

Leo appreciated this final jest. "I'll probably swill it to the dregs," he said. And he reeled off down the road, pretending to lift the bottle to his lips, upending it in the process. When I think, Kate said to herself, that Lord Peter Wimsey wouldn't even let anyone *dust* a bottle of wine. There's no question about it, we live in parlous times.

14

A Little Cloud

"As far as I can see," Grace said, coming up to Kate, "there's nothing wrong with that little boy. Of course I'm a childless old maid, and wouldn't know."

"Aren't old maids usually childless?" Kate asked.

"You're not. You've got Leo."

"Only for the summer, thanks be. How's Lina doing?"

"Waiting for William to come back from Williams—what an uneuphonious sentence."

"My advice to her was to try to think less about William."

"Have you noticed how advice like that always seems to have the opposite effect?"

"Now that you mention it, I have. Grace, this whole business is getting more and more disturbing. Emmet now thinks that a valuable Joyce letter, perhaps more than a letter, has been stolen."

"Does he indeed?"

"You scarcely sound surprised."

"I scarcely am. You can't put all that temptation under the noses of three people whose academic careers depend upon the chance to make a publishing coup—and not expect trouble. 'Lead us not into temptation,' the prayer says."

"You're terrifying me. Which three people?"

"William. Mr. Mulligan. Emmet himself."

"Mr. Mulligan? He's already a full professor."

"I know. He'd still love to make a coup, I'm sure. As to Emmet, who knows when the letter was stolen, or when, so to speak, he decided to discover it was missing?"

"Grace, you shock me."

"For the second time in two days—not bad, for an aged, cast-off lady."

"You resent it like hell, don't you, being retired?"

"Like hell. I try to recognize that retirement laws are important; we must get rid of old fuddy-duddies automatically, to keep from breaking hearts. But I do wonder sometimes if the cure isn't worse than the disease—it so often is, you know, in academic life. Perhaps I'm an old fuddy-duddy and don't know it, but I really think I still have all my marbles, and they are quite a handsome collection of marbles by this time. Something too much of this. What about you, Kate?"

"I? Don't ask me for an answer about anything. Maybe I'm just waiting for this murder to dim with time—maybe I'm just lying fallow, like one of Mr. Bradford's fields. I'm getting old, Grace. Don't laugh. There's old and old."

"I had no thought of laughing."

"Reed's asked me to marry him. It just goes to show, we all fall apart in the middle years. The one thing certain about Reed and me was that we would never really matter to each other. Grace, if a man hasn't married before he's in his forties, I don't think he ought to marry. I mean, one can't take up marriage as though it were the violin—to fiddle with in one's off moments."

"Jung has a theory about human life I'm rather taken with. I know the Freudians all frown on him, but to a literary mind, or perhaps I mean a mature mind, he speaks of possibilities beyond those offered by the viscera. As I said, a childless old maid. At any rate, he thought that about age forty—a few years more, a few years less—a human being needed to remake his life because, in a certain sense, he had become a different person. It was the unconsciousness of this which caused many breakdowns in middle age. Jung didn't believe in looking back to childhood sexual patterns. He believed in discovering who it was you were trying to become."

"Grace . . ."

"Don't argue. Think about it all, and we'll argue another time. I wonder if you didn't get involved in this peculiar summer because you knew this kind of stasis was somehow needed, the protection of the womb before birth."

"Some womb."

"A womb with a view, as a wit remarked. You can't stand still, Kate. You've got to keep going, and changing, or die. Remember Emmet's saying some are dead though they walk among us; others have never been born. Personally, not to change the subject, I've always found Simone de Beauvoir hard to take, largely, I think, because even past forty, she kept right on acting like George Sand."

"So Lina's been talking to you about my talking to her."

"We all of us talk a great deal too much. Here comes Leo, about to drop the cake. Will Reed be back soon? He's the only one around here who ever seems to *do* anything."

Reed returned a little after five, seemingly intent upon refuting Grace's compliment. He was met in the driveway by Emmet, and the two of them began strolling down across the fields, obviously deep in conversation. After a time they headed back, and Reed, capturing Kate, took her for a long walk in another field. He explained about Mr. Mulligan, but seemed unwilling to assume that that mysterious gentleman was guilty of anything more serious than stealing Kate's license and Reed's registration and generator wire. Kate told him of her day: her morning with Molly, and Emmet's discovery. "Emmet has already told me about that," Reed said. "Tell me about your conversation with this Molly: all you can remember."

"I'm not Archie Goodwin, who has total recall."

"We ought to hire him in New York, whoever he is."

"He's got a very good job already."

"Well, just try telling it as though you were one of those boring ladies on a park bench. 'And then she said, and then I said,' you know the sort of thing."

"You want me to be boring?"

"To be honest, I doubt if you could accomplish it. But try."

Kate tried. She was surprised at how a conversation came back, once she began trying to recall it. Reed listened attentively. Then he wandered off, and Kate was not *really* surprised to see him again in conversation with Emmet. She had gone inside when Reed again captured her and led her out onto the lawn.

"Kate," he said, "will you do something for me and ask no questions?"

"Not unless you tell me what. I've had a trying day."

Reed lit her cigarette. "I'm going to make it far more trying," he said. "I want you to go with me to a drive-in movie."

"You must be mad."

"Leo, who after all has been undergoing rather a rigid schedule, deserves a treat. Emmet will come with us because he likes new experiences on which to try his wit. William will come because you will expect him to accompany Leo, and Lina will come because William is going. Whether Grace comes or not is up to her; we need not urge her, if she doesn't mind staying home alone."

"Are you suggesting we all go in one car? It won't be a drive-in, it will be a squeeze-in."

"I'll drive, with Leo next to me, and William next to him; in the back seat will be Emmet and Lina and you. Of course, Lina too may decide not to go, but I doubt it. Needless to say, we will again take your long-suffering brother's car."

"I'd like to know what's long-suffering about my brother. He's in Europe, the lucky bastard."

"My language was inexact. I should have said, your brother's long-suffering car. Remember, you think the idea of a drive-in is too exciting for words."

"Reed, I hope you know what you're doing; it seems to me the sad deterioration of a first-rate mind. What's playing?"

"I have no idea."

"Don't you think my enthusiasm might be a little more convincing if I knew what the picture was?"

"Certainly not. The chances are ten to one it will be something you would never dream of seeing, like Elvis Presley. Your line is that you've been overcome with a need to experience American culture, regardless of the movie."

"Reed, I will *not* see Elvis Presley."

"Yes you will. Be good, Kate, and do as I say. I'll buy you popcorn at the drive-in, *if* you behave."

To Kate's astonishment, her suggestion of visiting the drive-in after dinner, which sounded to her ears about as convincing as a recommendation that they all play a fast game of touch football, was met with enthusiasm and a burst of high spirits. Leo, of course, was largely responsible for this. Once the possibility of such an adventure had been mentioned, it became inevitable. Emmet so amazed Kate with his eagerness to see a movie from a car that she suspected him of having had too much to drink. William showed signs of wavering, but Leo's "Ah, come on, William," was enough for persuasion. Lina said that she too would come, partly perhaps to be with William, but mainly, Kate thought, because she was the sort who would always rather do things than not.

Grace flatly refused to consider the whole thing, even if Reed offered to take his Volkswagen to make more room for her. "Preposterous idea," she said. "Looking at a movie through a windshield. I can't think how such an idea ever caught on."

"The boys at camp say you go there to love someone up," Leo announced.

"*Leo!*" came out in so emphatic a chorus from Kate and William that they could only laugh. "What," Emmet asked, "would Mr. Artifoni say if he heard you?"

"We don't let him hear us all the time."

"If you want to know the truth," Emmet said, "I read somewhere that drive-in movies are attended mainly by families; the children come in their pajamas and fall asleep as the evening goes on. The parents drop them into bed when they get home. No need for babysitters, and the drive-ins provide bottle warmers and everything else needed for the care and feeding of the human young."

"The things you pick up," Kate said.

"Are you sure you don't mind staying here alone?" Kate asked Grace, when they were preparing to depart.

"Absolutely certain," she said. "Mrs. Monzoni will be here for a while, but in any case I'm not the sort to worry. Mr. Bradford is just down the road, should I need assistance in I can't imagine what contingency."

"Well," Emmet said, "I for one am selfishly glad you're staying. Pussens hasn't been feeling well"—Emmet picked up the cat, stroking it—"and I feel much better knowing she won't be all lonely-byes. I hope you don't loathe cats, Professor Knole."

"Not at all," said Grace. "In fact, I welcome the chance to make the closer acquaintance of one. I'm thinking of acquiring a cat *and* a canary."

Emmet had been quite right about the drive-in. In all the cars Kate could see were families with incredible numbers of pajamaed children. Kate began to have the direst forebodings about a generation brought up on late nights in cars, receiving, as it were, movies subliminally. The movie was called "Moon-something"—Kate had already forgotten what—and had been produced by Walt Disney, thus confirming Kate's worst fears, since she had never really believed Reed would expose her to Elvis Presley. At least the movie wouldn't be too wildly inappropriate for Leo, which was a load off her mind. "I can't wait to see Hayley Mills get her first kiss," one popcorn-laden girl said to another, passing by. Kate sank deeper into the seat of her brother's luxurious car and groaned.

The movie turned out to be a not greatly edifying example of the sort of story she and Grace had been discussing: much derring-do and some mystery, all of it revolving (literally in the case of one windmill scene) around the most extraordinary adventures. The lovers—doubtless one should call them the ingenues—were very young. "It is necessary," Kate reminded herself, "to remember that fifty-seven percent of the population of the United States is under twenty-five." That Kate and her contemporaries found the throes of first love agonizingly boring as not likely to be of the smallest interest to Walt Disney, who knew well what he was about.

The picture, having achieved at least fourteen climaxes, seemed, by the sheer necessities of time, to be drawing to a close: at least the heroine was confronting a woman who kept a pet leopard when Emmet, perhaps driven by an association of ideas, mumbled something about finding out how his pussens was. He left the car—a departure to which no one but Kate paid the smallest attention. It seemed to Kate that no great amount of time had passed when he returned, clearly the bearer of great tidings: "My god," he said, "troubles never come singly. First his wife, and now his barn. Thank heaven there were no animals in it, except a few calves, which he rescued. Grace says it started with a little cloud of smoke, but now the flames are probably visible five miles away—a barn packed to the rafters with hay."

Emmet had spoken in a strong whisper to Kate, and the others wrenched their attention from the movie only slowly. "You mean his whole hayloft's burning?" Leo said. "Emmet, William, Reed, Aunt Kate—" he appealed to them all, leaving the young heroine to be eaten by the leopard should it choose. "Let's go back and watch it burn."

"Absolutely not," said Reed. "We'd only be in the way, and a danger to the fire department."

"Of course," Emmet said, "we should stay right here. Grace said they have the road cordoned off. They're just trying to keep the house from catching—it's all they can do. All that hay, it's hopeless. Thousands of bales of hay . . ."

"We've got to go, you fool," William shrieked, punching Reed as though to awaken him. "Drive. We've got to get back. They've got to put out the fire—the hay can't burn, do you hear, it can't burn, *it can't burn.*" By this time his screams were so loud they attracted attention from the other cars. There were stares, and shouts for quiet. "Drive! Drive!" William shrieked. "They have to save the hay. Merciful God." He leaped from the car and started racing across the gravel, shrieking.

"Come on, Emmet," Reed said. "Kate. Drive Leo home. Now. Lina, stay with her."

But Lina had dashed from the car after William. As Kate moved into the driver's seat and began to maneuver the car out, she saw Emmet and Reed catch up with William. One of the attendants was already running toward him, and as she pulled past, quickly, so that Leo might not see much, she heard the scream of sirens coming toward them.

15

A Painful Case

"You may say what you want about Mr. Artifoni's camp," Kate said, "but if it were not for those sessions with first aid and basketball, I would hardly know what to do with Leo these days."

"The entire point of camps," Emmet said. "My objections were not to Mr. Artifoni, but to his maxims, so banal, and so oft-quoted. Ah, Reed at last."

"Will Cunningham defend him?" Kate asked.

"Let me at least get him a drink," Emmet said. "Have you left Lina there?"

"She hoped they might let her visit him. They've sent for a priest too, someone for whom William has a lot of respect—a friend really, I gather. Thank you. I need this. Cunningham will defend him, though whether the charge will be different, or the defense much changed— nothing has been decided."

"They won't—they can't execute him, can they?"

"No. Cunningham will certainly not allow that it was premeditated murder. That's going to be tricky, since of course he did get hold of the bullet, but Cunningham's going to maintain he found it more or less at the last minute—I gather that's somewhere near the truth, or as near as we're likely to get. Cunningham says thirty years, as an absolute maximum."

"Thirty years!"

"Twenty, more likely; eight, with parole and time off for good behavior. And Cunningham hopes to get him psychiatric help—there may actually be a possible insanity plea, though, as the law reads, that's almost hopeless. It's ghastly, I know, but look at the bright side. William will be helped, and Emmet and Mr. Mulligan and Mr. Bradford and his children, not to mention Mr. Artifoni and the Monzonis and the Pasquales, will be cleared of all suspicion. And of course, Kate.''

"Surely no one really suspected me?''

"Not especially. But it is just as well, if one has any sort of highly responsible position, not to have even a suspicion of murder hanging about one.''

Kate glared at Grace, who continued to listen to Reed with an air of unshatterable innocence.

"I,'' Emmet said, "will forever have the shadow of vile deception hanging about me, as far as Leo is concerned.''

"He simply could not believe the barn wasn't burning. He kept running hopefully to the window—really, small boys are ghouls.''

"What would you have done,'' Grace asked, "if William hadn't reacted?''

"If our plot hadn't worked, you mean?'' Reed asked. "Emmet was taking that chance.''

"Suppose I'd gone to the movie,'' Grace said, "and Emmet couldn't have pretended to call me?''

"He would have pretended to reach Mrs. Monzoni, still held to the house by the fire.''

"Go on, Reed,'' Kate said. "Sum it up. You know how to begin: 'The case as I first saw it seemed a simple matter of accident; but that was only as I first saw it.' ''

Reed got up to refill his glass.

"You might have let me in on it,'' Kate said.

"It was bad enough counting on Emmet's histrionic powers; I didn't want to count on anyone else's. Not that I underestimate Emmet's talents for drawing-room comedy, but melodrama seemed rather out of his line.''

"Besides,'' Emmet said, "any risk, even so small a risk as of appearing an ass, was mine to take. In a sense, it was my fault.''

"It was all our faults,'' Kate said. "Lead us not into temptation, as Grace said. I ought to have thought more.''

"The only real sinner,'' Reed said, "though doubtless we are all too thoughtless of one another, was the woman he killed. It at least provides me with some satisfaction to know that it was not the innocent who suffered for Mary Bradford's sins.''

"Did you think from the beginning it was William?" Grace asked. "The obvious man to the police, I think you said."

"Not from the beginning, but soon after. The more I thought about it, the more I realized that only a maniac would have taken the chance of leaving a loaded gun lying about. And for all the reports of that early morning target practice, would anyone really count on that as a way to murder the woman? Even if they thought the chance worth taking, the threat to the boy, to all of us, was preposterously great. It was the judge's horror of the gunplay at William's arraignment that made me realize that. And then, it was always Leo who shot the gun. Why not this time, if indeed there had been a plant by someone else of which William knew nothing? However terrible a deed William did, he did not let Leo shoot that gun. He was incapable of that, of letting Leo commit the murder, however innocently. Yet it was the fact that Leo did not shoot the gun which convicted William in my eyes."

"That's why I wondered about it so myself," Grace said.

"I know. The difficulty was, of course, while I'd decided William had loaded the gun as well as fired it, there wasn't a ghost of a motive. The woman may have been a monster—I think we all agree that she was—but William had never laid eyes on her before. How could he hate her enough for murder? Reluctantly, I began to look about elsewhere for my suspect—and for a time lit, as Professor Knole did, I think, on Mr. Mulligan. Upon investigation, however, Mr. Mulligan's innocence seemed assured, almost absolutely."

"Shall we ever know about that?" Grace asked.

"Forgive me for being mysterious. I shall have to ask for amnesty there. However, when I returned from New York and had two conversations, one with Emmet and one with Kate, the whole thing suddenly seemed to fall into place. I ought to mention, incidentally, that it has only been my recent association with Kate, my nearness to her in the same house, that apparently allowed me to learn from her the leap of mind necessary to, for me, so uncharacteristic a construction of events. To my honor, I was beginning to think like a professor of English."

"Most gallantly put, dear sir. But though pleased with the compliments, I am still bewildered by your conclusions."

"Emmet had discovered something missing, something that a letter from Joyce to Lingerwell had mentioned. There was always the chance that Emmet had taken it himself—though again, it is to Kate's credit that she was a good enough judge of character to think that unlikely." Emmet glanced at Kate, who flushed. I have grown not one whit better at accepting compliments, she thought. Damn.

"It was Emmet who did most of the guessing here, but of course, being a literary-type chap, he was used to letting his ideas leap about illogically."

"It begins to come naturally, after you've read Joyce awhile. It's more an association of ideas than a logical sequence."

"Sounds like *Tristram Shandy*," Grace said.

"Is like, in a way."

"Tell them how your mind went," Reed said. "I don't think I could do it justice."

"First of all, I'd been thinking about *Dubliners*. That's why I gave our funny policeman 'Ivy Day in the Committee Room' to read. You know, he saw right off the solution was in those letters, and when I told him I'd been working on Joyce, he wanted to know about Joyce. He wasn't at all slow, for a policeman whose mind in no way resembled the White Queen's. Then there was a sentence of Harry Levin's, I don't know what the grounds for it were—here, I better quote exactly: 'Mr. Bloom's day first occurred to Joyce as the subject for another short story.' Add this sentence to the fact of the lost document, and—well—it suddenly seemed possible to me that *Ulysses* had started as a short story for *Dubliners*, and that Joyce, who of course waited so many years for publication of his stories, meanwhile decided that *Ulysses* would be his masterpiece, and withdrew the story from *Dubliners* before publication. He kept it though, as he kept *Stephen Hero*, an earlier form of the *Portrait of the Artist as a Young Man*, and it was this manuscript, or so I believed, which he sent as a gift, the most valuable thing he had to bestow, to Lingerwell. But he wanted it kept from the public. Why? That's still anybody's guess. Maybe he wanted *Ulysses* read in its own right—Lord knows, that hope succeeded beyond even his wildest dreams, I'm sure of that.

"This, as Reed or any of you would have pointed out, was only the wildest supposition. I hadn't a breath of proof for any of it. But I began to wonder, suppose there was such a story, suppose William had stolen it, hoping later to be able to claim he had found it, where would he have hidden the story? Not, I was reasonably certain, in this house. Of course, I searched. But if the story were found in this house, little of the credit would be William's. Lingerwell's daughter would dispose of it as she would dispose of all the other papers. But if he could find it in a dramatic way, a way similar to many of the literary discoveries of recent years, he might be allowed to bring it out; at the very least, his name would be connected with it. But where could it be hidden?

"As you can see, I wasn't a bit closer to a solution, but I was beginning to think like William; suppose, I thought, I walked the fields as he did with Leo, would the hiding place strike me as it struck him? I thought at first he might have taken Mary Bradford into the plan and then have had to kill her, but that seemed too wildly improbable. There was absolutely no questioning William's loathing for Mary Bradford. Anyway, though I actually tramped over the fields, I didn't think of anything. But I did talk to Reed about the missing story and tell him my theory."

"Before you spoke to me?" Kate asked.

"Yes. I felt he was likelier than you to call me a fool. And I couldn't let you live with the possibility of such a theft unless I really believed in it. Ultimately I did tell you, though not that I suspected William. After that," Emmet said, shrugging his shoulders, "it's Reed's story."

"I grabbed the stick, so to speak, from Emmet's faltering hand. Not a bad image, really, for my purposes. I came to it fresh, a new runner. He was already tired. In the end, however, I too nearly dropped with fatigue until I started recapitulating my whole visit here—one of the most wonderful and dreadful visits I have ever paid—and I remembered my first morning, being instructed in and bounced mercilessly about on Mr. Bradford's baler. I remembered also that Mary Bradford had seen me out there. Remembering all this, I again walked across the fields, and as I was watching that machine forming a bale, it came to me suddenly how even a good-sized manuscript could be neatly hidden in one of those bales, if one merely dropped it into the machinery when Bradford was looking the other way.

"I thereupon asked Bradford, with what I fondly hoped was a careless air, if the machine would wrap a wad of paper up with the hay? 'That's the second time I've been asked that question in as many weeks,' Bradford said."

Grace Knole whistled. "What a hiding place. To hide a needle in a haystack."

"But, of course, one must have a chance of recovering the needle. I went on talking to Bradford, and discovered that William had approached him for a job as handyman, to begin work in September. He spoke of needing a job while working on his dissertation, of wanting to do physical work, and so forth. He knew of course how hard it is for farmers to find hired men these days.''

''And he intended to 'find' the manuscript while working for Bradford. Ye gods, did Bradford hire him?''

''No. Bradford was rather circumspect here, but he *seemed* to be suggesting that he suspected William of having had an affair with his wife.''

''So that was it,'' Kate said. ''Molly said—but I never thought . . .''

''Naturally not,'' Reed said. ''There's so much we can't know, and probably never will, though with luck and the grace of God, a psychiatrist or a priest, perhaps between them, may unearth it. I think she seduced him—perhaps out of sheer malevolence, or a mad kind of lust. All that is certain is that she saw him put something into the hay, and learned that it was something he treasured; her knowledge put him in her power. I can't believe he ever told her what it was, which is, you know, the saddest part of all. Because had she known it was a story, she probably would not have thought it worth bothering about. I'm certain she had never heard of James Joyce. God knows what she thought it was.''

''For some horrible reason,'' Emmet said, ''I imagine it was in that very hay, where his treasure was, that she made him make love to her. It must have been, if Bradford found them. Perhaps he wouldn't have killed her for either thing alone, the story, or the assault on his chastity. Or perhaps the thought of her leering at him as he searched, as he had to search, through that hay, was more than he could bear.''

''Whatever way it was,'' Reed said, ''when Kate recounted to me her conversation with Molly, the girl Bradford loves—it all fell into place. It explained Lina, it explained so much.''

''And on that walk back from Mr. Mulligan's party,'' Kate said, ''I thought he was talking about me. I should have known he would never . . .''

''Oh yes, it all fits, once you think about it. Emmet and I agreed. But there wasn't a shadow of proof, not a glimmer. And what Molly said to you, Kate, was truer than you admitted. Bradford would have been doomed with having murdered his wife in any community, considering the motive he had.''

''So you tried your little act with the fire?''

''It seemed harmless enough. If it hadn't worked, we would have lost nothing but face—Emmet's face—and he was ready to risk that.''

"Do you mean to say," Grace said, "that there is a priceless, unpublished James Joyce manuscript wrapped in one of thousands of bales of hay on the top of Mr. Bradford's barn?"

"Oh yes, it's there all right. William had the letter on him when the police took him away. He hid the manuscript but he kept the letter. It just said: 'Here it is, Lingerwell. Bloom's first appearance in print.' ''

"I can't wait to read it," Emmet said. "Do you suppose Bloom was seen as part of the general paralysis, as in the other *Dubliner* stories, or was he already the apostle of love?"

"What I want to know," Kate said, "is what I am going to do with the four thousand bales of hay I have today purchased from Mr. Bradford. Where does one keep hay in New York City?"

"I only hope," Emmet said, "he starts today using some other hay for his cows. Can you imagine that story, that precious story, in the stomach, one of the four stomachs, of a cow, slowly being churned into manure or fertilizer? What a horror!"

"An event, nevertheless, which would vastly have amused Joyce," Kate said. "Read *Ulysses*."

Epilogue

THE chairman of the James Joyce Society rose to speak.

"Ladies and gentlemen. The sixty-second anniversary of Bloomsday has passed," he said, "to be followed by an event so earthshaking that one could scarcely have conceived of anything so magnificent. Incredible though it may seem, a sixteenth story originally intended for *Dubliners* has been discovered. A story which may well have been the first to tell of Mr. Leopold Bloom. Here, to recount the fascinating details, is Mr. Emmet Crawford."

There was applause and many eyes glistened, most of them male. In the back of the room, unobtrusively seated, were a lady, a gentleman, and a small boy looking quite pleased with himself. Emmet Crawford arose.

"Thank you, ladies and gentlemen. We all share, I am certain, the same excitement. But, alas, neither I nor any of us has a new manuscript by James Joyce. We have only what is perhaps little more than a wild hope for a manuscript by James Joyce. What we have at the moment, ladies and gentlemen, is four thousand—no, let me be accurate, as Joyce would have approved—three thousand, two hundred and thirteen bales of hay!"

Poetic Justice

Note

It will, of course, be obvious to every reader
that the quotations at the heads of the chapters,
and most of the poetry scattered reverently
throughout this work,
are from the writings of W. H. Auden.
The author is grateful to Random House, Inc.,
for its permission to quote from the copyrighted works of Mr. Auden.

Contents

PART 1

BEFORE DEATH

Prologue

though one cannot always
Remember exactly why one has been happy,
There is no forgetting that one was.

PROFESSOR Kate Fansler mounted the stairs to the upper campus where the azalea bushes were just coming into bud. She did not yet know, on that May morning, that the students had already occupied the administration building. Few knew as yet; tomorrow, it would be front-page news around the world. Now she walked past lawns just turning rich with green. The students, damn them, were trampling thoughtlessly across the new grass, heedless of all the cautionary signs and fences erected by the University's tireless gardeners. The annoyance she had always felt at this desecration had grown, if anything, more acute with the years. She reprimanded herself for crotchetiness. " ' . . . unready to die,' " Kate thought, " 'but already at the stage when one starts to dislike the young.' " The lines were Auden's and, as always, they gave Kate special pleasure. She was going that afternoon to see him receive a gold medal for poetry.

Kate had never met Auden and was unlikely ever to do so. Yet there had existed between them for over ten years what she considered to be the perfect relationship. That it was wholly satisfactory to Auden was to be inferred from the fact that he had never heard of it; its satisfactions for Kate rested securely on the knowledge that he never would. Auden's private person did not interest her. But, over the years, his poetry and such delightful facts about him as appeared in books by his friends had given her a new awareness of life. She had never read a word of criticism or scholarship about him and, safely and professionally ensconced as she was in the Victorian period, planned never to do so. Which just goes to show, as, indeed, did everything happening that day, that foresight is not a human attribute. At that very moment the students had opened the President's files and begun to read his letters.

> *Abruptly mounting her ramshackle wheel,*
> *Fortune has pedalled furiously away;*

but Kate, who did not know that, sat down and pleasurably regarded the newly blossomed tulips.

Kate had first seen Auden a decade before on a television program which, since she did not own a set, she had gone to considerable inconvenience to catch. (Her hosts had been more inconvenienced still, since the program had begun at nearly midnight and went on into the small hours of the morning; abandoning Kate, Auden, and their living room, they had finally gone to bed.) Kate could no longer remember the occasion for the program, nor exactly what Auden and the others had been discussing, but she did remember that throughout the long hours Auden had called loudly and unsuccessfully for tea: apparently as difficult to obtain in a television studio as Coca-Cola in a four-star Parisian restaurant. Kate had never forgotten Auden's frown. Reportedly, he had been frowning since boyhood. "I see him," Christopher Isherwood had written, "frowning as he sings opposite me in the choir, surpliced, in an enormous Eton collar, above which his great red flaps of ears stand out, on either side of his narrow, scowling, pudding-white face." They had been at school together: Isherwood was to present Auden with his gold medal that afternoon.

"And so, after all these years, I am forcibly evicted from my office. They have taken over the College building too."

"Who has?" Kate stared at the man standing beside her.

"Fate," Frederick Clemance observed, "has, I see, granted you some additional moments of blessed ignorance. And what were you thinking of, sitting there contemplating tulips?"

"Auden," Kate said.

"You don't say?" Clemance sat down beside her on the bench. "Do you know his poetry well?"

"I browse in it," Kate admitted, "as though it were a meadow."

She regarded Clemance with a certain degree of discomfort. She had admired him for years, had studied with him as a graduate student (which for a woman had been a singular honor indeed), had followed with interest and devotion his growing reputation—he was now one of the University's luminaries. She was, indeed, technically speaking, his colleague, but she had never before chatted with him.

"There they go, you see. Crawling around the ledges like so many monkeys and shouting obscenities. If you come close enough, they will spit down on you. Can it be a new form of panty-raid? At least," Clemance added, "no one ever before involved me in that sort of escapade."

By standing on the bench they could indeed see the students, mostly bearded, and looking, even at that distance, unwashed, posed out the windows, hanging on the bars. "Perhaps, Miss Fansler," Clemance said, climbing down, "you could do me a favor." Kate smiled nervously. So, she imagined, Frederick the Great might have spoken to one of his courtiers.

"If I can, of course," she said.

"It's about Auden."

Kate stared at him blankly. Neither of them, of course, knew yet that their world had changed. For them, the academic machine was still grinding on. Had anyone suggested then to Kate or Clemance that they would soon see their colleagues obscenely mocked by students and clubbed by policemen, they would have questioned his competence. We shared, Kate would think later, a last hour of innocence.

"I am directing a dissertation on Auden; it's finished, actually; the work of a brilliant young man who's eager to have the dissertation examination soon. Professor Pollinger is also on the committee. I was about to look for someone to take over in the final stages, because of all the pressures I'm under. You see how lucky I am to have found you. Do you know Auden?"

"No," Kate said. "And I've never approached his work academically. I really don't feel qualified."

"You'll do beautifully. Knowing Auden, I've never been able to feel properly academic about his work either. I'll tell them at the English Office. Many thanks; I shall be off now and see where all this is leading. I am glad, in more ways than one, that we have met before the tulips." He smiled and walked away. And indeed, in the next day or two, the academic machine, not yet sputtering, ground out an official notice to Kate: "Title of Dissertation: The Poetry of

W. H. Auden; Name of Candidate: R. E. G. Cornford; Chairman of
Dissertation Committee: Professor Fansler.''

By two thirty that afternoon the students had taken a third building and delivered a series of ultimatums to the President of the University who, as usual, was somewhere else. Rumor announced that
he was flying home. Meanwhile, the faculty had begun to meet in
groups, discussing what action they might take. The Vice-President,
temporarily in charge, began to talk of calling the police. Kate hailed
a taxi and asked to be driven to the American Academy of Arts and
Letters.

But she was not to see Auden in person; that much was immediately clear. At the annual ceremonies of the American Academy of
Arts and Letters, the members, and those who are to receive awards
or be inducted into membership, sit on the stage in numbered seats.
The programs held by the audience contain a diagram of the stage
indicating who is to occupy each seat. Neither Auden nor Isherwood
was there. At the end of the program, Mr. Glenway Wescott agreed
to read both Isherwood's speech presenting the gold medal to Auden
and Auden's acceptance of it.

The audience was disappointed, but Kate, seated in the balcony,
was strangely satisfied; it had always been their words she cared for,
not their presences. Isherwood's short speech spoke of ''the transformation of seven-year-old Auden Minor into the sixty-one-year-old
poet whom we honor today,'' and ended with Isherwood's taking
''advantage of his non-presence to tell him how very proud I am to
be his friend.'' ''Dear Christopher,'' Auden's acceptance speech began; and then: ''For me, poetry is firstly a game.'' Which, Kate
thought, listening to the voice of Mr. Wescott, is why we can allow
him to be profound. Who but Auden could have written so fine a
poem about his bedroom:

Don Juan needs no bed, being far too impatient to undress,
nor do Tristan and Isolde, much too in love to care
for so mundane a matter, but unmythical
mortals require one, and prefer to take their clothes off
if only to sleep.

It was, in fact, an odd poem for Kate to have thought of—had
she, perhaps, possessed that day unrecognized prophetic powers? For

at her university no one was to undress and go to sleep for an entire week. By the time Mr. Cornford's dissertation arrived at her office, Kate was far too tired even to resent on Auden's behalf the hand of academe.

1

Though mild clear weather
Smile again on the shire of your esteem
And its colors come back, the storm has changed you:
You will not forget, ever,
The darkness blotting out hope, the gale
Prophesying your downfall.

THAT classes at the University began, as they were scheduled to, on September 17, was a matter of considerable astonishment to everyone. There was not a great deal to be said for revolutions—not, at any rate, in Kate's opinion—but they did accustom one to boredom in the face of extraordinary events, and a pleasant sense of breathless surprise at the calm occurrence of the expected. Kate said as much to Professor Castleman as they waited for the elevator in Lowell Hall.

"Well," he answered, "I might have found myself even more overcome with amazement if they had not managed to put my course in historical methods, which never has less than a hundred and fifty students, into a classroom designed to hold ninety only if the students sit two in a chair, which, these days, they probably prefer to do. Though come to think of it," he added as the elevator, empty, went heedlessly past, apparently on some mysterious mission of its own, "I don't know why students should expect seats at lectures, since audiences can no longer expect them at the theater. We went to a play last night—I use the word 'play,' you understand, to describe what we expected to see, not what we saw—and not only were there no seats, the entertainment principally consisted of the members of the cast removing their clothes and urging, gently of course, that the audience do likewise. My wife and I, fully clothed, felt rather like missionaries to Africa insufficiently indoctrinated into the antics of the aborigines. Shall we walk down? One thing at least has *not* changed in this university: the elevators. They have never worked, they do not now work, and though an historian should never speak with assurance of the future, I am willing to wager that they never will. Where are you off to? Don't tell me, I know. A meeting. What's more, I can tell you what you are going to discuss: relevance."

"That," said Kate, "would be the expected. As a matter of fact, I have a doctoral examination: the poetry of W. H. Auden. He wrote a good bit of clever poetry to your muse."

"Mine? Gracious, have I got a muse? Just what I've needed all these years. Do you think I could trade her in for a cleaning woman, three days a week with only occasional ironing? My wife would be prostrate with gratitude."

"Trade Clio in? Impossible. It is she into whose eyes 'we look for recognition after we have been found out.' "

"Did Auden write that? Obviously he's never been married. That's a description of any wife. I thought you were in the Victorian period."

"I am, I am. Auden was born in 1907. He only missed Victoria by six years. And don't be so frivolous about Clio. Auden called her 'Madonna of silences, to whom we turn When we have lost control.' "

"Well, get hold of her," Professor Castleman said. "I'm ready to turn."

The dissertation examination was not, in fact, scheduled for another hour. Kate wandered back toward her office, not hurrying, because no sooner would she reach Baldwin Hall, in which building dwelt the Graduate English Department, than she would be immediately accosted, put on five more committees, asked to examine some aspect of the curriculum about which she knew nothing (like the language requirement for medieval studies) and to settle the problems of endlessly waiting students concerning, likely as not, questions not only of poetry and political polarization, but of pot and the pill as well. Kate strolled along in the sort of trance to which she had by now grown accustomed. It was the result of fatigue, mental indigestion, a sense of insecurity which resembled being tossed constantly in a blanket as much as it resembled anything, and, strangest of all, a love for the University which was as irrational as it was unre-warded.

She would have been hard put to say, she thought looking about her, what it was she loved. Certainly not the administration (had there been one, which, since they had resigned one by one like the ten little Indians, there wasn't). Not the Board of Governors, a body of tired, ultraconservative businessmen who could not understand why a university should not be run like a business or a country club. The students, the faculty, the place? It was inexplicable. The love one shares with a city is often a secret love, Camus had said; the love for a university was apparently no less so.

"Kate Fansler!" a voice said. "How very, very nice. 'I *must* telephone Kate,' I have said to Winthrop again and again, 'we must have lunch, we must have dinner, we must meet.' And now, you see, we have."

Kate paused on the steps of Baldwin Hall and smiled at the sight of Polly Spence. Talk of the unexpected! Polly Spence belonged to the world of Kate's family—she had actually been, years ago, a protégée of Kate's mother's—and there emanated from her the aura of St. Bernard's—where her sons had gone to school—and Milton Academy, the Knickerbocker dancing classes and cotillions.

"I know," Polly Spence said, "my instincts tell me that if I wait here patiently you will say something, perhaps even something profound, like 'Hello.' "

"It's good to see you, Polly," Kate said. "I don't know what's become of me. I feel like the heroine of that Beckett play who is buried up to her neck and spends every waking moment rummaging around in a large, unorganized handbag. Come to see the action, as the young say?"

"Action? Profanity, more likely. Four-letter-word-bathroom, four-letter-word-sex, and really too tiresome, when I think that my own two poor lambs were positively *glared* at if they said 'damn.' It's not an easy world to keep up with."

"But if I know you, you're keeping up all the same."

"Of course I am. I'm taking a doctorate. In fact, I've almost got it. Now what do you think of that? I'm writing a dissertation for the Linguistics Department on the history of Verner's Law. Please look impressed. The Linguistics Department is overjoyed, because the darlings didn't know there was anything new to say about Verner's Law until I told them, and they've been taking it like perfect angels."

Kate smiled. "I always suspected an extraordinary brain oper-

ating behind all your committee-woman talents, but whatever made
you decide to get a Ph.D.?''

"Grandchildren," Polly said. "Three chuckling little boys, one
gurgling little girl, all under three. It was either hours and hours of
baby-sitting, to say nothing of having the little darlings cavalierly
dumped upon us at the slightest excuse, *or* I had to get a job that
would be absolutely respected. Winthrop has encouraged me. 'Polly,'
he said, 'if we are not to find ourselves changing diapers every
blessed weekend, you had better find something demanding to say
you're *doing*.' The children, of course, are furious, but I am now a
teaching assistant, very, very busy, thank you, and only condescend-
ing to rally round at Christmas and Easter. Summers I dash off to do
research and Winthrop joins me when he can. But you look tired,
and here I am chatting away. Let's have lunch one day at the Cosmopolitan Club."

"I'm not a member."

"Of course not, dear, though I never understood why. Why *are*
you looking so tired?"

"Meetings. Meetings and meetings. We are all trying, as you
must have heard, to restructure the University, another way of saying
that we, like the chap in the animated cartoons, have looked down
to discover we are not standing on anything. Then, of course, we
fall."

"But everybody's resigned. The President. The Vice-President.
We've got an Acting President, we're getting a Faculty Senate, surely
everything's looking up."

"Perhaps. But the English Department has discovered there is no
real reason for most of the things they have been happily doing for
years. And the teaching assistants—where, by the way, are you being
a teaching assistant? Don't tell me the College has reformed itself
sufficiently to be hiring female, no-longer-young ladies, however talented . . .''

"Not them; not bloody likely. I'm at the University College. *Very*
exciting. Really, Kate, you have no idea."

Kate, looking blank, realized she hadn't.

"Really," Polly Spence said, "the snobbery of you people in
the graduate school! We're doing *splendid* work over there . . .''

"Didn't the University College used to be the extension school?
Odd courses for people at loose ends like members of labor unions
who only work twenty hours a week and housewives whose children
are . . . ?''

"That was a hundred years ago. There are no more courses in basket-weaving. We give a degree, we have a chapter of Phi Beta Kappa, and our students are *very* intelligent people who simply don't want to play football or have a posture picture taken."

"Forgive me, Polly. As one always does when one speaks from ignorance and prejudice, I'm sounding a lousy snob."

"Well, you'll be hearing more from us, just you wait and see. Meanwhile, you must come and have dinner. When I tell Winthrop I've met you, he'll insist. He always finds you so entertaining, like Restoration comedy."

"And about as up-to-date. I'm faltering, Polly. If you want to know the truth, I'm thinking of taking up bridge, if not palmistry, astrology, and the finer points of ESP. One of my students has offered to introduce me to a medium with electronic thought waves."

"There is no question about it," Polly said. "We must have lunch at the Cosmopolitan Club. It reassures one."

Kate, walking up the stairs of Baldwin, waved a dismissive hand.

"Kafka," Mark Everglade said, meeting her in the hall outside her office, "where is thy sting?"

"I take it," Kate said, "that is a perpetually appropriate remark these days."

"Perpetually. Would you mind teaching a text course next year in the novels of Bulwer-Lytton?"

"You have to be joking. And what, while I'm doubled over with hilarity, is a text course?"

"One that uses books, of course. I know we're all tired on the first day of the semester, Kate, but surely you could have seen that. You remember books? They're what we used to read before we began discussing what we ought to read. The students have spent the entire summer reforming our course offerings, and it's now to be text courses."

"I have never read Bulwer-Lytton. I have never even discussed reading Bulwer-Lytton, except with some strange student who used to turn up every seven years with another thousand pages on the development of the historical novel. Ah, I see, *The Last Days of Pompeii* is now considered relevant. Perhaps it is, at that."

"If only," Mark Everglade said, "a volcano would come and cover us all with dust. We have done away, as you would have known if you had ever listened at all those meetings this last summer, with lectures and seminars. We now have text courses, preferably in texts nobody ever heard of before, like Bulwer-Lytton and the literature

of the emerging African nations. While I think of it, we are in the
market for someone who reads Swahili, if you should ever hear of
such a person.''

"So mysterious," Kate said. "No doubt there are scads of fascinating literary works in Swahili. But I spoke just the other night to
someone returned from Africa. He said that in Ethiopia, for example,
there are seventy-five different dialects, and that the tribes can only
converse with each other in English. In Nigeria, I understand, there
are two hundred and twenty-five languages, with English again the
common tongue for conversation. Why don't we train people to teach
English in Swahili, instead of training people to teach Swahili in
English, or is that a particularly reactionary observation?"

"Not only reactionary," Mark said, "but probably in itself
grounds for occupying this whole building. Now as to the catalogue . . ."

"Why are we discussing next year's catalogue on this year's first
day of classes?"

"As you will see when you meet with the student-faculty committee for finalizing the revisions of the catalogue, everyone keeps
changing his mind, so that we've got to get the damn catalogue for
next year into print so that no one can change it and we can argue
about the year after."

"I am not on the student-faculty committee to finalize anything,
and I will not serve on any committee with so barbaric a word as
'finalize' in its title, and that's final," Kate said.

"The title is open to discussion," Mark said, "but I'm afraid
you've absolutely got to be on the committee because you've been
on it all summer and are the only one who knows what's going on."

" 'We have no means of learning what is really going on,' Auden
says."

"I had no idea Auden was so relevant; the ultimate compliment."

"Well, he may be," Kate said, "but I'm not. Do you think that
could be my whole problem?"

"It's the problem all right. We are not only magnificently irrelevant, but are prevented, mysteriously, from enjoying the fruits of
irrelevance, which are frivolity and leisure."

"I wish I were an African nation," Kate said. "It must be so
comforting to think of oneself as emerging."

Kate had time only to dive into her office, add the mail she had
collected from her box downstairs to that already on her desk uno-

pened, grab the dissertation on Auden, tell three students who appeared from nowhere that she was *not* having office hours or consultations of any sort, and listen, with perfect impassivity, to the ringing of her telephone. Kate did not claim to have learned much during the previous spring's disruption or the summer's hard committee work, but she had learned one thing: it is not necessary to answer one's telephone. One can always suppose that one is not there. This vaguely existential decision meant, therefore, that Kate avoided for another two and one half hours what her governess used to call a rendezvous with destiny. A nice phrase. But Kate had early on discovered (though considerably after the reign of the governess) that one cannot 'avoid' a destined rendezvous. Rendezvous are either inevitable or impossible.

It was by no means usual for the dissertation examination, the final examination for the degree of Doctor of Philosophy, to be held on the first day of classes. In fact, like so much else now going on, it was hitherto unheard of. But the spring revolutions had meant the inevitable postponement of many doctoral dissertation examinations, partly because the Committee of Seven appointed by the Dean of the Graduate Faculties could rarely be collected (most of them were either wrestling with plainclothesmen at the time, examining identification at the University gates, or begging the mayor to intervene in the University's problems). And even had it been possible to get all seven in one place, it was not possible to find the place. The head of the Graduate English Department, a man for whom, Kate had decided over the summer, the term 'longsuffering' was meiosis, had held several examinations in his living room (to the evident distress of his children, who had planned to watch television at the same time), but after a while all such efforts were given up. When it reached the point where one examination committee (which fortunately included no lady members) met in the men's room of the Faculty Club, and two of those who had been asked at the last minute to serve had never, it soon became evident, heard of the subject under discussion, the office of the Dean of Graduate Faculties declared itself officially closed. For one thing, with all the student raids on the administration buildings, the secretarial staff became so unnerved at the necessity of shoving all records and dissertations into the safe at the threat of occupation that they flatly refused even to come to the office until things had "quieted down."

Today four members of the examining committee had shown up,

which was a quorum, and an enormous relief to Kate and the candidate, who had flown in from his teaching post in California especially for the examination. All is, thank God, minimally official, Kate thought, taking her place as chairman at the head of the table. To Kate's right sat the other member of her department, Peter Packer Pollinger, the official sponsor of the dissertation. To her left sat the two necessary representatives of other departments, Professor Kruger from the German Department, and, next to him, Professor Chang from the Department of Asian Civilization. Professor Chang was present as the result of total desperation, but someone else outside the English Department was required, and, after all, Auden, together with Christopher Isherwood, had gone to China in 1938 and written a book about it. The Department of Asian Civilization had told Kate that Professor Chang had never been to China, but one couldn't ask for everything in outside examiners.

All began properly enough. Kate asked Mr. Cornford to leave the room and told the committee what facts about Mr. Cornford, provided in a special folder by the office of the Dean of Graduate Faculties, seemed relevant: his education, present position, date and subject of his master's essay. "Perhaps, then, we can ask the candidate in for the examination," Kate hopefully said.

"Clarification, please," said Professor Chang.

"I beg your pardon," Kate said. "I didn't mean to seem to be rushing. Is there a question about Mr. Cornford? About Auden?"

"Please. I have read dissertation with great interest and attention. But I would like to point out I am not from Department of Asian Civilization. I am from School of Engineering."

"Engineering?" Kate said faintly. "I'm afraid there must be some confusion."

"Mr. Auden is most interesting writer," Professor Chang said, "but are there many limestone landscapes in China?"

"Limestone landscapes!" Professor Kruger said. "It is more a question of the Weimar Republic. Auden does not realize that the love of death and the rejection of authority . . ."

At this point Professor Peter Packer Pollinger began blowing through his mustache, always a sign, as Kate well knew, that he was about to burst into speech. Professor Pollinger had only three kinds of speeches. The first was about punctuation, particularly about the necessity of keeping all punctuation marks *inside* quotation marks. He had been known to go on about the unbelievable dangers involved in placing punctuation marks *outside* quotation marks for close on to two hours. His second speech had to do with Fiona Macleod, the alter ego and pseudonym of a turn-of-the-century Irish author named William Sharp. He had managed (William Sharp, not Professor Pollinger, although the confusion did appear to be in some mysterious way appropriate) to get himself so perfectly, so schizophrenically divided between himself and his pseudonymous alter ego (who was, of course, a lady) that he had been known to fall down in a fit if William Sharp and his wife were invited to a dinner party and Fiona Macleod overlooked. Professor Pollinger had for the last ten years devoted himself (he was now sixty-seven) to the collection of every possible datum about William Sharp, and he was delighted, not to say compelled, to transmit whatever he had most recently learned to anyone he encountered. Thus despite a good deal of dodging behind doorways, everyone in the English Department, but particularly the secretaries, who, being rooted behind their desks, were less able to disappear, became authorities on the life and times of William Sharp/Fiona Macleod.

Professor Pollinger also had a third speech, which was unassigned: variable, as the mathematicians say. This speech might happen to do with any experience Professor Pollinger had recently undergone which had sufficiently caught his attention to be memorable: how a snow drift into which he had absentmindedly walked had overwhelmed him; the way he had heard the sound of the Irish Sea quite clearly in his ears for a solid hour before his wife returned to discover that the tub in the adjoining bathroom had overflowed, leaving Professor Pollinger ankle-deep in water; or, very occasionally, when truly impelled by circumstances, Professor Pollinger would deliver himself of a pertinent fact, which was always, as it was now, alarmingly germane to the discussion.

"Auden was interested in engineering," Professor Pollinger now announced, blowing through his mustache. "Wanted to be one. When the Oriental languages fellow dropped out, I suggested an engineer." Professor Pollinger puffed for a moment or two. "Glad to discover they had a Chinese engineer," he said. "That made it all right, I thought. Couldn't find you," he added, looking sulkily at Kate.

Kate coughed. "Then," she said, turning to the gentleman from Engineering, "your name isn't Professor Chang?"

"Is," that gentleman insisted. "Contradiction, please. Is."

"I see," said Kate, who didn't. "Well, then, perhaps we can begin. Will you, Professor Pollinger, ask the usual first question?"

"Certainly," said Professor Pollinger, puffing through his mustache. "What made you choose this topic, Mr. Whateveryourna-meis?"

"Please, Professor Pollinger," Kate said, "if you don't mind, don't ask the question until we get the candidate into the room."

"Very well," Professor Pollinger said crossly. "Very well." Kate, going to the door to summon Mr. Cornford, gave Professor Pollinger a baleful look. She seriously suspected him of putting them all on. Due to retire at the end of this year, he found it suited his peculiar sense of humor to appear gaga, but Kate suspected that a delight in confusion allied with a general resentment of the modern world was chiefly responsible for his eccentric ways. He had, of course, not really directed this or any other dissertation, although he did read right through all of them searching for punctuation outside quotation marks.

"Please be seated, Mr. Cornford," Kate said. The committee, as was customary, arose at the entrance of the candidate. "We will now begin. Professor Pollinger, will you please ask the first question?"

"Mr., er, Whateveryournameis," puff-puff through the mustache, "do you happen to know if Auden ever read the poetic dramas of Fiona Macleod?"

"Perhaps," Kate interjected, "Mr. Cornford could begin by telling us why he chose . . ."

"Tell me please," Professor Chang said, turning courteously in his chair, "in China your Mr. Auden found limestone landscapes? And what, please, is dildo?"

How they got through the subsequent two hours—for Professor Kruger was very interested in Auden's experiences in Germany, and Professor Chang in everything—Kate never properly knew. But such a good time was had by all that they quite happily voted Mr. Cornford a distinction (which he thoroughly deserved) and Kate was still congratulating him when the other three had bowed themselves from the room.

"My God," Mr. Cornford said. "No one will ever believe it. Can it possibly be official? I shall go to my death, which I hope is far distant, telling the story of this examination, and no one, no one on God's green earth will ever, ever believe it. And this is the world of scholarship I want to enter."

Kate laughed. "Well, according to T. S. Eliot, Auden is no scholar, you know."

"Eliot liked his poetry."

"Of course he did. But he insisted Auden was no scholar all the

same. Somebody asked why, and Eliot said: 'I was reading an introduction by him to a selection of Tennyson's poems, in which he said
that Tennyson is the stupidest poet in the language. Now if Auden
had been a scholar he would have been able to think of some stupider
poets.' And if you, Mr. Cornford, had been around this university as
long as I, you would know that it is better that a farcical examination
produce a first-rate piece of work like yours than that a brilliantly
run examination produce, as I have often seen it do, a farce.''

"So Auden was right," Mr. Cornford said. " 'Against odds,
methods of dry farming may produce grain.' But, oh my Lord. 'Your
Mr. Auden, he found limestone landscapes in China?' '' he mim-
icked.

Kate parted from Mr. Cornford at the door of the building; he
was due to make a midnight plane. This, she thought, has been a
day. But it has had its moments, she thought, chuckling to herself
over Professor Chang, bless his heart.

"Going my way, lady?" a voice said. "Or, more exactly, may I
be allowed to go yours?" With something of a flourish, a man who
had clearly been waiting for her removed his beret and bowed. "Bill
McQuire is the name," he said. "Remember me? Department of
Economics. Statistics is my specialty. I advised you once that some
figures you wanted to juggle could not reveal anything meaningful,
being self-selected."

"I'm going to get a taxi," Kate said. "Can I drop you somewhere?"

"I wanted to talk with you," McQuire said, "on a quite imper-
sonal matter. May I buy you a drink?"

"Can it be as important as all that? I've had a day."

"Very important. Dean Frogmore has been trying to reach you
all day, but your telephone never answers. I've been delegated to
drop round and catch you after your examination. Successful candidate, I hope?"

"Beyond my wildest expectations," Kate answered. "What's
this all about?"

"I realize," McQuire said, "that I am perhaps not the ideal man
to approach you. But when Frogmore asked, I had to say I was acquainted with you. Do you know of Boulding?"

"He isn't by any chance a character in a novel by Bulwer-Lytton
or a citizen of an Emerging African Nation?"

"He's an economist, and he announced one of the great laws of
modern times: if it exists, it must be possible. That's what I want to

see you about: something which exists, but which everyone is saying is impossible.''

"I have always thought," Kate said, "that you scientists and social scientists ought to emblazon on your walls a quotation from J. B. S. Haldane: 'How do you know that the planet Mars isn't carried around by an angel?' Will it express my utter confidence in your knightly qualities if I ask you up for a drink?"

"It will," Bill McQuire said, hailing a taxi. "Same place?"

"Same place," Kate said. "And who in hell is Dean Frogmore?"

Kate had consulted Bill McQuire some five years earlier, when the Admissions Office of the Graduate Faculties had co-opted her onto a committee to study the old patterns of admission and to evolve new ones. For the first time in her life Kate found herself confronted with statistics, with no knowledge what to do with them but a distinct sense that either the statistics before her or the conclusions to be drawn from them were faulty. Someone had suggested that she consult a statistician, and had suggested Bill McQuire. Professor McQuire had himself soon provided a new statistic in Kate's life. He was the only man she had ever gone to bed with on the basis of a ten-hour acquaintance, liked moderately well, and never, to all intents and purposes, seen again.

They had, of course, met from time to time on University occasions, in the Faculty Club, once on a dissertation committee when a student of Kate's had written on some abstruse topic concerning economics and literature. They greeted each other on these occasions not only with the pleasant formality their surroundings required, but with the pleasant indifference they both genuinely felt.

Now, when they had reached home, Kate left McQuire in the living room to fix himself a drink. It was, Kate thought, a room Auden would have approved of:

> *Spotless rooms*
> *where nothing's left lying about*
> *chill me, so do cups used for ashtrays or smeared*
> *with lipstick: the homes I warm to,*
> *though seldom wealthy, always convey a feeling*
> *of bills being promptly settled*
> *with checks that don't bounce.*

McQuire seemed to agree, for he was happily stretched out in her Knoll chair when she returned. "It is extraordinarily ungallant of me to say so,'' he laughed, ''but when I opened your liquor cabinet I had a most magnificent case of *déja vû*. I remembered looking into it, years ago, whenever it was, and thinking: My God, Jack Daniel's, and that's exactly what I did tonight. What can I get you?''

Kate asked for Scotch. She watched him as he fixed the drink. How old was he now, somewhere between forty-five and fifty? His curly hair was thinner, and gray; at least he doesn't dye it, Kate thought, and was surprised to have thought it. Bill had always worn his curly hair longer than the prevailing style—he was a distinctly Byronic type—and now that fashions had overtaken him he looked oddly more out of style than he had previously done. His face was lined, with that special crinkled quality of the skin which marks those who have drunk heavily and long. Turning to her with the drink, he found himself held by her stare. ''Portrait of an aging stag,'' he said. ''Dissipated but kindly. If you want to know the whole hideous truth, I like them younger and younger all the time, so that I am in danger of becoming a dirty old man. Humbert Humbert, I do pity thee. Well, no,'' he added, seeing Kate's eyes widen. ''Eighteen is still my under limit. Cheers.''

''I am trying to decide,'' Kate said, ''why it is that you are quite incapable of shocking me, even though I think your life reprehensible and I find promiscuity shocking, particularly in married men.''

''I'm sure you do. In fact, I have often noticed that those most shocked by marital infidelity are usually themselves unmarried. Cecelia, as it happens, has settled quite nicely into life, though she is pleased to see that neither of our sons at all resembles a rampant stag—that is, me. *You've* worn well, Kate. I like you and the way you look, and you're very decent to put up with me this afternoon.''

''I haven't worn all that well. Supposedly I shall always be tall and lean with a French twist and a face that shows all the worries in the world. Do you know what I like about you, Bill? It's only just occurred to me, so let me say it and then we can get down to whatever you and Dean Toadwell have on your minds.''

''His name is Frogmore. What do you like? My eternal evanescence?''

''The fact that however much you stalk your prey, you do not class women with motor cars if they are attractive and with eye-flies if they are not.''

''Eye-flies?''

''Well, something nasty. I was quoting Forster, who happened to be writing about India at the time, so it was eye-flies.''

"Somebody said once—unlike you I never remember where I read things—that if a woman is not beautiful at twenty, it's not her fault; if she's not beautiful at forty, it is her fault. Have you ever thought of getting married?"

"Once or twice, lately. The ramifications of university upheavals are endless. Do you think marriage advisable? One has such lovely friendships with men whose wives were beautiful when they were twenty."

"What a dreadfully cynical remark. Married women can have friends; the men feel, if anything, more comfortable."

"Meaning you would feel more comfortable now if I were married."

"Kate, don't put words in my mouth. I was . . ."

"Answer me honestly, if you want me to help with your beastly crisis."

"That's not fair. People who demand to be answered honestly have already decided what the honest answer is. But you'd be wrong. I wouldn't be more comfortable with you, but I think I would feel you were happier, particularly in these times of institutionalized uncertainty."

"I'll tell you one thing, Bill," Kate said, recovering herself. "I have believed, in the words of a first-rate woman scholar who lived to be eighty and was always falling in love with someone, that marriage for a woman spoils the two things that make life glorious: learning and friendship. Somehow, that no longer seems so unquestionably true. Fill up your glass and tell me about Toadwell."

"Frogmore. That you haven't heard of him is absolutely symptomatic."

"Oh, come on, Bill, how many deans have I heard of?"

"Can you name the Dean of Divinity? Law, Graduate Faculties, Public Administration, Business, Engineering?"

"Not Public Administration."

"My point still holds."

"I can only name most of the others because of the troubles last spring."

"Fair enough. But you can't name the Dean of the University College?"

"Frogmore?"

"Frogmore."

"You know, Bill, it is absolutely coming over me in waves that

I do not want to know the Dean of the University College, or University College, or . . ."

"Shall I tell you something? Last spring, when this place was blowing up, there was only one school in it that remained intact."

"Don't tell me, let me guess."

"The students of the University College occupied their own building and held it for themselves. They proved to be the only really loyal student body the whole blasted University possessed, and the University, with the gratitude and intelligence that has marked all its decisions, now wants to wash the University College down the drain."

"Bill, I'm in Graduate Faculties. I'm planning next year's curriculum there. I'm going to give a text course in the novels of Bulwer-Lytton, and maybe one in the literature of Emerging African Nations. I'm thinking of emigrating to an Emerging African Nation myself. Do you really think you want to try to make this my problem?"

"Yes, lady, I do. And when your fortieth birthday comes, I shall buy you a specially lovely present for a beautiful and humane woman."

"As Polly Spence would say—my God, Polly Spence—four-letter-word-bathroom. Bull's, that is."

2

In our morale must lie our strength.

"ALL I ask, Kate, is that you listen. Give it a chance. Try to remember that these are people fighting for the life of a school *they* do not need. They all have tenure in other branches of the University. It's a matter of believing in something."

"Even Dean Frogmore?"

"Even he." Bill McQuire and Kate were walking toward the Faculty Club next day to attend a luncheon with Dean Frogmore and some senior members of his faculty. Kate had had to cancel two appointments to come, and she did so, finally, only as a favor to McQuire. He had known, and Kate respected him for knowing, that she had learned to refuse any official request, but was still far from immune to personal ones. "Frogmore is offered a job every other day, as president of this college or that. Everyone's looking for administrators; they're almost as scarce as plumbers and doctors. Probably he'll go off to some rural collegiate paradise before long, but I think his devotion to the University College is unquestionable. Everyone has underestimated Frogmore from the beginning, I among them. But let me tell you two things about him: he's got guts you'll admire, and an oily surface you'll hate. For one thing, and I want to warn you about this in advance, knowing your prejudices, he calls everyone, *everyone*, by his first name the first moment they meet."

"Cripes," Kate said.

"I know; that's why I mention it. You're remarkably old-world in some ways, Kate."

"Remarkably. I don't mind going to bed at ten at night with a man I met at noon the same day, but I can't bear being called by my first name until a relationship has had time to mature. Very old-world indeed."

McQuire chuckled. "It's a maddening habit—Frogmore's, I mean. When I first met him he kept referring to Lou and Teddy, and the conversation had gone on for half an hour before I realized he was speaking of the President and Vice-President of the University. But don't underestimate him, Kate. He really and truly wants to put the University College on the map, when the easiest thing for him to do would be to cop out."

"It might be the easiest thing for all of us. Certainly for me. I can't imagine, truthfully, why you think I . . ."

"Yes, you can. Be good now. I'll give you a chance later to protest and thrash around, and I promise you, if your answer is really 'No,' I'll back you up."

"Which means if I act intelligently interested today, and ask leading questions, you won't assume I'm committed."

"Have I told you yet today," Bill said, "that you're beautiful?"

The luncheon party was held in one of the private rooms of the Faculty Club. The moment Kate and Bill McQuire entered, Frogmore leaped to his feet and rushed forward to greet them at the door. Somewhat overcome by his enthusiasm, the other gentlemen already seated around the table rose to their feet, awkwardly pushing back their chairs, dropping their napkins and brushing crumbs from their laps. (It was one of the unfailing characteristics of the Faculty Club that although service never began until the latest possible moment after one had sat down, there was always present, as part of the table setting, a large, exceedingly stale roll which one found oneself compelled, in time, to pulverize, showering oneself and the table top with crumbs.)

"Please," Kate weakly said. The academic community had taken longer than most to shake off old habits of gallantry. When Kate had first joined the faculty she had had to become inured to roomfuls of men rising to their feet as she entered. Gradually, of course, the custom had died out. Only Frogmore, with his bouncy manner and boy-scout demeanor, had trapped them into old habits.

"So this is Kate," Frogmore said. "Thank you, Bill, for bringing her." Kate, regarding Frogmore with a lackluster eye, avoided glancing at McQuire. Clever he: the blow fell less painfully, being expected. "Let me introduce you pronto to the others before getting under way; we've got a long agenda. What will you drink, Kate? This is on me; the Dean's slush fund.''

"A Bloody Mary please," Kate demurely said. (Reed had often remarked that when Kate came all over demure, it meant that what she really wanted to do was put a pillow over some chap's head and sit on it.) Kate did not like, in the ordinary way, to drink at lunch, a meal she avoided if she could, and certainly not when she was in danger of becoming involved in some internecine struggle. She had therefore hit upon the lovely stratagem of ordering a drink which was, at the Faculty Club, equal parts of Worcestershire sauce and watery tomato juice with as little vodka as made no difference to anyone not a teetotaler on principle.

"You know everybody, I'm sure," Frogmore said. "Luther Hankster of Biology." Kate, indeed, had stood side by side with Luther Hankster when the police had first and, as it turned out, abortively, been called to clear out the administration building. Playboy turned radical, Hankster kept more or less in the good graces of his colleagues by his unerring good manners and the careful use of a voice never, ever, raised. He was given to outrageously radical pronouncements which, had they been delivered in any but the voice of a man making secret love, would have instantly offended everyone.

"George Castleman, of course, is our guiding star." Kate wanted to ask Castleman if he had been tempted lately to public disrobement, but contained herself; she wondered anew at the passion for clichés which seemed, in Frogmore's case, almost to equal his passion for first names. Castleman, if not a guiding star, was certainly a power in the University, on all the vital committees and possessed of the kind of political acumen that was almost as rare in an academic community as inspired teaching.

"Herbert Klein, Political Science. Herbie, I believe you're not as well known to Kate as the rest of us." "Herbie," a man of enormous dignity and baleful looks, rose and shook Kate's hand with a firmness clearly indicating his wish to dissociate both of them from Frogmore's unearned intimacy. Kate wondered if anyone else had ever called him Herbie in his life. "We hope you will be able to help us, Professor Fansler," he formally said. Kate suppressed a grin.

"And," Frogmore went relentlessly on, "this is the other stranger to you, Kate: John Peabody, a student in the University College."

"Hi," said Peabody, to whom formality was unknown. Kate looked up in surprise. Although the principle of students serving on all the governing bodies of the University had by now been given token acceptance, in fact where there was a need for delicate decisions, students had so far not usually been present. Peabody, though, was older than any ordinary college man: he looked nearer thirty than twenty.

"And Tony Cartier is of course from your own department." Kate could never resist smiling at the sight of Cartier: his ill-controlled restlessness made luncheon meetings a torture to him; he would glance wildly about as though at any moment someone might lock the doors and keep him prisoner here forever.

The aged waiter took the order for the drinks and scrutinized it with exaggerated care. All the waiters at the Faculty Club were old and slow, though those chosen for the private rooms were, if not fast, because that was clearly impossible, at least not deliberately slower than age and rheumatism determined. Finding, perhaps to his sorrow, no esoteric and therefore unavailable drinks on the list, the waiter departed.

Frogmore began to speak. He had not spoken long before Kate became aware that he was, for all his foolish ways, a genius at committee work. Kate, who thought herself remarkably inept on committees, recognized the talent instantly. Thank God, Kate thought; were Frogmore a bumbler they would all be wasting their patience and their time.

"Now," Frogmore said, "let us run over the major points in a swift recapitulation, mostly for your benefit, Kate, since the rest of us have been kicking this thing around for quite a while. I don't want to be long-winded, so I'll get down to the nitty-gritty, the nuts and bolts." (Kate had, by the end of this sentence, ceased even to wince; she was taking her beating manfully. "There is one evil which . . . should never be passed over in silence but be continually publicly attacked, and that is corruption of the language . . ." Auden had written, but then Auden's hours were not passed amidst deans and social scientists.)

"As you know, Kate," Frogmore went blissfully on, "the University, which used to be a collection of baronies, has got to start operating as a whole if it's not to be part of the state system in ten years. There are certain changes we all agree on: it would take three million dollars to make our Dental School adequate; ten million to make it outstanding. Do we really need a Dental School? No, we do not. But, you see, restructuring is a convenient excuse for carrying out long-planned hanky-panky. I take it you are familiar with Pro-

fessor Jeremiah Cudlipp?'' Kate, who knew a rhetorical question
when she heard one, did not trouble either to nod or object. ''He, of
course, and his associate, Bob O'Toole, have decided that this time
of restructuring is just the moment to bounce the University College
off the campus altogether.''

''Bounce it?''

''Demolish it, phase it out, declare it null and void, give it the
ax.''

''But Cudlipp is only Chairman of the College English Department,'' Kate said.

''There is no 'only' about it, I'm afraid,'' Castleman said. ''For
reasons we do not wholly understand, he is determined that the University College must go. It gives a bachelor's degree that Cudlipp
claims dilutes the prestige of the degree given by *The* College, as
they so maddeningly call it. He has lots of other arguments. The point
is, since he is in the English Department, we felt we needed someone
in addition to Professor Cartier to help us in what is, I'm afraid, a
fight for survival.''

''The College feels,'' Luther Hankster whispered, ''like someone
with valuable suburban property whose neighbor threatens to sell to
a black.''

''Does Bob O'Toole go along with this? I have always thought
of him as a follower of Clemance.''

''So he is,'' Castleman said. ''But, as perhaps you have noticed,
he possesses arrogance and ambition in about equally large proportions, which puts him squarely on Cudlipp's side.''

''Where does Clemance stand?''

''Oh,'' McQuire said, ''he's with the College; always has been.
He suggests, in his marvelously reasonable way, that we are simply
not 'excellent' enough. Which is nonsense; we are the most excellent
college for adults in the country.''

''Have you had much to do with the College, Professor Fansler?''
Herbert Klein asked.

''Enough to know they are in danger of giving arrogance a bad
name,'' Kate lightly said.

''Exactly,'' Frogmore exclaimed, clapping his hands together.
''Well put, Kate.''

''O.K.,'' Kate said. ''You want someone from the English Department—which you gather, correctly, is fed up with Cudlipp's
throwing all that weight around.'' She hoped Frogmore would consider that well put too.

"And," Castleman said, "we need general sort of help so that when the Administrative Council next meets they will confirm the future of the University College in no uncertain terms. Needless to say, Cudlipp will do all he can to prevent that."

"Right," Kate said. "I see, or think I do. But why me? I don't even like teaching undergraduates."

"You are more decorative than our other colleagues," Cartier said.

"We did a lot of research, Kate," Frogmore said, "and we ran into very little flak when it came to you." (My God, Kate thought, he *is* smart; smart enough to know the we-chose-you-for-your-womanly-charms bit wouldn't work; good for him.) "From all sides we heard of your sympathy with students—your willingness, long before the roof fell in, to give them time. We also heard that you are opposed to the publish-or-perish racket, and to professors who have no time for anything but their own professional careers."

"All exaggerated, I assure you. I have no recent experience in undergraduate teaching and, to be brutally frank, not much desire for it. I like graduate students because they're self-selected." She winked at Bill McQuire.

"Why do you dislike teaching undergraduates?" Hankster asked. "Or did you just say that to startle us?"

"I said it because it's true—and tact isn't my most notable characteristic. Why is it true? Because of the age of undergraduates—delightful, no doubt, but not for me. As far as I'm concerned, youth is a condition which will pass, and which I prefer to have pass outside of my immediate field of vision. Of course, I have nothing *against* young people—apart from the fact that they are arrogant, spoiled, discourteous, incapable of compromise, and unaware of the price of everything they want to destroy. It's not that I disagree with their beliefs, or mind if I do disagree. I just prefer those whom life has had time to season.

"What a long speech. I am certain I ought not to be so emphatic; for one thing, it's unladylike and mysteriously unbecoming not to cherish the company of the young of one's own species. Someone must have asked me a question, and now I've come all over nasty about children, and quite forgotten what it was."

"We are answering the question of why you were chosen to join us," Klein said. "We felt we could interest you in a college whose students are no longer in the throes of role-playing: older, experienced in the ways of the world, mellower on the whole, and totally motivated—self-selected was, I believe, your own phrase."

"I see," Kate said. "And am I to be persuaded to some special action, or only encouraged to cheer in a general sort of way?"

"Let some of our students into your courses," Frogmore said. "Get to know them. Find out a bit about what we're doing, and give us a chance to impress you. Carry our banner in the Graduate English Department any way you see fit, but fight our cause there."

"I've certainly no objection to a few of your students in my courses, if I can interview them first. As to the fight in the Graduate English Department—you know, I don't as a rule drink at lunch, but right at the moment I feel the need of what Auden calls an 'analeptic swig.' "

"You've got to admit, Reed, it's not madly *me*. I mean, can you imagine *one* getting involved in a university power-struggle?"

"Then don't," Reed said. "What I can't imagine is why you don't just say no, but then I, like all outsiders, am having a certain amount of trouble understanding what in the world is going on in that university of yours. Surely you can send this Frogmore chap a firm but gracious note telling him you don't want anything to do with his silly college."

"But am I certain I don't want anything to do with it? It is, after all, awfully soul-satisfying of them to want me."

"And a very clever bunch they are, I must say. Though it is certainly by no means clear to me why the proposition of any old college gets the most careful consideration, while my . . ."

"I have yet to refuse one of your propositions, Reed, admit it."

"Kate, whenever you start talking like a bad imitation of Nancy Mitford I know that you are not only plastered but worried."

"Sweet, perceptive you. Though I must say, I really can't believe that Auden drank a whole bottle of Cherry Heering." They were in Kate's living room late that night and Kate, as she carefully explained, while she had long since admitted she couldn't write poetry like Auden's, wanted to discover if she had at least his capacity for alcohol. "You see," she had told Reed, "Auden went to spend the evening with the Stravinskys and Robert Craft, and he managed to drink a pitcher of martinis before dinner, a bottle of champagne during, and a bottle of Cherry Heering after. Craft thinks he thought the Cherry Heering was Chianti—I rather wish it were, actually. All that affected his labials only slightly and his wit not at all. It had no effect either, apparently, on his stomach, his liver, or his plumbing—not one visit to the loo. Well, I have failed the test—that is, my stomach is all right; I have, thank God, no way of knowing *how* my liver is; I'm far too comfortable to go to the loo; but I am not going to make it through this bottle of Cherry Heering. To join the fight or not to join the fight, that is the question. Whether it is nobler in the mind to defeat Jeremiah Cudlipp, which would be so pleasant in the gut, to say nothing of the good one could do, or . . ."

"Kate," Reed said, "what has happened to you this fall? Last spring, at least before all those students decided to occupy all those buildings, you seemed to . . ."

"Sara Teasdale."

"I beg your pardon?"

> *"In the spring I asked the daisies*
> *If his words were true,*
> *And the clever little daisies*
> *Always knew.*
> *Now the fields are brown and barren,*
> *Bitter autumn blows,*
> *And of all the stupid asters*
> *Not one knows."*

"I am certain," Reed said, "that Auden does not quote Sara Teasdale even after three bottles of Cherry Heering. What are you worried about, this University College?"

"There is my motto."

"Oh, my God, which motto is that? If a thing is worth doing, it's worth doing badly?"

"Not that one. The British Navy one: never ask for a job, never refuse one."

"I wonder if I, too, am not an honorary member of the British Navy: I'm thinking of leaving the D.A.'s Office."

"Reed Amhearst! Why? Surely you haven't tired of fighting crime?"

"I've been offered a job—actually a partnership—in a Wall Street law firm. Great rise in salary, among other things. A man might even consider supporting a wife and a small canary."

"Do you mean you would help people merge companies and diddle with their stocks and bonds?"

"No. That's what everyone else in the firm does. I would be

expected to rally round when their clients take time off and start diddling with things *other* than stocks and bonds. I am distressed, Kate, that the more certain I become of what I want, the more uncertain you become. I do realize that the University has got to go through a time of reorganization and re-examination, but—well, you seem positively driven . . ."

"To get plastered."

"Yes, but I was going to say—to examine every alternative as though you had somehow forfeited the right to say a simple 'no' to anything."

"But I have, you know. In former days, everyone found the assumption of innocence so easy; today we find fatally easy the assumption of guilt. The generation gap appeared somewhere between me and my brothers. They deny that they are guilty of anything but an excess of generosity, and I deny that I am innocent in anything except bumbling good intentions. Excuse me a minute, I think I'm going to throw up."

Reed, watching her more or less dignified exit, decided this was hyperbole. She returned, indeed, in a cheerful mood.

"I have thought it all out," Kate said. "Ready? The University College is a damn good idea, and there is nothing against it except the insufferable snobbery of the College. The fact is, now that I come to think of it, I know plenty of people of my generation of all sexes to whom an adult college of excellence would be the chance for a new life or a second life, which is becoming more and more necessary in the United States but which present institutions make impossible. Hooray, I'm going to make a speech. Ladies and gentlemen . . ."

"Right," Reed said. "Then drop Frogmore a short, gracious note saying let's fight together shoulder to shoulder for good old University College, sincerely yours, Kate Fansler."

"Just Kate. He never uses last names."

"Good. Then you join the fight for University, and I'll join my law firm. Why not?"

"Frederick Clemance."

"Our hero."

"You need not be vulgar. When you speak with admiration of all those musty forensic types, I do not sneer."

"I'm not sneering, simply surprised to have his name introduced into the discussion. What's he got to do with University College?"

"He's against it. Lock, stock, and barrel—or do I mean hook, line, and sinker? Anyway, he hates it, he wants to crush it under foot, he has joined with Jeremiah Cudlipp to defeat it, and do I want to go into battle with those two?''

"Why not? Growing up consists in fighting our former heroes."

"Maybe. I'm not that grown up. I don't want to get close enough to Clemance to discover he's not as great as I prefer to suppose he is."

"I don't know about the labials but the sibilants are doing fine. If I remember correctly Auden's poem on the death of Yeats, which isn't all that difficult since you cannot have read it to me fewer than eighteen times, Auden found no difficulty in recognizing that Yeats was magnificent and silly at the same time. Something about time forgiving those who wrote well. Clemance, if I am to believe you, wrote well. Let time forgive him, and get on with your college."

"But Clemance isn't silly; he's always been large of soul when all about him were nit-picking. Anyway, I've been hero-worshipping him since before I got into his special seminar as a student, and that, God help me, was nearly twenty years ago."

"If Clemance is as large-souled as all that, why does he associate himself with Jeremiah Cudlipp?"

"I don't know. Love for the College, maybe."

"Maybe."

Kate got to her feet and wandered over to the bookcase. Clemance's books were there, ranged together, biographies, essays, plays, poems—all together, a rare tribute in itself, since Kate divided her library ruthlessly into categories: poetry, fiction, drama, biography, criticism, cultural history, and books-not-worth-keeping-with-which-I-cannot-bear-to-part. "And if this were a movie," Reed said, "we would flash back to eager young Kate, eyes shining, hair streaming down her back, listening to Clemance in the glory of his prime, explaining us to ourselves."

"My hair never streamed down my back, surely it's the prime of his glory, and I wish they still made movies like that."

"He must be almost as old as Auden."

"We're all almost as old as Auden, 'in middle-age hoping to twig from/What we are not what we might be next.' "

"I'll tell you what you and Clemance are going to be next."

"What?"

"On opposite sides. Do you think I could be present at the opening fusilades of what promises to be a most interesting skirmish?"

"You can if you want to join us tomorrow. Frederick Clemance, though you may not believe it, has invited me to lunch. Why should you want to support a small canary?''

''Why should I want to support a wife? The only woman I think of marrying has long supported herself, with the aid of a meager salary and a large private income, and is presently concerned with founding a new college.''

''I'm not founding a college, I'm allocating resources—that is, if you're describing me. Are you thinking of marrying me for my money?''

''Odd you should mention that,'' Reed said. ''It's the only reason for marrying you I hadn't thought of. Now, when it comes to the reasons for *not* marrying you, there isn't an argument I've missed. But I'm like the Jew in Boccaccio who was converted to Catholicism on the sensible grounds that if the Church has succeeded despite all the corruption he found in Rome, it must have God behind it.''

''The world is full of beautiful young women aching for a handsome man like you, all graying sideburns and youthful demeanor. I am aging, cantankerous, given to illogical skirmishes and the drinking of too much wine. There must be at least fifty young women waiting for you, Reed.''

Reed walked then, in his turn, to the bookcase (poetry), extracted a volume and read from it: '' 'One deed ascribed to Hercules was ''making love'' with fifty virgins in the course of a single night: one might on that account say that Hercules was beloved of Aphrodite, but one would not call him a lover.' Nor is that all,'' Reed said, turning the pages. ''We have all agreed we live in uncertain times. Indeed, says Auden:

'How much half-witted horseplay and sheer bloody misrule
It took to bring you two together both on schedule?' ''

3

If equal affection cannot be,
Let the more loving one be me.

SATURDAY morning, and Central Park free for human beings to move at the speeds they might have attained at the turn of the century: horses, bicycles, and the almost forgotten pleasures of walking. Kate and Reed, whenever they considered the incredible series of disasters to which living in New York City regularly exposed one—strikes, garbage uncollected, snow unremoved, no transportation, no heat, no safety in the streets—or whenever they heard others complain of city living, would always think: they have taken the automobiles out of Central Park on weekends. It was the one urban blessing the decade had conferred.

"To return," Reed said, "to the conversation of last night, why has misrule and horseplay brought you to such a state of discombobulation? Or, since it has, may I offer my help in recombobulation? Does the University matter that much?"

"On Thursday, when the semester began," Kate said, "I asked myself that question—not, perhaps, whether it matters, which it so clearly does, but why?" Kate stopped to pat a puppy who came loping up anticipating admiration. "I can remember many stages of the revolution or insurrection or whatever it might be called. The exhilaration of the week when the buildings were occupied, the sense of absolute aliveness which, despite all the problems, one did so ringingly feel. I remember being shoved against a building by a plainclothesman with a club and thinking, this is it. I remember hearing the endlessly repeated obscenities from the students who stood about on the ledges and roofs of the buildings like acroterium, and wondering if indeed, as one of the characters in one of Forster's novels notes, they were out of fashion. I remember watching the flowers and grass being trampled, distinctly noticing as the last tulip was crushed. I remember, on the first day when they occupied the President's Office, walking by the administration building and thinking: so that's where the President's Office is, and never wondering, then, why in all the years I had been associated with the University I had never learned where the President's Office was, nor cared to learn. Later on, of course, we heard that the guards had entered the office, not to try to bounce the students but to rescue a Van Gogh which hung there, and I did muse then to think that I had never known the University possessed one of the world's great paintings.

"But none of that was the worst, you know; it only seemed the worst to those on the outside, who were appalled at the actions of the students, or appalled at the actions of the police—when what I became so suddenly struck with was the fact that there had never really *been* a university. That a bunch of half-baked, foul-mouthed Maoist students could bring a great university to a standstill, could be followed in their illegal acts by nearly a thousand moderate, thoughtful students, but above all could reveal that the University had never really been administered at all. We had a president whom no one ever saw, whose understanding of the true condition of the University could not have been more inaccurate if his job had been running a yacht club in East Hampton; we had a Board of Governors who had never, literally never, spoken to a student nor visited the University except for the monthly meetings, when their chauffeurs drove them to the campus; we had a faculty so busy with its own affairs that it had not troubled to observe that there was no university, only separate egos, departments, schools, programs all staking claims.

"Do you know, Reed, my brothers, who needless to say were outraged to the last degree that a bunch of unwashed radicals could be allowed to wield such powers, could never understand that there was any fault at work but that of the students and perhaps their overindulgent parents. They could not understand that a fumbling, withdrawn administration and a self-indulged, indifferent faculty were as much to blame as a youthful generation's failure to observe 'law and order.' There were students in those buildings, students I had known in class, who were no more Maoist than I was, who said that the communal life inside the buildings was the first vital experience they had had since they entered the University. We let it all go dead on us, Reed. Whatever may have happened in other universities, whatever may have been the destructive glee of radical groups at other places—Berkeley, Columbia, or wherever—the blame for what happened to my university was mine—mine and my associates.''

"Those kids were an outrageous group—the radical core.''

"They were. But to blame them for everything that followed is to blame the First World War on the assassin at Sarajevo. I am not, of course, very good at historical analogies. Auden says that:

> *at any hour from some point else*
> *May come another tribal outcry*
> *Of a new generation of birds who chirp*
> *Not for effect but because chirping*
>
> *Is the thing to do.*

I know all that; I know it is true of student rebellions at other universities now. But not of my university.''

"Are you going ahead with the University College crusade then in an attempt to grab some stones from the wreckage and build them into a more lasting edifice?''

"Sorry if I've been going on. All the same, it does intrigue me that the University College was the single unit in the University where the students, faculty, and administration did not automatically, or even eventually, assume they were working at cross purposes. The faculty at *The* College went about either in open disgust or like fathers who have done everything for their sons only to be sneered at, treated with disdain and ingratitude. The graduate students revealed that they had long suffered agony from the outworn structures and grading systems of their schools. But Frogmore's little domain held off chaos and went on with its work. That interests me.''

They stopped by the lake to watch the rowing. "Shall we rent a boat?'' Reed asked. Kate shook her head.

"Sorry to run on so,'' she said. "I keep trying to put it all into place. All right, I want to say, we were wrong; O.K., we were wrong, we will rebuild. But what a job! All the easy relations of the faculty, one with the other, gone. People have each other tagged now: radical, conservative, untrustworthy. Reed, I wanted to ask you something.''

"I know.''

"You do? How do you know?"

"Talented me, from the District Attorney's Office. I've known you awhile, Kate. I always know when you have a speech ready, and I know that you do not proceed through martinis and champagne to Cherry Heering because Auden did. You couldn't make the speech sober or, we now know, drunk. How about on a lovely fall morning? Shall we rent bicycles?"

"You have suggested everything but horses. And I haven't ridden in—oh, since another lifetime. We could of course take one of those horse-drawn carriages."

"Shall we?"

"Let's walk. We can get a beer at the boathouse."

They got the beers, walking in silence, and took them to a spot on a hill where they could watch the bicyclists, most of them pushing the bikes but a few riding, straining to reach the top. Kate liked to watch the moment when those who had struggled up on their bicycles let the wind catch them, going down.

> *"We may someday need very much to*
> *Remember when we were happy.*

The life before last spring seems to have been a time of innocence. I am no longer certain of anything, Reed, but I think that in my uncertainty, I would like to live with you, if you will have me."

"Live with me. What does that mean?"

"Even words don't mean anything anymore. Live with you. Occupy the same premises, have the same address. Pretend to be married."

"Pretend?" Reed leaned against a tree, with his hands in his pockets. "The one word I never expected to hear you use. I've asked you to marry me often enough; I don't mind if you ask me."

"I don't believe in marriage; not at my age, anyway."

"Kate, what I cannot pretend is that this University turmoil has improved you. You've developed all sorts of alarming symptoms, not least of which is a constant reference to yourself as on the brink of total decrepitude. People get married at your age, as you very well know, and indeed at twice your age. At any rate, if you are doddering, I am doddering even more, and do not find myself in the slightest inspired, as you seem to expect me to be, by the thought of a wife twenty years my junior, however luscious she might be."

"Reed, I—even Auden wrote a *Dichtung und Wahrheit* about

love, and not a love poem. There are no words for the words I want
to say."

"May I suggest some? Simple, straightforward, unmistakable?"

"They would not be for what I want to say. I've funked it. Why
the assurance of being me should be affected by the occupation of a
President's Office which I would not, in any case, have been able
even to find, I can't say. I don't know. Now, being a woman alone
doesn't seem as easy as it has been. I need, for a time anyway, the
sense of being part of a partnership; oh, I mean every petty thing you
may wonder about: all the confidence of having a man. But none of
that seems to me grounds for marriage."

"What a very odd idea of marriage you must have. The only
people who could possibly have lived up to it were Tristan and Isolde,
and all they could do was die. In fact, now I come to think of it, all
great lovers cannot choose but die because marriage is essentially
mundane and quotidian and useful."

" 'A game, like war, that calls for patience, foresight, maneuver,
for those with their wander-years behind them,' Auden once said."

"He has said a good deal, I'll grant him that. Do you know what
I think? I think you would have changed anyway, even if your university had not come falling down like London Bridge. It's simple
enough; all we do is find a pig with a ring on the end of his nose,
and get married."

"Reed, I do want a ring, from a pig or merely from Tiffany's, I
want to be half of a pair, as though the world and every dinner party
were Noah's ark and one could not attend except in pairs, but I don't
want actually, legally to get married. I want you to be legally free."

Reed laughed. "You want a sham, a plain, unadorned sham, because you won't allow yourself to be someone's wife, like any other
proper woman. You can't share my apartment unless you marry me,
so there!"

"It seems to me shameful to turn to you now and say let's get
married because I now need a security I didn't in the least mind
scorning before. What I meant about all the luscious young women
is simply a recognition of the fact that it is easier for men to marry."

"I am not 'men,' and I doubt that I should find it easy at all to
marry. Shall I tell you what worries you? No, don't stop me. I've
never known you to balk at the truth, and you shan't now. From
some new-found weakness, like one recovering from an illness, you
are seeking to belong—to me, as it so fortunately happens. Not only
does it seem unfair to you to capitulate in weakness to what you

refused in strength, but you know that the love you have for me is not of the same timbre, not even of the same scale, as the love I have for you. Don't protest. I know it makes little sense. I agree it makes little sense. I a handsome, talented, affable man in the prime of life, you an aging, argumentative, irrational spinster. But sense or not, I love you, and if we marry it shall be properly, with a ring and a judge and a license so that if you decide to leave me or I you I shall at least not be cheating some lawyer out of the chance to arrange a divorce. Do your brothers have to come to the wedding? I'm glad to hear they don't, because frankly the thought of your brothers terrifies me. Kate, let's get married on Thanksgiving. That way, we don't have to remember the date even, we can just celebrate on the last Thursday in every November—which will be a holiday, so much more convenient if you stop to think about it. Aren't you going to say something?''

"I was thinking," Kate said, "that I never really asked the daisies, and they never told me, but this fall, all the asters knew.''

"I am willing enough to put up with Auden," Reed said with lapidary phrasing, "I am even willing to quote a bit of Auden now and then on my own, but I want to make *quite* clear that I will not put up with the poetry of Sara Teasdale.''

4

*the funniest
mortals and the kindest are those who are most aware
of the baffle of being, don't kid themselves our care
is consolable, but believe a laugh is less
heartless than tears.*

KATE had been astonished at Frederick Clemance's invitation to lunch. She felt as nervous, she told Reed, as a teenager on a first date. I mean, she tried to explain, I have worshipped him, or close to it, and what can we possibly find to say now, over an atrocious vegetable omelette at the Faculty Club. I know, Kate said, I am terrified, in Auden's words, of discovering that a god worth kneeling-to for a while has tabernacled and rested.

Yet her first thought, when she and Clemance were seated, was how old he looked. The spring occurrences had aged him. He had allowed his white hair to grow long, which became him, since he now resembled not so much Emerson as Kate's idea of Emerson. Yet it was not his white hair nor lined face nor sixty years which most distressed Kate, sitting opposite him, as his indefinable air of regret, perhaps even of despair.

"So it took a revolution for us to lunch together," he said. "That is too bad. Well, perhaps it is all destiny—I think, you know, the Greeks were right: family curses are easier to live with than personal failure."

"Oh, I'm not so sure," Kate said. "It must be aggravating to find yourself in trouble 'because of a great-great-grand-mother who got laid by a sacred beast.' "

Clemance smiled. "How *was* the Auden dissertation?" he asked. "I quite forgot, with all these goings-on. You were good to help me out."

Kate decided that the details of that particular event were perhaps best glossed over. "It was an excellent dissertation—it managed to appreciate Auden's poetry without patronizing him or his life. Mr. Cornford was blessed with the understanding that while a new poem of Auden's is an event in all *our* biographies, we have no business meddling with his."

"Wouldn't you like to meet him, all the same?"

"No," Kate said. "Not for a moment. Oh, I do rather hope one day to hear him read his poems, or catch him again on the telly. But meet him: no. I should be afraid of boring him to death; or worse, going on, like the juggins he mentions in the poem to MacNeice, who went on about Alienation. If I met him I would be certain to be so nervous I would go on about *something*. Besides, Auden's just a man: as full of demons and petty irritations and unkindnesses as the rest of us—he's bound to be. What I cherish are the poems, and the persona, the literary biography of him I've accumulated over the years."

"Your instincts are probably right. As Auden says in one of his small humorous poems: 'I have no gun, but I can spit.' What are the main events you've accumulated in the biography of Auden's persona?"

Kate looked at Clemance. She admired enormously his attempts at lightness. Kate found herself thinking of Auden's poem to T. S. Eliot:

> *It was you who, not speechless from shock but finding the right*
> *language for thirst and fear, did much*
> *to prevent a panic.*

"Well," she said, "what I have is a series of snapshots, really, caught by Auden's friends. Isherwood describing Auden's hats: the opera hat, 'belonging to the period when he decided that poets ought to dress like bank directors, in morning cutaways and striped trousers or evening swallowtails. There was a workman's cap, with a shiny black peak, which he bought while he was living in Berlin, and which had, in the end, to be burnt, because he was sick into it one evening in a cinema.' There was a Panama with a black ribbon, representing Auden's 'conception of himself as a lunatic clergyman; always a favorite role.' Isherwood is really the richest source of Auden lore.

My favorite of all is Auden in China in 1938 listening with Isherwood to the translation of a poem written in their honor in Chinese. Not to be outdone, Auden replied with a sonnet he had finished writing the day before. Auden had a visiting card in China with his name on it: *Mr. Au Dung.*" Kate chuckled. "There's much more, but, of course, you know him, so it seems . . ."

"Do, please, go on," Clemance said.

"Some of Auden's anecdotes are unprintable, though of course I've seen them in print. I especially appreciate the critic who said of Auden that he is able to write prolifically, carelessly, and exquisitely without seeming to have to pay any price for his inspiration. He is the only poet I know of whom that is true—good poet, that is."

"I thought you didn't read critics on Auden."

"I don't; coming on that was just a bit of serendipity."

"Do you know Auden's explanation for today's educational difficulties?"

"I can't imagine. Not enough statues to defunct chefs?"

"You're close: not enough luncheon parties given by undergraduates in their rooms—of the sort Auden had at Oxford."

"Oh, yes," Kate said:

> *"Ah! those Twenties before I was twenty*
> *When the news never gave one the glooms,*
> *When the chef had minions in plenty,*
> *And we could have lunch in our rooms.*

Never having had lunch in my room, I wouldn't know. But Auden and I do have one oddity in common: we both grew so accustomed, as children, to being the youngest person present that even today we are likely to feel the youngest person in the room even if, as frequently happens, we are the oldest."

"Speaking of news giving one the glooms, as I suppose we must sooner or later," Clemance said, "I gather that you are supporting this University College, which I'm afraid I have always thought of as an extension school. I'm told that, unlike my colleagues Professors Cudlipp and O'Toole, you actually think the University College has greater value than the undergraduate college which I attended and where I teach. Cudlipp and O'Toole are both convinced that an undergraduate college for, as they put it, dropouts will undermine the value of any other undergraduate degree given in this University. I take it you don't agree with that?''

"No," Kate said, "I don't. Why should you have thought I would?"

Clemance laughed. "A good question," he said. "Why indeed? Kate Fansler, if I were to ask you, very rapidly, what you remember first of all, right off, about your childhood, what would you answer? You know, answer as in those association games we always used to hear so much about.''

"Rose petals," Kate said.

Clemance looked surprised.

"Yes, odd as it may seem, and not for the world would I admit it to my revolutionary students, but I remember rose petals in the bottom of finger bowls, even at Nantucket where we spent the summers. When I was a child growing up, there was a depression and then a war; yet it might have been the Edwardian era, when, as everyone knows, the sun always shone. We had a cook in the house in New York and in Nantucket, a laundress who sat for hours at a mangle, maids running up and down the stairs, and finger bowls at dinner with rose petals in the bottom. My brothers were away at school, and then at war; I had a governess. Does all that matter?''

"It's very Proustian."

"So I've begun to think. Although the Duchess of Guermantes would always have been strange to me, I could have known Aunt Leonie and the two country walks, and the hawthorn blossoms. Does this have some connection with University College that I don't understand?''

Clemance sat forward in his chair and pursed his lips in thought, evolving one of his deliberate sentences which would emerge only slowly. "I went to a public high school for bright boys," he said, "and when I came to the College it was only because I got a partial scholarship and could live at home, and because my parents had carefully saved money over the years so that I might come here rather than to City College. I know that the City College classes of my time and later produced some of the most brilliant men in our country, but there was something here I cherished which I can only call graciousness, and a kind of excellence which was not alone determined by ambition. I find I am offended by the manners, by the lack of culture in the deepest sense of the word, prevalent today. I think in order to give everyone an opportunity, we are sacrificing our gifted people.'' Clemance made an impatient gesture with his hand. "I'm

rambling," he said. "I can't think why I should have imagined you
would know what I'm talking about."

"The instinct was quite correct," Kate said. "I can't bear bad
manners and being called by my first name by strangers, yet I also
realize that superficial good manners may cover the most appalling
nastiness and hostility. My brothers have excellent manners, but they
are basically the rudest men I have ever met. You see, I'm rambling
too. My rudest graduate student went through Princeton on a complete scholarship, and as far as I can see he communicates either in
dialectics or exponibles, part of a mechanized generation to whom
haphazard oracular grunts are profound wisdom. Do you suppose the
University College students to be ruder than those in your own college? That isn't my impression."

"Perhaps I don't mean to talk about manners. Perhaps I mean to
talk about excellence."

"There I am with you. But Professor Clemance, academic excellence is not that easily measurable. More and more students are
getting perfect scores on college entrance tests—my graduate student
with the oracular grunts scored very high indeed—but excellence is
otherwise measurable, provided one maintains a minimum admissions
score. The graduates of University College go on to graduate school
in large numbers, astonishingly large numbers if one remembers the
average age of the students. I know that some of those older students,
especially the older women students, bore the boys in your college
if they turn up in the same classes but, to be frank, the boys in your
college bore me. I have never found youthful male arrogance, even
when combined with great talent, especially appealing, while you, of
course, have. In that, I suspect, we don't agree at all."

"You are accusing me simply of prejudice."

"Oh, yes, quite simply. And as to manners, your college boys
have fewer of those. They were the original, urinating-on-the-
President's-rug revolutionaries who called policemen pigs and the
administration a double-barreled epithet I will not embarrass either
of us by repeating. What I find difficult to understand is what it is
you fear so about the University College—all of you, I mean. Those
who are not satisfied to hurl from prep school through college and
graduate school into the family law firm or whatever seem to me
intelligent; it is surely the better part of wisdom to take time to think,
and a country like ours should have a college for those who have
gained wisdom and decided on a later, different college, or on a
chance for a second life."

"Miss Fansler, could your University College have produced Auden?"

"No. And neither could your college, Professor Clemance." (Kate, as an inheritance from days when children were "brought up," found she could not bring herself to call Clemance "Frederick," a difficulty which Reed, who had never had a governess, thought preposterous.) "Oxford didn't produce Auden, even if it did allow him luncheon parties; neither did his doctor father, from whose books Auden used to learn the facts of life he diagrammed on the schoolroom blackboards, nor his mother, whom he loved and resembled. What produces an Auden? Having a friend like Isherwood when you are young?"

"Wouldn't you like it if Auden were to dedicate one of his poems to you?"

"I've given up daydreaming. No, I should always be so hideously frightened, with Auden, of being a bore or a hideola. Imagine afterward; one would have to drown oneself to avoid the memories."

"He's not as forbidding as all that; he's a superb teacher, you know."

"All I know about his teaching is another peculiarity we have in common: we are the only two teachers of literature who have ever admitted in class that we have never read *Don Quixote* through to the end."

"It is a good thing I didn't know that before I voted for your tenure."

"Professor Clemance, I have often wished for the opportunity to tell you that you taught me more—about literature, something I can only call morality, and about the honor of the profession of letters— than anyone else in the University. But you seemed to wish only for young male followers, and I did not wish to burden you with an older female disciple. Surely you must know, however, that no teacher knows where his influence reaches."

"I remember that you did a paper on *Portrait of a Lady*. I have never especially cared for women students. I think perhaps I was wrong in that. Perhaps there are Isabel Archers at University College."

Kate looked at him for a time. "Perhaps there are," she said. "I hope there isn't anything terribly wrong—with you, I mean?"

"But there is," he said. "My heart is broken. I have a pain in it." Kate remembered how he was always able to say dramatic things simply, as though emotion did not frighten him. "This student revolution hasn't broken your heart, hasn't affected your love for the University?''

"No," Kate said. "Much as I loved the rose petals in the finger bowls, I know my brothers too well. I have never cared for playboys or reactionaries, and they were produced by the same process that produced the finger bowls. I love talent, but do not care for privilege which takes itself for granted. To put it another way, I do not care for a society which has a place for Oblonsky, but none for Anna and Vronsky.''

"What about Levin?"

"Levin without his estate and serfs would have been Anna. We are all Anna now."

Clemance sat silent for a time. "There is a Departmental meeting on Monday," he finally said. "No doubt the whole matter," he waved his hand in a familiar gesture, "will come up."

"No doubt."

"Jeremiah Cudlipp and Robert O'Toole feel very strongly about it; very strongly."

"So I have heard," she said. "Professor Clemance, let me tell you some non-University news: I'm to be married."

"Are you indeed? I am glad. It is good 'to be reborn, reneighbored in the Country of Consideration.' ''

"The Country of Consideration: what a lovely definition of marriage."

"Yes," Clemance said. "If one considers it in the middle years, the best definition I know."

When Kate had parted from Clemance outside the Faculty Club, she walked for a time around the campus; the autumn was her favorite season, she was to have dinner with Reed, she was happy. The campus looked peaceful, benign, perhaps falsely so, but "when was peace or its concomitant smile the worse for being undeserved?" Perhaps, she thought, Reed will be ready early.

She was surprised, though only mildly so, to find McQuire waiting for her at the bus stop.

"More propositions?" Kate asked.

"I am Frogmore's pander. I promised him I would try to bring you over to the Club for a conversation. We've heard the English Senior Faculty Committee meeting is Monday, and we'd like a word in your ear before then."

"I have only just been at the Club," Kate said; "inferior lunch,

superior quotations. I never even expected to be here Saturday when
I took up this line of work."

"Come back to the Club with me now. I faithfully promise this
will be the last time I abduct you."

"By the way," Kate said, as they walked toward the Faculty
Club, "what's your great interest in the University College? Surely
there aren't enough beautiful young things to be worth all this
bother."

"Well—the University College these days is an extraordinarily
vital place, while the College, let's face it, is catering first to a lot of
boys fed up with work in prep schools whose only ambition for their
college years is to get confronted and laid, preferably on alternate
days, and second to the college alumni who want Alma Mater to go
on unchanged, supporting the same prejudices and enthusiasms they
remember, or think they do, from their undergraduate days. As an
economist, I'm interested in the economically viable, and in the long
run I think that's an adult undergraduate school. Certainly in New
York City. I mean, it may be lovely to go and gambol by the Charles,
but the river in this city is not a river but an estuary of the ocean,
and it follows the tides of the ocean. I think we should stop trying
to be Harvard or Yale and find our own pattern. I ought to add that
St. Jude is my favorite saint: he of the lost causes—or has the Church
demoted him along with the others?"

"All causes are lost causes, as e. e. cummings used to say; otherwise, they're effects."

Frogmore greeted Kate with all the exuberance of a hostess who
had not really expected the guest of honor to appear. "Nevermind
how goody-good he comes on," McQuire had said. "It's no doubt
due to an oppressive upbringing. I've actually heard him use four-
letter words, when driven. I don't know why University College
should be a personal matter to him, but I think he would do almost
anything for the sheer joy of seeing Cudlipp's face when the Board
of Governors announce that they have voted to let University College
continue." Today Frogmore ("Call me Vivian," he said to Kate, who
was astonished; it seemed to her that any man named Vivian would
stick to last names as a mere matter of survival) did not come on
goody-good very long. "You'll never guess what that son-of-a—I
beg your pardon, Kate—has done," he said. "Managed to get one
of his pals in as Dean of the College."

"From the English Department? Do I know him? Or is his name unmentionable?"

"His name's O'Toole," Frogmore said. "Robert J. O'Toole. Ring a bell?"

"I don't believe it," Kate said. "Why should Robert O'Toole take a job like that? He's already a full professor and a leader of what I believe is known as the New York intellectual community, with influence even in certain parts of Connecticut and New Jersey. Why should he take . . . ?"

"Cudlipp has managed it. Of course, O'Toole's acceptable to the faculty because he's a name, and has a lot of university and extra-university weight to throw around. The only members of the College faculty who might have objected are those who can't stand O'Toole's guts, or those who don't think he's quite as good as he thinks he is . . ."

"Which is impossible on the face of it, from all I hear," McQuire interjected.

"And these, of course, were quietly persuaded by Cudlipp that it takes a . . ."

"Conceited, arrogant, insensitive bastard to win this fight," McQuire happily concluded. "Forgive me finishing all your sentences, Frogmore, but they all have such provocative beginnings."

"Which explains, I guess," Kate said, "why you want someone in the English Department on your side at the meeting Monday. Let's think about the English Department a moment, may we, if you can bear it?"

"That, Kate, is what I hoped you would say," Frogmore said, leaning toward her. "McQuire here can probably handle the Economics Department, but they will only give a certain amount of trouble—economists today, except for Bill, aren't really interested in undergraduate education—but if we can't do a little something in your department, Kate, we might as well turn in our badges. What will you drink?"

"Beer," Kate said. "It will remind me of how pleasant the park was this morning. O.K. We have Cartier committed to the University College, and also, if I may put order before modesty, you have me. Opposed to the University College you have Cudlipp, Clemance, O'Toole. But O'Toole as Dean will be off the College faculty. It's scarcely worth the price to us since he will be leading the fight in the main arena, but the odds on our side are small enough so that every advantage counts. From the rest of the Department we have the chairman, Michaels, who is, I would say, so fed up with Cudlipp and Clemance going over his head to the Acting President that he would probably welcome, in a properly decorous way, any plan which gave him some weight against those two. Everglade, the Secretary of the Department, is absolutely the sweetest guy in the world, but I don't really know what corner he'll be in. Probably ours. We have then Professor Peter Packer Pollinger, who is perfectly capable of voting on either side when it comes right down to it, depending on what he imagines Fiona Macleod would have done under similar circumstances, but as a matter of fact he dislikes Clemance so much for once having said that Fiona Macleod was a silly poetess whose rhymes were not improved by the fact that she was really a man that Professor Pollinger may vote with us if he remembers what it was Clemance said on the day he happens to vote.''

"Kate, dear,'' McQuire interrupted, ''I do hope you know what you're talking about. Frogmore and I aren't going to ask you to explain why a lady poet should be a man, but you might just assure us that you aren't, shall we say, rambling?''

"I assure you. The one who rambles is Peter Packer Pollinger. All right, then we have Chaucer, Medieval English, Comparative Medieval, Renaissance, Seventeenth Century, Eighteenth Century, Shakespeare. I don't know where any of them stands (I mention the fields rather than the names for the moment to give you the scope of the problem) but the older the field, the more conservative the views, as a general rule. The only trouble with that is that I'm not certain what they'll consider the conservative position in this case. Of the two people in the contemporary field, one is Plimsole, who is a College man and lost, I fear, to us, but he is so unbelievably longwinded that I can't believe even the College will consider him altogether an asset, though he's not a bad fellow if he could learn to stop talking when he gets to the end of what he wants to say. The other contemporary person is Emilia Airhart.''

"You must be putting us on. I never heard of her, I mean not as a member of the English Department. You aren't suggesting she made it out of the Oriental waters only to pop up here in a new life.''

"I hadn't realized, really, what an odd lot we were. Emilia's little known because she never turns up anywhere except to see students, whom she likes, and to write plays, which keep getting put on off-Broadway, but they are so very with it that no one in the whole Department realized for years that Emilia was writing them. She never has anything to do with anything in the Department, never goes to parties or gives them; she *might* come down on our side on this issue—it's not unlikely.''

"What does she look like?'' Frogmore said. "I thought I knew all the tenured English faculty.''

"What she looks like is the whole point, as you'd realize the moment you clapped eyes on her. She's a large woman with flat shoes, wide skirts, and glasses, who gives you the impression that she could actually be a *jolie laide* if someone with the combined talents of Sophie Gimbel and Yves St. Laurent would only take her in hand. She's got five children and a husband, and that's almost all I know about her, although I know her better than most people, since we're the only two women with tenure in the Department and we inevitably find ourselves together in the ladies' room from time to time. Her specialty's drama, and the only other thing I know about her is that when I once asked her what she thought of Clemance, she said that apart from the fact that he was pompous, a company man and a male chauvinist, she had nothing against him, which I suppose, is another good sign for us. All the rest of the Department don't have votes on the Senior Faculty Committee, being non-tenure, and need not concern us, though of course they wield more influence than is often realized. I hope I have made it quite clear that this is going to be an uphill fight.''

"You don't know how uphill,'' McQuire said. "It's on the question of promotions that I've had my troubles with the Economics Department. The point is, we want you to see that a couple of assistant professors who've been teaching at the University College get promoted.''

"You don't want much, do you?'' Kate asked.

"The thing about Frogmore,'' McQuire said, "is that easy fights bore him.''

"Listen, Kate,'' Frogmore said, "I don't want to be Dean of University College if it gets a new image, a new lease on life, and a new destiny. I want to be president of a girls' college somewhere very rural and genteel. But I want to see University College the model of the elite adult education for the whole United States, and I want it so badly that I'm going to get it.''

"What odd reasoning,'' Kate said.

"No, it's not,'' Frogmore said. "When you find a man who wants something very badly, and doesn't want it for himself, watch out.''

Kate stared at Frogmore awhile. "Do you know, Vivian," she said, "like the man, meaning McQuire here, said, you got guts."

"What happens at that Senior Faculty Committee meeting on Monday is going to show us a lot," Frogmore said.

"I can hardly wait," Kate laughed.

Then she hurried home to Reed.

5

There will be no peace.
Fight back, then, with such courage as you have
And every unchivalrous dodge you know of,
*   Clear in your conscience on this:*
Their cause, if they had one, is nothing to them now;
*   They hate for hate's sake.*

MONDAY, Kate reached Baldwin at two, in time for her office hour. The Senior Faculty Committee meeting was scheduled for four that afternoon, and Kate hoped, without too much conviction, to pick up a few tips before the meeting on the way the wind was blowing. So political a thought had not previously occurred to her and marked, no doubt, her initiation into the world of history. Clio, she thought, stand me now and ever in good stead.

"We have found no one for Swahili," a voice said. "How is Bulwer-Lytton doing? Look, the elevator is actually coming," Mark Everglade added. "There must be something wrong with it."

"I do think," Kate said as they got in, pressed '8' and watched the doors close, "that such consistent pessimism is surely the triumph of experience over hope, not to mention reason. Even this University's elevators must work occasionally. The law of averages..." Kate's voice faded away as, between the third and fourth floors, the elevator came to a reluctant, but by no means uncertain, stop.

"There is a law of averages," Everglade said. "There is also a law of falling bodies. We are about to prove Galileo's theory that two bodies of different weights will, if dropped from a sufficient

height, reach the ground at the same time and in the same state of
dejectedness. You ring the alarm bell; I will telephone.''

Kate pressed the alarm bell in much the same spirit with which
one accepts herbal tea from an ancient aunt: it probably won't help,
but it can't hurt. Mark, meanwhile, addressed himself to a little cupboard which housed the University's most recent attempt to grapple
with the problem of its elevators: a telephone. ''What do you dial for
emergencies?'' Mark asked Kate.

''I don't know. It says in the front of the campus directory, but
I'm afraid I never noticed.''

''Who, alas, has? We shall have to dial the operator, and we all
know where that leads.''

''Do you think there is sufficient oxygen?''

''For what? Compared to the air I've been breathing in most
meetings lately, there is probably here a smaller proportion of carbon
monoxide and irritating tars than most otherwheres.''

''May I help you?'' a voice said over the telephone.

''You certainly may,'' Mark happily replied. ''We are stuck in
an elevator and . . .''

''If you are on campus,'' the voice continued, ''you may dial
directly the number you want. Is this an outside call?''

''I can't even get outside this elevator,'' Mark said. ''Help, help,
help,'' he mildly added.

''I will connect you with maintenance,'' the voice said. ''If you
are on campus, will you dial one-two, one-four? Are you on campus?''

''Perhaps it's a recording,'' Kate said.

Mark pressed down the telephone button until he heard a dial
tone, then dialed 1214. There was a busy signal.

''Try calling the English Office,'' Kate said.

''A brilliant suggestion which I am hideously certain will not
work. Ah, well.'' Mark dialed the English Office.

''English,'' the secretary's voice brightly said, ''will you hold on
a minute?'' There was a click as the secretary pushed the 'hold'
button. Mark slammed the receiver down as violently as the small
cupboard allowed. Kate put her purse and case down on the floor.

''I am reminded,'' she said, ''of a story my father used to tell,
repeatedly, in order to drive home a moral whose application has,
until this moment, escaped me. He was a friend of the president of
some railroad, the New York Central or something, and one day my
father asked his secretary to find out when the next train left for

Tuxedo, where he was planning to meet someone. The secretary returned to tell him that she could not get through to railroad information because the line was continually engaged. 'Nonsense,' my
father called out. 'Get me the president of the whatever railroad.' The
poor secretary couldn't get the president, but she did get his private
secretary, at which point my father grabbed the telephone from her.
'I'm terribly sorry, Mr. Fansler,' the president's private secretary
said, 'but Mr. Whosis is out of town. Is there any way I can help
you?' 'There certainly is,' my father said; 'when is the next train to
Tuxedo?' Well, she managed to find a timetable and tell him; and
the moral of the story is: always go to the president.''

"I trust," Mark said, "that since we are without a President, the
Acting President will do."

"Perfectly," Kate said.

"And do you happen to know his extension?"

"Yes, I do. I was recently glancing through the new directory,
as one does when it first comes out, and I noticed that his number is
1837. Shall we try it?"

"How did you happen to decide to remember his number and
not the emergency number? Your father's advice?"

"Naturally not. I have never given a thought to my father's advice until this moment. Eighteen thirty-seven is the year of Queen
Victoria's ascension."

"Of course. Silly of me." Mark picked up the receiver and dialed
1837.

"President Matthewson's office," a voice cheerfully said. "Good
afternoon."

"Good afternoon," Mark said. "May I please speak to Mr. Matthewson? This is Mark Everglade of the English Department calling."

"I'm terribly sorry, Mr. Everglade, but President Matthewson is
at a meeting. May I take a message?"

"You certainly may," Mark said. "Tell him that Professor Fansler and I, both of the English Department, are stuck in an elevator
in Baldwin Hall and are rapidly running out of oxygen. I might add,
in case it will in any way goad you more rapidly to action, that
Professor Fansler and I are not of the same sex. Good afternoon to
you." Mark hung up the phone. "I give her fifteen minutes," Mark
said, "to check on us and the elevator. Shall we go over the catalogue, since the opportunity presents itself?"

"Mark, what do you think of Cudlipp?"

"He does his job, which is to represent the College. I do mine, which is to represent the Graduate School. Michaels, as chairman of the whole Department, complains about Cudlipp from time to time, but after all, everybody's got to do his thing, doesn't he?"

"I often ask myself," Kate said, "—does he? Do you know anything about University College?"

"Sure," Mark surprisingly said. "I've been letting its students into my classes lately; they're good."

"Funny, you never mentioned it," Kate said.

"To tell you the truth, I'm not certain it's kosher, so it seemed a case of least said soonest mended."

"Do you think Cudlipp would object if he knew?"

"No doubt. But he can't very well do anything about it, since the Graduate School doesn't give credit, and what credit the University College gives is its decision. He makes damn sure no University College students take any College courses, or vice versa, and that's exactly as far as he can go."

"Why is he so against the University College? I know all about the question of resources, but his passion has deeper roots than the University's operating deficit."

"Mainly, I guess, he thinks the University College degree threatens the value of *The* College degree. He wants undergraduate education at the University to be absolutely elite, and all those adults returning with their tired brains to school threaten him."

"Do I," Kate asked, "hear the calls of rescuers?"

"Professor Everglade," a voice called. "Switch the Emergency button to *off*, and push open the door."

Mark looked at Kate and shrugged. "Well," he said, "here goes. Are you prepared to dive down the shaft?" He switched the button and pushed at the inner door which, rather to his astonishment, opened. Below them, the door on the third floor had been pushed back. "Have you a lady in there?" the voice called. "Professor Fansler is with me," Mark said, winking at Kate, "if that answers your question. The point, I gather," he said to Kate, "is to drop down into their arms on the third floor but *not* into the elevator shaft. Chivalry demands that you go first, so that I may hand you down into their waiting arms. And we never even looked at the damn catalogue."

It was typical of Kate's post-revolutionary attitudes that being caught in an elevator, which might, at one time, have been an adventure, was now not even material for an anecdote. She rushed up the stairs from the third floor to her office on the eighth, apologized for her lateness, and plunged into interviews with four students from University College who hoped to register for her course in Victorian literature. She recognized John Peabody from the luncheon arranged by Bill McQuire. He introduced the others: Barbara Campbell, Greta Gabriel, and Randolph Selkirk. "No doubt," Mr. Peabody said, "you want to know something about us, how we come to be at University College, why we want to take your course, stuff like that. It's probably simplest if we just start in and tell you about ourselves." To Kate, who had been uncertain what inquiries she might decently make, given, particularly, her profound disinclination to ask personal questions, this blunt prelude was a distinct relief.

"We," Mr. Peabody began, "have all returned to college after what is known as a voluntary interruption in our education—though the word voluntary has to be pretty broadly defined. Anyway, we weren't bounced out of college, we bounced ourselves. And when, in the fullness of time, we decided to return to college, the last thing we wanted was dormitory life, rah-rah games, anybody being *in loco parentis* or the company of eighteen-year-olds. To us, therefore, University College seemed a kind of miracle. There aren't many adult schools in the whole country, not many even in New York—schools which give degrees, and aren't just places to take courses and wile away the time. University College had no athletic requirements, no organized social life, and some of us were a bit shaky at math at the time of our entrance examination. But we are all in college because we have decided to be; we are, as the saying goes, highly motivated; and most of us are even pretty bright. I might add, though Barbara can tell you more about this, that the women students are looking for a bachelor's degree, not for a bachelor."

Barbara Campbell was stunning, beautifully dressed, and appeared to be in her early twenties. "I'm fairly typical, I guess," she said with a smile which acknowledged that she certainly didn't look typical. "I went to an excellent prep school where I was mainly interested in what our antedeluvian headmistress used to call 'the lads,' and then to Bennington, where I spent three years—almost; I quit in the middle of my third year. I discovered at Bennington that I enjoyed thinking, and that if you work there are plenty of people who will encourage you. I worked like a demon for five days, when, since we were all girls, it wasn't necessary to wash your hands or feet or even face if you didn't feel like it, and every weekend I spent away from the campus with a man.

"Partly, I began to realize that I had been in an intellectual and emotional cocoon for years, and partly I just wanted to *bouleverse les parents*—at which I succeeded beyond my wildest expectations. They objected to the fact that I was living with a guy, they even objected to the guy, which at least made some sense, and they said if I didn't give him up they would stop paying for college or anything else. I didn't and they did. After a time I got tired of the guy, and of working in the glamour trades, and I began to want to study again. I saved enough money and here I am. My parents have since come round, but I don't take any money from them, though I have been known to accept an occasional lavish present. If I took their money they would assume, however tacitly, that I had accepted their values, and I haven't. I want to take your course because I've heard you're great, and tough, and it recently occurred to me how like a harem Bennington was. I don't mean just that all the faculty was sleeping with the students, I mean that all the faculty was male, and that the whole spirit behind the place was of girls sitting at the feet of men. I find the idea of a woman teacher invigorating. End of my speech— I'm to introduce Greta."

Greta Gabriel was in her middle forties, Kate guessed. Her story resembled Polly Spence's, though she had not yet reached the grand-mother phase and was not from the upper reaches of New York society. She was a suburban housewife who had decided that her life of being maid, chauffeur, and emotional wastebasket was insuffi-ciently inspiring. Everything about her new academic life was diffi-cult, from the commuting to the pressures of her life's multitudinous demands, but she felt alive for the first time in years, and indicated her gratitude for the uniqueness of University College, which allowed her really to work, not to dabble, and agreed to reward her work with a degree.

Randolph Selkirk was more unexpected. "I was at Yale," he said, "getting A's in everything and working all day six days a week to do it. I had a girl and one day she broke off with me, saying I wasn't human enough for her. It took me several weeks to calm down and discover it was quite true—I wasn't human enough for anyone. I stopped working so hard, and finally took a leave from Yale and went to work teaching in a slum school; then I married the girl, who had begun to find me more human. We had a baby, which seemed to us a proper affirmation of life, and after a time I wanted to return to school, and this was the only place that wasn't an undergraduate society for boys or a series of money-making courses for bored adults. My wife is working to help me finish, and I can't begin to understand why they should want to get rid of this place—University College, I mean. Still, I've observed that the boys from the College are radical enough when it comes to occupying buildings, but not when it comes to supporting an institution which might challenge the status of their own degrees. I've noticed nobody minds being revolutionary when he doesn't think he has anything to lose. Forgive the cynicism. If you want to know why I'd like to take this course, it's because I'm particularly interested in the ideas of the Victorian period.''

Kate leaned back in her chair and regarded the four of them. It seemed to her, oddly, that life had walked into her academic world, impressing her as not even the police or occupying students had done. She understood why McQuire found impressive the fact that University College students had been the only ones to feel loyalty to their school. Of course, she had sensed it from the beginning—which was why she had let McQuire drag her to that lunch and entice her into conversations with Frogmore. " 'Your presence exactly,' " Kate thought, looking at them, " 'so once, so valuable, so very now.' "

"You are welcome to the course," she simply said.

What with further student conferences, a delegation from the student-faculty committee on curriculum, a good many frantic telephone calls, and similar distractions, Kate was not able even to ascertain if there was a wind, let alone the direction in which it was blowing. At four o'clock, the hour of the Senior Faculty Committee meeting, she left her office and stopped off in the faculty ladies' room where she found Emilia Airhart looking at herself dubiously in a mirror. She turned, apparently with relief, to contemplate Kate. "How lucky you are!" she surprisingly said.

"I?" Kate asked. "I'm feeling lucky at the moment, for personal reasons. Does it show?"

Emilia Airhart laughed. "Probably," she said, "but I don't know you well enough to tell. Congratulations, whatever it is. The luck to which I referred had to do with your willowyness—I have always longed to be willowy; if only one could design oneself, instead of turning out to be some dreadful preordained shape. I would, like you, be tall and slim, with my hair gathered at the nape of my neck, attractive without being charming. You mustn't be insulted by the last item, which is, from me, a compliment. I dislike charm, having accepted Camus' definition of it: the ability to get the answer *yes* without having asked a question. I prefer people who have to form questions. Still, it is agonizing to have the soul of Greta Garbo in the body of Queen Victoria. Ergo, lucky you."

Kate laughed. "You don't look a bit like Queen Victoria," she said.

"Of course I do, if you could picture Queen Victoria in panty hose with flat shoes and her skirts above her knees. I take it you are going to the Senior Faculty Committee meeting?"

"Yes," Kate said. "And for once in my life I don't wish I could think of an excuse not to. I go with a purpose: I've decided to do what I can for the University College. Do you know anything about it?"

"Haven't a clue; ought I to have?"

"Probably," Kate said. "But there isn't time to go into it now. The College is trying to kill it off, which is rather too bad, I think."

"Nasty old Cudlipp, I suppose. Terrible man. If only he were more like Pnin."

"Who?"

"You know, Pnin, the man in Nabokov's novel. Cudlipp looks just like him, but, alas, couldn't be more different. I hardly like to say that if Cudlipp and Clemance are for something, I'm against it—it sounds so unscholarly and prejudiced, which it is—but at least I'm leaning in your direction, if that's any comfort."

"It's some," Kate said. "By the way, as to my being lucky, I'm getting married. I haven't told anyone in the Department yet, but I'll have to soon. Perhaps it's being unmarried that's kept me thin."

"Congratulations, or whatever the proper phrase is, though in a way I'm sorry." Kate raised an interrogative eyebrow. "Don't misunderstand me, but you're the only woman I've ever known who seemed unmarried as a wonderful choice, the combined influence of Artemis, Aphrodite, and Athene all in one. Please don't be offended."

"On the contrary," Kate said. "I'm honored." Emilia gave a pleased grin and preceded Kate out the door. But Kate stopped a moment in the hall. "You know," she said, "Forster sags in one of his novels that the abandonment of personality can be a prelude to love; for most women I think it certainly is. You've made me see that, for me, it hasn't been."

"Do you like Forster?" Emilia Airhart asked. "I see you do;

he's too effete for me. But he did say once that life is a performance on a violin which one has to learn to play as he goes along. A remarkable description of our times."

"Gentle, perhaps," Kate said, "not effete."

The Senior Faculty Committee of the English Department, which comprised all tenured members of the Department, used, in pre-revolutionary days, to meet several times a semester for the purpose of discussing promotions and additions to the faculty. While these meetings were grim enough, in all conscience, a certain degree of cordiality prevailed, so that, as Kate used to say, though it might be clear that one professor thought another a tiresome, pontificating, and deluded bore, he did not openly indicate this opinion. Since last spring, however, fatigue and the plethora of meetings which the process of restructuring inevitably entailed had taken their hostages, which were, as always, good will, courtesy, and graciousness. The professors were exhausted, and exhausted people are easily made first angry and then rude.

To make matters worse, exhaustion bred not only bad temper but long-windedness. The inability of certain men, once they got to their feet, to finish a statement and sit down, amounted, in Kate's view, to a disease as incurable as satyriasis and far more socially dangerous. She knew, as she seated herself in the room, that scarcely would Michaels, the chairman, have rustled his papers and made the few desperate grunts, punctuated by giggles, which constituted his reaction to exhaustion, than Plimsole would be on his feet and away. In fact, he was.

Plimsole was concerned, as he had been for months, as to whether teaching assistants should be considered primarily as students, which they were, or as teachers, which they were also. The question was certainly of importance and was one, moreover, on which the radical faculty felt a consuming passion the conservative faculty was not prepared to match. This, perhaps more than anything else, annoyed Professor Plimsole. Kate could well infer from the looks on the faces of those about her that had the senior faculty had an opportunity to hear Mr. Plimsole before his promotion, that event might well have never taken place. It was, Kate thought, a mark of the need for this revolution that the faculty of departments like this never met, and the senior members never really heard the junior members at all. But, since last spring, all the meetings except those of the Senior Faculty Committees had been open to junior faculty

and the long-winded Mr. Plimsoles might in the future be more suc-
cessfully nipped in the bud.

"I really do feel," Mr. Plimsole began, "that this body must
come to a decision about the professional autonomy of teaching assistants. It is not that I anticipate another series of events like those
which rocked this institution last spring; indeed, I would hate my
colleagues to think I spoke in anticipation or even expectation of any
such event, but I also do feel that we cannot allow our teaching
assistants to remain in doubt as to their actual professional standing,
and they are professionals, we must face that, for certainly the teaching assistants come into direct contact with students, both in actual
teaching duties and in the correction of papers, and it is surely insufferable and insulting that they should be loaded with the responsibilities of teaching and then be treated as students if they are found,
for example, occupying a building, though as I have indicated I do
not bring this subject up because I think buildings are likely to be
occupied in the near future. But once we have co-opted them into
our profession they must be treated professionally and not summarily
dismissed as teachers because as students they have acted against
what they consider inequitable policies on the part of the administration, whether or not those of us here consider the policies of the
recent administration to have been inequitable or not . . ."

"His hat!" Emilia Airhart, who had risen, shouted. "His hat!"
For a moment there was stunned silence as everyone tried to absorb
the evident fact that Professor Airhart had flipped; Mr. Plimsole was
certainly not wearing a hat, discourtesy having failed, as yet, to extend that far. Professor Airhart, having delivered her interruption, sat
down again. Mr. Plimsole, as though he were an old mechanical
Victrola, could be seen, metaphorically speaking, to be winding himself up again. But Professor Cartier, whose succinctness no revolution
could undermine, bounced up just in time.

"Mrs. Airhart, whose field is contemporary drama, refers to a
speech by a character called Lucky in *Waiting for Godot:* those of
you interested in the reference may have time to look it up this evening if this meeting is allowed to get on with its agenda. I congratulate Mrs. Airhart on the appositeness of her remarks, and remind
Mr. Plimsole that the question of teaching assistants occupying buildings is properly the business of the Committee on Graduate Studies.
I would like to put before *this* committee the promotion of Professors
Levy and Genero, presently teaching in the University College." He
sat down as abruptly as he had stood up. Kate grinned. She remem-

bered, as no doubt did all her colleagues, Lucky's speech, which, while it made less syntactical sense than Mr. Plimsole's, achieved at least the adumbration of significance.

Cartier's remark, as was inevitable, brought Jeremiah Cudlipp to his feet. "If Mr. Plimsole's contentions are misplaced before this committee, and I agree that they are [glare at Mr. Plimsole which Kate wanted to regret for his sake, but could not], so are those of Mr. Cartier. Assistant professors teaching in the University College cannot be considered for tenure by this committee until it is established that the University College is, in fact, a continuing part of the University. I suggest that it is not a continuing part, and ought not so to be considered by this committee." He sat down. Kate heaved a sigh. The fat was in the fire or, as McQuire would have said, the four-letter-word-bathroom had hit the fan. Michaels, the chairman, giggled, rustled his papers, and drew in his breath to speak. In vain. Clemance had risen to his feet.

"I support Professor Cudlipp," he said, as though that might be news to anyone, "but," and every head in the room came expectantly up, "I think perhaps we ought honestly to confront the problem before us. I have a sense of polarization having divided this committee, and that sense is profoundly disturbing to me. I think we ought to listen to what Professor Cartier has to say, and indeed to what any of us may have to say on this question, even if we cannot today vote to recommend the promotion of people in a school which may not for long exist."

At this precise moment—it was probably not planned that way, but Kate wouldn't put it past them—the door opened and Robert O'Toole entered. The myrmidons were gathering. Kate looked at Clemance. Why, she thought, is your conscience bothering you? Bless you. Robert O'Toole's thoughts, however, were clearly far from wishing to convey a blessing.

"I'm afraid I can't agree with Frederick," O'Toole said, calling Clemance by his first name. "It seems to me inevitable that his greatheartedness should lead him to such a sense of openness, and equally inevitable that we, his more narrow-minded friends, should recall him to the fundamental accuracy of things."

Professor Cartier again rose to his feet. "Mr. O'Toole's ability to answer questions he hasn't heard is certainly worthy of admiration. I should like to repeat my recommendation that we consider for possible promotion Professor Levy. He has done excellent work in the

Victorian field, and if I understand correctly departmental needs at the moment, we could use a man in the Victorian period.''

"I thought Professor Levy's book on Wilkie Collins excellent,'' Michaels said. "Have any of the rest of you read it?''

"I have,'' O'Toole said, extending his arms from his French cuffs and examining his fingernails. "It's a good enough book in its way, modest, unexceptional, competent, but small in its ambition. One can't condemn it nor, I think, is one inclined to praise it extravagantly.'' At this point someone tapped Kate's shoulder and handed her a note; it said, "Whatever that pompous s.o.b. is for, I'm against. EA.'' Kate grinned her appreciation of the sentiments expressed, and stuffed the paper into her purse. Several senior professors now began to argue about Mr. Levy's book and Kate, sensing some moments' respite, rested her eyes on Clemance. Was O'Toole, in a sense, a comment on Frederick Clemance, an inevitable commentary which now, like the notes to "The Waste Land,'' had to be considered along with the original document? O'Toole had been one of Clemance's most brilliant, most loved students, and had returned the affection wholeheartedly, not least by adopting every mannerism of Clemance's for his own. But he could never learn to temper his arrogance as Clemance had learned. Or would he learn in time? When Kate had first known Clemance, after all, when she had first sat in his seminar, Clemance had been almost as near to fifty as O'Toole was now to forty. Could ten years make that much difference? Kate doubted it.

The news of O'Toole's deanship was apparently not yet general. But that O'Toole had himself decided that the success of his tenure depended upon the demise of the University College was beyond question. At this point Professor Peter Packer Pollinger could be heard sputtering through his mustache; slowly the group's attention focused on him. "Why's he against it?'' Professor Pollinger was asking the world in general.

"Are you addressing me, sir?'' Clemance mildly asked.

" 'What is it that is moving so softly to and fro?' I asked,'' Professor Pollinger said.

Clemance regarded Professor Pollinger as though, were sufficient attention paid, some meaning might be discerned; the hope, however, proved illusory. "Is that a quotation,'' he patiently asked, "perhaps from some misty Maeterlinck-like drama?'' This question, which was not intended to be, and was not delivered as though it was, insulting, aroused Professor Peter Packer Pollinger to the highest reaches of indignation.

"Mist be damned," he said. "It is a question of symbolism, whoever you are. Same as the English toward the Irish; pure snobbism. That adult college is a symbol to you, and you and you," he nodded, causing his mustache to quiver as he indicated Clemance, Cudlipp, and O'Toole. "I know the reason. Cudlipp went to University College himself when it was still just a group of extension courses, after they threw him out of the College and before they took him back. I thought Levy's book large and exceptional, and I am inclined to praise it extravagantly. You," he said to O'Toole, "are lost in an obscure wood." He puffed again through his mustache, leaving his on the whole pleased audience to infer that the obscure wood occurred in one of Miss Macleod's misty dramas.

"Surely," Clemance continued, "we are wandering rather from the point. At least," he added, anticipating another outburst, "from my point. Whatever our views may be on the University College, they are not the most germane points to be made at the present time. The Administrative Council has, I believe, undertaken to study the needs of the University as a whole. Doubtless we will all be asked to present our points of view, if any. Meanwhile, it seems to me perhaps irregular to consider promoting to tenure assistant professors whose service is entirely in a school whose future in the University is problematical."

Are you just trying to smooth it all over? Kate thought. She wondered if Peter Packer Pollinger's allegations against Cudlipp could possibly be true. Interesting. Professor Goddard, who taught medieval literature and whose specialty was *Piers Plowman*, rose to his feet.

"I don't follow Professor Clemance's reasoning at all. In the first place, it is our business to promote people on the basis of their ability and possible service to the Department, not on the future of any school in the University. In the second place, I am on the Council to which Professor Clemance refers, and I don't think I'm betraying any confidences by saying that the Council is also studying whether or not The College has a place today in an urban university like this, whose reputation has been made largely through its graduate offerings. I don't mind saying that my own inclination is to consider that a college for adults is more to the point in New York than a college for overgrown schoolboys from whose ranks, I need not remind all of you, came most of the instigators of last spring's disturbances."

Into the awed silence which followed this remark Kate spoke. "I wondered," she said, "how many of us here do, in fact, have students from University College in our classes. The College, as we know, has always avoided cross-listing courses with the Graduate School, but I have only recently learned that University College does, in fact, encourage students to enter many of our courses. How many here do have University College students in their classes?"

"I might add," Michaels said, "that such a show of hands will be unofficial, and its results not recorded in our minutes. Is it all right with you, Professor Fansler, if your question remains unrecorded too?"

"Certainly," Kate said. "I asked it for my own information, and so that I might follow it with another question, also off the record if you like, at least for the present: How good are those students?"

Tentatively at first, and then with more assurance as the number of hands in the air increased, the professors indicated the presence of University College students in their classes. Professor Peter Packer Pollinger was of course one of the first to raise a triumphant hand, whether because he knew it would annoy Clemance, or because he had found a Macleod admirer was not, nor ever likely to be, clear. "And have you found them to be good students, or poor students, or merely satisfactory?"

"I object," Cudlipp shouted, running a hand over his bald head. He had a habit of throwing back his bald head as though he had, in fact, long hair which dangled in his eyes. "The question is irrelevant."

"Nonsense," Professor Goddard shouted, *"Piers Plowman* may, as my students persistently tell me, lack relevancy, but if you are damning a part of this University to extinction, I fail to see how it can be irrelevant to discuss the quality of its students. Perhaps Professor Cudlipp can enlighten me."

"Before Professor Cudlipp enlightens us," Michaels, the chairman, said, "may I be allowed a few words? I don't know if you are aware that I am running this Department, which is twice as big as the Business School, and almost twice as large as the Law School, with no administrative staff whatever—the Law School, I may remind you, has five deans, the Business School six—and I am teaching two courses in Victorian poets at the same time. Mr. Levy, whom, because he is in my field, I know better than I know Mr. Genero, would be able to help me considerably not only with my dissertation load, but with certain administrative tasks in the department. Though none of you can be expected to know it, Mr. Levy is a first-rate administrator. If we are to promote people on the basis of their usefulness to the English Department, I would like to point out that, whatever the abilities of the students in the University College, Mr. Levy is to be highly recommended.''

"I would like to second that," Mark Everglade said. "Mr. Genero, as it happens, is in my field, which is Comparative Renaissance, he is fluent in Italian and speaks and reads five other languages as well, and if I am to continue as Secretary I would like to suggest that his usefulness to me can scarcely be overestimated. Let me add, while I have the floor, that the students from University College who have been in my classes have been first-rate and have been, compared to the boys from the College, possessed of a higher degree of motivation and a considerably lower degree of arrogance.''

Cudlipp leaped to his feet. "I move that this meeting be adjourned," he shouted.

"I second the motion," O'Toole said.

"Now wait a minute," Cartier shouted.

"Motions for adjournment are not debatable," Cudlipp announced. Indeed, the faculty had learned Robert's Rules of Order in recent months.

"We shall have to take a vote," Michaels said. "All in favor of adjournment signify by saying 'Aye.' " There was a loud chorus of 'Ayes.' "Opposed."

"No," several voices trumpeted.

"The 'Ayes' have it," Michaels said. "This meeting is adjourned." He gathered up his papers and marched from the room lest any inclination to continue the discussion manifest itself.

"Interesting," Kate said to Mark Everglade, "and thanks for your support."

"It was heartfelt," Mark said, "and not at all disinterested. I'm conniving for Genero's assistance in a desperate way."

"What astonished me," Kate said, "is how many we've obviously got on our side—the side, I mean, of University College. The support is much greater than I dared think. Of course, alas and alack, Cudlipp must be aware of this as fully as I. What do you think he'll do next?"

"What you taught me to do in the elevator," Everglade said, "remembering, in your Proustian way, the stories your father told." Kate stared at him. "He'll go straight to the President," Everglade explained, "together with Clemance, the University's most renowned adornment, and O'Toole, Dean of the College—yes, I was passed a note during the meeting. Speaking to the President directly works for getting out of elevators, discovering train schedules, and killing schools and promotions.''

"Does Cudlipp really have that much power?''

"He does. What is more, all Michaels and I have been able to threaten him with is our resignations from the administrative posts in the Department we so reluctantly occupy; and since Cudlipp would be only too delighted to take on those duties himself, with all that means for his enemies, our threats can scarcely be dignified by the term idle.''

"Golly,'' Kate said.

"So,'' Everglade asked, "what else is new?''

"As it happens,'' Kate said, "I'm getting married.''

Enjoying the impact of this as a curtain line, Kate, who was still eschewing elevators, ran down the stairs and out of Baldwin, again to meet Polly Spence.

"I was on my way to see you,'' Polly Spence said, "absolutely on my way. Have you *heard* the news from the Linguistics Department?''

"They've disproved Verner's Law,'' Kate ventured; "they've discovered long E never shifted after all.''

"It's almost that amazing. They're firing the only specialist they have in the English language because they might have to give him tenure and he's primarily associated with University College.''

"The words are familiar,'' Kate said, "and I even think I recognize the tune.''

"Which will mean,'' Polly went on, "actually *mean* that the Linguistics Department will have a specialist in Chinese and *not* in English—can you believe it?''

"Oddly enough, I can,'' Kate said. "Who objects to the promotion from University College, have you heard?''

"Well, of course, I'm just a lowly teaching assistant, and none of my news can be called from the horse's mouth, or even from his immediate neighborhood, but the *general* word is that the College objects, and especially the new dean who looms on the horizon, though he is as yet nameless.''

"I believe,'' Kate said, "I could put a name to him. Polly, you've actually come up with something lunch at the Cosmo wouldn't cure. Give my love to Winthrop and I'll give yours to Reed.''

"Who's Reed?'' Polly Spence called.

"My husband, more or less,'' Kate called back, leaving Polly open-mouthed and speechless on the steps of Baldwin Hall.

PART 2

DEATH AND AFTER

6

Looking up at the stars, I know quite well
That, for all they care, I can go to hell,
But on earth indifference is the least
We have to dread from man or beast.

THE news that Kate was acquiring a husband became, as the fall semester got under way, the excuse for a bacchanal. Which is to say that the three secretaries in the English Department, certain that marriage is more important than revolution, planned a department party to celebrate. Kate and Reed were to be the honored guests, and everyone who was invited would contribute the necessary funds and come. One may insult one's colleagues, the administration, or the Board of Governors, but one does not offend secretaries.

"You," Kate said to Reed, "are my greatest accomplishment. I have achieved the apotheosis of womanhood. To have earned a Ph.D., taught reasonably well, written books, traveled, been a friend and lover—these are mere evasions of my appointed role in life: to lead a man to the altar. You are my sacrifice to the goddess of middle-class morality, as Iphigenia was Agamemnon's sacrifice to Artemis. Shall you mind the party frightfully?"

"I shall be giddily amused. Nor had I known the victim enjoyed the sacrifice. I can never remember having been so outrageously happy."

"Which merely shows how even the sanest man can be the sport of the gods. There are times, Reed, when I wonder if you know what you're taking on. But I suppose if one ever knew that, one would never do anything. May I urge you to back out, if you so choose, before the party? After it, you are more committed than if the banns had been read in St. Paul's Cathedral. Secretaries may not be trifled with.''

"What I don't understand," Reed said, as they set out for the party, which was being held in the English Department Offices (thus making it semi-official and obviating the necessity of asking wives), "is what Clemance wanted from you at your lunch *à deux*."

"I expect he wanted reassurance," Kate said.

"Clearly; but of what?"

"That he need not change his ways; that those who felt impelled to kill the University College need not be stopped by him."

"But why should he have expected you to provide the reassurance?"

"That is the question, I know. I think it must have occurred to him that, suffering like him from heartache, I might be induced to back him up in his old-fashioned opinions, particularly since, as he suspected, I had an old-fashioned background whose beauty I was not prepared to deny. You see, his moral nature or his imagination or both caught him up. Of course, Emilia Airhart thinks that he is a male chauvinist and a company man, and if she's right, the University College may well be doomed, but I take his choosing to have lunch with me as a sign that she may be wrong."

"My instincts tell me not to ask, but I will ignore them; who is Emilia Airhart?"

"You'll meet her tonight—the only other lady member of the department, of tenure rank that is, and therefore on the secretaries' most exclusive list. I think you'll like her, if you don't object to large, downright women on principle. She likes me because she thinks me willowy."

"You are," Reed said. "The willowiest of the willowy."

It was with some trepidation that Kate agreed to take the elevator to the eighth floor. After her dramatic presentations about the wild eccentricities of University elevators, Reed was mildly disappointed to arrive at the English Department with no undue incident whatever. He was immediately taken in tow by the secretaries, provided with drink, and paraded round for introductions for all the world, Reed said later, as though he were some unique specimen miraculously caught in the nets of matrimony—which perhaps he was. Certainly the young ladies could not have been prouder of him if they were planning to marry him themselves. Kate, meanwhile, accepted a drink from Professor Goddard, the medievalist, who offered congratulations.

"I cannot remember," Kate said, "when I have had so overwhelmingly the sensation of having done something devastatingly clever. As though I had been saved after days in the bottom of a well or lost in the depths of the forest. And yet you know," she added, in a more confidential tone of voice, "Reed and I have known and cared for each other for a long time."

"No matter," Professor Goddard said. "A wedding is destiny, and hanging likewise."

"Did *Piers Plowman* say that?" Kate asked. Kate's total ignorance of *Piers Plowman* was one of her most guilty secrets.

"No. John Heywood; too late to be in my period. But I shall find you a properly dull tag from *Piers Plowman* and have it framed for you both as a wedding present. It may serve, in these days of frantic relevance, to remind you of the importance of the useless."

"The useless is never important, it is only comforting," Robert O'Toole said, coming up. "I'm glad you're getting married," he added. "All women should be married. An unmarried woman is an offense against nature." He seemed to find this a marvelously witty remark, despite Kate's look, which indicated clearly to Reed all the way across the room that Kate was finding Robert O'Toole an offense against nature. Kate, who, when she was really offended, had to think with both hands for a fortnight before becoming possessed of a satisfactory retort, was fortunately saved from beginning on this endeavor by the voice of Emilia Airhart, who had joined them. "What I can never understand about you, Mr. O'Toole," she said, "is whether you think arrogant bad manners encourage the illusion of manliness, or whether you think that evident unmanliness is somehow obscured by arrogant bad manners."

Professor Peter Packer Pollinger interrupted whatever response anyone could possibly have found to make to this observation, which was delivered in the voice of one noticing, pleasantly, some mild natural phenomenon, by strolling up to Kate and handing her a book.

"Didn't wrap it," he said. "Many happy weddings."

"Don't you mean many happy returns?" one of the secretaries skittishly asked.

"Mean what I say. She's beginning late, but she may take to it and keep at it, you never know. Here you are, anyway, regardless." Kate was pleased to receive an old book from which all indication of title and author had long since been eradicated by use. She opened therefore to the title page. *The Mountain Lovers*, she read—Fiona Macleod. "Wasn't an easy choice," he said, "for your first wedding. *The Immoral Hour*, *The Divine Adventure*, or even, though I hope not, *The Dominion*, might have done equally well. Have you ever been lovers on a mountain?"

To this embarrassing question, which ought to have been answered in the affirmative for veracity's sake, in the negative for the sake of everyone's feelings, and for propriety's sake by what her mother used to call a deprecating *moue*, Kate was fortunately saved from responding. (I might, she later observed to Reed, have tried a deprecating *moue* and failed; how awful a thought.) Jeremiah Cudlipp had entered the room, announcing that he had had a terrible day in such stentorian tones that every conversation stopped in deference to him. Kate managed only to take Professor Pollinger's hand and thank him with the affection and gratitude she felt.

The room was now rather full, and almost all of Kate's colleagues had found an opportunity to converse with Reed. As an Assistant D.A. he had no doubt encountered worse ordeals, but this could scarcely be easy, and as Kate regarded the relaxed pose of his long, lanky form from across the room she was suddenly visited with an enormous affection. Odd that she should have to see him in a room full of academics before realizing wherein exactly his unique attraction lay: he was vital without being intense, confident without being assertive, assured without being pompous. She was certain he found this whole phenomenon amusing, and was particularly pleased to see him make his way over to Emilia Airhart—who, naturally, would not want to appear to be looking him over—and engage her in conversation. They appeared to like each other. Into this *tête-à-tête* plunged Jeremiah Cudlipp.

Before Kate could even consider the outcome of such a threesome, Cartier came up to her. He seemed to consider his presence sufficient comment on Kate's marital state, and plunged immediately into questions about University matters, though it was a moment or two before this became wholly clear. "What do you think," he asked, "are the chances for things turning out well? Do you feel doomed to frustration, or slightly optimistic?"

"Well . . ."

"The meeting of the English Department seemed to offer far more hope than I had thought possible; at the same time . . ."

"O'Toole being chosen Dean is not a hopeful sign," Kate said, pulling herself together.

"Most depressing," Cartier said. "Well, cheers," he inconsequentially added, and disappeared as Mark Everglade approached.

"I like your Reed Amhearst," he said. "I thought it only fair to admit that you and I had been stuck in an elevator together in the recent past, and he complimented me on such good company under the circumstances. He's the first lawyer I've ever really cared for, if you want to know. I wonder what the position of the Law School will be on the future of University College."

"I can answer that, I think," Kate said. "They will be for it, partly because they resent The College, which acts as though *it* were the University, but mainly because their secretaries take jobs in order to attend University College free; no University College, no secretaries. The same may be said of the School of Public Administration and probably of several others."

"It really is extraordinary," Everglade said, "the way one works one's ass off for important ideas and principles, only to find that decisions are made in the end for reasons of petty convenience by people who have no more stake in the quality or general movement of education than I have in the changing rate of arbitrage. I don't believe the Trojan War took place over Helen or anyone else. No doubt it began and ended because Hector needed a secretary and Thetis had some sort of working arrangement with Hephaestus about new shields."

"Homer told that story," Kate said. "But if, as Auden has pointed out, Hector or Achilles had written the *Iliad* in the first person, we should have had a comedy, as we have here. Besides, Clio did not love the commanders, the big swaggering figures of history, but those who bred them better horses, found answers to their questions, made their things. If Clio honors anyone, it's us, I think—not mere commanders."

"And Cudlipp is a mere commander?"

"Indubitably. Like boys in pimple-time, like girls at awkward ages, what does he do but wish?"

Everglade smiled. "What do *we* do but wish?" he asked.

The room by now was full to overflowing. Reed and Kate were tall, and their eyes met. Plimsole had caught Michaels in a corner and was making a speech of great length. But for Reed, everyone in the room was tired, wearied with meetings, the extra, unthought-of burdens revolution brings, the sense of impermanence which is perhaps the most wearying of all. For none of them had, previously, questioned the University's power to endure. Certainly one heard of financial crises, community troubles, but for the first time all of them at the University realized that the entire institution might come to grief. Yet, Kate thought, most of the faculty want only to get back to their work—many of them are probably considering offers elsewhere—more money, less turbulence, fewer students. Glancing at Cudlipp, who was now walking toward her, Kate thought of Auden's question: "And how is—what was easy in the past, A democratic villain to be cast?" Stage front and center, Kate thought.

"May I have a word with you, Professor Fansler?" Cudlipp said in his loud, deep voice. Characteristically, he did not wait for an answer. Why are his questions more insulting than other men's assumptions? Kate wondered. "I have had a short talk with Frederick Clemance tonight; he tells me that you two have discussed the future of University College, about which he appears to think there may be some question. He thinks we might at any rate consider the promotion of the two assistant professors we discussed at the recent meeting. I have never heretofore disagreed with Clemance, and I am sorry to do so now. But since you seem to be representing the fight for University College here in the English Department, I thought it only fair to tell you my views. The University College has to go; Bob O'Toole and I have . . ."

"Come now, Jerry," Clemance said. "This is a party for Kate and her charming lawyer, not for the thrashing out of departmental affairs." He placed a hand on Cudlipp's arm.

"I've got a frightful headache," Cudlipp said, acknowledging nothing. He reached into his pocket for a tube of pills, and shook two of them out into his hand.

"I'll get you some club soda to take them with," Clemance said. "You've really got to take it a bit easy, you know." But Cudlipp was gathering his forces. "Look at this catalogue," he began, haranguing Kate as Clemance came up carrying a glass and a bottle of club soda.

"Thank you," Cudlipp said at last when he had gulped the two pills. "I've spent the whole day listening to the representatives from your University College. Four students who appear to be in your class; Dean Frogmore, Bill McQuire from Economics, whom I really would have expected to have more sense; all of them going on as though that silly extension school, degree-granting though it may be, were actually viable, actually . . ."

Cudlipp turned white and apparently grew dizzy, for he reached out to balance himself against one of the desks. "My God," Kate heard him say, "aspirin. Aspirin." And before any one could move at all he had vomited violently, brown blood the color of coffee grounds.

Everyone except Reed was too stunned to move. "Call the hospital," he said to one of the secretaries, who had rushed over, "tell them we have an emergency case, hemorrhaging, blood loss from the stomach. You," he said, pointing to Plimsole, rendered amazingly silent, "help me get him into the elevator. We better not wait for an ambulance. Isn't the hospital right down the street?"

Plimsole helped Reed to lift Cudlipp, no mean weight. With the assistance of two other professors, they were able actually to carry him. Kate ran ahead to ring for the elevator which, for a miracle, was waiting at the eighth floor. She held the doors open as they carried Cudlipp in. While the doors were closing, Kate saw Cudlipp vomit again. Plimsole pressed the button and the elevator started. Everyone stood there, uncertain what to do next. "Perhaps I'd better run down and help them," O'Toole, who had seemed too stunned to move, said. He raced down the stairs, followed by Clemance, who moved more slowly.

But, as it happened, the elevator reached the main floor many minutes after O'Toole and Clemance. It had stuck between the third and fourth floors, Cudlipp had continued vomiting, and by the time they got him out of the elevator and to the hospital it was too late. He had lost great amounts of blood, and they could not revive him. He died that night.

It was almost morning when Kate opened the door to Reed, and for a moment, seeing each other, they remembered the reason for the party that had so abruptly ended and were glad in spite of everything.

But sooner or later they had to talk about it. "It's quite a while," Reed said, "since I watched a man die, though technically he wasn't yet dead when the hospital carted him off. The appalling irony of it is that he had time to call out 'aspirin,' and there were God knows how many people in the room who could interpret that remark—I'll explain it to you in a minute. I knew exactly what to do, we all did exactly the right thing, but the elevator stuck, the mucous membrane of the stomach began to erode very near to a major artery—talk about destiny. He's dead. How much difference will that make in the whole University picture?"

"I've no idea. Does it really matter?"

"I think it might; I very strongly suspect that he was murdered."

Kate stared at him. "But you've only just now said that given your presence, and lots of other factors, it was really only the most extraordinary bad luck that he died."

"Perhaps you're right. If I decide to run someone over with my car, injuring him sufficiently so that he will be out of commission for a good while, and by mistake I skid and kill him, would you or would you not call it murder?"

"Great Scot," Kate said. She was, when really affected, likely to revert to the innocent ejaculations of her childhood. "What's it all got to do with aspirin?"

"Like many other common medicines, aspirin is a poison to some people."

"I never knew that. Aren't Americans supposed to gulp down millions of aspirin tablets a year?"

"They are not only supposed to; they do. Not to mention the aspirin they swallow in Alka-Seltzer, Coricidin, Pepto Bismol, and fifteen other household remedies you might care to mention. But to some people aspirin is a deadly poison. The moment it is absorbed by the blood stream—and that doesn't take very long, nor, which is more mysterious, does the amount of aspirin taken matter—an allergic person begins to suffer erosion of his mucous membrane. He feels dizzy and weak, he vomits—you saw before you a classic demonstration. There is, I now learn, more and more question whether aspirin ought, in fact, to be as readily available as it is."

"What would they have done if they had got him in the hospital on time?"

"An interesting point we need now never really explore. Probably they would have wasted time doing blood tests, and so forth. They would probably suspect an ulcer or something of the sort. What is of special interest, however, is not only that there probably were many people in that room who knew Cudlipp was allergic to aspirin, but that I am still in the D.A.'s Office and able, therefore, to demand and get a certain amount of prompt action from the hospital. It's almost as though Cudlipp were given the aspirin under conditions guaranteed to prevent a fatality."

"Couldn't he have taken the aspirin by accident? I mean, couldn't it all have been a mistake?"

"Not a bit likely. Someone who knows he's allergic to aspirin—and Cudlipp knew—would have to be forced at gun point to take it. In fact, Cudlipp was in the habit of taking an imported product—made in England. I have it here." Reed put a bottle of pills on the table. "All labeled and clear. An analgesic without aspirin: in other words, a pain-killer which does not expand the blood vessels."

"Paracetamol, B.P." Kate read.

"B.P. is British Pharmocopoeia, in case you wondered. I discovered there is an American product, in capsule form, now available, but Cudlipp had supposedly got used to Paracetamol and continued to use it."

"Wouldn't he have tasted the aspirin?"

"What a clever girl you are, to be sure; it took me five hours to think of that question. But I know why you thought of it. What kind of aspirin do you use?"

"The cheapest sort they have in the drugstore. My doctor said aspirin is aspirin and it's preposterous to pay more than a dollar for five hundred of them."

"He's right, of course, except that if you don't happen to like the taste of aspirin, which will begin to dissolve on the tongue immediately, you pay considerably more than that and buy buffered aspirin—you are acquiring, in your new husband, a buffered aspirin eater, by the way—which doesn't taste any more than Paracetamol does; get it?"

"Someone, therefore, supposedly replaced Cudlipp's Parawhateveritis with a buffered aspirin that looked the same. How much else about you is there that I do not know?"

"I shall refuse to follow that entrancing thought, and plod on instead with the question of aspirin-analgesics. You know, in any case, how dull I am when puzzled."

"I was just thinking earlier this evening how enchanting you are at all times. You know, Reed, I think if you'd only come to a Department party earlier, and let me see you, beautifully lanky and relaxed among all those professors, I would have proposed long ago. Would you have accepted?"

"Probably with a lot less trepidation than I have now. You know, Kate, I've never really minded your being a sort of overage Nancy Drew . . ."

"Now that's unkind, Reed, that's downright nasty . . ."

"Forgive me. I guess I realized you were going to be smack in the middle of this business and I was hoping, in my manly way, that you might be willing to bow out—you know, just go on with what you were doing."

"But none of us can just go on with what we were doing; it's just no longer possible, not, at least, if you're the sort who listens and admits to being confused, which is something no one ever said of Nancy Drew. But why are you getting the wind up so? It's unlike you. I know it's a ghastly mess, but after all, it could have been an accident—or somebody may have put some aspirin in his British thingammies months ago.''

"They mightn't, as it happens. Naturally, that's the first thing I looked into. He was beginning on a new load of pills just today— yesterday, I guess, by now—and the entire bottle of two hundred tablets is O.K., so clearly, it was the small tube in which he carried a day's supply of pills around with him that had been tampered with. As it happens, the two he took at the party were the first of the new batch, but he might have taken them at any time—he was nervous, and prone to headaches. Someone got hold of that pill-carrier, sup- posedly after Cudlipp had filled it, and replaced the first two British pills with buffered aspirin.''

"There, you see," Kate said. "And he might have taken them anywhere, and I wouldn't have been at all involved.''

"You weren't near his office that day, no. But you had had lunch with Clemance some days before—though you had admired the man this side of idolatry for decades without finding it necessary to lunch with him before. And, as it happened, Cudlipp was talking to you when he decided to take the pills, and Clemance rushed right off and got him some soda water—right?''

"Right. Who noticed that?''

"Just about everyone.''

"Well, all it proves is that I couldn't have had anything to do with it. If he had just got the new pills today, I wouldn't have had time to substitute the aspirin for the pills in his pill tube.''

"You could have done it right at the party.''

"My dear man, I may be Nancy Drew; I'm not Houdini.''

"The fact is, anyone at the party could have done it. He carried the tube with the pills loose in his outer pocket; child's play. Or anyone who visited his office today—which includes students from your beloved University College (which should have gone right on being extension courses, if you want my candid opinion), Frogmore, McQuire, and one or two other chaps from that little luncheon you had before you asked me to marry you.''

"Reed, aren't you being a little over-dramatic? If anyone wanted to kill Cudlipp in that way, doesn't it seem likely that it was someone of a non-university sort? His wife, someone like that?''

"When you hear the history of the pills, I think you'll discount that."

"*Is* Cudlipp married?"

"He and his wife have recently separated, amidst much acrimony, I am given to understand."

"You've picked up more in five hours that I have in five years."

"You are not, I am pleased to say, a gossipy sort. What floors, by the way, were you stuck between when you and Everglade were in that elevator together?"

Kate stared at him. "The third and fourth. Why?"

Reed took her in his arms. "Why indeed?" he said. And then for a while forgot all about it.

7

Between those happenings that prefigure it
And those that happen in its anamnesis
Occurs the Event, but that no human wit
Can recognize until all happening ceases.

"To put it crudely," Frogmore said, "Cudlipp's death can be the end for us, or the beginning. I would not have lifted a finger to injure Cudlipp, but if his death can help the University College, I will make use of it. Need I say more?"

"It will scarcely help us," McQuire remarked, "to have the University College discovered to be the motive for the murder. It does seem to suggest that we don't produce people of the right sort. There is, after all, a distinction between occupying the President's Office and murder. Or so I assume."

"Correctly, I am certain," Hankster said in his hoarse whisper.

The same group who had met previously, when McQuire had brought Kate to luncheon, was now reconvened, minus the student (to Kate's relief). She did not doubt the judgment of students, which, in some cases, she valued over that of the faculty, but she did doubt their discretion. In a case like this, rumor could do irreparable harm, particularly if it were true.

Castleman apparently not only understood the power structure of the University with remarkable clarity but with ease shifted this understanding to problems of murder. "We have donned our academic gowns and attended a memorial service for Cudlipp," he said, "and we have all contributed to a fund to establish a prize in his honor."

"To be awarded, naturally, to an outstanding student in the College," Frogmore said.

"Naturally," Castleman acknowledged. "But we had better realize that the administration and the senior faculty are profoundly shaken by all this. Disruption is one thing, murder—however haphazard in appearance—another. It follows inevitably that if Cudlipp was given the aspirin accidentally, more or less at random as a flying brick may hit *someone*, that is one thing; if he was given the aspirin intentionally as part of some personal grudge or individual pottiness, that is another. If, however, he was poisoned fatally on behalf of any school in this University, or any group of students or faculty ..." Castleman shrugged, not bothering to complete his sentence.

"Whether fortunately or not." McQuire said, "we know exactly when Cudlipp got this latest batch of non-aspirins, so we know that the substitution of the pills must have taken place on that day, the day of Kate's party."

"I don't see how that really helps us," Cartier said.

"It helps the detective work, not us," Castleman pointed out. "It means that the aspirin Cudlipp took had to be given to him that day—they couldn't have been mixed in with his British pills, simply waiting for him to light on them. We know, furthermore, whom Cudlipp saw that day. Alas, having refused for weeks to talk to anyone from the University College, he appears, on the day of his death, to have decided to lend his ear if not his sympathy."

"That may have been thanks to Clemance," Kate said.

"Thanks are not, as it has turned out, what we especially want to offer," Frogmore said.

"That's unfair, I think," Kate said.

"Of course it is," Frogmore agreed.

"We know," Castleman went on, "that on the afternoon of the day of his death, Cudlipp saw McQuire and Frogmore and Cartier; he agreed to be called upon by four students from the University College; he also had a conference about the College English Department with Clemance and O'Toole. In the morning he had a class; he had lunch with Hankster and ..."

"And," Hankster added, "we were joined by Professor Emilia Airhart."

"Which does not, of course," Kate added, "necessarily account for everyone he saw that day. There are the secretaries, casual encounters on campus paths ..."

"And in the men's room," Hankster said. "Let's face it, anyone could have switched those pills, if murder were the intent. I don't believe it was. I think someone copped what he thought were a couple of aspirins, and then returned others, unaware of their lethal qualities for Cudlipp.''

"Then," Castleman said, ''we've got to find him—the innocent aspirin-changer.''

"Perhaps he will confess," Frogmore said. "Let us hope so. Meanwhile, I would like to know what the next move is—for University College. Whether or not we can find the person who caused Cudlipp's death, we can certainly determine the effect of the death on us. O'Toole will be taken up with running the College. Clemance, while not our advocate, seems actually to have some decent sense of reticence about wiping us off the face of the map. The Graduate English Department, from what I can gather, is all for promoting our assistant professors from the English Department, helping themselves and doing the College in the eye at the same time. I think we ought to move.''

"Move cautiously," Castleman said, ''but move—I agree with you. Let's discover, in an informal way, how the administration feels.''

"I thought we were clean out of administration," Kate said.

"The Administrative Council is still functioning," Frogmore said, ''and will go on until we get the Senate. The Acting President has promised that a statement of confidence in the viability of University College, and instructions to departments to promote its qualified faculty to tenure, will come before the next meeting of the Administrative Council.''

"Which is when?" Hankster asked.

"In three weeks, and every hour of that time has to be used to get us the votes we need—not only in favor of the motion, but also against a motion to table for any reason whatsoever—for example, so that all undergraduate education at the University can be studied. Because if the Administrative Council doesn't give us its mandate we're as good as finished. By the time we get a Senate and a new President it will be a whole new ball game—as Cudlipp knew.''

"So his being out of the picture will make a difference?''

"Oh, yes," Frogmore said, ''all the difference in the world. Cudlipp had a lot of favors to trade, and now isn't around to trade them.''

Kate walked from the meeting with Hankster; she fell in step beside him so that, without being rude, he had no choice but to proceed at her side—and Hankster was never rude. He had, since the spring, acquired a reputation for devoted radicalism; yet, *tête-à-tête* with him, one found it hard to believe. Not only the scarcely audible voice—the intimation was that he was unable to speak loudly, though Kate suspected strategic rather than physical inhibitions—belied the drama of radicalism. He was a gentleman, from the top of his sleek head, past the elegant clothes, to the tips of his beautifully made shoes. Kate, because she had come from his world, understood him, and knew better than most that there are those who cling to the finger bowls, those who dismiss them with a shrug but not without nostalgia, and those like Hankster whose life was devoted to smashing the finger bowls against privy walls.

"What did you talk about with Cudlipp, if I may be forthright enough to ask? If you don't want to tell me, don't; spare me the gentlemanly circumlocutions."

"I'm honored," Hankster said. "As I have gathered, you're often peppery, but seldom rude. You dislike me very much, don't you?"

Kate stopped a moment, with Hankster waiting patiently by her side. "Yes," Kate said, "I do. I think I always dislike people who are destroyers by principle, though I never really faced up to it, until this moment. Sorry. I've no right to ask you any questions at all."

"Sure you have. You really think, don't you, that we've seen the last of the troubles. That from now on, we just rebuild our university, better than before but not fundamentally different."

"Oh, I expect students will sit in buildings, or whatever the new ploy is, again this spring. But I don't think it will make any real difference; not here. We've had our moment of awakening. This spring, it will be other universities who have the uprisings; don't you agree?"

"Perhaps. But the whole system's finished all the same. Sure, you'll have your Senate, which will bring students and junior faculty into the system, and will perhaps keep an antediluvian administration from making the kinds of mistakes which, in any case, they aren't going to make anymore, because no university will ever again have so basically stupid a president as this university had. But it's only reaction you're institutionalizing. Administrators on the whole, you know, are more up-to-date than the senior faculty. That's where the bastion of conservatism is, if you want to know. And this Senate will simply give them more power. So—when the big break comes, it will be a lulu."

"And you look forward to it, hope for it, will work for it?"

"It will happen whatever I do, though I'll lend a hand if I can. I don't know what revolutions you're dreaming of, Professor Fansler, or hoping for, or fearing."

Kate laughed. "You're accusing me, in your ever-polite way, of being like the dreaming lady in an anecdote of Kenneth Burke's. She dreamed a brute of a man had entered her bedroom and was staring at her from the foot of her bed. 'Oh, what are you going to do to me?' she asked, trembling. 'I don't know, lady,' the brute answered; 'it's your dream.'"

Hankster laughed. "It is delightful to talk to someone who enjoys one's point, even against herself."

"I know. It's our guilts and our hidden desires that you work on most, you radicals. We shall destroy ourselves in the end, whether because we understand the radical students too well or too little."

"But it's not just the radical students; it's all students. There simply is no longer any reason for their being in college—not the smart ones, anyway. The engineering students, those on their way up the social ladder, the blacks—college has some point for them. But for the bright kid who's been to a first-rate high school, what's he got to learn at college? He no longer comes to college for his first drink, his first woman. Until college becomes a privilege again. . . ."

"But that's the point of the University College—for the older students. Education is again something they've had to earn."

"The University College, and places like it, are the future. Whether this University has the sense to see that or not is important only to us here, now, but in the end it will make no difference. The question is not *if* the state will take over this University, but when. Every year, also, fewer kids make it through undergraduate education uninterrupted. To leave college is the norm, not the exception now. The whole picture's changing. That, if you want to know, is what I talked to Cudlipp about at lunch. Since I teach in both the adult and the boys' colleges, he wanted to know where my loyalties lay."

"And what did you tell him?" Kate asked.

"That I was a smasher of finger bowls. But ask your colleague Emilia Airhart. She joined us near the beginning."

"How come?"

"I met her and asked her to."

"Didn't Cudlipp mind?"

"Horribly. He dislikes women if they are not beautiful, not slender, not stupider than he—or willing to pretend they are—and not flirtatious. Mrs. Airhart made a clean sweep. You would do better, or would have done; we will never know now.''

"I am quite past deciding if that is nasty or nice. Anyway, I like Emilia Airhart.''

"So do I. And if you ask her, she will tell you that Cudlipp tried to co-opt me and I said no. The system's finished. You and I came out of the same world, but only one of us dreams of going back.''

"I know I can't go back,'' Kate said. "I just don't hate the memory. What's Frogmore going to do now?''

"What everyone must do: reach every member of the Administrative Council; tell each one a vote for University College is a vote against the growing power mania of *The* College. We'll come through now. It's truly amazing what aspirin can cure, wouldn't you say?''

Kate found Emilia Airhart in her office riffling, as one seemed to do these days, through mimeographed pages. "Come in,'' she called to Kate. "I was just about to write you a note. One less dirty piece of paper, thank God. I knew I had lost my interest in revolution when I lost my interest in mimeographed announcements from every splinter group on campus demanding this, foretelling that, condemning the other. There is now even an organization for liberating women—utter nonsense. Women are liberated the moment they stop caring what other women think of them.'' With a gesture of great delight she dumped the whole package of papers into the waste basket. "I hear you're an admirer of Auden's and have just sponsored a brilliant dissertation on him.''

"Yes, though the less said about the dissertation defense, the better. There was a moment there when I feared for the whole future of the academic world.''

"Do tell. Professor Pollinger mentioned it as the most interesting dissertation defense he had been to in years. What *do* you admire about Auden, by the way, if you can enunciate it in several well-chosen sentences—a talent of yours, I'm told.''

"I can't imagine by whom. As a matter of fact, I babble on, hitting the truth occasionally by happenstance which inspires students by the sheer surprise of it; the rest of the time they just feel comfortably superior. As to Auden, he's interested in squares and oblongs, rather than in sensory effects, which I like; that is, he understands that men always have moral dilemmas, which makes him intelligent, and he is able to present these structurally, which makes him an artist. The structures he uses are patterns of words, which make him a poet. He's conceptual rather than descriptive, and he always sees objects, natural or not, as part of a relationship. He knows that, first and last, a poet has to express abstract ideas in concrete forms, his own words, as it happens. How's that for a one-minute lecture?''

"Brilliant."

"Thank you. I stole it from Richard Hoggart's introduction to Auden's poems, which Mr. Cornford in turn quoted in his dissertation. If you want to know what I personally admire, well Auden knows that poetry 'makes nothing happen,' though it is of supreme importance: the only order. And Auden is the only poet I know whose poems are serious and *fun*. He refuses to let poetry be pompous *or* empty. That's why he appreciates Clio, and leaves the other muses alone. Clio 'looks like any girl one has not noticed,'

> *Muse of the unique*
> *Historical fact, defending with silence*
> *Some world of your beholding, a silence*
>
> *No explosion can conquer but a lover's Yes*
> *Has been known to fill. . . .*

Think of that in connection with Cudlipp for example. An explosion of sorts conquered him, but can you think of him as filled by a lover's Yes?''

"Now that you mention it, no. He was always empty and scorned girls one had not noticed. I'm wondering, actually, about the plays Auden wrote with Isherwood."

"Must you?"

"Duty calls. A student wants to work on them, and who am I to say him nay? Will you kind of advise on the Auden part?''

"All right. But I don't look forward to the dissertation defense."

"Our examinations are all wrong. In Sweden, the whole thing is done what I call properly. There's a professor who attacks the work, a professor who defends it, and a third who makes humorous remarks, which of course we're all dying to do but never can do properly in this country. Then when it's over the candidate gives a ball, white tie and long dresses. I'm thinking of emigrating.''

"It's true," Kate said. "When formality went from life, meaning went too. People always yowl about form without meaning, but what turns out to be impossible is meaning without form. Which is why

I'm a teacher of literature and keep ranting on about structure. Perhaps it's different in the drama.''

"On the contrary. When a culture no longer agrees on form, it loses drama. Certain ardent souls, to be sure, try to get effects by undressing on the stage, having intercourse in front of the audience, perhaps even getting the audience to join them, but it won't work. That's why films are the thing today—perceived in loneliness, like novels.''

"I thought the young were all mad for film-making today—quite ritualistic and groupy.''

"Making them, perhaps. But one *sees* a film in the dark, alone. Isherwood and Auden plays, though, could count on an audience of the left.''

"Sure—like today. The bad guys were in, and the good guys wanted to get them out. Things were simpler then, though. I have often wished I were not among the Epigoni:

> *No good expecting long-legged ancestors to*
> *Return with long swords from pelagic paradises. . . .*
> *Meanwhile, how should a cultured gentleman behave?*

Which reminds me, what about your lunch with Hankster and Cudlipp?''

"Well, Cudlipp disliked me, and Hankster disliked Cudlipp and wanted to make him uncomfortable. It was one of those situations no one could get out of without being brutal, and so far one doesn't openly snub a colleague in the Faculty Club. In short, Cudlipp wanted Hankster to admit he was a gentleman and come in with the College in some grand though unspecified position; Hankster declined.''

"Was Hankster alone with Cudlipp at all in the Club that day?''

"They were at a table together before I came—not for long, I think. They were together in the men's room, one supposes; I was in the ladies' room and can't be sure. I was alone with Cudlipp for a minute; I ought to tell you that. Hankster got up in search of a bottle of ale, the waiter having apparently gone on some extended errand in another part of the forest, you know how it is in the Faculty Club. When are you getting married?''

"I don't know. Reed says we'll talk about it tonight, if we can get our minds off Cudlipp's aspirin. Emilia, did Cudlipp ever promise you anything to get your support for the College?''

"Yes. He promised me positions for women in the College,

which he thought dear to my heart. What does it matter now? Anyway, why shouldn't you have your University College? A new experience, like getting married.''

"I hadn't looked at it in that light. It really represents new experiences for everyone.''

"Essential to a well-lived life. Take loneliness, for instance. Terrible in its way. And yet, for me, a few days of complete solitude in the country, away from an outrageously happy marriage, work I love, and noisy, gifted children is a joy so intense that perhaps not even Auden could describe it. But one day too much, and one plunges into the abyss of enforced solitude, of not being wanted or missed. I don't know if you or Auden ever noticed it, but the only earthly joys are those we are free to choose—like solitude, your college, certain marriages.''

"And what about unearthly joys?''

"Ah, those, if we are fortunate, choose us. Like grace. Like talent.''

Mark Everglade caught Kate as she emerged into the hall. "Just the person I wanted to see. We shall want your advice. We haven't done too well with Swahili, but we're interviewing someone who reads and writes Ndebele. You needn't look blank; as everyone should know these days, that's a dialect of Zulu, and contains the greatest literature of Africa not in English. We're stirring up people to come and chat with him tomorrow between two and four. Do try to come.''

"But what on earth will I talk to him about?''

"Offer to help him translate the novels of Bulwer-Lytton into Ndebele. A way of preparing for next year's text course.''

"But why do we have to teach Ndebele literature in the English Department?''

"The Elephant's Child,'' Mark Everglade said. "There you go again. We are restructuring after the revolution, remember?'' And Kate, remembering, went off to teach her class in Victorian literature.

She returned home somewhat late that afternoon, showered, dressed, and went to meet Reed at his apartment where, he had announced, he was preparing dinner. "My plan is this,'' he had said. "If we are going to get married, there are bound to be evenings when we will not feel like eating out. There is a place which, with ample notice and heroic payment, will send up some sort of casserole all ready to be popped into the oven, but the way I figure it, once or twice a week we will want to eat in and *cook*. I know you can cook at least three dishes, because I've eaten them, and I've just learned from a friend that if you have a fireplace like mine you can buy little thingamajigs with which to make logs out of *The New York Times* (I'm getting quite the married man, you see, finding a use for everything), and then we can grill steaks over an open fire, but I still ought to be able to make a contribution. I have therefore learned to cook one dish and will soon learn to cook another, both in an electric frying pan which a bachelor friend of mine gave me. (I took that, by the way, as a sure sign that I ought to get married.) You are to come and eat sausages and peppers with crisp bread, cucumber sticks sprinkled with fresh-ground pepper, red wine, and black coffee. I've discovered that to appear a gourmet, one serves too little food, highly seasoned: the sausages are hot.''

He greeted Kate with a book in hand. "Here," he said, "listen to this; it should make anything delectable.'' The book was *Letters from Iceland*, and Reed read from Auden's tourist guide: '' 'Dried fish is a staple food in Iceland. This should be shredded with the fingers and eaten with butter. It varies in toughness. The tougher kind tastes like toe-nails, and the soft kind like the skin off the soles of one's feet.' Bound to make peppers and sausage luscious, don't you agree? Sit down and let me fix you a drink. Then I'll give you my news.''

"Here's a passage you missed,'' Kate said, reading from the book. '' 'A curious Icelandic food,' he says, 'is Hakarl, which is half-dry, half-rotten shark. This is white inside with a prickly horn rind outside, as tough as an old boot.' Auden seems to have become a foot fetishist in Iceland. 'Owing to the smell it has to be eaten out of doors. It is shaved off with a knife and eaten with brandy.' Do you think he can be serious? 'It tastes more like boot polish than anything else I can think of.' I'm not at all certain,'' Kate said, accepting her drink from Reed, "that I want to eat at all.''

"When you hear my news you'll want to eat even less. I have had visitors from your glorious University, not to say from one of your select, conspiratorial lunches. Marrying you makes for a busy life, that much is clear.''

"Frogmore and McQuire, by any chance?''

"Castleman and Klein. Castleman, it turns out, knows some of my associates, and Klein knows others, so they decided to trust me. They were further encouraged in this decision by the fact that I was present when Cudlipp took the aspirin, and as helpful as possible when he died, which isn't saying much. They were very kind, formal, discrete, and honorable, and I didn't envy them their mission at all.''

"Reed! They came to ask you to be President of the University! You've no idea the trouble everyone's having finding presidents these days. Who wants the job? It was bad enough when one had to raise money and talk to rich alumni, but these, however stupid and trying, never occupied one's office or ransacked one's files. I hope you turned them down flat.''

"They came to ask if I thought you had interpreted their plea for help at luncheon and Frogmore's enthusiasm for his school as a mandate to put Cudlipp out of commission. Their motive in inquiring, I gathered, was not law and order but simple clarity: they wanted to ascertain who had slipped Cudlipp the aspirin in a wholly admirable effort to establish who had *not*.''

"But why on earth me? I didn't even know about Cudlipp's blasted British pills, I haven't that sort of mind, and while I have admittedly become devoted to the cause of the University College, there are limits to my devotion even to so worthy a cause. Do you think it's blackmail?''

"By God, Kate, for the first time I have come to appreciate your blasted revolution. Such sangfroid well becomes you. I remember once, years ago, having to tell you that you were suspected of murder and you burst into tears and had to be comforted with pats on the head and hot coffee.''

"What a long memory you have.''

"It didn't have to be all that long to enable me to recall that you were standing with Cudlipp when he took the aspirin. In fact, he was arguing with you at the time.''

"Arguing is a bit strong—for Cudlipp, who never did anything else. I'm sure he was bald because he'd torn out his hair so often it decided to give up the struggle. He was wielding the University College catalogue, as a matter of fact, presumably prior to letting me know how inferior the offerings were—or am I theorizing ahead of my data?''

"Since, short of seances, that's as much data on Cudlipp's intentions as we're likely to have—no.''

"What else, if anything, did Castleman and Klein want—after you convinced them that I was Nancy Drew and not Lucretia Borgia?''

"They wanted to know if I'd help.''

"Clever of them; but didn't they guess I'd have asked you already?"

"Their asking me made it semi-official."

"Like our relationship now. I can hardly wait for Thanksgiving."

"Thanksgiving is only four weeks away."

"Reed, that is the most ungallant remark you have ever made, and that's saying a good deal. I know I said you couldn't back out after the secretaries' party, but after all, we hardly expected Cudlipp to pop off like that, so you can always say there were extenuating circumstances. Only be kind enough to remember that *I* only asked to move in with you and have you cook sausages and peppers in your new electric frying pan; *I* never asked for legal assurances."

"Kate darling, that was not a remark, it was an observation, and the 'only' referred not to my implied regrets about my wanning days of bachelorhood, but to the fact that the meeting of the Administrative Council which is to decide the fate of University College is scheduled for one week before Thanksgiving. As Castleman and Klein point out, if the question of Cudlipp's death isn't closed by then, the matter of the University College may be. It is being widely suggested to the Board of Governors, the administration, and everyone else in sight that no move should be taken in the matter while any suspicions about Cudlipp's death remain. Castleman's sense of things is that if approval doesn't come at the next meeting, it will likely never come at all. In fact he quoted the line about a tide in the affairs of men and so forth. Cudlipp's death has got to be cleared up a week before the four weeks to Thanksgiving—hence my unfortunate observation."

"Well, I'm mollified if not reassured. Are you supposed to deliver the murderer's head on a platter—that is, with enough evidence to prosecute—or is the Board of Governors' knowledge of what happened sufficient?"

"It's not only sufficient, it's advisable. After all, the chances are still open that it was all an accident. Castleman and Klein, who are men of real substance, want to be able to give their word to the Board that the accident was *not* the work of anyone from University College. Then, supposedly, the Administrative Council will proceed. I gather the Board never overrides the Administrative Council."

"They never have, no. And of course once the new Faculty Senate is in business, which should be by the New Year, the Administrative Council will dissolve itself. I agree with Castleman about the tide."

"I didn't actually give Castleman an answer; I said I wanted to

talk to you first. I hope I did assure them that not only were you
wholly incapable of carrying out such a plot, you were even not likely
to have thought of it, among other reasons because, as I would be
prepared to swear, you had never heard of the deleterious effects of
aspirin until I pointed them out to you. Do you think I ought to help?
It's all right with the D.A., by the way, who turns out to be a friend
of someone or other.''

"Of course you should help. Wasn't that your first impulse?''

"My first impulses, like most people's, are generous. That's why
Talleyrand told his ministers to resist first impulses. Not, however,
being involved in the French government, I may decide to indulge
myself. What fascinates me, you know, is the fact that the aspirin
had to be substituted that day. It's impossible that someone had, from
whatever motives, dropped two aspirins into his supply at a previous
time. That means we can really concentrate on the people Cudlipp
saw that day, and we've got his day pretty well covered. That he
happened to have spent it almost exclusively in the company of people from the University College is certainly unfortunate.''

"Didn't he see anyone else?''

"Clemance and O'Toole. What with the revisions in the College
English Department and everywhere else—I will say for you academic people, once you start revising you really make a job of it—
he was seeing both of them fairly regularly. With O'Toole about to
be Dean, they had plenty to talk about.''

"Who'll be chairman of the College English Department now?
It's been Cudlipp for years and years, and O'Toole was the heir
apparent.''

"An interesting question. Do you think you could find out?''

"You're not suggesting someone bumped him off to get the job?
I do assure you, Reed, except for Cudlipp, who was power-mad, no
one takes the job except as a service to mankind. Look at poor Michaels and Everglade in the Graduate English Department; nothing
short of an elephantine sense of duty could have persuaded *them*.''

"Perhaps. Haven't you some brilliant ex-student now teaching in
the College who would be pleased to visit you and spill the beans?''

"I might. You realize, of course, that almost anyone might have
dropped into Cudlipp's office and diddled with his pills. English Department offices are very milling-about sorts of places.''

"I know. That's why I shall begin with the Department secretaries. Now let's see. We've got McQuire, Frogmore, and Cartier,
each of whom saw Cudlipp in his office, by appointment, on the day

he died. Then there are your four students; you might, simply oozing tact and discretion, get them to tell you about their conversation.''

"Reed, you know perfectly well I never ooze tact, and will either ask them flatly what happened or not mess with it.''

"There is tact and tact. Very well, I'll take on the students. Then there's Hankster and your Mrs. Airhart. Anything likely there?''

"I wouldn't put much past Hankster. But how could he have replaced the top two pills at lunch without Cudlipp noticing? Reed, wait a minute, I've got an idea. Suppose at lunch Cudlipp takes two of his British pills, which are, of course, harmless, and says something to Hankster about them—take these instead of aspirin, ha, ha, or something—and Hankster asks to see the tube, and replaces the top two pills with two aspirin.''

"Which he just happened to have on him?''

"Why not? Anyhow, we'll never know now, since he won't have them on him anymore. Maybe that's the whole solution.''

"Mrs. Airhart also had lunch with them. Castleman told me. Wouldn't she have seen them diddling with the pills?''

"It would have been before she joined them; in fact, Hankster probably asked her so that he would have a witness for most of the lunch.''

"For that matter, Emilia Airhart could have done the same trick with the pills.''

"True. She told me she was alone with Cudlipp while Hankster went for an ale. But he probably just went to cast suspicion on her. I *like* Emilia.''

"I too like Emilia. I like everybody concerned except the victim.''

"Could the victim's estranged wife have sent round doctored pills—suppose she put two regular aspirin in and Cudlipp got them at the first shot?''

"Even if he managed to get one aspirin at the first shot, his chance of getting both was, statistically speaking, nonexistent. If we're going to have to count on a long shot like that we'd better give up before we start.''

"Speaking of starting, whatever is happening to your sausage and peppers? Don't you think . . .''

"No,'' Reed said, "I don't. The great thing about electric frying pans, my bachelor friend said, is that they can be ignored for hours and hours.''

8

but we, at haphazard
And unseasonably, are brought face to face
By ones, Clio, with your silence. . . .
your silence already is there
Between us and any magical center
Where things are taken in hand.

THE next morning Kate was able to reach on the telephone a young man presently teaching at the College whose dissertation she was directing. He had been a member of her Victorian Seminar several years back and had, after one-and-a-half semesters of the soundest work on the Corn Laws, Reform Bill, Carlyle, and John Stuart Mill, developed a frivolous and unaccountable passion for Max Beerbohm: not his life, nor his times, nor even his works as such, but his sentences. Since it is impossible to study all of a writer's sentences in the ordinary way without a century of time, the young man (whose name was Higgenbothom, but whom Kate always thought of as Enoch Soames) had soon entangled himself with computers. With something between relief and dismay, Kate had handed him over to a stylistics expert, though she had remained on the dissertation committee. Higgenbothom agreed to come and see her at four, relieved and mystified to learn that his dissertation would not be the subject under discussion.

Having arranged that matter, Kate settled down to the reading of some student papers, and was soon lost in wonder at the inability of highly intelligent students properly to construct a sentence. It occurred to her to wonder if computers might be enlisted in her constant struggle against wobbly syntax and sociological jargon. "Being a young writer, the novel was filled with fresh ideas," was typical of sentences which greeted Kate's wondering eyes. Nor was this the worst. She read with horror of the subdued dynamics of Ruskin's interpersonal relations and could not at once hit upon a comment for the margin which was both succinct and mentionable in a scholarly ambience. Thinking of Max Beerbohm and then of her bright, reform-minded young students, Kate marveled not for the first time at the inverse correlation between moral outrage and sentence structure: apparently one could be radical or syntactical but not both; a disturbing thought. And where, Kate thought, her mind dwelling on interpersonal relations, would Reed have got in his investigations?

Reed, at that moment, was vamping the secretary of the College English Department, a pitifully easy thing to do. He had been considering, on the subway, alternate possible approaches to a subject which, simply stated, was a demand to be told when Cudlipp received the bottle of pills, and where and how and what he did with them. The question was how to counter the inevitable "Who are you and why do you want to know?" which, while easily answered in a way, would immediately put the lady on her guard and negate the possibility of always-useful gossip. As it turned out, he need not have concerned himself. Miss Elton was a type with which he was agonizingly familiar. She appeared to have been born with a smirk on her face; she was one of those whose chief reward in life lies in snubbing others, particularly women. But let any male treat her in a truly manly fashion—that is, combining the worst features of a spoiled teenager and an aging *roué*—and she would bat her eyelashes as readily as their great load of mascara allowed, and succumb. Before you could say Blazes Boylan, Reed was sitting on the edge of her desk discussing bottles of pills. Auden of course, Reed thought, had got it perfectly:

> *So pocket your fifty sonnets, Bud;*
> *tell Her a myth*
> *Of unpunishable gods and all the girls*
> *they interfered with.*

"He and his wife had separated," Miss Elton confided. "I know because I filled out the application for him to the University housing office; he wanted a small apartment for just him, with a room for the kids to stay once in a while. But the pills were delivered as usual to

his regular apartment, and his wife dropped them off here the morning he died. I took them into his office, and he said 'Thank God, I
just took the last two,' and he showed me that little gidget he always
carried them in was empty. He began opening the bottle, which always made him swear because it was sealed—like whiskey you
know—and then he started telling me all the things I had to do while
he filled the tube with the pills.''

"What things?"

"Well, I'd made the appointments the day before with those jerks
from the University College—Cudlipp couldn't stand them, but for
some reason he decided to see them; we all supposed Clemance had
talked him into it. I heard Cudlipp talking to Clemance recently when
they walked out of here and Cudlipp said, 'All right, I'll see those
students, but if one of them tries to pressure me, I'll throw him out.'
He used to, you know.''

Reed raised his eyebrows provocatively.

"Throw people out," she said, giggling. "He would open the
door and yell 'Get out!' and if they didn't, he'd put his hands on
their chests and push. With men of course. He didn't see women
much in his office.''

"Was there any chance he would have considered hiring women
teachers in the College?" Reed asked, remembering what Emilia Airhart had told Kate.

"I hope not. What a dreary bunch *they* are, all brains and messy
hair. The College boys wouldn't go for that, believe me. If we ever
get women working around here, I quit; I'd never work for a
woman.''

"Did all the people Cudlipp had appointments with come to his
office or did he go to theirs?"

"You a detective or something?"

"As a matter of fact, I am, but keep it secret, honey. It'll be a
real feather in my cap if I can clear things up—you know, universities
don't like hanky-panky.''

"You ever been a spy?"

"I go where the money is, so long as there's plenty of it. So all
of Cudlipp's appointments came here?"

"Yeh. Here's the appointment sheet, Mr. Bond. Though really,
I ought to turn my back so you could steal the page underneath the
one I wrote the appointments on—the one with the impressions of
the writing.''

"I'd rather have the writing and impressions of you. Did they all show up on time?" Reed asked, reading the list.

"More or less. He'd allotted half an hour for those students, but he threw them out after fifteen minutes, so he saw Clemance and O'Toole earlier than is down there. I called them and said he was ready. So in they came and shouted a lot, but I couldn't hear about what. Academic stuff, anyhow."

"Do you mean he put his hands on the chests of the students and pushed?"

"One of the men. 'Get out!' he screamed, 'and stay out. Go back to that half-baked school you come from.' "

"Some language from an English professor."

"Yeh. Then he lowered his voice real low and said, 'Miss Elton, tell Mr. Clemance I'm free now.' " Reed had heard Cudlipp only once, but the imitation seemed to him not bad.

"Who do you suppose will be in charge of things around here now?"

"Search me. Of course, there's a new piece of inside dope every other minute, but I figure I'll wait and see. If I don't like the guy, I'll split. There are plenty of jobs."

"There must be lots of high-paying jobs for an efficient, attractive girl like you. Why work in a college where they pay less than a business does?"

"I like being around literary types—I like an intellectual atmosphere. And the young English professors are real brainy and cute."

"Like Robert O'Toole?"

"He's not young—he's a full professor—and what a stuffed shirt! Thinks he's a big deal. Mr. Know-it-all. Tries to imitate Clemance. Now there's a nice old man, really dignified and cool. Always calls me *Miss* Elton. But he's fading away."

"Clemance? He can't be that old, surely. Barely sixty."

"That's ancient. I feel sorry for the old coot. His days of greatness are behind him."

"Sic transit etcetera. Tell me, Miss Elton . . ."

"Jennifer."

"Jennifer. Did Cudlipp ever go to the men's room, or to someone else's office, and leave his tube of pills on his desk?"

"Look, sweetie, I'm the secretary here, not anyone's valet. Your guess is as good as mine."

"Well, thanks, Jennifer; see you around."

"Anytime, poopsie. Take it easy."

Reed waved to the other secretaries in the office who apparently typed for the lower ranks. It had been clear to him early on that Cudlipp and the other full professors in the English Department here were Jennifer Elton's property and none of theirs, so he did not stop to question them. Well, Reed thought, consulting Cudlipp's appointment sheet, here I go. And he headed across the campus to the building that housed the University College and Dean Frogmore.

To Reed's mild surprise, Frogmore agreed to see him almost immediately. Apparently Castleman had cleared the ground.

"Come in, Mr. Amhearst. Please, don't apologize. As a matter of fact, you give me the perfect excuse to get out of a rather boring meeting. I do hope we can settle this Cudlipp business—it's very disturbing, you know."

"Helpful, too, is it not, Dean Frogmore? Speaking frankly."

"It could be very helpful, if we're to be allowed to make use of it. Cudlipp had a great deal of direct power—and he liked to wield it. He was damn clever in the personal deals he made, and he was absolutely set on destroying University College; it was an obsession. Some of the students went to see him, you know, the same day I did, thinking to tell him how great this place is, and he literally threw them out of his office. Frankly, if I'd heard Peabody had hit Cudlipp over the head with a bat, I would have been grieved but not surprised. I'm sure I don't need to mention that Peabody didn't even know about this aspirin business."

"Is there any chance I could talk to Peabody, do you think?"

"I'll do the best I can for you; hold on a minute." Frogmore went over and stuck his head out the door: "Miss Philips, would you see if you can locate John Peabody? And let me know when you do. It's rather important. Thank you." He shut the door and returned to his desk. Academic secretaries, Reed observed, were cherished; they were not issued orders over the telephone.

"Had you heard," Reed asked, "that Cudlipp had attended the University College during his own undergraduate days?"

"I had heard, and it's quite true, interestingly enough. This place was called the extension school then, and it had even less prestige, university-wise, than it has now." (Reed wondered if Frogmore had used "university-wise" to Kate, who hated the word formation. "Do you know what the mama owl said to the papa owl?" Kate would ask; "How's the baby wisewise?" The only harsh criticism she had ever been known to make of Auden had been on this score: "something odd was happening soundwise," he had, unforgivably, written in a poem.) "I guess it's the typical syndrome," Frogmore said, blissfully unaware of his offense. "Cudlipp, we now know, was simply incapable of any objectivity on the question of University College. And, of course, he managed to carry the College faculty and alumni with him."

"Of course. Snobbism transforms itself into intelligent discrimination when practiced by ordinarily rational people."

"That's nice, Mr. Amhearst. I like that. You've heard that we began by trying to convince them that we were good—and then one day at luncheon Professors Castleman and Klein, whom you've met, told us we had to begin to attack politically. We did begin—with the Graduate English Department; and we were doing very well when this happened. "Don't misunderstand me, Mr. Amhearst. With Cudlipp out of the way we have a much better chance. But O'Toole and some others have convinced the University that the whole issue can't come before the Administrative Council while there's any question about Cudlipp's death. So, if there's anything I can do to help you . . ."

"You're certain in your own mind then that no one connected with the University College could have given him the aspirin?"

"Yes. That sort of thing just doesn't occur to academic people, Mr. Amhearst."

"You'd be surprised what occurs to academic people these days, Dean Frogmore. Let me tell you something about the D.A.'s Office that has changed since your now historical events last spring. It used to be if a college kid got into trouble, if anyone connected with the academic world got into trouble, the lawyer would come to the D.A.'s Office and say 'Look, he's a college kid, you don't want to press charges.' And we didn't press charges. If you were connected with a university or college it was assumed you were probably straight; certainly you got the benefit of the doubt and then some. Now? All the D.A.'s Office has to hear is it's a college kid, and they're pressing charges so fast the lawyer can't even follow the handwriting. As troublemakers, the members of the academic world have lost their amateur standing. The question here is: did you know about Cudlipp's allergy to aspirin?"

"I did know, though I'd forgotten I knew. Bill McQuire reminded me. A while back he said something about Cudlipp being so tensed up he was living on those British pills of his. I thought Bill was referring to birth-control pills, actually, which is what the word 'pill' seems to mean these days, and I said I didn't get it. Then Bill told me about Cudlipp's headaches and how he couldn't take ordinary aspirin. But believe it or not, Mr. Amhearst, the news just didn't sink in; it wasn't of interest.''

"Do you think the students knew of it?''

"I can't imagine how. But my experience with students like Peabody is that they know everything there is to know, and a lot that hasn't been thought up yet. I wonder if Miss Philips was able . . .''

"Dean Frogmore, what did you feel about Cudlipp personally? I mean, did you have the sense he was not a bad guy underneath, did you think he would give in the end, had you become fond of him for all his prejudice and churlishness, or did you dislike him rather intensely? I'm not looking for a motive, sir. The motive is screaming itself all over the place. I'd just like a sense of the sort of feelings Cudlipp aroused in someone outside the English Department.''

"I hated him, and so did all of those in the inner circle of old-timers here. There's no sense side-stepping that. I think the man was demented, if you want to know the truth, and so beside himself with vengeance and rage that he was perfectly capable of not knowing aspirin from peppermint Life Savers. I realize there is a lot of pressure from the College alumni, and I know the University is hard-up for funds right now—student disruption hardly stimulates giving—and that our alumni don't fork it over the way the College alumni do, but none of that explains his animus. I don't mind admitting that if I could have got Cudlipp an unrefusable offer from somewhere a thousand miles away, I would have grabbed at the chance; but that's a long way from murder.''

"From all I've heard, part of Cudlipp's dementia was his devotion to the College. Apparently neither he nor Clemance would ever consider going anywhere else. And of course, Dean Frogmore,'' Reed said, rising, "whoever gave Cudlipp the aspirin wasn't necessarily planning murder; aspirin allergies are dangerous, but rarely fatal.'' Reed had planned to exit on that line, but there came a knock at the door. Miss Philips stuck her head in. "John Peabody is here, Dean Frogmore.''

Frogmore introduced them: "John, this is Mr. Amhearst.''

"Hi,'' John Peabody said. "How about some lunch?'' Clearly, informality was going to be Mr. Peabody's keynote.

"Fine,'' Reed said. "Thank you, Dean Frogmore. I may be back with more questions, if you'll allow me, but I can't think of any more at the moment.''

"Any time, any time," Frogmore said. "Glad to have you aboard."

"You must really be Some-Body," Peabody said as they walked out, making it two words. "You the D.A. or just his brother?"

"Has something noteworthy occurred?"

"Frogmore never called you by your first name. Man, he must really be impressed."

"I never told him my first name."

"He picks up first names the way radar picks up moving objects. Regular bar and grill O.K. by you? We might even have a beer."

"Suits me," Reed said. He found himself amused by John Peabody, who looked not only as though he had slept in his clothes, but as though he had spent his whole honeymoon in them. Why wear a tie when it is not tied, a shirt when it is not buttoned, Reed wondered? Still, his tie is not psychedelic and he does not wear beads; there is always much to be thankful for.

The 'regular bar and grill' turned out to be a largish restaurant with beer on draught, and Reed settled comfortably into a booth with John Peabody, who fetched them each a stein. "Here's to it," Peabody said. "I didn't bump Cudlipp off, but, brother, I sure would have, given the chance. Man, we used to have fantasies—me and the other guys at U.C. Maybe we'd kidnap his kids and say, 'O.K., mac, you get them back when you lay off old U.C.' We dreamed about holding him prisoner in a cellar and beating him with wet ropes until he begged for mercy, and then we planned to say: 'After you call the Acting President, mac, and make it O.K. about old U.C.' So help me, if I'd known of this aspirin dodge, I'd have forced them down his stinking throat myself. He actually pushed me out of his office. I know he's old enough to be my father, which would have made it one great big pleasure to lay him out flat, but he closed the door, and the other guys held onto me." Peabody concluded with a few up-to-date epithets. Odd, Reed thought: When we were young we mouthed niceties and thought nastily. Mr. Peabody sounds like a horror and it's perfectly obvious he's nice as pie underneath. At least, so I assume.

"I thought two of the students with you were women?"

"Sure. And Randy Selkirk. All good guys."

"I see. What happened exactly?"

"You want a sandwich? I'll be glad to get us each one, if you've got what it takes. I'm stony."

Solemnly Reed handed over some money. "Ham and cheese on rye for me," he said.

Peabody returned in short order—clearly he was known here and got immediate service—with two sandwiches and two more steins of beer and a pack of cigarettes. "You need cigarettes?" he asked Reed.

"I gather," Reed said, "that you are fresh out."

"Man, you learn fast," Peabody said. "We like your bird."

"I'm lost again," Reed said. "I thought it was ham and cheese."

"Professor Fansler, man. She's your bird. Fun and games in the Graduate English Office, when Cudlipp took the wrong pills. She's real sexy on the Victorian novel."

"Sexy?"

"Good, man, good."

"Yes," Reed said. "Thank you. Now—about your meeting with Cudlipp. Could you give it to me slowly and in something approximating standard English?"

"There's nothing to give. We went there, the four of us, armed with our stories. We're used to giving them—we did that bit for your bi—for Professor Fansler. The point is to give someone an idea of how great U.C. is. What it's meant to us. We're all different types, but all kind of impressive, if you follow me. But I hadn't even finished my piece—I sort of M.C. the show—when Cudlipp lost his cool; man, he flipped. I found out why after: I'd said something about U.C. not just being a place to take some courses and wile away the time—I always say that—and of course he'd been bounced from *The* College a hundred years ago, when he was a lad, and had taken courses at U.C., then called extension, to wile away the time till he could get back in with the upperclass lads."

"Did anyone else say anything?"

"Didn't have a chance. He went for me. The others had to help me—boy, I was powed. But that Barbara Campbell is a cool chick. After they all got me out, and before Cudlipp could slam the door, she turned to him—of course her clothes are by Dior out of Bergdorf—and said, 'Professor Cudlipp, a man of your standing should have better control of himself.' Just like that. He slammed the door so hard I thought its hinges would spring off. And that's all there is to that story."

"Not much help, I'm afraid," Reed said. "You optimistic about the Administrative Council's actions?"

"Well, we got to clear up this mess. What about the elevators,

man, carrying on like that. Beer tastes better in a stein, don't you
think, and certainly better on draught. Want another?"

"No, thanks. What about the elevators?"

"What about them?"

"Didn't you say . . ."

"Man, you better take it easy. You're pushing too hard."

"Right." Reed pocketed his change. "It was a pleasure, Mr.
Peabody."

"Likewise. Take it . . ."

"I know," Reed said. "I plan to."

Reed had an appointment downtown; one cannot, after all, spend
one's entire day vamping and drinking beer with undergraduates, but
he dropped into Castleman's office, just on the chance. Castleman
was, Reed learned, at lunch at the Faculty Club. Reed said thanks
and strolled toward the Faculty Club, not quite clear in his mind what
he wanted to ask Castleman, but figuring he better have a look at the
Club anyway, since that seemed to be where everybody spent all their
time laying plans, nefarious or other. Entering the Club, he met Castleman coming out.

"Ah," Castleman said, stepping aside with Reed. "Any progress?"

"Tell me," Reed said, "is there somebody in the administration
with whom I could discuss elevators?"

"Will I do? Or do you want the maintenance department?"

"I'm not sure what I want. I take it my question does not surprise
you."

"Not unbearably. Shall we sit down a minute? Have you had
lunch?"

Reed nodded. "Let me just say 'elevators' and you tell me what
comes into your mind."

"The Acting President mentioned it to me this morning, as it
happens. I never thought of there being a connection with the Cudlipp
business—but of course he was caught in an elevator, wasn't he?"

"Fatally, as it turned out. Or probably so."

"I see. This has got to be strictly confidential, Mr. Amhearst.
Not part of any report or officially noticed at all."

"I have seldom found any use for information that isn't off the
record," Reed said, "but if an actionable crime has been committed,
I can't blink it away."

"No, naturally not. I was referring to the general University problem. But I know, who better, that you can't ask someone to do a job and then bury him in *caveats*. The trouble with discretion in a university, I've been learning, is that if a man is discreet, it turns out his friends are the only ones in the dark. Everyone else, of course, has been consulting like mad. The line between full consultation and decent discretion is finer than the razor's edge. Well, elevators. The elevators in the University have always been a blasted nuisance, an irritating joke. They are much overused, and by a community of youngsters whose gentleness with feedback devices is not noticeable. Still, it was never a serious problem. What usually happens is that an elevator which you have ridden for what seems like millennia in order to reach the top floor would decide one floor from the top that it was going no higher, and deposit you back on the ground floor minus two. Like that game my kids keep playing where you land on the wrong square and return to go. Annoying, but all in a day's work. Quite often the elevators going down would simply refuse to stop at all, but we always suspected they were secretly geared that way as a hint that we ought to walk down.''

"I lived once in a *pension* in Paris," Reed said, "where you were only allowed to take the elevator up. I found it extremely annoying at times, particularly if one were descending with heavy packages.''

"It is annoying. But that was about the size of it until this fall. Then, elevators began stopping between floors, sometimes in one building and sometimes in another. There was a great rash of that, and then the elevators took to stopping only during special hours, days or evenings when there was a meeting in a building, or all the deans were on their way to see the President, or, for example, when the whole senior classics faculty was in the elevator. Occasionally an hysterical student would get stuck and have to be treated for shock. Only very recently did we officially begin to wonder if it was actually part of some subversive plan.''

"To what end?''

"Disruption. Confusion. One more inducement to lose confidence and believe in the general ineptness of universities. It's a clever trick, really, better in its way than class disruption, because no one's caught at it, no one organizes against it, and its effects are more subtle and therefore longer lasting.''

"You mean objectless hostility builds up?''

"Exactly. Anger, or hostility if you prefer the term, is one of those forces modern society hasn't devised any really good way of dealing with. Kicking an elevator you're locked into, or an elevator door which shows no sign of opening, is humiliating and unsatisfactory—so one takes it out instead on the next student or colleague one meets. Yet stopping elevators isn't really a major crime. Whoever does it probably isn't even trespassing, according to the letter of the law, and they aren't really causing any damage that can be laid directly to them. Always supposing we knew who 'they' are.''

"But how are the elevators stopped, do you know? It sounds a bit dangerous.''

"That's what had puzzled us for so long. This whole business seemed to require a high degree of technical knowledge and timing. Then one day we nearly caught one of the culprits, or at least, Cartier thinks he nearly caught him. Cartier had dashed to the basement of the building once when he heard an elevator stop, just in time to see someone sneaking out. Cartier, who has more nerve than sense if you want to know, almost grabbed the guy, but not quite. Anyway, when he looked at the place where the miscreant had been standing he discovered the power box.''

"So they simply turned off the juice?''

"As simple as that. We couldn't lock the damn thing; one has to be able to get at it in case of emergencies. The campus guards tried keeping an eye on the elevators, but, needless to say, they couldn't be everywhere at once. No doubt someone was waiting to tamper with the elevators in Baldwin the night Cudlipp died, knowing there was something going on up there. Simple enough, when you figure it out.''

"Is this the sort of thing these radical groups go in for?''

"No, it isn't. That's the most surprising aspect of the whole thing. They want publicity, some big, showy gesture which embarrasses the greatest number of people in the most flamboyant possible way, and puts the authorities immediately on the spot.''

"The word is confrontation, isn't it?''

"Exactly. Whereas confrontation is what one doesn't have here. Just a rather diabolic scheme by someone who's more interested in annoying the University than confronting it; someone with a twisted sense of humor; if you want my guess, it'll turn out to be someone who got bounced out of here and is still simmering. The sort of people who used to sue the University for failing to fulfill its contract after they had flunked out, in the good old quiet days. But it's anyone's guess.''

"Well," Reed said, rising, "it's not a pretty mess, but I don't suppose it's got anything to do with the present investigations."

"Let me know if I can be of help in any other way. There's no question that time . . . Hi, Bill. I'd like you to meet Reed Amhearst from the D.A.'s Office; he's looking into Cudlipp's death. Bill McQuire."

"If you're walking to the subway, Mr. Amhearst, I'll go with you and see if I can be of any help. My office is in that direction. You interest me."

"Do I? Why?"

"Lots of reasons. Let's say I think it's going to be uphill work, finding out who slipped those aspirin into Cudlipp's pocket supply. Let's say, what I happen to believe, that the University killed him."

"Now that's an interesting idea. Why?"

"Because he was doing his best to kill the University. Oh, he thought he was saving it, of course. But he was pushing the College out of all proportion. I think he would have been willing to see the rest of the University go if he could have used the resources for The College. Even if you could find out how the aspirin got into Mrs. Murphy's chowder, would it matter?"

"It seems it will matter to the University College quite a lot. The Administrative Council won't move if this matter isn't cleared up."

Bill McQuire whistled. "That sounds like the work of our friend O'Toole. Well, it's the last gasp. Do you know everyone Cudlipp saw? Someone must have done some hanky-panky with those pills of his."

"I've got a pretty good line on most of them now. What do you think of Cartier?"

"He's in the English Department; hated Cudlipp's guts, but that hardly makes him even noticeable in that crowd. I'm an economist myself."

"Someone suggested, in passing, that Cartier was perhaps somewhat hot-headed."

"He is. He doesn't talk much, but he's always popping around and turning up in odd places. During the police bust last spring, he was hit on the head by a policeman and carried off in a paddy wagon and damn near charged before anyone identified him, and all because he got into an argument with a student about the indecency of calling any human beings, even policemen, pigs. When he got out the students said surely he'd changed his mind, but he said no, policemen were unnecessarily brutal, probably sadistic, and certainly ill-advised, but they weren't pigs.''

"Might he have been impulsive enough to pull the aspirin trick?''

"I can't see it. He and I saw Cudlipp together the day he died.''

"I know.''

"Were you working up to asking me about it? Because I've got to make a class in a minute.'' Reed nodded. "We tried to urge Cudlipp to soft-peddle it a bit, but he wasn't having any. Cartier said . . .''

"Yes?''

"He said, 'You're asking for trouble, Cudlipp; violence and trouble.' But I'm sure he was just speaking generally.''

"What did you say to Cudlipp?''

"I told him if he kept on the way he was going, someone would break his goddam neck for him. Well, let me know if I can help.''

Reed took the subway downtown and was so engrossed in the problem that he forgot to get off at Franklin Street.

Mr. Higgenbothom turned up promptly at four.

"And how,'' Kate asked, "are the computers?''

"You must let me show you through the computer center one of these days.''

"I should like that,'' Kate said. "If only I had a problem a computer could solve this very moment. But I gather computers can give you answers only if you give them all the relevant information and ask all the right questions. Alas, I haven't either.''

Mr. Higgenbothom sat down and looked politely expectant.

"As you have no doubt heard,'' Kate rather ponderously began, "Professor Cudlipp died at a party given in my honor the other evening.'' Mr. Higgenbothom nodded. "His death was, of course, the result of several unfortunate accidents, but the University would like, if possible, to establish some of the facts surrounding the case. Which means, in English that cats and dogs can understand, that I want a worm's-eye view of the College English Department—and what is nearer a worm than a teaching assistant?''

Mr. Higgenbothom grinned.

"And,'' Kate went on, "if you say a word about discretion, I will throw something at you. I am willing to let you use a computer on Max Beerbohm, who couldn't even stand the simpler inventions of the twentieth century, so you've got to be willing to let me have your impressions—at least, I hope you'll be willing.''

"I could quote Max Beerbohm in connection with Professor Cud-lipp," Mr. Higgenbothom said. "If two people disagree about a third, the one who likes him is right, always."

"I'm to gather that you liked Cudlipp?"

"Yes, very much. He was very nice to me indeed. He let me experiment with my freshman English group—I spent the whole year on linguistics and stylistics and the students actually liked it—but it took some believing in me on his part. And then, he was very devoted to the College, and so am I. He believed it could really be an exciting educational place, because we were all ready to experiment, and Rob-ert O'Toole was going to be Dean and do the first exciting things to be brought off in education in the last forty years. I know Cudlipp didn't think highly of the University College, and I understand that you believe in it, but he knew perfectly well that there had to be only one undergraduate school here, and that first-rate. I agreed with him, and still do. I think Cudlipp had courage and he worked for what he believed in. I admire that. So many men just let things slide."

Kate leaned back in her chair and laughed. "Sorry," she said to Mr. Higgenbothom when she had recovered herself. "I'm laughing at my getting so cocksure as to forget there are two sides to every question, and I damn well ought to remember that. Would you be willing to tell me who's likely to be new head of the College English Department?"

"At the moment it seems to be a standoff. I hear there's been some heated discussion."

"Between whom, mainly?"

"You're remembering, Professor Fansler, that this is a worm's-eye view?"

"By all means. I would apologize for asking these forthright questions when you can scarcely avoid answering them, Mr. Higgen-bothom, if there were the smallest point in apologizing for what one has every intention of doing."

"The rumor is that Clemance wants us to think about it a bit, sort of struggle on for a few months and not put a Cudlipp man right in. He says he's willing to take on some of the work for the rest of the term, and no one's exactly prepared to argue with that. I'm sorry there are more ill feelings; we ought to be healing up the wounds. We're getting together a memorial volume to Cudlipp, by the way. I hope you'll feel better about him by the time it comes out, which, given the schedules of scholars and university presses, should be in about three years."

"I'm certain to feel better about him long before then. Thank you for coming, and good luck with Max's sentences."

In fact, it was one of Max's sentences Kate quoted to Reed when he asked her how her day had gone. " 'To give an accurate and exhaustive account of that period would need a far less brilliant pen than mine,' " she wearily said.

"Likewise," said Reed. It was uncertain what a computer would have made of that.

9

Our race would not have gotten far,
Had we not learned to bluff it out
And look more certain than we are
Of what our motion is about.

THE week that followed was marked for Kate not primarily by attempts to solve the puzzle of the elevators and the aspirin, but by the presence together of Reed and herself on the campus. She was startled to discover that she had always held the University and Reed quite separate in her mind, as though her place of work existed, as far as Reed was concerned, as the source of news and problems and experiences which she might bring home and lay as tribute at his feet.

But now he had joined her in the problems and experience and news, and she found she enjoyed enormously walking with him on the campus, bidding him at its center a formal farewell which seemed to include their love more easily than any public embrace could ever have done. Reed, for his part, admitted the fascination of the campus and his eagerness to leave it as having equal force with him. Certainly he did not want to leave it until he could provide it with the knowledge it required for peace. Disruptions of communities, like illnesses, are not cured by being named; but if one names them, one isolates them from their allies: unreasoning fear, anxiety, and trepidation. The magic of doctors, for all their research, Reed pointed out to Kate, is still their power to name. He had the power now; he wanted to use it and be gone.

In the past week Kate had had probing conversations with such involved students and faculty as she met and, since the troubles of spring, one seemed constantly to meet people and to stop and talk. From resembling a club where only the oldest members recognized and spoke to one another, the University had come to seem like a small town where everyone knew and greeted one another, and usually had news, gossip, or rumors to exchange. As always, Kate thought, it was danger and shared experiences which made the modern world like a village—not television, as that dreary medium-message man had said. She had talked to many and learned a good deal, but none of it seemed to move them very far forward.

Frogmore reported that he had talked with almost all the members of the Administrative Council, and there was no question that University College had an overwhelming number of votes with which to carry their motion *if* they could ever get it before the Council. A number of members on the Council came from schools not immediately connected with the Undergraduate or Graduate Faculties of Arts and Sciences, and they clearly saw no reason why one branch of the University should be able to eliminate another—not without more cogent reasons than were being mentioned. Frogmore, as he told Kate, only hoped it would be that simple.

McQuire, who sought Kate out to tell her how superior he thought Reed, said that he now believed Cudlipp had committed suicide as the best way to kill the University College. "Call it a kind of hari-kari," he said. " 'I'll go down and take the enemy ship with me.' " In that case, Kate had pointed out, it would have made more sense to accuse his putative murderer before collapsing instead of merely yelling "aspirin" in that unhelpful way. McQuire only shrugged. "There is no question," he said, "that the whole plan went awry. We shall probably never know. He has succeeded all the same, and I'm powerfully gloomy. Let's get a drink."

But Kate had gone on to talk to Cartier, who was beginning to intrigue her a good deal. He was the most restless man Kate had ever seen, almost as though he suffered from some muscular ailment which caused him to begin twitching if he stood or sat in one place too long. He would greet one pleasantly enough, with some provocative remark ("I'm on my way to interfere with a few elevators, how are you?" was a fair example) but after extracting a certain amount of information and imparting as little as he decently could he would twitch away as though some unseen string attached to him had been jerked offstage. A good deal of his restlessness, Kate surmised, came from his hunger for information and his utter inability to impart any.

Since most people would rather talk than listen, Cartier's method worked up to a point. He would listen, nodding furiously, and then, when questioned in turn, would depart in a stammered explanation of pressing engagements. But after a time Kate, and no doubt others, began to realize that the exchange of information was not mutual, that Cartier could not bring himself to trust anyone else's discretion. Kate faced him with this one day, and he accepted it, in his usual curt style, nodding his head and thrusting out his arms in his puppet fashion. "What elevators, for example, are you going to interfere with?" "Oh, just a joke, just a joke," he replied, retreating exactly, it seemed to Kate, like some actress playing Tinkerbell whose apparatus is not working properly.

On the day when she had talked to McQuire she had gone to look for Cartier in the lounge of the Faculty Club. It was the best place to pick up information, and Cartier could never avoid it for long. She had, indeed, found Cartier and, with great difficulty, induced him to sit down with her on a couch. He offered every possible excuse, from imminent disasters to rising ill health, but Kate was firm: "I'll only keep you a minute. Please sit down. I'm not feeling at all well." This, while untrue, made Cartier's refusal impossible. He perched on the couch, his weight on his toes and his knees drawn up, for all the world, Kate had thought, like a Victorian maiden lady anticipating an indecent proposal. Yet, Kate had thought, he is the only man I know who can resemble Little Miss Muffet without looking in the least effeminate.

She had reported McQuire's theory to him. "Interesting," was his comment, "but I don't believe it. The aspirin were merely the result of an unfortunate accident, pharmaceutical more likely than not; no one seems to have thought of that. The important question is the elevators." Cartier always stopped talking as abruptly as he began, one of his more appealing characteristics these long-winded days.

"Have any elevators been stopping lately that you know of?" Kate had asked. "And," she had added ominously, "if you try to leave I shall sit in your lap until you answer me."

"Wonderful," Cartier had surprisingly said, pushing himself back on the couch to make more lap available.

"I'm sorry," Kate had said. "The ultimate sin: pigeon-holing people, thinking you always know what they will say." Cartier took the apology as dismissal, but then paused as Kate allowed her unanswered question about the elevators to echo between them.

"There's a meeting of the Chemistry Department late this afternoon," he had said, departing. Kate had remained on the couch, treasuring this piece of information. She could not imagine what possible use it could be, but it was the only fact which Cartier had ever imparted to her. It was unfortunate that she had not taken it more to heart, or at least reported it immediately to Reed, because when she ran into Professor Fielding of Chemistry several days later, he mentioned that the whole Graduate Chemistry Faculty had been stuck in the science building elevator for forty-five minutes on the day of their meeting.

Reed in the past week had interviewed maintenance men, guards, deans, secretaries, and receptionists until he was weary of endless opinions on the student generation, dire predictions about the future, and completely useless information. He told Kate as they emerged from the subway in time for her afternoon seminar that he hoped today would yield something, but he doubted it.

In this he was wrong.

To begin with, they ran into Castleman. He stopped to talk to them, resting his briefcase on the ground. "I have seen more progress," he said, "made by an inchworm on frictionless terrain. Oh, not your fault, not mine, not anybody's. Cartier thinks he'll catch someone at the elevators, but it will be the same story over again. Whoever is doing this isn't going to walk into any trap. If someone's there, they go away; if someone comes in on them, they run faster."

"Is there a meeting of some sort today?"

"Yes. Political Science."

"Why haven't you tried to keep these meetings secret?" Kate asked.

"We thought of it—and then we thought a bit more. First of all, it's impossible; if you have a meeting of eight people, there are at least double that number or more in the world who have to know it; we aren't running a secret organization, God forbid. Besides, our only chance is either to get the offenders to stop out of sheer boredom, or to catch them. It isn't as though there were any real danger; people terrified of being caught in elevators walk—they always have at this place anyway. Let's face it, the elevators, even in the best of times, were problematical."

"What time is the meeting?" Reed asked.

"Four. It could go on till six. And chances are nothing will happen." He wearily picked up his briefcase and left them.

Kate and Reed continued across the campus, feeling defeated and eager to act if only some possible action presented itself. Reed was just leaving Kate at the entrance to Baldwin when Clemance came along.

"You two," he announced, "the first really pleasant sight in days." He smiled his characteristic, sideways smile and stopped a moment with his oddly courteous air, implying that if they had anything to say he was delighted to hear it, but that he was bereft of the power of speech.

"I must be getting very old indeed," he finally murmured. "I actually find myself dreaming of the old days here, when we attended chapel in our gowns with fair regularity. I suppose what I'm trying to say is that this used to be a world of gentlemen, and I wish it still were. Nostalgia is a dangerous disease."

"You're just gloomy about this Cudlipp business, and no wonder," Kate said, really worried about him. "What's dangerous about nostalgia is that it's phony. It's a daydream in reverse. Like thinking we loved the books of our youth, when all we love is the thought of ourselves young, reading them."

"You're right. I resent so much being old, and being thought stuffy, that out of a kind of childish petulance I talk as though I were considerably older than I am. I don't mind telling you there are moments when, quite apart from wanting Cudlipp back again, I wish that someone had handed me a poison, instead of him."

"You must be pleased about O'Toole becoming Dean of the College."

"I guess I must. My daughter's going to have a baby."

"One's daughter's having a baby must, in a certain way, be the most shocking thing that can happen to a man," Reed said. "I've seen it often."

"You're probably right," Clemance said. "Anyway, it's getting to be winter, and that's always dreary. Let's hope that this will be a better spring—that the grass will not be trampled to dry earth, or the tulips crushed and broken." He raised his hat and left them.

"So he noticed exactly what I did—the death of the grass and flowers. The war-torn countryside is always desolate; grass only grows later, among the crosses."

"For God's sake, Kate, I'm glad you at least waited till he was gone to make that heartening observation."

"I can't see making him greet a grandchild as the mark of doom as exactly designed to cheer him up."

"It at least gives him a natural cause for feeling glum, instead of despair about the University. Where does the Political Science Department keep itself?"

"In Treadwell Hall—over there."

"I'm going to reconnoiter. Kate . . ."

"Yes?" Kate said when he did not seem to be continuing.

"Oh, nothing. I'll see you later."

"Yes. I must give some thought to my seminar. We all of us spend so much time at committee meetings that we forget what we're really here for." She waved at Reed as she walked away.

Reed waited, he scarcely knew for what, in the basement of Treadwell Hall. It was dimly lit and unfinished. Reconnoitering, he had discovered the door leading to the tunnels connecting the buildings. They had been used for years, Kate told him, by professors who did not want to emerge into the cold in winter, the rain in spring, or student greetings at any time. Another door apparently hid some machinery which made a good deal of noise but seemed otherwise of no interest. The box with the switches for the elevator was, as might have been expected, in the darkest corner. Reed looked at his watch. He went back upstairs and out onto the campus and walked about, thinking.

When he returned it was to contemplate the extremely wide pipes that ran along the basement about a foot from the ceiling. He jumped for one, but found he could not reach high enough to pull himself upward. He tried a running jump, but the basement did not provide adequate leaping room. Finally, he opened the door leading to the tunnel and pulled himself up on it until one of his feet rested on the knob. As he climbed he had to keep pushing the door, whose nature was to close itself, open with his other foot. At last he worked himself into a position to swing from the door onto one of the broad pipes. The door, relieved of his weight, closed. He was able to lie across the broad pipe on his stomach, resting his head on his hands. He was not invisible to anyone who looked up, but people do not normally look up in empty basements. Should he be discovered, Reed thought, he would merely go about the business of climbing down and make as ignified an exit as was possible under the circumstances. But he hoped to remain unnoticed long enough to see who came, and why.

His position was not uncomfortable. It interested him to realize that for all the physical vigor of the storybook detective, this was the only time he had had the crease in his trousers endangered by anything more extraordinary than the heat of a courtroom. After a time, he began almost to doze.

But not quite. As the door from the stairway opened, he came fully awake. A man entered silently and hurried noiselessly across the basement to the door behind which was housed the machinery. He opened the door with a key and, reaching inside, extracted first a wooden door-stop with which he braced open the door, and then a long, hollow tube with which he moved to the center of the room. Raising the tube above his head, he proceeded to slip it over the light bulb and turn it until the light went out. Fortunately the man, who was Cartier, had his back to Reed while he worked. Having plunged the basement into darkness, Cartier, carrying his tube, retreated into the machinery room and closed the door behind him. All was dark and silent.

Not long after, the door from the stairway opened again, and another man entered—Reed could not, in the darkness, tell who it was. The new arrival walked over to the corner near where the power box for the elevator was and crouched down, resting, Reed supposed, on his heels. Again there was silence. For a great period of time, it seemed, they waited. Periodically, Reed could hear the elevator motor start up and then stop. He longed to switch his position on the pipe, but dared not. From time to time he felt rather than heard the man in the corner shift his weight.

Up in Mabel's room, Reed thought, and we shall all be here until morning. And at the thought of explaining to Kate how he had happened to spend a whole night on a pipe in the basement of Treadwell Hall, Reed began to feel himself hideously on the verge of the giggles, about the only calamity, he thought, which never befell Sam Spade or Philip Marlowe.

How long it was until the door from the stairway opened was a question which might well have inspired agonized deliberations about the relativity of time. When the door did open, however, whoever entered was clearly bewildered to find himself in darkness. He listened—as Reed, holding his breath, listened, as the other two, he was certain, listened; but there was no sound. Running his hands along the wall to find his way, the last arrival moved around until he was in front of the elevator. Reed saw him take out a tiny pocket flashlight and consult his wristwatch. Before long, the elevator machinery could be heard running: the elevator had been called, one supposed, to a top floor. There was a pause as the light which indicates when the elevator is in motion went out; then it lit again. The listeners could hear the elevator descending. The newcomer moved toward the box containing the elevator power switch and the silence broke into clamoring noise. The door to the machine room was flung open, several men seemed to be grabbing one another, there was a scuffle toward the doors, Reed heard a man's voice whisper: "For God's sake get out of here," and then there was the sound of a pressurized can being sprayed. "You goddam idiot," the same voice whispered. By this time Reed had dropped down from the pipe and was guarding the door to the stairway. A man rushed against him and they were both propelled into the lighted stairway hall. The man with Reed was Hankster, and he was covered with bright, luminous paint. As they stared at each other, speechless, they were joined by Cartier who simply announced "Ha!" in pleased tones, and refused to utter another syllable. The fourth man there, whoever he was, had vanished.

It took several hours to straighten the whole thing out, if "to straighten out," as Reed later said to Kate, was possibly the correct verb.

Cartier was mightily pleased with the success of his "spy kit." He had apparently begun his James Bond operations with a camera equipped with extremely fast film or, in the event of almost total darkness, a strobe light. This, he readily admitted, had been a dismal failure. Either he was not quick enough in handling the equipment, or the camera was not focused on anything very enlightening. Cartier had already, he said, come close enough to touch at least two of the elevator interferers, but even if he pursued them into a lighted area, they mingled with groups of students too quickly for him to feel certain of identifying them. Hence the pressurized paint can: it covered its victim with paint so that he could be readily recognized; melting away into a crowd would not be possible.

The only problem in this case was, as Hankster pointed out to Cartier in agonized whispers, the wrong man had been sprayed, the wrong man's expensive clothes had been ruined, and they had all made idiots of themselves.

"Then what *were* you doing there?" Cartier had not unnaturally asked.

"Trying to prevent a misguided youngster from getting himself into serious trouble for the wrong cause," Hankster said.

"One of your radical students, no doubt," Cartier said.

"Perhaps, as you say, a radical student, though hardly mine. The idea of disrupting the University by elevator hanky-panky did not originate with me, or him, or any radical in the ordinary sense of the word.''

"With whom, then, did it originate?'' Reed asked.

"Cudlipp, of course,'' Hankster said. "Didn't you guess?''

They both stared at him for a moment. "And,'' Reed asked, before Cartier could make some remark as rude as it was concise, "would you be willing to arrange for us to meet one of the students involved in this at Cudlipp's instigation?''

"No,'' Hankster said. "I'll do my best to stop this business, if I have enough influence to accomplish it, enough persuasive powers, and am not poisoned by all this paint, but I won't give you a single name. Sorry about that.''

He marched out, probably the first man, as Kate later observed, to desert a conversation with Cartier before Cartier did.

"But,'' Kate asked Reed that night, "can Hankster's accusation possibly be true?''

10

A truth at which one should arrive,
Forbids immediate utterance,
And tongues to speak it must contrive
To tell two different lies at once.

THE following morning's mail brought an invitation to a poetry reading from the Graduate Students' English Society, The GSES, clearly
proud of itself, announced its poet with a flourish and a photograph:
W. H. Auden. Kate looked with pleasure at the picture of the white,
marvelously rumpled face. Of Icelandic descent, Auden possessed, in
the words of Christopher Isherwood, "hair like bleached straw and
thick, coarse-looking, curiously white flesh, as though every drop of
blood had been pumped out of his body." The lines in Auden's face,
originally formed, Isherwood said, by "the misleading ferocious
frown common to people of very short sight," had, over the years,
deepened and softened: the expression, Kate thought, looking at the
photograph, was less ferocious than experienced, life-tossed. She
looked forward to the poetry reading. I wonder, she thought, if Clemance will be going. It seems, somehow, suitable that he and I and
Auden should be in the same room together in these strange days.
But of course he knows Auden and will probably want to see him
first.

   It would all have to be arranged soon. Auden's reading was not
far off and must have been arranged hurriedly, but the new GSES
was doing well. The previous organization of Graduate English students had, in fact, belonged to the students only nominally; the fac-

ulty had used it to try out members from other institutions whom it might later choose to woo. Since the revolution, the GSES had been wrested from faculty hands and devoted to readings and discussion which the students thought interesting: everyone considered the arrangement a wonderful improvement as God knows it is, Kate thought, marking the date down on her calendar.

She was interrupted in this observation by the ringing of the telephone. Clemance, as though in answer to her thought, asked if she were going to the reading and if she would accompany him. Auden, Clemance said, would not be dining at the University but would arrive just for the reading. Somewhat astonished, Kate agreed to meet Clemance outside the auditorium. "I had just opened the invitation myself," she said, "and was thinking that you must be planning to go."

"Oh, yes," Clemance said. "I have always, of course, admired his poetry, but it is truly eerie how near he is to the bone these days. Do you know the lines:

> *What have you done to them?*
> *Nothing? Nothing is not an answer:*
> *You will come to believe—how can you help it?—*
> *That you did, you did do something;*
> *You will find yourself wishing you could make them laugh;*
> *You will long for their friendship.*

He is so right in those lines," Clemance went on, "about how one feels, even toward those students who have most cavalierly and with least thought destroyed the confidence and cordiality it took years to establish. And so right, of course, about guilt. We who in the turmoil of today can continue to believe that we did nothing—we are the generation, are we not, who is finished? Will you bring Reed Amhearst?"

"To the reading? Certainly, if he wants to come; he hears so much Auden these days he's quoting it himself. But I suspect there will be an awful mob."

"I think I can reserve three seats," Clemance said. "My influence, though waning, extends that far. A quarter of eight then, Friday evening?"

When he had rung off Kate pondered a bit about the fancy Clemance had taken to Reed, who appeared oddly skittish in the presence of the famous professor. Certainly that remark about the horrors of daughters having babies had been the absolutely most uncharacteristic remark she had ever heard Reed make. Well, it was probably one of the happier effects of the turmoil that people no longer sorted themselves out so neatly. Reed, indeed, had become a more rigorous attender of the University than she. He was there now, hanging from pipes no doubt and contemplating elevators.

Reed, at that moment, was thinking of elevators, though not hanging from pipes. He was in fact smack in the middle of the campus contemplating Hankster's suggestion about Cudlipp. A red herring? The determining factor was, of course, when precisely . . . Reed turned his steps toward the Administration Building.

"To see President Matthewson now?" The secretary was clearly unhappy, and Reed could well guess why. The Acting President, compensating for the almost total inaccessibility of his predecessor, had made a point of being readily available to all comers. But of course, in his position, this was a difficult principle to implement: one could scarcely allow oneself to be broken in on by every petulant complainer at every hour of the day. So Matthewson's much-tried secretary had learned to parry requests. "But," she plaintively said, "he's in an important conference."

"Tell me, Miss Franklin," Reed said, reading her name from the sign on her desk, "do you remember when you were called by two faculty members who were stuck in an elevator?"

"I certainly do," Miss Franklin said with emphasis. "A *most* disturbing conversation."

"Did you subsequently report it to President Matthewson?"

"I told him about it that very afternoon. He chuckled, in fact. But of course when more and more faculty members started getting stuck in elevators, and senior faculty for the most part. . . ."

"His chuckles became noticeably less robust, as I can well imagine. Tell me, Miss Franklin, and please be sure of your answer: was that occasion when Professors Everglade and Fansler called you from the elevator the first time senior faculty, shall we say as a group, were stuck in an elevator between floors?"

"Oh, yes, I can be quite certain about that. In fact, President Matthewson mentioned it again to me only the other day."

"I see. Miss Franklin, I'm sure you will be immeasurably relieved to know that I no longer have any need to see President Matthewson. His conference may continue undisturbed, at least by me."

"I'm exceedingly glad to be of help," Miss Franklin faintly said.

She did not pretend to understand the conversation she had just taken part in, but if a crisis, in these days of continuing crises, had been averted by the exchange of inconclusive remarks, she was not about to complain.

Feeling considerably more buoyant than he had in days, Reed set off for the bar and grill where he had lunched with Peabody. The man, Reed thought, who speaks in two languages, one in a university and one in a bar and grill. He called Kate my bird, said she was sexy about the Victorian novel, told me nothing, made me pay for the lunch, and yet left me with the feeling that I had profited by the whole occasion. Which I had.

Sure enough, Mr. Peabody was in his accustomed booth, drinking beer and holding forth.

"May I ask you a question privately?" Reed asked. Peabody stepped aside with Reed.

"I sometimes take the Fifth, but probably not with you," he said.

"Do you remember," Reed asked, "the day you and three of your fellow University College students, who are, I understand, a sort of traveling P.R. arrangement for your Alma Mater, first called on Professor Fansler?"

"Sure I remember; I told you about it. Get to the nub, man."

"Miss Fansler was stuck in the elevator that day, and kept you waiting."

"Not really. You seem to keep mentioning elevators. Have you noticed it? Look into it, man, that sort of thing can become serious."

Reed decided to ignore this disingenuous remark. "How many people knew you were going to talk to Professor Fansler, to ask for the first time to be officially admitted to a Graduate English class?"

"Everyone, man. We were like publicizing it. We'd had it with that boys' group always having us on the defensive—we told the world we were going to move, we announced our schedule of offensives. Your bird was the first."

"Professor Fansler," Reed said, frowning slightly, "was carefully picked for this offensive."

"Natch. We had to decide—old Vivian even consulted with some of us students before deciding which faculty member would be the best to begin on."

"Vivian?" Reed faintly said.

"Frogmore. We all came up with the name of your Professor Fansler, and we told the world. A compliment, really; don't get uptight about it."

"On the contrary," Reed said. "May I contribute," he asked, reaching into his pocket, "to the beer or cigarette supply?" In his day, Reed thought, such a request would have been considered insulting and patronizing; he would have been lucky to get away unassaulted. Because money was scarcer then? Or more sacred? Peabody's response was simple.

"That would be much appreciated," he said, "in these penniless parts." Reed handed over the money, and thought to himself as he walked back to the campus that money became desanctified only to those who had neither earned it nor done without it. The question was, was that a good or a bad thing?

So it *was* Cudlipp who had started the elevator business; madly to disrupt the University as the hated University College moved toward power? Only one more errand, Reed thought.

And he set his wandering feet on the path to the Dean's Office, now occupied, in the legal sense, by Robert O'Toole.

O'Toole was moving in and out of the Dean's Office like a reverse spectre—someone, that is, who haunts the place he is soon to inhabit. The Acting Dean was only too happy to vacate; indeed, his eagerness to depart the office bordered on the indecent. Kate was right: administrators were not going to be easily come by in the days that lay ahead.

Half expecting a snub, Reed was pleasantly surprised to find himself being ushered into O'Toole's office, offered a seat with a certain flourish, and encouraged to settle in for a cozy chat. Life was certainly very odd. But, as Kate had observed to Reed, the need to talk had markedly overcome many since the passage from the old life—and, to be sure, an unwillingness to chatter had never marked the academic profession.

"You have pleasant surroundings for your new and onerous tasks," Reed observed. The room was a lovely one, paneled, high-ceilinged, with the graciousness no new building, however elegant, could achieve.

"My main reaction to it," O'Toole said, "is a desire to run and not to stop till I hit some pleasant spot in the middle or far west."

"Surely there are no hiding places," Reed said.

"Obviously not. Have you noticed *The Times* is devoting a special section, complete with index, to the turmoil in the colleges? Perhaps we, like plague victims who have recovered, will be safest of all."

"I have often wondered if the carrying on with one's daily life is not the most difficult part: no excitement and glory, just plain hard work."

O'Toole nodded. "You want, I assume, to talk about Cudlipp's death."

"If you don't mind."

"I don't mind, but I can't help. The whole thing seemed so shocking, even in a place by now inured to shocks."

"You mean there is no inherent logic in the situation?"

"Yes," O'Toole said. "I guess that's what I mean."

Reed paused. "You are widely known as—I believe the word 'disciple' has actually been used—of Clemance. Is he as great a teacher as they say?"

"Absolutely great; almost *sui generis*, if you know what I mean, as though one had to judge him by special standards." O'Toole leaned back in his chair. "He taught us to think, those of us who came with the necessary equipment for thinking, which is rarer than you might suppose. We did not always draw the same conclusions he did, but he was a good enough teacher, even, to be pleased with that. And then, so much of what he has himself produced is first-rate; some of it errs, but none of it is cheap. He has even written plays, which means he understands something of literary creation, but, most important, I am inclined to think, he is never esoteric, scholarly, or turgid. What he has to say is available to any cultured, intelligent man who will read with care. But I sound as though I were writing his obituary, which God forbid. When your teacher becomes your colleagues, there is a tendency to think of him as two people: from then, and now."

"What of Cudlipp, whose obituary you could be writing?"

"Cudlipp was a more ordinary academic; an interesting scholar and a good teacher to those who could stand his rasping ways. Absolutely devoted to the College. I admire loyalty and devotion."

"What I've seen of your work seems very good to me," Reed said. "In the Clemance line: socially relevant discussions of literature with intimations of morality. Will you have time for work when you are dean?"

"I hope to have, but no doubt every new dean beguiles himself in that way. The secret, I suspect, is to be able to sleep only four hours a night."

"Let me ask you a pointed, not to say barbed, question, Mr. O'Toole. Do you intend to continue fighting, as Cudlipp did, the continued functioning of University College? I know you've told the Board of Governors and the administration that, as a new dean, you don't feel the Administrative Council should be allowed to so much as vote on expressing confidence in the University College until the mysteries surrounding Cudlipp's death are cleared up. But, should that . . .''

"As a matter of fact," O'Toole said, "I've changed my mind. To be frank, the pressure from the alumni of the College is enormous, but I'm inclined to think that we ought to let the vote go through; certainly we ought not to hold it up because of Cudlipp's death. There is really no question, is there? Cudlipp's death was an accident. It isn't as though he had been shot or anything. I admit that immediately after his death I was moved to follow a policy which he would have approved as a delaying tactic but—we are the living. The University must adopt the attitude that Cudlipp's death is a closed book; we must proceed to rebuild the University. I'm about to get in touch with Castleman and Klein and the Acting President and tell them.''

Reed regarded O'Toole for a while. Kate's adjective for him had been arrogant, and Reed had learned to trust Kate's adjectives. But the man in front of him was not arrogant. "I think your change of mind is understandable," Reed said, "and almost certainly best for the University. Except, of course, that you have, by your previous attitude, stirred up a certain amount of investigation, and it is easier to begin these operations than to stop them.''

"But surely there isn't anything to discover, is there?''

"There is the problem of the elevators.''

"You mean, to the extent that the elevator stoppage was responsible for Cudlipp's death?''

"That stoppage, and others. Mr. O'Toole, I believe I know who was behind the interference with the elevators, but I would like confirmation; hunches have little legal standing. I'm looking for some College students, one, two, perhaps three. I wondered if you could help me to find them.''

"I'm not even officially Dean yet.''

"I know, and I apologize for importuning you so early, not to say prematurely, in your administrative career. I believe there are one or two young men who may, as a prank of course, perhaps rather radical youngsters . . .''

"Why do you think they're radical? Because only radicals do mischief?''

"No. Because they are students Hankster was particularly interested in. I may have drawn an incorrect conclusion. That, however, is not the point. All I want is a statement from those students of what they were doing, and assurances that it will stop. The whole matter need not go outside University disciplinary procedures, nor even that far if you do not choose.''

"What makes you think I know who they are?''

"Perhaps, as the new dean, you can guess. Will you look into it and let me know? Is that a bargain?''

"You might call me in a day or two and see what I've decided,'' O'Toole said.

"All right, I will. Thank you for your help.'' Reed was amused and a little relieved to see the old arrogance returning. ''I'll telephone tomorrow,'' he said. ''And I do want to wish you all good fortune in your years as dean. You may be inaugurating an important new policy, where faculty members give a few years to administrative work out of devotion.''

O'Toole stood up and, with great formality, bowed Reed from the room.

11

That fellow was back,
More bloody-minded than they remembered,
More godlike than they thought.

KATE and Reed met Clemance outside the auditorium. Clemance had succeeded in reserving three seats, and they were ushered, past glaring standees, to their places in the third row.

"I've had a word with Auden," Clemance said. "I suspect there's a good deal of kindness in his presence here; he knows a few of the students. He's going to read his poems and answer a few questions and then he's got to be off. So there's no chance of a party or anything for him afterward."

Here Auden was led onto the stage by the student head of the GSES. Kate could not think back to a day when so prominent a poet would not be introduced by someone at the University at least half as prominent in his own right. But achievement, these days, gave place to youth.

"We are honored and grateful," the student said, "to have Wystan Hugh Auden with us tonight to read his poems. He has said that after the reading he will answer a few questions if they are relevant." Auden's slight look of surprise at this suggested to Kate that this was a free translation of anything Auden might have said. But it received a grateful laugh soon followed, as the student sat down and Auden rose, by thunderous applause. "I mount the rostrum unafraid," he had written in a marvelously funny poem, "On the Circuit," which Kate found herself recalling with delight.

Auden read some recent poems, and some older poems, and a fairly recent poem to Miss Marianne Moore on her eightieth birthday: "It's much too muffled to say," he concluded, "how well and with what unfreckled integrity It has all been done."

"What a tribute to have earned," Clemance said to Kate, beneath the applause.

In the question-and-answer period which followed, Kate found herself remembering, not Auden's exact phrases, but their purport: no game can be played without rules. A secondary world must have its laws no less than a primary world. By "secondary world," Auden meant a work of art, but it occurred to Kate, thinking of the present university situation of turmoil, to wonder whether the secondary worlds the revolutionaries were trying to create were not, so far, dangerously lawless. Or did the young not realize the necessity of law? "Absolute freedom is meaningless," Auden said. One is free to decide what laws there shall be, but once imposed, they must be obeyed. A troubling thought applied to anything but art. And Kate remembered one other phrase of Auden's she had wanted repeatedly to quote to the young, though he had intended it only for poets: those who refuse all formal restrictions don't know what fun they're missing.

Auden concluded by saying that the life of a poet is a balancing act between frivolity and earnestness. Without the frivolity he is a bore, without the earnestness, an aesthete.

I must remember to tell that to Emilia Airhart, Kate thought; that, I shall say, is Auden's greatness; he is the best balancer of all.

"Will you come home for a drink?" Kate asked Clemance, when they again stood outside the auditorium. "I shall soon be leaving the apartment in which I have been very happy, and it seems to me that it would mark the formal closing of that happiness most fittingly if you would spend some time there."

"A most gracious invitation," Clemance said. "How fortunate you are to go from remembered happiness to anticipated happiness. Is it agreeable to you if I accept the invitation?" he asked Reed.

"Perfectly," Reed said. "Let's get a taxi."

Yet when they were all seated in Kate's living room, all supplied with spiritous liquors, Clemance seemed strangely silent. Kate spoke of Auden, of her thoughts during Auden's remarks on the need for law in secondary worlds.

"My mind was working much the same way," Clemance said.

"I expect I was so drawn to literature from the beginning because it is the only way in which man can create worlds: his godlike faculty. The only mistake is not to understand the necessary distinction between the laws of the primary and secondary worlds—the primary world being, of course, the actual world we inhabit."

"Surely something of what we learn from literature can be used in life," Kate said. "Our greater awareness, if nothing else."

Another silence. Then Clemance said: "It begins to look as though your University College is to get a new lease on life. I have no doubt it will be given a vote of confidence by the Administrative Council, perhaps as its last act before the Faculty Senate takes over. A most significant act, I dare say. You must be feeling glad of that."

"I am, of course," Kate said. "But you do realize, don't you, that until the beginning of this term, I had never given the University College a single, wandering thought? I can't imagine how it became such a crusade with me, even if my help was sought out. I suspect I was outraged at those who didn't want their status symbols interfered with. I mean, it was so clear the fight wasn't over academic excellence, but over snobbery and a wicked kind of prejudice."

"I like the word 'wicked,' " Clemance said. "No doubt you realize, at least, and I'm certain as can be that Reed Amhearst realizes, that I've come tonight to talk about Cudlipp, the College, the whole mess. You *know*, don't you?" he said to Reed.

"Yes," Reed said. Kate stared at them.

"How did you guess?" Clemance asked. "Idle curiosity on my part, since I intended to tell you anyway. A process of elimination?"

"How could I have helped but guess?" Reed said. "Everything in your actions, afterward, made me certain. It was easy enough to guess you had done it, but how to know? Finally, it was a very slight thing that told me. That day we met you on the campus. I became so nervous when I knew I had the truth, I spoke to you idiotically about your daughter."

Clemance listened, with what those who do not understand like to call an academic interest.

"Everyone else," Reed went on, "in discussing the aspirin, spoke of them as being somehow put into the tube in which Cudlipp carried his British pills. Everyone assumed the substitution had been made in his supply. But you, in speaking to Kate and me, referred to the person who had 'handed' Cudlipp the aspirin. I knew, of course, that they had to have been handed to him; no other method would have worked. And you handed them to him, right in front of

Kate's eyes. I don't think, even at the end, that Cudlipp suspected you. He, too, I'm certain, thought it was an accident; something that had gone wrong at the source.''

"I never meant to kill him. Need I say that?''

"I never for a moment thought you did," Reed said.

"We cannot guess the outcome of our actions—how often I have said that in discussions with students. Which is why our actions must always be acceptable in themselves, and not as strategies. Kant put it differently and better.''

"It is most unusual for aspirin to kill that way. And then there was the complication of the elevator.''

"Neither did I think," Clemance went on, as though he had not heard, "that the crime would be laid at the feet, so to speak, of the University College. It's strange, really, how that seemed so germane to it all, and yet had nothing to do with it.''

"Not in your mind. But Cudlipp's actions against the University College must have gone some way toward making you realize the strangeness of Cudlipp's behavior. He was mad, wasn't he, or near so?''

"Oh yes," Clemance said. "At the end I think he was probably certifiably mad. But who was to certify him, or even, if it came to that, to notice, till the damage was done? A number of faculty actually cracked, you know, under the strain of last spring's events; it took different people different ways. One extremely prominent member of the faculty, whom Kate probably heard, ranted on to his colleagues one night in a completely vile and incoherent way. It was assumed by most people that he was drunk. But he wasn't drunk. He suffered, not from alcohol, but from fatigue and psychic strain.''

Kate rose to fetch them all fresh drinks.

"Cudlipp, alas," Clemance went on, "had cracked up. This anti-University College mania—he actually organized some students to stop elevators—was only a minor symptom, really. He was becoming paranoiac and utterly power-mad. He persuaded Robert O'Toole to become Dean of the College. Oh, I know what you must think—that I was jealous that Robert transferred his devotion from me to Cudlipp—but if I was jealous, that was only a small part of it. Cudlipp was corrupting O'Toole, as he was corrupting others. Not that it will matter if O'Toole is Dean for a while now. I imagine he may even do some good.

"What you must try to realize is the great affection I had for Cudlipp—years of affection and admiration before he went to pieces.

It took me a good while to face up to the truth about him. And then I had to decide what to do. Some action was clearly necessary. He couldn't be allowed to go on. He wouldn't take a leave, take any time off. But I hoped, if he were ill and forced to take a leave of absence, he might reconsider, recover, return to his former self, or some new-found self. His marriage was wrecked, you know, along with everything else. I tried to talk to his wife, but she assured me that he was sick and past being reached by any means she knew of.

"I had known for years about the aspirin. It was never suggested, by Cudlipp or anyone else, that aspirin could be fatal. Such a possibility never occurred to me. But we are not gods, and the laws of our primary world inevitably operate. I hoped Cudlipp would be immobilized for a time, given time to think, made ill, perhaps frightened into reconsidering. I don't want to suggest I wasn't aware of the seriousness of what I was doing, but I had to act. I waited until a day when he had a new supply of pills, so that there could be no question of suspecting anyone; so my essentially non-criminal mind worked. Funny, isn't it?"

"Do you mean," Kate said, "that I watched you hand Cudlipp those aspirin?"

"Yes, you did. Your party, as it turned out, provided the perfect chance which I had not found earlier that day. I am so terribly sorry that I did not properly think how I might affect . . ."

"Don't worry about that," Kate said. "As you realized, that party was none of Reed's or my doing, but rather an aboriginal celebration of a marriage rite. But I keep trying to think back to the moment when you brought the soda water . . ."

"Yes. I had a bottle of soda water in one hand and a glass in the other. Cudlipp was holding his pills in one hand and the University College catalogue in the other. I put down the bottle of soda water and took the pills from him, handing him the glass instead. Then I filled the glass with soda water, and handed him back the pills as he put down the catalogue. It sounds complicated and intricate, like a ballet or conjuring trick, but it was ridiculously easy. Had it turned out not to be, I should simply not have gone ahead with the substitution. As it was, the pills I handed him were two ordinary aspirin. I knew they were dangerous for him; I never thought they could be lethal."

"Buffered aspirin, as it turned out," Reed said. "So that he did not immediately taste the aspirin and spit them out."

"My God," Clemance said. "I never thought of that. It does

sound a diabolic scheme. They were simply the kind of aspirin I use. No doubt,'' he added, ''a good prosecuting lawyer could make much of that.''

They were all silent for a moment.

''I cannot see,'' Reed said, ''that there need be a prosecuting lawyer, or a trial. Had I thought the possibility of such a trial existed, I should not have allowed this conversation to take place. Perhaps,'' Reed said, ''this is the nearest I shall ever come to creating a secondary world.''

''No doubt it will sound unbearably pompous and unsuitable coming from me, but I cannot add to murder the sin of allowing you to be party to a crime.''

''What better way to celebrate my marriage to Nancy Drew and my probable departure from the D.A's Office?'' Reed smiled. ''No,'' he said, ''I would do neither of us any favor to cover any of this up. But we need not publicize it. I shall introduce into the file an account of how you must have given Cudlipp the aspirin; an accident will be assumed, and indeed, his death was an accident if I know the definition of the word.

''You have nothing to fear from anyone but yourself. If I might presume to persuade you of anything, it is to try to find the courage to continue in your work. You are essential to your university, and your instincts about Cudlipp were all correct. I do admit, however, that I have used a certain amount of blackmail to establish the truth of Cudlipp's tricks with the elevators, and to save students from such further nonsense.''

''With O'Toole, I suppose?''

''Yes. He will produce the students. And in his work as Dean, he will need your support and help.''

''Did he guess?''

''Yes. No doubt of it. I was certain as soon as I heard of his intention to call off his demands for forestalling the University College. He still admires you, you know, and I think, was not a little concerned about Cudlipp himself.''

''If you want,'' Kate said, ''in the old moral way, to pay a price, remember that the University College is now almost certainly assured of continued existence and development. Perhaps that is not something you would have wished for.''

''You wished for it,'' Clemance said. ''It will be my wedding present. I hope I find the courage to continue my work. As to the price I pay, you need never concern yourselves about the appropriate enormity of that.''

12

Clio,
Muse of Time, but for whose merciful silence
Only the first step would count and that
Would always be murder, whose kindness never
Is taken in, forgive our noises
And teach us our recollections.

BY the middle of November, the evenings were drawing in. The campus was almost dark by the time the offices closed and the secretaries went home. Kate, walking in the dusk toward the subway, was again visited by this sense of—what did one call it, affection, love, devotion?—and again wondered: toward what do I feel this sense of loyalty, a quite out-of-date emotion? Kate, in a way, sympathized with the younger generation who considered loyalty a typical demand of the establishment. Loyalty, after all, like patriotism, is the last refuge of scoundrels. Yet how explain this love? Suffice it perhaps to say that here was an institution for which she would willingly work; the University was not, for her, simply a place wherein to pursue a career. I recognize the claim, she thought, even if I cannot recognize what it is that makes the claim.

The University College had been affirmed in its existence. It had won the credit to be a full-fledged undergraduate college in a first-rate university, though certainly it had achieved this status by a strange route. "Dare sound authority confess," Auden's poem asked, "that one can err his way to riches, win glory by mistake?" Well, Clio had known.

Meanwhile, academia ground on its way.

Professor Peter Packer Pollinger, to the amazement and delight of everyone, brought out a book on Fiona Macleod with such insight into the odd dual nature of William Sharp that Professor Pollinger's colleagues looked at him with new attention. But he continued to puff through his mustache and grew, if anything, more vague and petulant. He delighted Kate by informing her one day that he had been reading the poetry of Sara Teasdale and that it was perfectly obvious no such person had ever existed. She was the alter ego of Vachel Lindsay. He had made a profound study of their imagery and was prepared to defend his thesis.

"I don't suppose," he said, puffing, "that you know *her* poem about the daisies and the asters."

"As a matter of fact," Kate smilingly said, "I do."

"Well, you see," Professor Pollinger went on, "the secret's there. Daisies and asters are both carduaceous plants, having, that is, discordant and radiate heads. But one appears to supply simple answers and the other shares its name with a biological phenomenon of achromatic substance found in cells which divide themselves by mitosis."

"They do?" Kate said. "I mean, it does?"

"Naturally. The aster originated in China, that is to say the Orient, never hot for certitude but full of the rhythm of life. The daisy originated in Europe, with its chief religions of simple answers and the simplistic beauty of its natural world. Both sides of the same person."

"But," Kate began, "there is a great deal of clear evidence that . . ."

"Have you had your wedding yet?"

"No," Kate said. "Not yet."

Kate met Polly Spence for lunch at the Cosmo Club. "Buffet now, dear," Polly had said, "so get there early or all those vigorous ladies will have grabbed the tables."

Kate entered the Club like a revenant returning to an earlier life. When she had been a girl and it had not occurred to her or any member of her generation to refuse to go to all the benefit dances arranged for boys and girls from the proper schools, she had come to the Cosmopolitan Club where, somehow, they were always held. She remembered the steps down, after one had entered, to the ladies' room on the left where she and a couple of girls from Chapin and

Sacred Heart had hidden out during almost all of one dance; she remembered the balconies, and the library where no one ever went.

"The library's changed, of course," Polly Spence said, when Kate had mentioned this, "all the latest books circulating like mad. They put me on the library committee and I said, 'Let's keep it old and stuffy and the way it always has been, where superannuated students like me can come and have a peaceful hour,' but activity is the order of the day, even here. Busy, busy. And what is your news, dear? When is the wedding to be? Why not have it here? Perfect."

"It's to be on Thanksgiving, with no one but two witnesses and a judge friend of Reed's."

Polly Spence sighed. "I remember your brothers' weddings," she said. "St. Thomas's and everything just so."

"That was never my style, you know, even in those days."

"I dare say. But you have done well, I think. You must bring your Reed to dinner and he and Winthrop can talk about all those dreary things lawyers always do talk about, and I can tell you about my wonderful new job."

"Tell me now."

"I don't dare, because it hasn't *absolutely* come through yet. But I'm so pleased. Imagine starting to teach linguistics at my advanced age—I'm really considered a coming scholar, even if I'll be gone before I've finally come. And I'm so excited about University College. We're actually beginning to get tenure for people. Do you suppose this spring we'll be at the barricades again, filthy language, long nights, and all the *desperate* excitement of revolution?"

"My opinion, for what it's worth, is that we won't. Some other places may be, though. You know, the only thing I really remember about the Cosmopolitan Club, apart from the dances for the benefit of blue babies or whatever it was, are the macaroons. Do they still have those fantastically good macaroons?"

"Certainly they do, my dear, though now, of course, one serves oneself. Winthrop says pretty soon they'll be selling a mix for them, and they will begin to taste like the glue on postage stamps, but I tell him not to be such a confirmed pessimist. I really do think life is just too wonderfully exciting, especially now that I don't have to look after grandchildren anymore. My children point out that *I* was able to hire governesses, and I point out that *I* never contradicted my mother, but after all, *autre temps, autre moeurs, n'est-ce-pas?*"

"And what do they say to that?" Kate asked, munching macaroons.

"They don't say much, dear, but they glare, and I know what they're thinking: four-letter-word-sex you, meaning me, of course. *Tant pis.*"

For Clemance, Kate felt an aching need to offer comfort and knew no comfort existed on earth.

"There is," he told her, "a terrible need to demand punishment—to punish oneself. Resign, retire, go quietly and miserably mad in a richly deserved and dreary solitude. We never know, these psychological days, when we are fooling ourselves, but it seems to me that since I destroyed Cudlipp for the sake of the young men in the College, I ought to stay to serve those same young men—those, at least who care for what I say. Yet, you know, it seems to me there is never a half hour together when I do not re-live that moment of handing him the aspirin."

"And how," Professor Castleman said as he and Kate waited for the elevator in Lowell Hall, "is the proclaimer?"

"The who?" Kate asked.

"Clio, your muse of history. Kleio in Greek is the Proclaimer."

"You don't say. I never thought of her as proclaiming, I suppose because Auden never mentioned it."

The elevator, going down, passed them without stopping.

"If your Clio is going to proclaim any change," Castleman said as they started down the stairs, "I wish she would begin. The elevators do not stop, and the room I'm in now, while larger, is still not large enough."

"Standing-room-only is a compliment," Kate said.

"Which reminds me. We went to the theater again. Dionysian rites, as I live and breathe. Nude young women pretending to tear nude young men to pieces. Oceans of blood."

"Did they try to persuade you to take part?"

"Alas, no. Not, that is, that I actually want to tear anyone apart—not even my students, bless them, who refuse to believe one can learn from history. Do you suppose," he went on, "if we were all to enter the classroom nude—and Lord knows, it's overheated enough for that—the younger generation might be willing to pay their tribute to Clio?"

Kate met Emilia Airhart in the ladies' room, where she was regarding herself miserably in the mirror.

"My plan," she said, "was always to avoid mirrors, the sight was so demoralizing. Do you know, I had actually learned to put on lipstick and comb my hair without looking at myself? But I will escape no longer. I am going to look and look and perhaps the continual shock will actually force me to diet. I will never be willowy, but at least I can be slightly angular."

Kate smiled. "You are probably no one's idea of either Aphrodite or Artemis, but you are wonderfully you and I doubt, really, that you ought to consider changing. The trouble with Queen Victoria was not her figure but her opinions. Are you writing a new play?"

"I am, actually. It's a comedy with supernatural bits. A community of middle-aged parents and teen-aged children, and they change places—keeping, of course, their original ideas. The result is that the colleges and prep schools become frightfully proper and *comme-il-faut*, but the banks and brokerage houses keep having disruptions, and the different partners keep occupying their Wall Street law firms. Meanwhile, on the floor of the exchange, the radical brokers take over the ticker tape and demand open admission for all seats on the exchange. Of course, the college students insist that any broker who interferes with the workings of the market will lose his right to a capital gains . . ."

Cartier would not stop long enough to talk. "Have you heard," Kate asked him, "that they have found the students who caused the elevator trouble?"

"I did hear something," Cartier said, fairly dancing to be gone. "Sorry, but I must prepare a class." He rushed off and then, to Kate's astonishment, allowed the strings of restlessness to twitch him back.

"Hope you will sit on my lap one day," he said, and then was gone.

Epilogue

Our bodies cannot love:
But, without one,
What works of Love could we do?

KATE and Reed were married on Thanksgiving and, since she had only four days, and a class to teach on Monday, they spent their honeymoon in Reed's apartment cooking all their meals in the electric frying pan, which required very little attention.